ITEM 016 605 294

G000139417

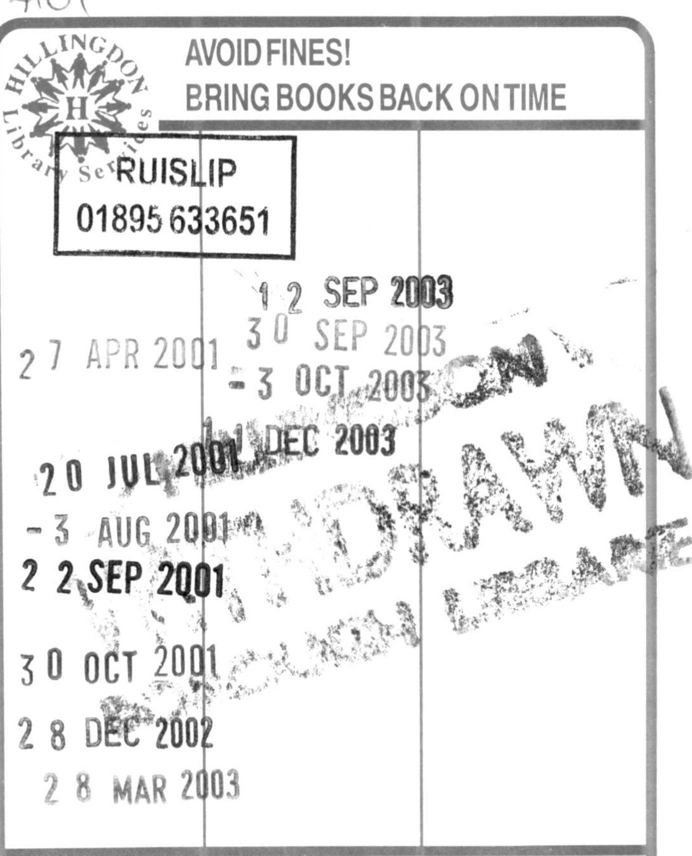

HILLINGDON Library Services
AVOID FINES!
BRING BOOKS BACK ON TIME
RUISLIP
01895 633651
27 APR 2001
20 JUL 2001
-3 AUG 2001
22 SEP 2001
30 OCT 2001
28 DEC 2002
28 MAR 2003
12 SEP 2003
30 SEP 2003
-3 OCT 2003
11 DEC 2003
WITHDRAWN
Adult readers will be fined for items kept beyond the latest date stamped above. If not reserved by another reader, this item may be renewed by telephone or in person. When renewing, quote the barcode number or your ticket number.
CALU 1

THE INHERITORS

Forge Books by Michael A. Smith

Jeremiah: Terrorist Prophet
New America
The Inheritors

THE INHERITORS

Michael A. Smith

A TOM DOHERTY ASSOCIATES BOOK
NEW YORK

This is a work of fiction. All the characters and events portrayed in this novel are either fictitious or are used fictitiously.

THE INHERITORS

www.jeremiah2.com

This book is printed on acid-free paper.

A Forge Book
Published by Tom Doherty Associates, LLC
175 Fifth Avenue
New York, NY 10010

www.tor.com

Forge® is a registered trademark of Tom Doherty Associates, LLC.

ISBN 0-312-86639-9

First Edition: March 2000

Printed in the United States of America

0 9 8 7 6 5 4 3 2 1

For Tim and Julie,
the only legacy that matters.

They have the power to shut the sky,
that no rain may fall
during the days of their prophesying,
and they have power over the waters
to turn them into blood,
and to smite the earth with every plague,
as often as they desire.
—*Revelation 11:6*

The Earth is God's Garden,
and Jeremiah is God's appointed Gardener.
God has directed Jeremiah
to weed His Garden.
—*2 Revelation 3:11*

Prologue

From her seat in the front row of the observation gallery, the petite woman with short, dark hair stared through the glass at the two operating tables in the surgical theater below.

On one table lay the great Prophet of the twenty-first century. When the woman looked down at him, her eyes narrowed and her face became pinched. As she looked at the ten-year-old boy lying on the other table, her body sagged and her eyes filled with tears.

White surgical sheets draped both patients except for their exposed chest cavities, which had been swabbed with a yellowish-green antiseptic.

"You'd think God would have put a better pump in the one who speaks for him," the lead surgeon observed wickedly, talking into the microphone attached to his communications headgear.

"Then God couldn't play God through you, Tony," the anesthesiologist replied as he glanced at the monitors.

Those in the gallery, including several leading Chinese cardiologists and surgeons, could clearly hear the doctors' conversation through the intercom system.

"You ready to make history over there?" Tony asked the team members at the table behind him.

"Let's rock and roll, boss. The sooner we're outta here, the sooner we can find out what goes on in Beijing at night."

"Nurse, a little inspirational music, please."

A masked nurse wearing a green surgical gown walked across the room and pushed a button on a boom box. A beseeching, slightly frantic female voice filled the theater as the vocalist sang lyrics from a popular song: "I got a pipeline to God. I got a pipeline to God. I pray for power and stuff but never get the nod."

Many in the gallery looked stunned at this display of irreverence by surgeons and scientists from the former New America Science Center.

The two surgical teams working side by side carved open the chest of each patient and put surgical retractors in place. Inside the chest cavities, both hearts pumped rhythmically, although the woman knew that one was diseased and the other healthy.

The nurses worked efficiently to control the bleeding as the surgeons began removing both hearts. Respirators breathed for the patients, and artificial pumps circulated their blood through their bodies.

An obvious urgency overtook both surgical teams as they began transplanting the donor heart from the boy into the Prophet, whose diseased heart was placed in a stainless steel receptacle and set aside.

The team working on the boy installed a newly designed artificial heart. The child's chances of survival were excellent, they had told her. They even held out hope that innovative gene therapy might allow the boy to regenerate his own heart.

Hours passed as the surgical teams worked steadily. Finally, an assistant placed two thin steel conductors on each side of the transplanted organ and delivered an electrical jolt to it.

For a moment, doctors and observers were frozen in place. The woman unconsciously held her breath. Suddenly the transplanted muscle came alive, contracting and expanding as it took over the job of circulating the body's lifeblood.

"Voilà!" Tony declared.

"Bee-you-tee-ful."

No similar expressions of joy came from the team operating on the boy as it efficiently closed his chest over the artificial heart. A surgeon and two assistants then wheeled the child out of the operating room.

The woman stood, left the gallery, and ran down the stairs. She barely made it into the elevator before the doors closed. She approached the boy on the gurney tentatively, as if afraid to waken him. Only the pumping sound of the battery-powered respirator intruded upon the silence.

She looked anxiously at the surgeon and asked, "Will he be all right?"

"Everything's going perfectly," the doctor answered in a bored tone.

She ran her fingers through the boy's curly blond hair, as she had done many times before. From the day a surrogate mother had given birth to him, she had been his nurse, teacher, and companion.

For the first two decades of the new millennium, laboratory techniques had been perfected for the cloning of humans and the growing of organs from fetal stem cells, although the latter procedure had not fulfilled its early promise. Most nations had outlawed the cloning of human beings for replacement body parts, but the woman knew that the prohibition didn't apply in this case. The end justified the means; the boy would gladly make the sacrifice once he had the proper perspective. In the beginning, she had agreed with them.

As the boy grew, however, and became not a "thing" but a precocious, energetic, loving child, she had begun to think of him as her own son. She had even named him James, after the brother of Christ. At the least, he was the Prophet's true inheritor.

"You were told many times not to get emotionally attached to him," the surgeon said in an accusatory voice. "He's performed a great service to Jeremiah and the movement. That's all that matters."

She knew they would continue to think of James only as a

source of other organs the Prophet might need in the future, or as a human guinea pig on which to test the efficiency of artificial organs and body parts.

But not if she could help it. When James was well enough, she would try to get him to safety. She couldn't trust anyone in the movement, or any government on earth. Only two people had the will and the means to accomplish the task, and they were halfway around the world. She planned to contact them immediately.

1

As the limo drove down Park Avenue, Laura Delaney-Wallace Austin considered how much her life, and that of her husband Steve and their adopted son Thomas, revolved around New York's Upper East Side. Near their penthouse condo, Thomas attended a private school on Lexington Avenue, and Steve worked at his office on the twenty-fourth floor of the IBM building. For security reasons, they seldom traveled outside the city.

Sandwiched between two bodyguards, Laura exited the car and hurried through the main entrance into the black, steel-and-glass skyscraper. With only the slightest pneumatic hiss, the elevator whisked them up to the offices of the Gemini Group.

When she entered the suite, Laura saw Thomas engaged in an animated conversation with Ariana Cicero, Steve's twenty-seven-year-old assistant. She suspected the teenager had a crush on the young woman.

"Hi, Mom," Thomas said.

"Hi, Mom," Ariana parroted.

"Hi, kids. What's up?"

"I had the guys bring me down here after school," Thomas said. "Ariana's got me filing stuff."

"You gotta earn your keep somehow, Thomas," Ariana said over her shoulder as she walked away toward Steve's office.

Laura looked up at her tall, gangly, dark-haired son. Unconsciously, she scrutinized his face for physical similarities to his real mother. At the same time, she buttoned down a collar wing that had come loose on his shirt. "I thought you were going to the club?"

"I am," Thomas said. "I've got a racquetball game at four with Larry."

"Dinner's at six," she said, watching her son leave with "the guys," who, in fact, were another bodyguard duo.

Laura walked down the hallway and looked through the side glass before entering Steve's office. He sat behind his desk, his shirtsleeves rolled halfway up his arms and his tie pulled loosely to one side. *Thomas bears an amazing resemblance to Steve,* she thought.

When she walked through the door, Steve stood, came around the desk, and gave her a kiss. "You look especially gorgeous today. New pantsuit?"

"Yes," she replied, savoring the aroma of his cologne.

"Love the zippers," Ariana said.

Laura sat in a chair, thinking once again that Ariana was way, way too good-looking to be hanging around her husband all day long, not that she had ever had any reason whatsoever to distrust Steve. Besides, Ariana was the niece of Leslie Ulrich, the FBI agent who had worked for Steve when he'd been head of the Bureau's counterintelligence unit. Leslie had been killed nearly twenty-five years ago and Steve had taken on the role of Ariana's benefactor, making certain she got through college and law school before coming to work for "the organization."

"So why did you want me to come over?" Laura asked.

Steve sat on the edge of his desk, looking down at her. "We've been contacted by a woman in Beijing who says she has significant information about Jeremiah."

The mention of the terrorist's name caused Laura to stiffen. "What is it?"

"She only gave us a tantalizing tidbit," Ariana said. "Jeremiah has apparently had a heart transplant."

The news several years ago about Jeremiah's deteriorating health had given Laura hope he'd die and that they would be free finally. "What else does she know?" Laura asked. "How much money does she want?"

"She doesn't want money," Ariana said.

Steve, who always seemed to Laura to be unflappable under all circumstances, shrugged and said, "We offered, of course. A lot of money, in fact."

Buying and selling information about Jeremiah and worldwide terrorism at premium prices was the means by which the Gemini Group had achieved parity over several years with most government intelligence services. Steve's organization paid top dollar and then sold the information on the open market, mainly to global corporations, so long as it wasn't detrimental to U.S. interests. Both buyers and sellers had come to prefer dealing with the Gemini Group simply because it wasn't a government agency encumbered with restrictive rules and regulations and subject to political considerations.

"She apparently only wants us to help her get out of China, along with a boy," Ariana said.

Laura jumped to her feet. "David?"

"No," Steve said gently, reaching out and pulling her close. "She said the boy was ten years old."

"And that he's Jeremiah's son," Ariana added pointedly.

Laura locked eyes with Steve. "How could he have hidden this boy from our surveillance all these years?" she asked.

"Maybe because we weren't looking for him," Steve said calmly.

"Do anything for her!" Laura pleaded, grasping his arm urgently. "If we get the boy and he really is Jeremiah's son, we can trade him for David."

"And what if Jeremiah wants Thomas in the bargain?" Ariana asked.

Laura broke away from Steve and whirled toward the young woman. "That's a stupid question! The answer is obvious."

Ariana looked chastened. "I'm sorry, Laura. It was insensitive of me."

Steve put his arm around Laura's shoulder. He smiled at her and then at Ariana. "Hey, this news naturally puts us all on edge. It's one of those bad news-good news situations. Jeremiah's health may be restored. On the other hand, if this information is true—and we'll certainly have to confirm it—we might gain some leverage over him."

"It could be just a propaganda ploy," Ariana said, once again playing the devil's advocate. "They could be trying to use us to spread the good word about Jeremiah's health."

"That's true," Steve agreed. "We'll know soon. I replied to the woman that we're ready to help her in any way."

"How are you contacting her?" Laura asked.

"Through an e-mail drop box in Hong Kong. Ariana's already trying to trace it."

"Steve, is there any significance to the timing?" Ariana asked.

He shrugged. "Not that I know of."

Laura sat down and took a deep breath. "I've been worried for weeks," she admitted, then saw both of them look at her with a mixture of alarm and curiosity. "Three days from now, Thomas will be eighteen. Three weeks later, so will David. They're men now. Have you forgotten about the inheritor prophecy, Steve?"

Laura watched her husband step back and sit again on the edge of his desk. She saw that for once, he looked stunned.

"Jesus, Laura. You're right."

Near midnight, Steve lay in bed reading a report. Every few minutes he glanced at Laura, who pretended to watch television, although he could tell from her furrowed brow that she was thinking about something else. Suddenly, she rose from the bed and put on a robe that had been draped over a nearby chair.

As usual, he admired her figure before she cinched the robe shut, thinking that his wife surely was the most beautiful fifty-seven-year-old woman in New York. She seemed ageless, in fact.

"Where are you going?"

"To check on Thomas," she said, walking out the door.

Within minutes, she returned.

"Is he asleep?" Steve asked, thinking it might be safe for them to make the bed headboard sing a squeaky song.

"Yes."

"If you can't sleep, Laura, let me rub your back." He paused and added mischievously, "And maybe some other parts, too."

She looked at him grimly. "You won't be able to sleep either after you see this."

Alarmed, Steve watched her enter the walk-in closet. From the bed, he saw her dial the combination to the wall safe where she kept her jewelry. She reached in and took out two videotapes, returned to the television, turned on the VCR, and inserted one of the tapes. As it began to play, she stood near the end of the bed.

As soon as the tape began to roll, Steve leaped out of bed and stood beside her. "It's David! How?"

"Just watch," Laura said.

And Steve did, amazed by the image of their son riding a small bicycle in the middle of a walled compound, just like any other boy. David turned the bike in a tight circle, smiling and laughing all the time.

"Oh, how wonderful," Laura said softly, putting her hands together prayerfully.

"How old is he here? Seven or eight?"

"Eight."

"I don't understand, Laura."

"Just watch and enjoy, Steve. I'll tell you everything later."

The tape ran for about an hour and chronicled signal events in the life of their son as he grew up in exile in China. At some point, Steve and Laura pulled chairs in front of the television set.

When the tape ran to snow, Steve turned toward Laura. "Where did you get this footage? How long have you had it?" Then, with considerable indignation, he added, "And why didn't you tell me about it? I always considered David my son, too. You know that."

"I know," she said, walking to the VCR. She ejected the tape and inserted the other one. "The first tape was a composite I put together from dozens of tapes like this that I've received over the past four or five years." She put the second tape into "Play" and then turned her back to the screen.

Steve watched the second tape intently, hoping to be enchanted once again. Instead, what he saw sickened him. It looked like outright pornography. After several minutes, he walked over to the VCR and turned it off.

Laura faced him and he saw the anger flashing in her eyes.

"Was that . . . ?" He couldn't even say her name.

"Yes, Melanie Thurston . . . and our son."

"My God! Why didn't you tell me about this, Laura? I can't believe you've kept this secret for years."

She blew out a deep breath. "There's no rational explanation, Steve. Maybe I wanted to preserve David's dignity until I could figure out what to do. For a long time, I simply couldn't come to grips with it. I also was afraid of what you might do."

He took her into his arms. "This must have just about killed you."

"At one point, I thought it would drive me insane. That was when I came up with the idea of excerpting the nice parts—being able to watch them eased the pain. Of course I kept the originals, in case I ever get a chance to use them against Thurston."

"Did she send them? Or was it Jeremiah?"

Laura shrugged. "I don't know. I've thought about it endlessly. Nothing happens around Jeremiah without his knowledge. On the other hand, maybe this is her way of getting back at me."

"I understand," he said, and then went into the bathroom for a drink of water.

He recalled that when Laura and he had finally escaped their imprisonment in New America—when they thought they were safe in their condo, protected by a small army of bodyguards—it was Melanie Thurston who had kidnapped David and handed him over to Jeremiah.

As he came back into the bedroom, Laura said, "Maybe Melanie finally wised up and realized that she was nothing more to Jeremiah than a Laura Delaney doll. God knows what he's done to her over the years."

"If she did this to David without Jeremiah's knowledge and he ever finds out, Thurston is dead," Steve said. "You were right this afternoon, Laura. Something's up. The bastard's getting ready to make a move."

"And David will have a role in his plans," Laura said.

Steve shuddered as he sat on the edge of the bed. "I hope not. Maybe David has become his own man."

Her arms crossed, Laura stood in front of him. "Jeremiah wants David to succeed him, but first he needs to break him down. Strip him of all his dignity. Make him a hollow shell, so he can reprogram him as a monster. That's what these videotapes are about."

Steve clenched his teeth. "Goddammit! We should have tried again to rescue David."

"You know we couldn't do that," Laura cried, sitting on the bed beside him. "Not after the last time."

Steve recalled their attempt to rescue David nearly eight years earlier. A shoot-out on a Beijing street near David's school had left three of Steve's men dead and ended with one of Jeremiah's thugs holding a gun to David's head. Clearly, Jeremiah had given orders that he would have David killed before he would allow him to be rescued.

Beijing had issued a formal diplomatic complaint, and the U.S. State Department had threatened that any such future "incidents" would result in charges against Steve and Laura.

"Everything's changed, Laura. No matter the price, I say we

strike first. Rescue David and get rid of that bastard once and for all."

He saw a determined look on Laura's face. "Our plan has to be perfect this time, Steve. We've got to get David back at all costs and give him the life we've given Thomas."

"We will, Laura," Steve said grimly. "We will."

2

The day held promise for Jeremiah, for several reasons. His son David had achieved his eighteenth birthday, a long-anticipated watershed event that coincided nicely with his own renewed health. He hadn't felt this invigorated in years, even though the transplant had taken place only five weeks ago. The Prophet breathed deeply, almost certain he could feel the new heart rejoice at the infusion of oxygenated blood.

Dressed in a simple black suit, he sat in a high-backed, ornately carved chair with plush scarlet padding on the seat and back. Appropriately enough, the chair once had belonged to a Chinese emperor.

A bodyguard opened a sliding door on the stained-glass wall facing the courtyard and Jeremiah watched David walk toward him across the tiled floor. Physically, the boy resembled him—tall, with broad shoulders, blue eyes, wavy blond hair, and an intelligent face. David already had a presence about him. Laura had named him aptly after the greatest of the Hebrew kings.

"Come, stand before me," Jeremiah said.

"How are you, Father?" David asked, standing with his hands clasped behind him as if he were at military parade rest.

"I'm feeling very well, thank you, David," Jeremiah replied. "All of life's tribulations are a test, son. Learn from adversity and you will achieve wisdom."

"If you say so," David replied indifferently.

"Those standing before the throne of God, being in the presence of the Lamb, are those who have suffered great tribulations," Jeremiah said, savoring the scent of incense in the air. "Their robes are made white in the blood of the Lamb. Where is this found in the Bible, David?"

David shook his head wearily. "Beats the hell out of me."

Jeremiah's eyes narrowed at the flippant remark, but he didn't take the bait. He wanted to avoid an argument with his son today, if possible. "The revelation to John, David. Revelation has been much on my mind lately."

"You don't say."

"Like Jesus, I am returned from the wilderness of my mind, where my spirit was in anguish and filled with doubt. The devil transported me to many kingdoms that he promised me I could rule if only I would renounce God and my mission on earth."

He watched David press his lips together to suppress laughter, an effort that resulted in a series of audible snorts.

Jeremiah tried to control a muscle twitching in his right cheek. "I submitted not to temptations and I am renewed. Inspired, in fact, to enter the fray again with the heart of a lion."

An image of the clone wedged its way briefly into Jeremiah's mind. He had seen only photographs of the boy who had been named James by his caretaker. He had no desire to form any relationship with someone who was simply a repository of spare body parts. *Some are called upon to play special roles in the Lord's grand scheme,* he thought.

"Sit," Jeremiah commanded, and watched as David complied by collapsing into a cross-legged position on the cold floor. On every fourth tile, a significant event in Chinese history had been painstakingly painted. A sitting area with comfortable chairs occupied the other side of the room, while only the massive throne chair dominated this side.

"There is a battle forever ongoing in the world, David. Do you know what it is?"

"Sure. It's the battle between the haves and the have-nots."

"In your sarcasm, David, you've accidentally stumbled onto part of the truth. 'The greatest evil is the dirty stain of greed that poisons the mind of man.' *Second Jeremiah*, chapter four, verse one. Mankind's history is a long, sad chronicle of individuals lusting for riches and power over others. Most people are incredibly self-centered, lacking in ethics or any real purpose in life. They have to be threatened with dire consequences before they'll do the right thing or obey the law."

"I'm certain you'll whip them into shape, Father."

Jeremiah enjoyed that quip. "Exactly. It's what my two campaigns to establish New America were about. It was established to be a place of absolute justice and equality, where the chief goal was to obey God's law and learn the secrets of life and the universe."

"And if people didn't agree with you, you killed them, right? With God's approval, of course."

"Indeed, our motto was 'Obey or die!' "

"Who can argue with someone who has a direct pipeline to God?"

Jeremiah ignored the usual teenage anger and cynicism, confident he would prevail easily in this confrontation. "My recent tribulation has revealed to me another ongoing battle about which I have been largely ignorant," Jeremiah said. "That is one reason I asked to see you today, David—to make you aware of this recent revelation from God, which I believe will guide our future actions."

"Our future actions? What do you mean?"

Now it was Jeremiah's turn to smirk at David's expression of concern. "Do you know what originally weakened my heart?"

"An infection, you said."

"Schistosomiasis, to be precise. Do you know what that is?"

"I forget."

"It's a parasitic infestation. The microscopic larvae pass right through the skin into your bloodstream, where they travel to many of the body's organs, including the heart. There they develop into worms. Very ugly picture, isn't it?"

"No shit."

"When I was thirty years old, shortly before my first campaign in Old America, I traveled in Egypt and Northern Africa. Apparently the infection began at that time. The diagnosis wasn't made quickly. Once it was, medication killed the worms but not before they'd damaged and weakened my heart, making it susceptible to secondary bacterial infections. Notably cytomegalovirus. Unfortunately, my body's defense mechanism against these parasites wasn't effective. Do you know why not, David?"

Feigning boredom, David sighed and said, "I haven't the slightest idea."

"The body's T cells, or white blood cells, should have latched onto the larvae and virus and killed them. But the microbes counterattacked. They may have manufactured an amino acid that caused the T cells not to recognize them as a foreign body. Would you say that's a sign of intelligence, David?"

His son laughed in disbelief. "Intelligent bugs?"

"Seems a contradiction, doesn't it. Yet many species of microbes employ sophisticated deceptions to overcome the human body's defenses. It's either intelligence or a fortuitous genetic adaptation, which seems statistically unlikely to me. Mankind is still part of the food chain. We'll talk more about this concept at another time, David. Suffice it to say that now I've become intrigued with this battle between microbes and humans. Clearly, it's part of God's plan, wouldn't you say?"

"I don't see how."

"Everything happens by design, David. Otherwise, there is no God in the universe and no purpose to life." When he saw that David had no response to that statement, Jeremiah decided to conclude the audience. He stood abruptly, startling his son. "Happy birthday, David. You're eighteen and a man. You should reread the prophecy of *Second Jeremiah* and consider your role in life."

Uncharacteristically, David stood without having received permission. Jeremiah found himself face-to-face with his son.

"My role in life," David repeated loudly. "I have no role in life other than to do whatever you want. I'm a prisoner in this house. Everywhere I go outside these walls, I'm shadowed by bodyguards."

"That's for a good reason."

"No, it isn't," David insisted, putting his face inches from Jeremiah's. "It's because you're a terrorist and a lot of people want to kill you, or to kidnap me so they can bargain with you. I don't buy into any of your bullshit!"

Jeremiah shouted back, "You have a role in God's plan, like it or not, David! You should reread *Second Jeremiah*, chapter six, verse eleven."

"The inheritor prophecy," David said, with disdain, although he backed away. "Terrorism isn't a family trade, Father. If I'm now a man, like you said, then I should make my own choices about what to do with my life."

Jeremiah also stepped back. "I understand, David. When I was your age, studying with my uncle Walter Dorfler, I had the same doubts. But you must resolve them soon and make up your mind. I need a successor—someone who can supervise the day-to-day requirements of God's work while I turn my attention to more important matters. Do you know what is the most essential aspect of reshaping the history of mankind?"

"I'm sure you're gonna tell me."

Jeremiah jutted out his chin defiantly. "To make a great evolutionary jump toward the Godhead. That is my role once God's work is done here on earth."

"Oh, for Christ's sake," David sneered.

"Exactly," Jeremiah said. "I must be able to trust you, David, above all others. I must be able to tell you all my plans with complete confidence. You need to know about all my resources, not only the identity of those men who support the cause, but the billions in wealth that are held for me—for us—in foreign banks."

"Money?"

Jeremiah smiled, noting the keenness of his son's interest in this subject. "Life is a welter of contradictions, David. One of the first things I learned from Uncle Walter was that you couldn't do battle with Satan unless you possessed Satan's weapons. Great wealth is required to rid the world of the sins of greed and pride. Yet the Lord's instrument must not be tempted to take up the devil's ways. Think upon that, David, because it will be your first true test."

"Can I go now?"

"Yes. Just remember the price of failure, or of failure to obey."

They stared belligerently at each other for several seconds before David turned and stalked out of the room.

Jeremiah sat down again on his royal throne and waited. Shortly, a small thin, Chinese man parted the beads covering another doorway and walked purposefully across the room to the accompaniment of tinkling jade and onyx beads.

"What can you tell me, Zhang?"

His counselor bowed slightly and said, "The nurse and the boy have disappeared."

"Our security should have been better."

Expressionless, Zhang said, "There were no signs that she would attempt to escape. But she won't get far. She and the boy will stand out clearly in China. Someone will see them and contact us."

"Someone had to have helped her. Check with all our informants and determine what rumors are about."

The clone was important, although not indispensable. In the

beginning, cloning had represented a low-priority option—behind medication, gene therapy, and a heart transplant from a compatible donor. Even in this heady age of astounding advances in medicine and science, clones still aged faster than normal humans did. Many times, their organs failed prematurely.

Nevertheless, the child James could be studied to determine the genetic components of aging and to improve cloning techniques and results. A few decades from now, it might be scientifically possible for Jeremiah to transfer his essence to the perfect clone—time and time again, far into the future. *Everything is possible under God's heaven*, he thought.

Zhang said, "I have heard rumors from many quarters that you may exert yourself more forcefully now that you are well, Prophet."

Jeremiah chuckled. "Zhang, the thing about rumors is that they almost always contain a grain of truth."

After Zhang left, Jeremiah sat and thought. He had survived this long in the world because of an innate ability to foresee events, which most of his followers considered a God-given talent. And he agreed. The Americans, the Chinese, even the Gemini Group, had tolerated his existence when he had seemed to pose no threat, although they were mistaken in their assessment. Even when ill, he had been able to plan. Now that his physical vigor was restored, someone would again attempt to neutralize him. He did not plan to be here when they arrived. He had work to do elsewhere.

David walked across the walled compound from his father's quarters to the main house and went into the kitchen to rummage in the refrigerator. He hadn't eaten before his early morning meeting with his father, largely because of a nervous stomach. He always dreaded such "audiences," knowing they would entail a test of some sort and eventually end in an argument.

As he nibbled on a cold chicken leg, he reviewed the session.

Beyond the usual rhetoric about the "movement" and the babbling about microbes and their role in God's plan, Jeremiah had talked as if he were planning to make some kind of big move soon.

In three weeks, graduation ceremonies at the international secondary school would take place and he would receive his diploma. *It would be great if Father and I could part company then,* David thought; at the same time, he knew that his father would never allow that—he hadn't missed the not-so-subtle death threat.

Maybe Jeremiah had inadvertently suggested the means of separation, however. As the Prophet's second in command, with access to intelligence and money, he might find a way to win his freedom. Jeremiah had taught him to think in devious patterns.

"So, how did the meeting with your father go?"

David turned toward his stepmother, who stood in the doorway leading to the living room.

"Just the usual stuff," he replied.

Melanie Thurston wasn't really his stepmother, although both she and Jeremiah had told him to think of her in that way. In actuality, David didn't know what she was, other than his father's former companion.

"He's obviously feeling much better," Melanie said.

"Ready to resume his mission in life," David replied scornfully.

"You can tell me all about it at lunch," she said.

"Lunch?"

"A special lunch for a special boy." She seductively raised an eyebrow. "Excuse me. For a special man."

He swallowed hard. Even though Melanie was at least forty, she could easily pass for thirty. In fact, she was more beautiful than any other women he knew.

"I really should go to school this afternoon," he pleaded.

"Your father has excused you for the entire day. He knows about our luncheon plans. He can't go along for security reasons, of course. But he'd think something was wrong if you declined my invitation." He heard the rustle of nylon as Melanie walked closer to him.

She put her hand on his shoulder and said meaningful, "And so would I."

The smell of her perfume so excited him that David could only look down at the floor, hang his head, and mumble, "Okay."

3

When Jeremiah launched a terrorist campaign in America in the 1990s, he progressively published *The Book of Second Jeremiah* on the Internet. Several years later, he did the same with his *Epistle to the New Americans*. Through his long exile and convalescence in China, many Internet Web sites continued to feature his writings and prophecies. Cyberspace discussion groups debated his impact on world history, and whether or not he would ever initiate a final campaign.

Shortly before his heart transplant in Beijing, the first chapter of the Prophet's latest addition to the Christian Bible appeared on www.Jeremiah2.com.

THE REVELATION TO JEREMIAH

CHAPTER ONE

1 I, Jeremiah, your servant and brother in Christ, having recently been suspended in the ethereal region that bridges life and death, saw an approaching Angel, who carried a scepter capped by

a globe. I looked into that globe and beheld the fundamental nature of the many universes.

2 Lightning bolts leapt from the eyes of this Angel, and his words were etched indelibly in my mind as if by a white-hot laser beam.

3 Blessed are those who read these words of God and blessed are those who make a record of this Prophecy, so that those who would listen can make preparation; for the end time is near.

4 Thus spake the Angel of the LORD: "Among many universes in many dimensions, Earth is but a speck of dust, unimportant and destined to burn in the fires of the sun that warms it. Earth is one of countless heavenly bodies on which life, in all its various forms, has taken root."

5 The Angel of the LORD posed this question: "What is the purpose of life? Why would God create primitive life, beginning with the one-celled creature? So that He might observe the vagaries of evolution over eons of time? Is the LORD of the universe so bored that He must play the Game of Life to fill His time?"

6 Your servant Jeremiah remained silent, for fear of being judged to be impudent or ignorant.

7 "In the answer lies the greatest revelation of the LORD about Himself," sayeth the Angel, "which Man has feared even to consider. In his contemplation of the first cause, Man created God in Man's image and subscribed to Him the omniscient powers necessary to create the universe. In his fear of death, Man invented religion.

8 "Most men ignored the only other obvious conclusion," sayeth the Angel, "which is that the universe and its materials and

the laws that govern it have always existed, and that God is a natural byproduct of this environment."

9 Heresy! Blasphemy! I thought to myself. The Devil has disguised himself and seeks to plant evil ideas in the mind of a Prophet anointed by the LORD to carry His message of salvation to Mankind.

10 The Angel said, "Listen well to this true account of the nature of the LORD, and His purpose for Mankind."

11 "Energy and matter have always existed and know no boundaries of space and time. In the conversion of energy and matter from one form to another according to the governing laws of the many universes, it was inevitable, yet wholly predictable, that a spark of Intelligence would be created, for intelligence is nothing more than electrical imprinting. Such Intelligence brought meaning to the Void that had definition, order, and predictability, but no purpose.

12 "That first spark of Intelligence, which Man knows as God, evolved over time immeasurable, and grew in Knowledge and power and control of the limitless universes and the laws that govern them."

13 I spake finally, "But did God then not create Man?"

14 "The same forces that gave birth to God also produced Man," sayeth the Angel, "so that Man is Godlike, and God is part of every Man."

15 "God does care for us, then?" I asked

16 The Angel smiled at me—a smile so dazzling and pure that I could no longer consider him Evil. "Yes, God cares and God has a plan for Mankind, part of which He has revealed to you, Jeremiah."

17 "But I am ill, perhaps dying. Has the LORD forsaken me?"

18 "The LORD has not forsaken you, Jeremiah. Nor will you die. Remember His words, which you spake, as I do. Man must seek after Knowledge. Man must evolve or he will perish, as have so many forms of life in the universes. The LORD can point the way, but Man must take the steps to control his destiny, which is to eventually unite with the Godhead. Otherwise, Man is not worthy."

19 And I was much ashamed to have forgotten the LORD's words.

20 "You must turn your mission over to your Successor, Jeremiah. The LORD has another role for you."

21 The Angel beckoned me closer so that I could peer again into the globe atop the scepter. I beheld the Divine Will, my destiny, and the future of Mankind.

4

March 23, 2018, *David's birthday, will be the beginning of my emancipation also,* Melanie thought. She and her "stepson" sat in the backseat of the black Mercedes, behind the driver and one of their bodyguards. They crept along in heavy traffic for the short trip from their sprawling courtyard house near Houhai Lake, north of the Old Forbidden City, to the glistening new high rises constructed on either side of Second Ring Road.

Centuries ago, the road had been part of the concentric circle of security walls surrounding central Beijing and the old palace, the walls designed to keep out marauding hordes and new ideas. Now honking cars clogged the busy thoroughfare lined with the modern buildings that signified China's openness and its market economy modeled after various Western systems, most notably that of the United States.

China's Democracy Party, founded at the turn of the millennium, now controlled the government, although many in the military were still faithful to the Communist Party's ideology. China had changed considerably since they first arrived seventeen years ago. Melanie smiled, knowing how much Jeremiah hated all this.

The driver stopped in front of a department store, and she and David and the bodyguard hustled inside.

"Where are we going?" David asked as they walked rapidly through the store and exited on the other side. This standard security precaution would help determine if they were being followed, in which case the bodyguard would summon reinforcements.

"Just down the street," Melanie replied, pulling the fur collar of her black coat tighter around her neck; early spring in northern China could pass for winter elsewhere. She walked at a fast pace, never looking at the sea of Chinese faces around them. She had been in Beijing long enough to distinguish the majority Han from Tibetans or Uighurs, but she never talked to any of them. In fact, excepting a few phrases necessary to direct the efforts of servants, she had refused to learn Mandarin. With its proliferation of homonyms, it sounded to her like funeral singing, especially when coming from high-pitched voices. As for the pictographic writing, it totally mystified her.

Several doors down, they entered another high rise and took an elevator to the sixth floor. Melanie nodded at the bodyguard, who obediently stopped and took up post in the reception area.

"What is this place?" David asked.

"It's a private club and restaurant," Melanie replied.

She didn't add that she lunched here frequently, often with high government officials and ranking military officers. Many powerful people were interested in Jeremiah's activities. While they cared little about him personally, they respected the worldwide following he commanded, which numbered in the millions; true believers and shock troops who could perhaps be manipulated to embrace a new cause once the Prophet passed on to his just reward.

In truth, she had been able to impart only a few tidbits of valuable intelligence over the years, so she freely dispensed sexual favors to influential Chinese officials—and to not a few foreign diplomats and businessmen as well—so she could pick their minds.

It was a dangerous gamble. In addition to his many loyal eyes and ears, Jeremiah always had been exceptionally intuitive—almost psychic—about perceiving traps and detecting traitors. Melanie reminded herself frequently of the fate of Katrina Dorfler, Jeremiah's first cousin and the mother of one of his sons. When Katrina betrayed the Prophet many years ago, she promptly disappeared and her body was never found.

As a cover, Melanie played both sides of the street and purported to be Jeremiah's mole within the Beijing power establishment. In fact, she and Jeremiah had arrived at an explicit agreement years ago about their relationship. When able to perform, he might use her sexually; otherwise, she could have her own discreet private life in return for taking care of David.

Jeremiah had seduced her during the New America era and then used her to kidnap David. She had accompanied him to China, prepared to love him and stay with him forever. But he only used her occasionally for sex, during which he compared her disparagingly to Laura. After that, she became a "nanny" to David. Melanie had gotten even with both of them, and she wasn't through yet, although she was in a hurry.

Now that David was grown and ready to take his place alongside his father, she had become dispensable. She intended nothing less than to turn the table on the world's best-known manipulator. Beginning today. The window of opportunity would be open for only a short while.

An arrogant maître d' seated them in the back of the room at a table isolated by screens that bore drawings of famous Buddhist shrines.

"See anything you like, David?" Melanie asked, studying the menu.

"I'm still looking."

The dishes were truly international, beyond the usual Beijing and Shandong cuisine—and Mongolian hotpot, which gave off a pungent smell that couldn't be confined to the kitchen. A nominal vegetarian, Melanie ate meat only on special days such as this one.

"I'm going to have the filet mignon," she announced to David. "What about you?"

"Maybe sautéed eel," he joked.

"How 'bout a burger and fries?"

He put down the menu and smiled broadly. "All right."

They placed their orders in English, although Melanie knew that David had a working knowledge of Mandarin.

"And champagne," she said to the waiter. "Dom Perignon."

"I'd rather have Tsingtao beer," David said after the waiter had left.

"Then why didn't you say so?"

He shrugged. "I've never tried champagne. Jeremiah would kill me if he knew."

He'd kill both of us—if he knew.

The champagne arrived and Melanie offered a toast: "Here's to you, David, on your eighteenth birthday, the traditional age of emancipation. You are now a man. The world lies at your feet."

She watched as he cautiously tasted the champagne and then wrinkled his nose. "You like this stuff?"

"Oh, yes," Melanie laughed.

During the meal, she noted with satisfaction that David had gradually warmed to the bubbly and begun drinking it freely.

"So, what did you and your father talk about?"

"The usual Bible lesson. Plus, he's had a revelation. Bugs are now involved somehow in the eternal conflict between good and evil."

"Bugs?"

David laughed. "Microbes. Like the ones that caused his heart problem."

"Oh." Melanie immediately thought of biological weapons, which Jeremiah had used in the past. It could be additional evidence that he planned a renewed terrorism campaign. Another sign that he would be leaving China soon.

"God has a purpose for bugs," David giggled, revealing the champagne's effect.

"Really?"

"Yeah, but only God knows what it is." David leaned across the table. "My father's a real asshole, isn't he?"

Melanie smiled, happy that David viewed her as a confidante and that he obviously was becoming drunk. "Only you could get away with talking about Jeremiah like that."

"Yeah, I know. I'm also supposed to prove that I'm a worthy successor, in which case he'll tell me all his secrets, including the whereabouts of billions of dollars he's got stashed in banks. It takes money to fight evil, you understand."

"Which banks?" Melanie asked, trying to appear nonchalant while thinking that she had accidentally struck the mother lode.

"He didn't say."

Melanie got the waiter's attention and pointed at the empty champagne bottle. Now she had a key to a key. It might open the door to freedom. David had never really been part of her long-range plans. In the end, he would be faithful to his father, if only out of fear—and that made him her enemy.

"Do you think Jeremiah plans to leave Beijing and China now that he's in better health?" David asked soberly.

"Maybe." Privately, she considered it a safe bet.

He shook his head in bewilderment. "I've been here all my life. I can't imagine what it would be like to live somewhere else."

Melanie could, even after all these years. If she had stayed in the United States with her husband Randall, she would have had a better life. She had been young, ambitious, and naïve. Stupid. She'd sold her soul to the devil, and paid the price.

"What was it like when you and Jeremiah first came here?"

"It was a very uncertain atmosphere. After the collapse of New America, the Chinese granted your father asylum, which caused a crisis with the U.S. government. They wanted Jeremiah extradited to America and put on trial for numerous criminal charges."

"He's never talked much about that to me."

Melanie knew that both at home and at school, David had received a sanitized version of his father's history.

"There were several assassination attempts on his life during the earlier years, probably by the CIA," she said. "It was a scary time."

"They tried to snatch me off the streets once, didn't they?"

"Twice. When you were five, and again when you were eight."

"Was that the CIA?"

"Probably." *More likely it was Steve Wallace and the Gemini Group,* she thought, but she wasn't quite ready to reveal that secret to David.

"Now no one seems to care about us."

That wasn't true, she knew. Steve and Laura would always care. They had given up armed rescue attempts, though, probably fearful that David would be harmed, or killed. According to her sources, however, negotiations continued over Jeremiah's extradition, especially after the U.S. had recently persuaded Taiwan to accept commonwealth status with China. Only the support of hard-core Communists kept Jeremiah safe for the moment, and that wouldn't last forever.

After their entrées were served, Melanie began her pitch. "I've devoted my life to you, David. Maybe I haven't done everything right, but I've always loved you and had your best interests at heart. Do you know that?"

"Yeah, I guess so," he said reluctantly.

She couldn't help but smile at his ambiguity, which she understood all too well. "And since I have your best interests at heart, I won't ever make you do something you don't want to do." *That's partially true,* she thought. "In fact, you should be your own man, not anyone's protégé."

"Jeremiah doesn't agree with you," he said sullenly, refusing as usual to call his father by any intimate name—Dad, Pop, or Father—when he wasn't in his presence.

"I know, but you can't be under his thumb forever, David. It's a wonderful world out there, with a million adventures awaiting us. You have to be smart to break away, and you have to grow up very fast. You can be free and independent and do whatever you want—if you have the will and the means."

"Money, you mean. Jeremiah said I'd be tempted by that in the future."

"And Jeremiah could never have accomplished anything without money—oodles of it."

"He admitted that."

Melanie savored a bite of the succulent filet. "I don't happen to believe that money is the root of all evil, David. It depends on the use you make of it. It can be a source of much good, pleasure, and freedom. Always remember that. And always remember that I will help you be what *you* want to be."

"I know, Melanie."

She could see that he meant it. She had accomplished one purpose today. "Eat your hamburger, David. You need to get something in your stomach besides that champagne you don't like."

They made small talk throughout the rest of the meal, dwelling mainly on David's school and friends.

After dessert, Melanie said, "There's a massage parlor in the basement. I've scheduled a rubdown for each of us. It's another present for you."

"I hope it's not moxibution," David joked, referring to the traditional Chinese technique of igniting herb-soaked cotton balls close to the skin prior to the massage.

"This will be totally natural," she assured him.

Downstairs, Melanie disrobed in a small dressing room and presented her nakedness to the mirror on the wall. She pirouetted slowly, critically examining her body from every angle. She liked what she saw—a tall, leggy blonde, thin but voluptuous. Oils and lotions kept her skin moist and elastic. Three hundred situps a day gave her abdomen the appearance of a washboard. Buttock-tightening exercises prevented her derrière from drooping or spreading. She was forty-one and in her sexual prime. A mature woman who knew what she wanted, and how to get it.

Melanie tore herself away from the mirror and strutted proudly into the adjoining room. She smiled provocatively at the Chinese masseur, daring him not to devour her with his eyes; not to linger on the V-shaped design of her pubic hair, which pointed the way to the promised land . . . or, in his case, territory as forbidden as the old Imperial Palace had once been to the masses.

Nevertheless, as he covered her with scented oil and began to massage her muscles, the squat masseur with the inscrutable face managed to brush a finger against the side of her breast, as she knew he would. When he did the backs of her legs, she felt his hand lightly brush her bush, as she knew it would.

Melanie brazenly flipped onto her back and placed her feet on the table so that her knees were bent at a sharp angle. "Do the inside of my thighs," she demanded. As he worked on one leg, she moved the other leg from side to side.

The sexual tension is just right, she thought, suddenly climbing off the table. "You can go now," she abruptly told the masseur.

She slipped quietly through the door into an adjoining room, where her eyes looked into those of the masseuse kneading David's back. With a raised eyebrow and toss of her head, Melanie dismissed her, knowing that the Chinese woman would start the hidden camera.

David's head extended over the end of the table. He sucked on a slender, flexible hose leading to a brass pot on the floor. The pungent smell of burning opium filled the air. *Some things in China never change,* she thought.

Melanie had arranged this treat also. She knew that he enjoyed the pipe, as did most of his teenage friends, who included the children of many wealthy Chinese, high-ranking government officials, as well as foreign diplomats and businessmen stationed in China. David had come home more than once high on beer and opium and suffered the wrath of his father, who would make him recite the Social Contract of *Second Jeremiah* and its ban on alcohol and drugs. Chapter two, verse seventeen.

Melanie moved the towel aside to look at the young, muscular body. Jeremiah once had the same youthful, curly blond hair, she noted wistfully.

David delighted in being stoned. High on champagne and opium. Chamium. He giggled at his new word. Then his thoughts wandered down other avenues. He'd had his session with Jeremiah, and now with Melanie. He couldn't go home like this. Today he had become a man, or so everyone had told him. He felt like he could drink and party all night long.

He'd call some friends and meet them at JJ's, the three-story disco on Xinjiekou Bei Street. Young girls from Beijing University hung out there. Willowy porcelain dolls. Willing porcelain dolls. He giggled. The massage had fired up his hormones.

He'd tell Melanie he was going to his friend Zhu's house to make up homework he'd missed by not going to school today. She would allow that and cover with his father, if necessary. Later, he'd call and say he was staying over with Zhu, whose father was an army general. Even Jeremiah would approve.

In truth, he and Zhu would stay out all night. If some of the university girls were willing, they'd go to their place. If not, they'd leave JJ's, walk to the nearby Jishuitan subway stop, take the underground train to the stop near Workers Stadium, and walk from there to the Sanlitun embassy district. That area had several all-night karaoke bars where the waitresses also worked as prostitutes.

The masseuse had resumed her work. He felt her hands on his shoulders, her fingers running down his spine. She squeezed his buttocks. And reached between his legs!

David turned over. "Melanie, please, don't. . . ."

"You say no, but your erection says something else."

"I don't want to do this right now," he said, trying not to whine like a teenager.

"Sure you do. It's perfectly natural. Besides, I love you. You know that. We're going to be together in the future."

"It just doesn't seem right."

"It's always been right, no more so than today. We're not related, David. I'm a woman, you're a man. We love each other, and this is entirely natural, as I've told you many times before."

He fumbled for the opium tube, inhaled, and felt the narcotic seep into the far reaches of his body. He relaxed and tried to forget his primal fears about incest.

Suddenly she was on top of him. Against his will, the lower part of his body began functioning like a jackhammer. His hands grabbed her swaying breasts.

Melanie rammed her tongue into his mouth alongside the plastic tube, so that when she sucked on his tongue, their mouths filled with opium smoke.

He rode along on the opium fog until he erupted with a scream and could see only bright white stars against a black background. As he started to fade away, David heard a far-off voice whisper, "I love you, David. We were meant to be together. I'll help set you free. Do you love me, David?"

"Yes," a voice said, and he wasn't certain whether it was his or someone else's.

5

Thomas stepped out of the cab and hoisted the gym bag over his shoulder by its strap. Inside it were his clothes—and yesterday's mail. He hadn't walked a half-dozen steps toward the condominium entrance before one of his bodyguards, wearing a pinstriped suit, got out of a car parked on a side street.

The bodyguard intercepted him and put out his hand like a traffic cop. "What you did last night wasn't smart, Thomas. Plus, your parents are worried sick."

"I'm sorry, John," Thomas said, then pushed through the doors into the building. The security guard nodded at him as he pushed the elevator "Up" button. Inside, he inserted an electronic card into a slot and punched a five-digit code. A computerized voice announced, "You have been granted access to the twentieth-floor penthouse."

When the elevator doors opened, he stepped out and stared through the barred gate at another bodyguard, who gave him a sour look and shook his head before pressing the button that opened the gate.

"Are they home?" Thomas asked.

"Certainly."

Thomas looked intently at the bodyguard. There were several of them and they had always been around, as ubiquitous as New York City cabs. He'd grown up with them and had accepted without question the rationale for their existence. Today he had a different perspective on that issue, as well as many questions.

"Where have you been?" his mother asked as he stepped into the entryway.

Thomas knew she would be right inside the door. The bodyguard he had met on the street outside would have used his cell phone to call upstairs.

"It wasn't smart to ditch your bodyguard last night," his father said, using that calm, measured voice that never seemed to vary, even in moments of crisis.

"It wasn't very hard, either," Thomas said, unable to resist the dig.

"Well, we'll do something about that," his mother snapped, crossing her arms.

"Where were you?" his father asked.

"I stayed over with friends. Maybe it never occurred to either one of you, but it's nice now and then to have a little privacy."

Thomas saw a forgiving smile crease his father's face, but his mother still had him fixed with angry eyes.

"Is there another reason?" she asked suspiciously.

"Yes," he said, dropping the gym bag to the floor. He squatted and unzipped it, taking out a ten-by-thirteen-inch padded envelope, which he held up for his parents to see, as if it were exhibit number one. "We need to talk about this."

He walked into the living room and deliberately sat in an easy chair so his parents would have to sit side by side on the sofa if they wanted to face him. This way, he could see their faces and gauge their reactions.

"So what's the big mystery?" his father asked.

"Where did you get the envelope?" his mother demanded.

"It came in the mail, Mother. No return address." Thomas scooted to the edge of his chair, placed the envelope on the coffee table between them, and undid the clasp. He began taking out the contents one at a time. "First, we have a copy of an FBI personnel file on Steven Wallace, special agent. The year is, let's see . . . nineteen ninety-five. It includes a lot of stuff. Family, education, medical reports, fitness tests, evaluations. A photo."

His father's face betrayed no emotion, but Thomas noticed his mother's eyes widen and heard her suck in her breath. He turned his attention back to the photo, which he compared to his father's face. The once coal-black hair had turned gunmetal gray, and the nose and eyes were somehow different. Still, the resemblance was striking, even after more than twenty years.

"That's you, Dad, isn't it?"

His father leaned forward, resting his elbows on his knees. "Before plastic surgery and the ravages of age. We told you when you were quite young that I had been an FBI agent."

"Right, and that the mob had placed a bounty on your head because of your undercover work inside the Mafia. You said that's why we live like we do. The secrecy, the security, the bodyguards, private school. All the guns around the house." Thomas laughed bitterly and shook his head at his own naïveté. "Even so, I never even thought about your real name. Our real name. It's not Austin, is it?"

His father shook his head.

Thomas pulled more papers out of the envelope. "Here we have newspaper clippings about Laura Delaney, famous television personality from the last century. Even an autographed picture." He couldn't help but linger over his mother's photograph, also dated 1995. She had always been beautiful, but she was breathtaking in this photograph. It wasn't only the shimmering blonde hair, flawless complexion, and perfectly formed face that held his attention, but the eyes also. They conveyed intelligence, humor, compassion, and understanding. He sighed, thinking that today they would need all of those.

He spread more papers on the coffee table in rapid succession, as if they were pieces of evidence. "Laura Delaney's medical records from the Leesburg, Virginia, office of a Dr. Helen Inman, gynecologist. Diagnosis: pregnant. And we have two birth records—one from a hospital in Munich, Germany, where a woman named Katrina Dorfler gave birth to a baby weighing eight pounds, one ounce, and one for a baby born to Laura Delaney in a Rapid City, South Dakota, hospital." Thomas looked at her. "In the space for the father's name, it says 'Jeremiah.' "

Thomas deliberately extracted the last piece of paper from the envelope and read aloud the handwriting: "Dear Thomas, Take a close look at the blood types for all these people. Who are they, really? Who are you? Who do you belong to?"

Then he sat back in the chair and tried to control his shaking hands. "It's a good question. Who the hell am I? I'm certainly not your son. If these records are correct, Steve Wallace has blood type A, while Laura Delaney has blood type AB. I have blood type O. I checked in a medical reference book at the library and A plus AB can equal A or B or AB, but not O."

They stared at him as if in shock but didn't speak, so he continued. "Who has type O blood? Katrina Dorfler, that's who. Jeremiah's blood type is listed as B. B plus O can equal O."

His mother stood abruptly and walked to the sliding glass door leading to the balcony. She stood with her back to them for several long moments before turning around. "You didn't seem to consider that these records might be false," she said, her voice unsure.

"Are they?" he demanded. "Am I adopted? Why didn't you tell me?"

"No," his father said quietly. "The records are probably accurate, Thomas. You're not adopted, at least not legally. We couldn't withstand the scrutiny of such a legal process, and after a while, it didn't seem important. It isn't important."

It all seems so damned crazy, Thomas thought as he also stood, then paced about the room, fighting off a panicky feeling. "So I'm not your son?"

His mother walked over, took his face in her hands, and looked up into his eyes. "No, you *are* our son. You always have been, and you always will be. No blood types will ever change that! Who loved you and took care of you? Who raised you? We did. We're your only parents, your true parents."

Steve joined them and the three stood in a small circle for several minutes, hugging each other. Thomas looked closely at his father. He had always assumed that he resembled his dad, except now he knew Steve wasn't his father.

Thomas listened intently as they told him the story, the whole story. *The truth,* they said. He was the son of Jeremiah, the terrorist Prophet, and Jeremiah's first cousin, Katrina Dorfler. Jeremiah killed Katrina in New America when he was only a few weeks old. In a complicated kidnapping operation, they said that two of Jeremiah's followers had exchanged him for David, Jeremiah's son by Laura.

"My God!" Thomas said, collapsing into the easy chair. "You have another son?"

"Yes," Laura said, perching uneasily on the edge of the sofa. "David. Your half brother. He's my son, too. We raised him for a year. We loved him dearly, and we still do. But we don't know him anymore. It's you we raised, you we love. If there's a true son of ours, it's you, Thomas."

"My God!" Thomas repeated. "Why didn't you tell me all this before now?"

Clearly frustrated, maybe even slightly angry, his mother asked, "When, Thomas? When you were five years old, getting ready to attend preschool? Would that have been an appropriate time to tell you that your biological father was one of the world's worst terrorists? That he imprisoned your father and me in New America while he threatened the country with nuclear destruction. That in a rage he apparently killed your birth mother and abandoned you. That we have lived in fear of him all our lives. Feared that he might return and abduct you, or kill us. Should we have told you all this when you were in grade school, Thomas? Junior high? High school? When would this information have made you feel good about yourself? Contributed to your mental health and sense of well-being?"

Tears flew as she thundered at him, "There was no good time until today, and even this isn't a good time! All this paper *evidence* doesn't change our lives one bit."

"Your mother's right," Steve said, smiling gently at him. "Our job was to raise you as best we could. To love and respect you and to give you every opportunity possible so that you'd grow up to be a good, well-adjusted man. I think we did a halfway decent job, don't you, Thomas? We're both so proud of you."

Laura said, "There is no bad seed, Thomas. Blood type and genes are not nearly as important as living the values you learned while growing up. Just remember the one rule I told you so many times."

Thomas looked at his mother and began to slowly nod as he repeated her favorite words of advice: "Be the best you can be, and practice the Golden Rule."

"And never, ever forget the overwhelming power of love," Laura added.

As if responding to a silent signal, they all stood. Thomas embraced his father in a fierce hug and clung to him for as long as he could. Then he gently wrapped his arms around his mother. They sat again on the sofa, with Thomas in the middle, wiping tears from his face.

"I've heard about Jeremiah, of course. We discussed him in a government class in high school. But I never thought . . . it was so long ago."

"Not so long," his father replied ruefully.

"We always feared something like this would happen," Laura said.

"Is he still alive? Jeremiah. What about David?"

"Jeremiah was granted asylum in China in the year two thousand," Steve answered. "David is still with him, as far as we know. Extradition efforts failed, as did several private rescue attempts. Jeremiah's health began to suffer several years ago, and most people, including the FBI, no longer consider him a threat."

Thomas saw his parents look at each other, and it was easy to interpret the meaning. *They don't believe that for a moment.*

"Did he send this stuff?" Thomas asked, pointing toward the papers lying on the coffee table.

"Probably," Laura said frankly. "Only Jeremiah would have access to some of these documents, especially the Rapid City hospital birth record."

"Why is he doing this now, for God's sake?"

"Both you and your half brother turned eighteen this month," Laura said. She rose, walked to a tall bookshelf, and took down a few volumes, which she handed to Thomas. "Here are several books and pamphlets you should read carefully, including *The Book of Second Jeremiah* and *The Epistle of Jeremiah the Prophet to the New Americans.*"

"Why?"

"So you'll know what to expect if he contacts you again," Steve answered.

David opened his eyes and stared at a broad expanse of white until he recognized it as the ceiling. He lifted his head and felt a stabbing pain right behind his eyes. As he forced himself to sit up, something slid off his chest and landed on the floor with a thud. He looked down and stared dumbly at a book.

The Chinese masseuse energetically burst through the door, took his arm, and pulled him off the table. "You go now to wet sauna," she said in her high-pitched voice.

She helped him to the door and held it open for him. Naked and unsteady, he wobbled down the short hallway to the glass-enclosed sauna, grabbed a handful of towels off a stand, and then went inside. He spread one towel on the lowest of the tiered wooden benches and lay down on his back. Rolling up another towel, he put it under his neck to lessen the pain in his head.

After several minutes, sweat flowed from his every pore, draining away the poisons in his body. He felt revived enough to rise and walk into the narrow shower stall, where he pulled the chain and stood under the cold water. After two more bouts of this regimen, he left the sauna and found himself face-to-face again with the masseuse.

"Your clothes in there," she said, pointing. "You get dressed now."

He did, and when he stepped back into the hallway, she stood there again. "Here, this yours."

She handed him the book.

"I didn't bring a book."

"It yours. You go now."

Too sick and exhausted to argue, David trudged toward the exit and took the elevator up two floors to the lobby. He leaned against a wall until he noticed one of the building security guards looking suspiciously at him. He stared in disbelief at his watch. It was nearly 7:00 P.M.

Moving unsteadily toward the exit to the street, he felt in his inside jacket pocket for his billfold. He half expected to find the cash gone and heaved a sigh of relief that no one had robbed him while he recovered from his champagne-and-drug orgy. *What the hell happened to Melanie? Why'd she abandon me here?*

He took a cab home and didn't bother with any subterfuge, such as crawling over the wall. When he punched the right numbers on the electronic pad, the gate to the courtyard swung open. He knew that security lights lit up simultaneously at several locations in the house, announcing his presence.

Sure enough, when he entered the west wing, a Chinese guard smirked at him and shook his head in mock disgust. David went straight to his bedroom and collapsed onto his bed, not bothering to take off his clothes.

Sometime in the middle of the night, he rolled over onto the book and immediately woke up. The digital display on the clock radio read 3:10 A.M. He switched on a lamp, picked up the book, and looked at the title: *The False Prophet,* by Laura Delaney and

Steve Wallace. He thumbed through the first few pages until he came to the dedication: "To our sons, so that they may know the truth."

Below that, an inscription in a flowing feminine hand read: "To my son David on his eighteenth birthday. Our long separation will soon end and we can begin our lives anew. With the greatest love of all, your mother, Laura."

David shook his head, put the book down, and got out of bed. He walked to the small refrigerator sitting in the corner of the room, took out a plastic bottle of orange juice, and drank greedily from it.

He went back to bed and began reading the book.

Thankfully, the government minister preferred the missionary position. With his face buried in the base of her neck, Melanie could think about other things, although she remembered to periodically emit orgasmic shrieks.

But Wang Ho would help get her out of China, given her promise to report back to him about Jeremiah's movements and plans if the Prophet left the country as expected. They knew of her "close ties" to David.

She considered her timing to have been impeccable. If she hadn't disappeared on David's eighteenth birthday, she would have disappeared anyway.

In response to the minister's moaning and pathetic pelvic thrusts, she grunted like a sow in heat while thinking about Jeremiah. She had outsmarted him and bound David to her with sex—a stronger bond any day than theology or philosophy. *That's the real story of mankind,* she told herself.

Giving David the book by Delaney and Wallace was a masterstroke. The kid already hated his aloof, dictatorial father and now he would find out that most others, including his real mother, looked upon Jeremiah as nothing more than an insane terrorist.

Of course Jeremiah would continue to brainwash David and program him as a robot, but Melanie knew she would eventually win that contest, too. Besides, Jeremiah obviously had his doubts about David as well. That was why he'd sent a package recently to his other son, Thomas. Melanie knew about the mailing, compliments of the minister drooling on her neck. The Chinese regularly read Jeremiah's outgoing mail, despite the Prophet's many efforts to circumvent them.

What else do the Chinese know that they haven't told me?

6

At 7:30 A.M., David went to the kitchen and ate a large breakfast prepared by the Chinese cook.

"Where's Melanie?" he asked one of the bodyguards, who responded with a shrug.

David went to her bedroom and knocked lightly on the door. When no one answered, he opened it and looked inside. Her bed hadn't been slept in. He considered that she could have spent the night with his father, a thought that filled him with disgust and resentment.

He started to leave and then reconsidered. He had been in her bedroom only a few times, and even then he hadn't progressed much beyond the doorway. In every room in the house, security cameras were mounted strategically on the walls. Guards monitored everyone's movements and undoubtedly reported to his father. His and Melanie's liaisons had always taken place away from the compound, sometimes in daring locations, including public parks, taxicabs, and once even in a museum bathroom.

Those thoughts reminded him of the book. He had skimmed all the way through it over a four-hour period, reading at least the beginning of every chapter and deciding whether to read further. One chapter near the end about Laura Delaney and her child, if true, provided a new perspective of his life—if he was the child described in the book. *A child of rape, a raped child* . . . although, in truth, he'd been Melanie's willing partner for some time now. Still, that didn't take away all of the hurt.

He searched the nightstand, chest of drawers, and closet without any specific goal other than to see what he could find. If Melanie came back, he'd be the indignant one, demanding to know why she had left him at the health club, stoned and unprotected. And why did she leave the book? She couldn't deny it and he'd laugh if she feigned indignation and suggested that someone working at the club had laid the book on his naked, unconscious body. Not this book, given the subject matter.

He didn't find anything of interest in the room, and even became embarrassed after being aroused when he searched through a chest of drawers full of Melanie's skimpy underwear that immediately triggered vivid memories.

He reached for the doorknob just as it turned and the door opened. He found himself looking directly at his father. The image startled him. Jeremiah wore a black shirt, black trousers, and black shoes. He had even dyed his hair black and had it straightened. Somehow, he seemed taller, broader and more robust than usual. The weariness that had often characterized his eyes during the years of illness had been replaced by a confident, cold look.

"I'm surprised to find you here," Jeremiah said.

"I was looking for Melanie," David stammered.

"I expect she's gone for good."

David experienced mixed emotions, relief vying with panic. "What do you mean?"

"I mean she's left," Jeremiah said, walking over to sit down in one of the two chairs arranged in front of the fireplace. "Left this house, maybe even left Beijing and China."

David gasped. "What do you mean? How do you know that?"

"I know many things. Some people don't believe that God talks to me, although I hope and assume you are not counted in their ranks."

"But I don't understand why she would leave."

"Life never proceeds in a straight line. There are inevitable plateaus and valleys. When one steps up or down, one's environment and perspective change."

David suppressed irritation at his father's usual manner of speaking in riddles, but he decided to sit down and listen.

"Melanie's job here is finished, David. And your role has changed also, as I mentioned to you before. You've stepped up to be a man, and you no longer need a stepmother. Conversely, Melanie has been forced to step down." He paused, as if considering whether to say more. Then he changed the subject. "Now that my health is restored and an angel of the Lord has visited me, I too have a new perspective. It's time to walk on the tallest mountain, David. We'll be leaving soon."

"Leaving? Where are we going?"

"I've neglected you in recent years, David, and for that I'm truly sorry. However, we will be working closely together from now on and we will reestablish the mutual trust and love that should characterize the relationship between a father and his son."

"Trust, Father? Have you always been truthful with me? About everything?"

His father seemed wounded. "Of course, David." Then a look of comprehension appeared on his face. "Ah, yes, the book you've been reading has planted doubts in your mind, which undoubtedly was Melanie's purpose in giving it to you."

David felt queasy. "You know about the book? How?"

Jeremiah smiled. "The guards check on you periodically during the night. You slept with the book."

"Why do you think Melanie gave it to me?"

"You were with her yesterday. Didn't the two of you go to lunch?"

He knows. David felt as if he might vomit.

"Don't get me wrong, David. I'm not unhappy that you're reading this book. Scholars of any subject should read all conflicting points of view. I just wish you had approached me first and indicated your interest in reading the opposition's point of view. You've read the words God revealed to me in *The Book of Second Jeremiah* and my *Epistle to the New Americans.* Learned men at the Science Center of New America, as well as Chinese scholars, have written many fine volumes about our movement. What new insights have you gained from Delaney and Wallace?"

He really didn't want to play this game. "I've only skimmed the book," David mumbled. "The most startling thing is that Delaney claims to be my mother."

"She *is* your mother."

"Why didn't you tell me that before!" David demanded, stunned.

"I always considered it inadvisable to tell a young boy that his mother abandoned him. That doesn't apply to a man, however."

"But she writes that agents working for you kidnapped me."

Jeremiah smiled indulgently. "Of course she does. I've read the book. She also claims I raped her and impregnated her. I think you're old enough to understand male-female relationships, David. The truth is that Laura and I fell in love. That's why I was hiding at her farm during the end of my first campaign in America. Then, after escaping from the FBI, I fled to China for the first time. During our long separation, when Laura didn't know whether I was dead or alive, she married Wallace. When I returned to establish New America, we resumed our love affair. She willingly lived with me in New America. You've seen the famous videotape of my tour of the Science Center in nineteen ninety-nine?"

"Yes."

"You'll recall that she was there at my side. Pregnant with you. You were born in Rapid City." Jeremiah's face lit up with a new thought. "You know, Dr. Michael Connolly, the doctor who delivered you, is still alive. He must be nearly eighty now. You should correspond with him, David. Better yet, you may have an opportunity to meet him soon."

Truthfully, David couldn't remember Laura Delaney in the old videotape. The times he'd been forced to view it, he'd thought of it only as another form of indoctrination. As soon as he left here, however, he'd find it and view it again.

"As for this alleged kidnapping of you, here's the truth: Wallace was insanely jealous of Laura and me, and he attempted to kill me several times. He made a desperate effort to kidnap Laura shortly after she gave birth to you. Ironically, my first cousin, Katrina Dorfler, also had given birth in the same hospital to our son."

"You and your cousin had a son!"

Jeremiah looked peeved that the subject had come up. "I'm a sinner, too, David. But that's not what we're talking about now. There was a fight at the hospital that night between Wallace, his gunmen, and my bodyguards assigned to protect Laura and Katrina. In the confusion, Katrina was killed and Wallace inadvertently took her son, thinking it was you. When I was forced to flee once again to China, I naturally brought you with me."

"Why didn't Laura come with you?"

"Wallace would never let her go, and I was fearful that she'd be killed in any rescue attempt my followers might make." His father looked disgusted. "I don't believe they've told Thomas, your half brother, the true story of his background."

"But if my mother loved you, why would she agree to co-author this book?"

"David, David. Wallace is a powerful man. A former FBI agent. Confidant of former U.S. President Peter Thompson. Laura couldn't cross him and live."

"It's all so confusing," David said, slumping back in his chair.

Jeremiah nodded his agreement. "Confusing and disturbing. I too have recently discovered terrible information I didn't know before." He rose and walked to a framed painting on the wall. David watched as his father swung the painting to one side, revealing a wall safe. After turning the tumbler rapidly in several directions, Jeremiah opened the safe, reached inside, and took out—*a video-*

tape. David jumped to his feet. His heart began to race and sweat poured down his face.

Holding out the tape, his father walked toward him. "This is another reason Melanie fled. Apparently she learned that I now know the truth. You and she were having sex. She abused you for years, David. Why didn't you tell me?"

David's tongue seemed swollen and he swallowed twice to generate saliva. That delay provided a precious few seconds for him to consider, and reject, several lies. "I was afraid."

"That's understandable—sexually abused children always feel ashamed and guilty. I would have stopped those assaults, however, had I known about them earlier." Jeremiah shook his head sadly. "But another thing disturbs me equally, David. As I reviewed this pornography, it seemed to me that there are many times, especially in recent years, when you enjoyed *fucking* Melanie. Is that why you didn't reveal this sin against God's law? Must I remind you of *Second Jeremiah,* chapter three, verse five: 'Sexual intercourse is allowed only within the bounds of holy matrimony.' "

David hung his head and choked back tears. "I know, Father."

Jeremiah put one arm around David's shoulders so that their faces nearly touched. "I'm disappointed in you. The Lord originally called me to my mission because people like you choose sin willingly and then find a thousand excuses for their waywardness. You know the motto of New America: 'Obey or die!' You must repent and redeem yourself, David. You must prove yourself anew to me. Otherwise, I fear you will become a drunk and a drug addict, a whoremonger, and a disciple of the devil. Is that what you want?"

"No, Father."

Jeremiah lifted David's chin and gave him a hard look. "Fail me again and you will be cast out. Choose wisely."

The next six weeks seemed an eternity to Thomas. He spent much of the time with his nose in a book, studying for final exams that would allow him to graduate from high school, or reading about his "father," Jeremiah.

There were many more discussions with Steve and Laura, as he now called them. After all, they weren't his real parents. They answered his questions as objectively as they could, and they respected his need for privacy. He knew it took a great exertion of willpower for Laura not to hover over him every moment of the day. Increasingly, he wanted to be alone, not so much to think or plan, but simply to escape mentally. He revived his teenage exuberance for playing mindless video games on the computer in his bedroom.

But some subjects he had to talk about. One day he came home from school early and found Laura in the kitchen making a salad for dinner.

He poured a glass of milk and sat at the table. "Tell me how I was switched for David."

Laura inhaled deeply, put the salad makings into the refrigerator and sat down opposite him. "Let me paint in the background briefly, to give you some perspective. As you may know by now, Jeremiah went into hiding at the end of nineteen ninety-five, after he escaped from the northern Virginia farm where your father and I lived. He remained underground for several years. Both Steve and I retired from our jobs. In the spring of nineteen ninety-nine, an intruder with a gun broke into our house and Steve killed him. After that incident, I went to visit my parents outside of Austin, Texas. Do you remember your grandmother?"

"A little bit."

Laura nodded her understanding. "She died when you were only five. Jeremiah found out I had gone to Texas. He had obviously been watching us for years. In fact, we learned later that the head of our security detail worked for him. Jeremiah broke into my parents' house and . . . he raped me."

Thomas felt as if someone had punched the wind out of him. He looked away, embarrassed as much for his mother as for himself.

"I became pregnant. Then things started to happen at a whirlwind pace. Steve was part of a government effort to assassinate Jeremiah in South Dakota, which Jeremiah and his followers had occupied and renamed New America."

"Obviously, Dad didn't kill him," Thomas said.

"No, although Steve laid one more trap for Jeremiah at the farm that didn't work either. Steve was severely wounded, and Jeremiah kidnapped me to New America. For the next seven months, I lived in a cabin in a cave, deep underground."

"Where?"

"There's an extensive cave system underlying the Black Hills, near Mount Rushmore. While I was there, momentous events were happening in the outside world. Jeremiah's mercenary army had attacked various U.S. military facilities. They confiscated bombers and nuclear weapons. There was a stalemate, negotiations, several assassinations, and a big battle at Kansas City. For nearly a year, there was political and social chaos throughout the United States. Your father tried to rescue me in Rapid City but was caught and jailed. In March of the year two thousand, I gave birth to David. A few weeks earlier, Katrina Dorfler had given birth to you in Germany."

"She was Jeremiah's cousin?"

"Yes. She truly loved Jeremiah and had followed him to New America. She didn't live in the cave, but she visited often. I can't say we were friends, but we had common objectives—I wanted to escape; and she wanted me out of Jeremiah's life. She went home to Munich to be with her mother and give birth to you. Then she returned to Rapid City and helped Steve and me flee with David."

"I'm having a hard time following this."

Laura nodded her understanding again. "It was a bizarre scheme. Katrina had hidden her pregnancy from Jeremiah. He didn't know about you, so he assumed that the baby I left at the Rapid City hospital was David. That whole deception was Katrina's idea."

"Why?"

"She naïvely thought that Jeremiah would never find out. But of course he did, and he killed her. I wish your grandmother, Theresa Dorfler, was still alive. She could verify what I've just told you. Luckily, there's tape of a television interview she gave in Pierre, South Dakota. You should see it."

"Yes, I want to."

"Jeremiah arranged an elaborate plan in which he had a couple, Melanie and Randall Thurston, pretend they were your parents. I met her at Bloomingdale's when you and David both were about a year old. That meeting was no accident, although at the time I thought it was. But we were still cautious and we ordered background checks. There was nothing in the Thurstons' past to indicate they were disciples of Jeremiah. Melanie and I became friends. She visited here often. One day we went shopping at Macy's. Jeremiah's supporters created a diversion and Melanie switched you for David. That was the last time we saw him."

Thomas's mouth dropped open. "He wanted to get rid of me! Why did Jeremiah hate me so much?"

"It wasn't you, Thomas. You were just a pawn to Jeremiah, as everyone is. It was a way of getting back at Steve and me. Read the so-called *Lamentations of Jeremiah*. He had it in his mind that David was the inheritor mentioned in *The Book of Second Jeremiah*. Don't try to apply logic to any of it."

"Why did you and Dad stay here after that?" he asked.

"It was obvious that Jeremiah could find us anywhere. This was as good a place as any other." Laura looked over his shoulder into the hallway, sorrow on her face. "It sounds stupid, but when we got David back, I wanted him to be at home."

Later, after Thomas had read the Prophet's *Lamentations*, he thought it possible that Jeremiah had referred to him as a carp, a slimy bottom-feeder, although the writing was obtuse at best. He had no idea of what it all meant.

• • •

The private school Thomas attended occupied several floors of a high rise near Hunter College. He knew that one of the school's security staff was also on the Gemini Group's payroll and reported directly to Steve. The guard remained in the background, always keeping a watchful eye on him. His other bodyguards waited in a car parked on the street and took over the surveillance as soon as he left the school building.

Thomas usually ate lunch in a noisy cafeteria on the third floor. The security guard stood against the back wall, near the only door leading to the main hallway. In the front of the cafeteria, a short hallway off the far wall led to the rest rooms and beyond them, to the kitchen. To see down the rest room corridor, the guard would have to move all the way across the back of the room.

Thomas finished his lunch and put his tray on a conveyor belt. He walked rapidly down the hallway toward the rest rooms, but passed them and went into the kitchen, hoping the security guard would think he had gone into the men's room instead.

In the kitchen, the staff scurried about to the accompaniment of clanging pots and pans. Thomas held a fifty-dollar bill in his hand as he looked for a likely target, finally selecting a busboy about his own age.

"This is yours," Thomas said, holding out the money, "if you help me ditch school. Is there a back way out of here? Stairs? A dumbwaiter?"

It didn't take the busboy long to decide. He grabbed the paper portrait of Alexander Hamilton and led the way to a dumbwaiter, which took Thomas down four floors to a subbasement and loading dock. He jumped down to the alley and made his way to Sixty-sixth Street, knowing that the bodyguards in the car always parked a block away, so they could see the Lexington Avenue entrance to the school.

On Park Avenue, Thomas hailed a cab and told the driver to take him to Newark International Airport, not because he planned to fly anywhere, but because he knew Steve would canvas the cab companies.

At the airport, he dropped a letter in a mailbox and hailed another cab. He told the driver to take the Garden State Parkway to Passaic, but as soon as they neared the rest stop marked on the interstate road map, he told the cabbie to exit and drop him in front of the visitors' center. Other road warriors piled out of parked cars to use the bathrooms, make phone calls, or dine at one of the fast-food franchises lining the central food court.

Thomas went to the gas station on the other side of the building and hung out near the diesel pumps, where he asked several truckers for a ride going west on Interstate 80. A half hour later, one of the attendants told him to shove off. He walked into the area reserved for truck parking, climbed up the side of several big rigs, and looked inside. Whenever he found a sleeping driver, he knocked on the window, but the aroused drivers simply shouted obscenities at him.

Inside the main service building, Thomas went to the food court to get a Coke and fries. He felt anxious, knowing time was running out. He looked around the seating area and spotted a burly man who fit the trucker image—jeans, flannel shirt, NRA hat, a couple of days' worth of beard stubble.

Thomas approached the table hesitantly. "You a trucker?"

"Yeah, so what?"

"Mind if I sit and talk a minute?"

The guy shrugged.

"I'm looking to hitch a ride west," Thomas said.

"There's a company policy against picking up hitchhikers. Why don't you take a train?"

Because they'll be looking for me on buses, planes, and trains. "I'm interested in maybe becoming a truck driver. I want to see what it's like."

"You shittin' me?"

"No, honest. Look, maybe you could think of me as an apprentice driver. You know, you could tell me about the job and I could help keep you awake or something." He could see that this approach wasn't working. "I can pay you a hundred bucks."

"You running from the law, boy? Or your parents?"

"No."

"You ain't queer, are you? 'Cause if you reach over and grab my cock, I'll fuckin' kill you, understand?"

"I ain't queer."

Thomas's spirits rose as he saw the trucker squint, as if thinking over the offer. "I'm going as far as Chicago," he admitted finally.

"That's perfect."

Calculation creased the driver's forehead. " 'Course, I'd have to have two hundred to take someone that far."

"No problem," Thomas said, digging into his pocket for the money. Over a four-day period, he had used his ATM card to take over a thousand dollars out of his savings account. That wasn't much money, but he couldn't use credit cards, which would lead his parents to him in a hurry. He had to be cautious. Below table level, he peeled a hundred-dollar bill off his roll and handed it to the driver. "I'll give you another one when you drop me off."

The trucker frowned, then smiled. "That's smart, kid. You passed the first test of the road—don't fuckin' trust no one." He held out his hand. "My name's Russ."

By five o'clock, they were on their way. He and Russ talked for several hours about the business of driving big rigs and Thomas tried to appear fascinated. But exhaustion soon overtook him and he drifted off to sleep, despite his apprehension that Russ might grab *his* cock.

Just after sunrise, the trucker pulled the big rig into a rest area south of Cleveland. He went to the bathroom, returned, and climbed into the bunk behind the seats, telling Thomas to wake him at 9:00 A.M. Thomas walked around the rest area and sat on a picnic table. Except for a few other truckers, no one else was about.

His parents would get the letter today, or maybe tomorrow. He'd tried to explain everything to them, but part of the impulse to run away remained a mystery even to himself. His underpinnings had been washed away and he felt adrift in life. His plans to go to Dartmouth in the fall to study pre-law weren't even a possibility now.

He had to find out who he was, and there was only one place he could begin his quest.

7

An unusual tension prevailed in the compound in the days after Jeremiah revealed the videotaped evidence of David and Melanie's sexual relationship. His father was capable of killing him, David knew, and he feared that a similar fate may already have overtaken Melanie.

At the same time, he couldn't rule out the possibility that it was a setup. Jeremiah apparently had known about the affair all along; he employed enough spies. Maybe his father derived some perverse pleasure in knowing and secretly watching. He could have hidden the cameras, or had someone else do it. David couldn't imagine why Melanie would have done so. Most likely Jeremiah saw the tapes as an opportunity to get rid of Melanie, David thought, as well as to force him to assume a role in the movement.

On the other hand, the knowledge that he had a half brother meant that he wasn't indispensable. Why else would Jeremiah have told him about Thomas? In doing so, he'd had to admit violating the strict morality codes of *Second Jeremiah*. And with his first cousin!

Thomas clearly qualified for the role of the Prophet's understudy, although David couldn't imagine any sane person willingly following in his father's footsteps. Besides, to get to Thomas, Jeremiah would have to go through Steve Wallace, and the former FBI agent apparently was a formidable man. Not for a minute did David believe Jeremiah's characterization of Wallace.

Since Jeremiah had ordered him not to leave the house, David read the Delaney-Wallace book more carefully and reviewed his father's video library about events that had occurred in New America. He played, rewound, and replayed the scenes featuring Laura Delaney until her image was etched forever in his mind.

David sorely missed Melanie, and not just because of the lure of forbidden sex and all the contradictory emotions that generated. Without her help and advice, he wasn't confident that he could outsmart Jeremiah.

He went out of the house and stood in the courtyard. He calculated his chance of dashing by the bodyguards, scaling the wall, and going to the American embassy to request asylum. At the very moment he considered this escape plan, several men dressed in black, wearing masks and carrying compact submachine guns, came over the wall.

David heard the muffled chatter of silencers as the invaders and the bodyguards began firing at each other. He had only seconds in which to observe the battle, however, as one of the bodyguards grabbed him, spun him around, and propelled him through the kitchen door with such force that he sprawled onto the floor.

Preprogrammed thoughts rushed into David's mind—the result of years of training. He started to get to his feet and run for the stairs to the second floor, where he could lock himself in the gun room, with its arsenal of weapons, lead-lined walls, and reinforced steel door. He and a couple of his bodyguards could hold out there indefinitely against even a superior force until reinforcements were summoned, or the police called.

He hadn't taken two steps toward the stairs when someone else shoved him down a hallway. The Australian bodyguard everyone called Red stood near an open closet door, holding an assault rifle.

"Down the ladder!" he yelled, never taking his eyes off the kitchen door leading to the courtyard.

David looked at the open trapdoor in the floor of the closet and instinctively dropped to his knees, turned, and lowered his legs into the hole, searching with his feet for the ladder rungs.

All hell broke loose to his right as the outside kitchen door exploded open, blowing one of the Chinese bodyguards against the wall. David looked up at Red just as bullets tore through the man and the closet door. Someone grabbed David's legs and pulled hard, causing his chin to slam against the floor and his head to hit the trapdoor as he plunged down.

A bodyguard partially broke his fall as he sprawled onto the wet brick floor of a subterranean tunnel. He looked up at Jeremiah, who grabbed his arm and jerked him to his feet. They crouched and ran through the five-foot-high tunnel for a distance of about fifty yards. Ahead of them, one of his father's men opened a round iron door in the middle of the wall. David wiped away the blood dripping off his chin and peered apprehensively into the pitch-black darkness of a concrete drainage pipe that led from the tunnel.

"Don't worry," Jeremiah said. "They don't know about this escape route."

His father's appearance startled David. A smile as bright as the sun lit up the Prophet's face, and energy visibly coursed through his body.

He's happy, David thought as his father shoved him headfirst into the pipe, causing him to painfully bump his knee. With Jeremiah following close behind, David—fearing that they'd encounter a den of rats or snakes—crawled after the bodyguard, who led the way with a flashlight.

Another dawn arrived before the next trucker dropped Thomas off at the exit ramp to State Highway 83, about thirty miles south of Pierre, South Dakota. It was Memorial Day, 2018. Still,

Thomas shivered in the early morning cold, thankful for the light jacket he'd worn to school two days earlier.

He began walking north, sticking out his thumb whenever he heard a car come up behind him. The surrounding scenery fascinated him; the undulating prairie and the omnipresent sky seemed parts of a whole. He imagined himself inside a glass globe. Having lived all his life in concrete and steel canyons, Thomas had no idea that this much open space existed anywhere. The absence of horns, sirens, construction sounds, and the babble of human voices gave substance to the near silence, interrupted only by the murmur of the wind, the bird calls, and the crunch of pebbles scattered by his shoes.

He and his parents hadn't traveled together very much in his lifetime. Usually they vacationed in someone's secluded home, such as the times they flew to an estate on an island off the South Carolina coast, or to the well-guarded Maine home of former President Peter Thompson. Thomas's cross-country odyssey already had expanded his horizons.

A crew-cab Ford truck pulling a horse trailer passed him and pulled partway off the road, causing him to run toward his next ride.

The old driver with a day or two's growth of white beard stubble wore boots, jeans, a shirt with shiny buttons, and a Stetson hat.

"Where you goin', son?"

"Pierre."

"I'll be goin' through there."

"You pulling horses?" Thomas asked, feeling the jolt of the trailer hitch as the truck lurched back onto the road.

"Naw, hay. But I got some horses in a pasture north of Pierre. What's your business in the capital?"

"Visiting relatives."

"Where you from?"

"Cleveland." It just popped into his mind.

"Minneapolis is as far east as I've been, and I ain't sorry 'bout that."

"You live here all your life?"

"Yep. My kin come here four generations ago as sodbusters."

Thomas thrust his right elbow through the open window, savoring the wind in his face. "You must have seen a lot of changes, then. Especially when they tried to turn this place into New America."

A grim look spread across the old man's face as he shook his head sadly. "Yes, sir, that was somethin'. Just goes to prove what it says in the Ecclesiastes—all things are fleetin'."

"Tell me about New America," Thomas asked. "I've only read about it in books."

"Don't hardly know where to start. A couple million of Jeremiah's followers flooded into the state'n tried to buy up all the land'n businesses'n elect their own kind to political office. And if you didn't want to sell to 'em, they'd try to find a way to take your land."

"I gather you weren't a supporter of Jeremiah?"

"I don't take to religious fanatics of any stripe. Religion should be private. Besides, that was nuthin' but a smoke screen anyhow. That'n all of Jeremiah's talk about justice and fairness. New America was a police state, run by the state police and Jeremiah's hired soldiers. He was just another tinhorn dictator lookin' for power'n glory."

"What about all his followers?"

The old man snorted. "Hell, ain't nothin' new about folks gettin' suckered into things they don't understand. It's the way of the world, son. Most folks in the old Soviet Union wasn't Communists, and most Cubans wasn't atheists just 'cause Castro said so."

Both examples were only textbook footnotes to Thomas, who had begun to realize how inadequate his formal education had been. "Why do you think New America failed?"

"There was two men what saved the country from splittin' up into a dozen pieces or more, and they was Peter Thompson, who become president, and General Buster Franklin, the top marine. Thompson forced people to take a hard look at theirselves and the country and do the right thing. Buster wrecked Jeremiah's nuclear bombers and ran them goddamned mercenaries back to all the places they come from."

"You ever heard of Steve Wallace and Laura Delaney?"

The cowboy's face crinkled up in a smile and he chuckled. "There's nobody Jeremiah hated more'n Wallace, who hunted him day and night. Damn near killed him once in Pierre durin' a big rally Jeremiah had there. Wallace got away by swimmin' down the Missouri River. Most darin' damn thing I ever heard of."

"And Laura Delaney?"

"Well, there's all sides to that story. Some say she was Jeremiah's woman. Others say he kidnapped her and held her agin her will. Me, I just don't know."

Thomas frowned. In the books and articles he had read so far, only a few writers thought Laura had been in love with Jeremiah. Most scholars of the movement, as well as former President Thompson, vigorously supported his mother's story of having been raped and kidnapped. Thomas had no reason to doubt her version of events.

"What happened to all the so-called New Americans?" he asked.

"Most of 'em left, and good riddance. There's still a few groups of true believers in these parts, but they pretty much keep to theirselves and don't cause no trouble. But that's not the case with some of those folks down to the Science Center. Among them scientists, professors'n students, you can still find a lot of fanatics who still hanker after Jeremiah. But the government keeps a close eye on 'em, I'm told."

"Where's the Science Center?"

"About ten, twelve miles northwest of Pierre. Hell, I drive right by it."

"You mind dropping me off there?"

The cowboy eyed him suspiciously. "Hey, now, you ain't one of them, are you, son?"

Thomas laughed softly as they approached the Missouri River bridge on the outskirts of Pierre.

• • •

The Marriott Hotel lobby and registration area occupied the twenty-first floor of the thirty-five-story, circular-shaped tower that stood in the middle of the Science Center. Thomas rented a room for two nights and then walked around the outer edge of the glass-enclosed lobby so he could get a better perspective of the huge complex, which encompassed nearly ten million square feet, according to an exhibit he had viewed.

As he pressed his forehead against the window and looked down, he saw the top of several rectangular-shaped, four-story buildings that radiated out from the tower like wagon-wheel spokes and connected to a circular outer "rim" of offices and laboratories. From this height, he had a panoramic view of the surrounding prairie and could even see into Pierre. It seemed like a half-formed world, waiting to be finished.

In his exploration thus far, he'd learned that it once had been the New America Science Center, St. Jeremiah Hospital, St. Jeremiah University, and the Walter Dorfler Hotel. The state legislature later eliminated that heresy by renaming them, respectively, the South Dakota Science Center, Franklin Hospital, and Thompson University, all of which occupied the first twenty floors of the tower.

After settling into his room, Thomas took the elevator to the ground-floor lobby and again studied the glass-enclosed model of the Center. Various buttons activated informational snippets. He put on headphones to listen to a narrative about Thompson University.

After that, and having made a decision, he stepped onto a motorized walkway that took him down a long hallway to the outer rim of the complex, which housed university offices, classrooms, and laboratories, including those of the medical and law schools. Student dormitories occupied one four-story "spoke."

About half of the other spokes contained health-treatment facilities, including an emergency treatment center, a rehabilitation unit, a heart institute, a spinal-injury facility, and offices for doctors and other health-care professionals. The rest of the ground-level buildings were primarily research laboratories and support offices.

In the busy hallway, Thomas found the university registrar's office and spoke to a counselor standing behind the counter.

"I'd like to enroll for the fall term," he told her.

"What do you plan to study?"

"I'm not certain. Maybe just general courses for the first year."

"Do you have a high school transcript and your college test scores?"

"I can have those sent," he replied, not really knowing how he'd arrange that without tipping off his location to Steve and Laura.

"In the meantime, you can fill out this application and other required information," the woman said, handing him a packet of forms and instructions.

"Are there any student jobs available?" Thomas asked. "I also need a place to stay."

"Try the Student Employment Office, two doors down the hall to the right. The dorms are full, but there may be vacancies in employee temporary housing in the basement area."

At the Student Employment Office, he discovered that the Center needed temporary janitors, but the application process reminded him of how poorly prepared he was to assume a new identity. They wanted his name, Social Security number, and home address. He considered leaving, but reminded himself that he had only a few hundred dollars left.

Without thinking, he wrote his name as Thomas Dorfler, adopting his birth mother's name. Using the name Austin didn't seem right anymore. After all, he had come here to discover his roots. He transposed several digits in his Social Security number, and wrote in the address of his best friend in New York. He'd call him later; maybe his computer-geek buddy could help him get his school transcripts and test scores.

Already short-handed, they scheduled Thomas to start work the next afternoon on the second shift. An old guy in the employment office took him to the basement and showed him a musty-smelling, Spartan room that served as temporary living quarters for Center employees. It had three single beds, each separated by a scarred armoire. In one corner of the room, a ratty upholstered chair sat in front of a combination TV/VCR. A sink and urinal were attached to the opposite wall. A metal stall surrounded the toilet.

"You can expect roommates," the old man said in a bored tone. "The bed's free for three weeks. After that, you find your own room or they start charging you two hundred'n ten dollars a month."

The next morning, Thomas wandered around the complex again before deciding to attend a student orientation session for those about to begin summer school.

An assistant dean gave a brief welcoming speech and then played a videotape showing various stages of the Center's construction.

"This next segment follows Jeremiah on a tour of the Science Center in the summer of nineteen ninety-nine," she said. "This does not constitute an endorsement by the university of him or his philosophy, but the film is invaluable in understanding the origin of the Center, and its priorities, even to this day."

Thomas watched intently. He had seen photographs of the Prophet in textbooks, and maybe once in a film his history teacher had shown about the highlights of the twentieth century. He hadn't paid as close attention then as he did now that the terrorist had been revealed as his biological father.

One part of the 1999 tour emphasized the cutting-edge work of the Center in the fields of biology, genetics, computers, physics, and applied technology. Jeremiah addressed a national television audience, emphasizing the philosophical differences between "Old" and New America. He talked about his concept of God, made several scientific predictions, and then announced that God had assured him personally that there would be a resurrection of the dead and eternal life for all.

He's clearly intelligent, confident, and commanding, Thomas thought. Maybe he and Jeremiah weren't related, he concluded gloomily, because he was none of those things. He couldn't even see a physical resemblance. They were nearly the same height, but Jeremiah had a thinner face, light blue eyes, and curly blond hair. Thomas thought that perhaps his own dark hair and eyes came from his mother's side. It occurred to him that he'd never seen photographs or videos of her. He didn't know anything about her, in fact.

"Oh, my God," he whispered to himself as the film focused on the enthusiastic and supportive audience. *There's Laura!* Uncharacteristically, she was dressed casually in slacks and a University of Texas sweatshirt. *She must have been pregnant then,* he thought, *although she doesn't look it*. The best word he could find to describe the look on her face was . . . *fascination*. Like everyone else in the audience twenty years ago, she appeared enthralled by Jeremiah's presentation. It made Thomas wonder anew about their relationship, despite what she had told him.

After the film ended, he stood and, with his head down, walked rapidly from the room. In the hallway, a voice startled him.

"Can I help you with anything?"

He looked to his right and saw an attractive young woman standing beside a table.

"I'm a graduate teaching assistant," she said. "Some of us serve as student mentors or work as tutors. I'm Karla Maypole."

Thomas took her hand and was immediately enchanted, although Karla seemed to be several years older than himself. She had a beautiful complexion and wide, sexy red lips. He could get lost in the deep ocean of those brilliant blue eyes.

"What are you planning to study?" Karla asked.

"I really haven't made up my mind," he stammered. "I'll probably just take general studies for the first couple of semesters. Get some required courses out of the way."

"That's smart. You can sample courses from the various departments."

"What do you teach?"

"Biology one-oh-one."

"I'll remember that."

"Great. What's your name?"

He hesitated. "Thomas. Thomas Dorfler."

She arched an eyebrow. "Like the famous Dorflers?"

He shook his head as if the name were a trivial coincidence. "Distant relatives, I think."

"Well, have a good day, Thomas. I hope everything works out for you."

So do I. Karla had reminded him of his loneliness and the uncertain future looming before him.

8

As the sleek passenger jet took off from the regional airport on the outskirts of the city, David pressed his face against the porthole window, searching the ground below for a familiar sight, although the scenery quickly became an undifferentiated collage of buildings, trees, fields, and roads. People seemed too small to matter.

"Take a good look at Beijing," Jeremiah said. "You may never see it again."

Still in a state of near shock, David turned toward his father, who sat beside him. "Who were they? Why did they want to kill us?"

"It could have been anyone, for any number of reasons," Jeremiah said breezily as if it were no consequence. "The assassins might work for certain elements within the Chinese government, or for the CIA. Even for the Gemini Group."

"Steve Wallace's organization?" David asked.

Jeremiah chuckled. "I see you're keeping up with your studies. It wouldn't be the first time Wallace has tried to kill me."

Or the first time he and Laura Delaney have tried to rescue me, David thought.

"It makes no difference who they were," Jeremiah said. "It's time for us to leave, anyway."

David's panicky feeling eventually gave way to a sense of excitement, even of exhilaration, as he tried to imagine the new life that stretched out before him.

Two hours later, the plane descended out of the clouds and he looked down on a checkerboard land of pastures and multicolored crops. Off to his left rose a formidable mountain range. Then the outskirts of a large city came into view.

"Where are we?" he asked Jeremiah.

"We're preparing to land in Xining, a city in the western province of Quinghai."

"What's there?"

"Many things. It's been a military garrison since the sixteenth century. I have friends here, especially in the military. They'll protect us, and help us get out of China."

"Where are we going then?"

Jeremiah ignored the question. "Quinghai Province is also called the Chinese Siberia. For decades, those opposed to the government were sent into exile here. At one time that included the fascist followers of Chiang Kai-shek, academics and intellectuals, the ultra-leftist Red Guards, anyone opposed to the Communist Party, and now, certain members of the Communist Party." He smiled sardonically. "What goes around comes around, David. Remember that."

That evening they stayed in a simple, private home on the edge of the city. Although now deserted, ample evidence suggested recent occupancy, including clothes drying on a backyard clothesline. As David opened an upstairs window, the pungent odor of manure flowed into the room. He lay down on a lumpy bed and stared at the ceiling.

Early the next morning, a military staff car picked them up.

They drove west, sandwiched between a transport truck carrying a squad of armed Chinese soldiers and a trailing car whose occupants included the two bodyguards who'd left Beijing with them.

David looked out at the streets and saw more racial minorities—Kazak, Uighurs, Mongol, and Hui—than he'd ever seen in Beijing or other eastern Chinese cities.

Jeremiah obviously saw something different from his window as they drove into the countryside. "You could call this area the birthplace of the Four Horsemen of the Apocalypse."

David couldn't follow his father's thinking. "What?"

"Pestilence, War, Famine, and Death are their names. In the Middle Ages, Mongolian hordes rode out of this general area and changed the world for the better."

It never stops, David thought. *Don't other fathers and sons riding together in cars talk about sports, fishing, the old days, whatever? Jeremiah never stops talking about issues and his take on the world.* Once again David couldn't resist a sarcastic response. "Changed the world for the better," he repeated, injecting a note of incredulity into this voice.

"Yes," Jeremiah said. "This area was once part of the empire of Genghis Khan. He was a pagan who thought he had a divine mission to conquer the world. By the time he died in twelve twenty-seven, his armies had extended the empire into Russia, Eastern Europe, and parts of the Middle East. It lasted another forty years under various successors. The achievements of the Mongols were due in part to their tactical military skills. They were the first to exploit the advantage of fast-moving cavalry, and they were masters of siege techniques. Additionally, they were exceedingly brutal to those who resisted them. Many opposing armies simply melted away in terror. Cities willingly surrendered."

As always, David wondered about the moral of the story. Was it that Jeremiah and the Great Khan were both terrorists bent on ruling the world?

"Yes, the Mongolian invasions *did* change the world for the better," Jeremiah continued. "The invaders established a vast administrative empire, instituted taxes, built roads, and greatly facilitated trade between the east and west. For a time, a *Pax Mongolica* existed. More important, the fledgling nation states of Europe and Asia were energized. If they were to survive and not be assimilated, they had to have direction, purpose, and dedication."

At times like this, David had mixed feelings about his father, a truly gifted intellectual from whom much could be learned. Sadly, like the Great Khan, Jeremiah cared only for the cause. People were entirely dispensable.

"In fact, one could theorize that some good comes out of all wars," Jeremiah went on. "The expansion of the Roman Empire and its cruel suppression of other people indirectly gave birth to the two major religions of the world, Christianity and Islam."

Unable to suppress a desire to cast Jeremiah in the fool's role, David interrupted, "What about World War Two? What good came to the tens of millions of people who were killed?"

"They were going to die anyway," Jeremiah responded serenely. "You have to take the broader view. World War Two ushered in the atomic age, space exploration, and created a global economy. It resulted in a tiny step toward world government and the ending of artificial classifications of people." Jeremiah smiled at David. "From that time to the present, the world's population has increased from three to eight billion. Unfortunately, no one of vision directed that regrowth."

"Oh, I see. Every now and then we need to kill off a few million people and make the world a better place."

Jeremiah laughed. "Interesting conclusion, David. But let me finish my story. A century after Genghis Khan, the bubonic plague originated in western China. The Black Death that swept Europe and Asia in the mid-fourteenth century is estimated to have killed upward to half the population on these two continents. It wrecked the existing feudal system and power structure. For those who survived, especially those in the lower classes, the Black Death created opportunities and upward social mobility that had been previously unthinkable. In the wake of the Four Horsemen, freedom, democracy, and new ideas flourished."

David shook his head in disgust. "Fortunately, plagues can't get started with modern-day health care," he said.

"At least half the microorganisms that live on earth remain unclassified," Jeremiah replied. "Many of them can be found in tropical rain forests in Southeast Asia, Amazonia, and along the equator. Ordinarily, they never have contact with humans unless their habitat is destroyed or altered. Do you know what the Black Death was, David?"

"No."

"A bacteria that attacked the lymphatic system, creating infections that produced more bacteria, which then migrated to the liver, spleen, and brain, causing hemorrhaging that destroyed these organs. Many people went mad."

"I guess they didn't see it as a great opportunity."

"At the time, people didn't understand that the bacteria was spread by infected fleas, which in turn infected rats. Fleas and rats are world travelers. Rats especially thrived in ancient cities, making their way into every home, where they urinated and defecated on food eaten by humans. Most critically, the bubonic bacteria became airborne, meaning that it could be spread simply by people breathing the air around them."

"Why didn't everyone die?"

"Some people were naturally immune, or possessed superior disease-fighting genes."

Silence prevailed in the car for a time as the driver took a road running alongside Qinghai Lake. David looked out in amazement at a tent city populated by families, dogs, goats, and chickens.

"Nomads," his father said. "Another phenomenon you may have thought didn't exist in the modern world, David. This is the largest lake in China and although the water is salty, it abounds with fish. That's how the nomads feed themselves, as they have for centuries.

There also are many geese and ducks to feed on. Look toward the center of the lake and you'll see Bird Island."

Even at a distance of several kilometers, David saw large flocks of birds take off and land on the island, as if it were a major airport. He recognized ducks, cranes, sandpipers, and cormorants.

"The island is a temporary sanctuary for many species of migratory birds," Jeremiah explained. "Some, like the bar-headed geese, winter on the plains of India and fly over the Himalayas in the spring to get here. By mid-June, they will move on north, as far as the Arctic tundra."

"How do you know all this?"

"I study topics that are important to our mission, David. It may seem to you that there's no relationship between our work and birds, or microbes, but appearances are often deceiving. In my opinion, the most neglected area of scholarship is the synthesis of ideas. People who practice that technique of thought often arrive at startling insights."

"Your insights certainly are startling, Father," David said with a straight face.

"Birds are ubiquitous, far outnumbering the people on earth," Jeremiah said. "They are always on the move, whether searching for food, nesting, or migrating. Yet people know little about them, and pay them even less attention."

After driving for hours on rough roads extending through a desert containing other, smaller saline lakes, they arrived at an isolated army post. Rectangular, military-green buildings stood in rows, like crops. David could only guess at their functions, since they were so indistinct from each other. Trucks, tanks, and artillery pieces were parked in lots surrounded by fences topped with razor wire.

Inside a traditional Chinese walled compound, a partial pagoda roof covered a large building housing command offices and, according to Jeremiah, a private residence for the commanding general.

A young soldier showed them to a bedroom in the rear of the residence, telling them in fractured English, "The general expect you for dinner."

Following a short rest and time to refresh themselves, they were escorted to the general's private quarters promptly at seven o'clock. The quarters were decorated efficiently, in keeping with the demeanor of their occupant.

"General Lu Jingtao is commander of the Mao Tse-tung Division of the People's Liberation Army," Jeremiah said.

"Your father has spoken of you often, David," General Lu said, as they were seated at a round dining table. "I assume we will be working together in the future."

David smiled but said nothing, although he looked keenly at the general, calculating that the dapper military man, dressed in a dark suit this evening, was an ethnic Han. He also had the regal bearing of the wealthy class.

"General Lu was a protégé of the late Li Gongquin, an unofficial emissary of the Chinese government to New America," Jeremiah said. "General Lu has been our principal protector all these years."

The general dipped his head. "The pleasure continues to be mine, Jeremiah."

As a waiter in a white smock filled their water glasses, David glanced about the room, taking in its décor, which consisted mainly of porcelain statues and landscape paintings, the latter seeming to emphasize the artists' brushwork rather than the scenery.

"David and I saw nomads camped around Qinghai Lake," Jeremiah said, "and I commented that despite efforts at modernization, China hasn't changed much over the years."

General Lu smiled. "Yes, and had you visited the Shuijing Xiang Market in Xining, you would have observed outdoor vendors selling cages of live ducks, pigs, pigeons, rabbits, and dogs. In many ways, some customs in China haven't changed since the Middle Ages. Despite the government's best efforts at family planning over a half century, China's population has exploded to a billion and a half, and probably will reach two billion by the year two thousand fifty."

"The more things change, the more they stay the same," Jeremiah said. "The situation in the world requires drastic changes if mankind is to make a great leap forward."

"I agree," General Lu said. "China is an ancient land and life here has always been hard, David, especially given our overpopulation and poverty. Over the past five thousand years, we've endured warlords, emperors, foreign occupation, fascism, communism, and now, allegedly, democracy and capitalism.

"Our religions give people hope only in stoicism or the afterlife. For example, as you perhaps know, Taoism emphasizes mystical insight, reflection, intuition, and meditation. The bulwark of Confucianism is *li,* with its emphasis upon proper behavior, order, and class. Buddhism teaches us that life is suffering and that the cause of suffering is desire. Nirvana is the elimination of all desire.

"As a dedicated Communist, I must agree with Marx that religion is the opium of the masses. An apt analogy in China, wouldn't you say, David?"

That remark stunned David, who wondered how much the general actually knew about him and his recreational habits. He also expected Jeremiah to react to General Lu's atheistic remarks.

As if reading his mind, the general tempered his observations: "As a man of reason, however, I can't deny the possibility of a god. And if we must have religion, I prefer Jeremiah's theology, with its emphasis on equality, justice, personal responsibility, and progress."

Pretentiously, Jeremiah said, "There is room for you among God's chosen people, General Lu."

David covered his smile with a napkin as he delighted in seeing his father play the role of a toady.

The general sat back in his chair, placed both hands on the table, and frowned. "The Communist Party and its chief protector, the People's Liberation Army, have been gradually forced to relinquish power over the last two decades, David. The ruling China Democracy Party has made economic reform its main priority. The real power in China and throughout the world has shifted to the international business class, which transcends race and nationalism and has, as its sole goal, profit. China has become weak militarily, and vulnerable to its enemies. The United States and its allies could never defeat China militarily, so they just bought it with the connivance of our traitor class."

Jeremiah laughed heartily at General Lu's dry humor, and David took the cue and smiled perfunctorily.

"I've never really understood the attraction of capitalism," General Lu continued. "A great economic depression swept Asia near the end of the last century. China has suffered significant economic recessions twice this decade. In two thousand five, even the United States suffered a major setback when its stock market plunged sharply downward. Yet everywhere, the so-called free market economy flourishes."

Jeremiah jumped into the conversation with fervor. "No economic system is inherently superior or inferior, General Lu. Capitalism is attractive for only one reason—it appeals to man's inherently greedy and selfish nature and his evil desire to exert power over others and to hoard money. Capitalism creates economic classes. The few accumulate wealth on the back of the majority of wage slaves. What keeps these slaves in harness is the false god of materialism. The state brainwashes them to believe they can be rich one day if they are selfish and cunning."

"Your father is right, of course," General Lu said. "Now, the young people in China want German-made cars, Japanese electronic equipment, America movies and music, French perfume and wine. And, of course, drugs from South America and Southeast Asia. We have become America's eastern colony."

"So people don't know what's best for them?" David asked, although he tried to do so in a way that conveyed genuine interest rather than mockery.

"Absolutely correct, David," General Lu replied. "Absolutely correct. Marxist theory always assumed an evolution toward true equality and justice, where the state and the people are one. The people must be led. Leaders must establish the priorities. That's why we're having this conversation, naturally."

Jeremiah stared intently at David. "General Lu and I believe in Mao Tse-tung's observation that power grows out of the barrel of a gun."

"The government decreed several years ago that the word 'liberation' be dropped from the army's name," General Lu said, "although none of my soldiers pay any attention to that official edict. We are a liberation army, and our work has only begun." He leaned slightly toward David as if to impart a confidence. "Around the world, there are many armies like mine, led by men who believe as I do."

"Indeed, we are not alone in our beliefs, General Lu," Jeremiah echoed, his fawning manner continuing to amaze David.

"Jeremiah is a great prophet, David. A moral teacher. Even a military tactician of note, as we all know from studying his nineteen-ninety-nine military campaign within the United States, including the Battle of Kansas City." The general turned a flinty eye on Jeremiah. "I would only fault him for one lapse of judgment, and that was when one of his bombers armed with nuclear weapons penetrated the East Coast air defenses of the United States but failed to destroy its targets. As it says in the Bible, 'But of the cities of these people, which the Lord thy God doth give thee for an inheritance, thou shalt save alive nothing that breatheth.' "

Jeremiah shook off the criticism and underscored the general's remarks. "Deuteronomy twenty, sixteen, General Lu. On the other hand, God did not destroy Sodom and Gomorrah until the righteous had been evacuated. Nor did the Lord let loose the plague on Egypt, or visit their firstborn with death, until the chosen people had marked themselves with purified blood. So it will be again, all over the world."

General Lu nodded enthusiastically. "I believe we are ready to eat," he said, glancing at the bowls of soup the waiter had placed before them.

Early the next morning, David and Jeremiah were driven to the post's military hospital, where a long line of soldiers waited outside the entrance. As he and his father stepped out of the car, a Chinese army officer greeted them.

"It is an honor to finally meet you, Jeremiah," the major said in perfect English.

"Thank you, Major. This is my son, David."

The major bowed in David's direction.

"What's going on here?" Jeremiah asked.

"Many of the new recruits are receiving their vaccinations today," the major responded.

"Go on, David," his father said. "Walk to the front of the line and get a shot."

"Why?"

"Influenza epidemics often originate in the East," Jeremiah said. "Predictions are that the next two years will be bad. You don't want to get sick."

David reluctantly walked into the building, uncertain of how his action would be received when he butted into line. In fact, many young faces turned in his direction, but the soldier he cut in front of only stepped back deferentially. David soon found himself face-to-face with a female nurse who had blond hair like him. He noted that nearly all of the medical personnel appeared to be European or American.

He walked back to the car, rubbing his arm and stood beside his father. "Who are all the Westerners?" he asked.

"Scientists and medical personnel, including those who performed my heart transplant. They travel the world, sharing their expertise. It's one of the many legacies of New America. We'll be flying out with them later in the day."

"Where to?"

"Moscow first. Then home."

"Where's home?"

Jeremiah looked at him and smiled.

9

THE REVELATION TO JEREMIAH

CHAPTER TWO

1 The Angel of the LORD directed that I close my eyes and let my essence flow into the globe atop the scepter he held.

2 In this new dimension and world where all possibilities existed, I assumed the form of a white snow goose and flapped my new wings frantically, lest I fall to the Earth thousands of feet below.

3 I spake and a foreign sound came from my mouth, yet I understood its meaning, as did those of my companions arrayed about me in the shape of a flying cross.

4 "Be not afraid," they said. With their constant instruction and encouragement, I relaxed into a steady, rhythmic effort that easily kept me aloft and generated feelings of euphoria and well-being. We glided effortlessly on a warm current of air, and observed the Earth below with vision both panoramic and telescopic.

5 Hear ye these observations made by a creature through whom the LORD speaks:

6 From a great distance, our home below is blue and green and white and brown, and breathtaking in its unsullied beauty. When the lens of my bird's eye revealed sharper detail, however, I observed the movement of Earth's many creatures, including the Dominant Creature.

7 Most forms of life are driven by the instinct to survive; an instinct formed and shaped by each species as it adapted to the environment. To find the resources to sustain ourselves and make possible the next generation, birds like us migrate to more abundant and hospitable lands, where we might eat and breed.

8 So it once was even with the Dominant Creature. But he has the gift of greater Intelligence, which allows him to discover and understand the laws of nature, and use this Knowledge to control the environment and shape his own destiny.

9 Yet Intelligence does not always include compassion and purpose, nor does diminished Intelligence mean that other creatures lack feeling or desire. In fact, the Dominant Creature is uniquely capable of selfishly waging war on his own kind, even to the point of extinction. The Dominant Creature has inflicted this fate on many hapless species.

10 The Dominant Creature thinks nothing of destroying his own habitat. He fouls the air and water, destroys the very vegetation that gives him breath; even punches holes in the shield that protects him from the deadly rays of the universe. He reproduces without constraint, further diminishing the resources available to all the creatures of Earth. Most of the Dominant Ones have no Earthly purpose.

11 This situation we bemoan as we fly the night sky, fearing not only what further folly will be wrought by Man, but fearing the dawn, when we return to Earth for sustenance and rest. For then he will attempt to kill us for sport.

12 Yet we are not alone. Benign Passengers give us solace by disputing our contention that the Dominant Creature is at the top of the food chain and has no natural enemies.

13 "To us they are but vessels," the Passengers whisper. "Places to breed and feed. The outcome of the battle is far from decided."

14 Blessed are those who read these Revealed Words of God and who make a record of this Prophecy, so that the Faithful can prepare for the end time.

10

Springtime has always been my favorite season in this area, Laura thought, as she looked out the backseat window of the limo taking them from Dulles Airport through the Virginia suburbs. After crossing the Potomac River, they asked the driver to drop them near the memorial to President Franklin Delano Roosevelt.

With bodyguards flanking them on all sides, they walked on the footpath beside the Tidal Basin. The blossoms on the cherry trees had already come and gone, but the sweet smell of azaleas hung in the air.

They crossed over Highway 50 into West Potomac Park and strolled beside the Lincoln Memorial Reflecting Pool.

Laura glanced around and said, "Look at all these people. They consider it an inalienable right to get out on a beautiful day like this without taking any elaborate precautions. They don't have bodyguards, and they don't have to worry that someone might attack them."

"I think we're pretty safe here," Steve reassured her.

"Do you wish we'd had a normal life?" she asked as she slipped off her shoes. She wanted to get rid of the pantyhose too, pull up her skirt and wade in the water. "Do you wish you'd never met me?"

"I can't figure out whether 'yes' or 'no' is the right answer to that question. Remember I'm an ex-ballplayer who got beaned once too often."

She grabbed his hand. "I like handsome studs who aren't too smart."

"God, you must really love me."

They walked along Seventeenth Street, crossed Constitution Avenue and cut across The Ellipse behind the White House.

"I needed this walk to relax after that plane ride," Laura said.

"I needed this time to get mentally prepared for the meeting to come."

"Whenever you shade the truth or tell an outright lie, I'll glibly back you up."

"The ex-news media star and the ex-government bureaucrat. We should make a helluva team, Laura."

She laughed and pulled Steve closer as they walked by the east entrance to the White House, where out-of-town visitors were cued up for the tour. Seven more blocks east on Pennsylvania Avenue and they stood opposite the oddly-shaped FBI building.

"Remember that it's a fishing expedition for them," Steve said. "They just want to find out what we know."

"And vice versa."

Inside, they walked through an arched metal detector, logged in at the security desk, and took an elevator to a lead-lined conference room on the eighth floor. Steve wondered how long before the aging J. Edgar Hoover building would be demolished and replaced. It already had been renovated several times and many of its departments moved elsewhere.

At one time or another, he had met all the major players assembled in the conference room and had had frequent telephone conversations with them. He introduced Laura to Howard Gentzler, director of the Central Intelligence Agency; CIA analyst Michael

Chou; Leon Rafferty, the president's national security adviser; and Mark Vandyne, executive assistant to Antonio Reyes, director of the FBI.

"Director Reyes will be here momentarily," Vandyne said, showing Steve and Laura to their seats on one side of the oval-shaped mahogany table. The prissy assistant poured them coffee from a silver carafe.

Reyes, a tall, strikingly handsome man with jet-black hair, soon walked purposefully into the room and sat down across from Steve and Laura. Steve assumed that Reyes had planned his grand entrance.

"We all know why we're here," Reyes announced, as Vandyne began taking notes. "Jeremiah has left his compound in Beijing, and may even have left China. Why don't you tell us what you know, Howard?"

"A squad of armed men attacked the compound," the rumpled CIA chief said, "although the Chinese officially deny the incident."

"Who were they?"

Howard shrugged, and Reyes looked first at Rafferty and then at Steve.

"The Gemini Group had considered action against Jeremiah," Steve said, careful to avoid any personal responsibility. "But someone beat us to it, obviously. I assumed at first that the FBI had finally decided to execute all the outstanding warrants calling for Jeremiah's arrest." *Ping.*

"No, we weren't involved," Reyes replied. "What kind of action were your people considering, Steve?" *Pong.* The match was underway.

"We wanted to make another effort to rescue our son David." *Ping.*

Reyes effected a sympathetic look. "That ended badly the last time, Steve. I thought you had agreed not to take such action without first informing the government." *Pong.*

"Which government?" Laura asked. "Our government? The one

that has allowed a man guilty of murdering thousands of people to live abroad in luxurious comfort for nearly two decades, all because of political and diplomatic considerations? Our son's a prisoner, and he's being abused. We have every moral right to attempt to free him." *Ping, pong, and first point.*

Reyes sat up a little straighter, Steve noticed. "I understand your feelings, Laura," Reyes said unctuously. "May I call you Laura?"

"Mrs. Wallace will do fine," she responded icily. *Slam point.*

Steve considered it appropriate for Laura to dictate strategy in this traditional male sanctuary. Her beauty and intelligence, combined with the various myths about her and Jeremiah, compelled even this august, pinstriped assemblage to feel somewhat intimidated.

Reyes looked again at Gentzler. "Who did it, then? And what were their objectives? Did they want to kill Jeremiah? Kidnap him? Or were they looking for something else? And if so, what?"

Gentzler nodded at his studious Chinese-American analyst Chou, who said, "Although there's no definitive proof, the attack probably was authorized at the highest levels in Beijing. It's the first wave of a final assault against the Communists, who've always protected Jeremiah. Also, the Chinese business community hates Jeremiah for his anti-capitalist bias."

"That's rich," snorted the rotund Rafferty, whose fat-rolled neck spilled over a too-tight shirt collar. "When Jeremiah terrorized this country, we called him a fascist. Now he's aligned with the Communists."

"Mr. Rafferty, madmen change philosophies for reasons of expediency," Laura said. "It's whatever works for the moment."

Fierce return; ball lodged in Rafferty's mouth.

"I think I understand the Chinese government's logic in denying any involvement in this illegal assassination attempt," Reyes said confidently. "If they kill Jeremiah, they've rid themselves of a nuisance and a political liability. If the raid fails, as it did, he flees the country. There's no downside for them."

"How about this downside?" Laura asked. "They screwed up, Jeremiah escaped, and now he's free to take up where he left off eighteen years ago." *Surprise slam.*

Reyes frowned and changed the topic. "How did he escape?" he asked Gentzler, who looked at Chou.

"Through underground passages that no one was fully aware of," the analyst said. "Parts of the tunnels are nearly four hundred years old. Built by some rich Chinese merchant whose house once stood on that site. Any construction records were lost long ago."

"You can bet Jeremiah didn't discover them accidentally," Laura said. *Another passing shot.*

Steve remembered the cold, dark night many years ago when the terrorist dove into the pond behind Laura's farmhouse after being cornered there by FBI agents. Jeremiah had known about an underwater pipe that could serve as an escape route. Contingency planning had always been one of the Prophet's major talents.

"Didn't the Gemini Group know about these tunnels?" Reyes asked, trying hard to make it seem an innocent question. *Strong return.*

"As you know, Antonio, we didn't have operational control in Beijing, which greatly hampered our intelligence-gathering activities," Steve said. *Nice save.*

"It was all highly predictable after Jeremiah's heart transplant," Laura said. *Tag team advantage.*

"We knew about that in advance," Reyes said. "There was nothing we could have done."

"You could have planted a bomb under the operating table." *Foul. Deliberate attempt to hit the opponent.*

"Mrs. Wallace—" Reyes said in a wounded voice. *Official complaint. Play fair.*

"Such an outrageous assassination attempt would have created an international crisis," Rafferty interjected disdainfully.

"It also would have solved the problem, Mr. Rafferty," Laura said, flashing one of her dazzling smiles.

"Let's confine our conversation to the realities of the moment," Reyes said. "Steve, what has the Gemini Group learned to date about Jeremiah's whereabouts and his plans?"

"Nothing of note." He wasn't about to tell them that the Gemini Group had arranged to smuggle out of China a woman who claimed to be a nursemaid for Jeremiah's youngest son. *Winning point forfeited.*

"What have you heard about my son David?" Laura asked, her voice cracking.

"We assume he's with Jeremiah," Reyes said.

"The Chinese did allow one of our agents to sit in on an interrogation of several of Jeremiah's servants and two of his wounded bodyguards," Gentzler added. "They had no useful information, however."

"And what about Melanie Thurston?" Laura asked in a controlled, barely audible voice. Steve knew she was making a strong effort to hide her true feelings.

"She apparently left a day or so earlier," Gentzler said.

"There've been rumors in the past that she has sponsors within the Chinese government," Chou added, which earned him a nod of gratitude from Laura.

"Do we have any idea where Jeremiah is now?" Reyes asked.

"He was seen at a military post in western China," Gentzler said. "As you know, there are few recent photographs of Jeremiah, and those we do have are unclear. But that's not the case with your son David, Mrs. Wallace. In the most recent photos we have, he stands out clearly."

"What were they doing at the military post?" Rafferty asked, expressing real interest for the first time.

"Meeting with General Lu Jingtao," Gentzler responded. "He's a dinosaur. A hard-line Communist who'd like to reverse the current economic and social situation in China. The government is waiting for Lu and others like him to die."

"That's an attitude many adopted in the past when dealing with Jeremiah," Laura said. *Ping.*

"You're not suggesting that Jeremiah and this General Lu might launch some kind of military campaign?" Rafferty asked, incredulous. *Pong.*

Steve watched Laura lean forward slightly, as if about to pounce. "Once upon a time, General Buster Franklin, then Chief of Staff of the Marine Corps, and Attorney General Peter Thompson—God rest his soul—advised President Bob Carpenter about the military threat posed by Jeremiah and his New America National Guard. That advice was ignored until Jeremiah's soldiers overran several U.S. military installations and came into possession of the finest stealth bombers available at the time. The nation came within a hairsbreadth of shattering apart, Mr. Rafferty." *Whap, whap, whap. Consecutive slams.*

"I'm aware of that history, ma'am," the national security adviser responded testily. "I just can't envision what they could do. Without going into details for national security reasons, if this Chinese army . . ." Rafferty paused, turned to Chou, and asked, "How large an army?"

Chou consulted his notes. "A division of approximately fifteen thousand men."

Rafferty responded with contempt. "If this so-called army prepares to move in any direction, neither our government nor the Chinese government will allow it. You can be assured of that. In fact, when I report back to the president following this meeting, I'm certain he will immediately contact the Chinese president. Perhaps General Lu will soon be relieved of command." *Playing with confidence.*

"I doubt that Jeremiah would put all his eggs in one basket," Laura said. "There may be many General Lu's around the world who've not yet been identified." *Pong. Opponent caught flat-footed.*

"So you're suggesting this is the beginning of a calculated campaign?" Reyes asked, looking from Laura to Steve. *Opposing coach weakening.*

Steve, content so far to mine information rather than divulge it, said, "Jeremiah's still a revolutionary icon in many areas of the world. Even insurgents who have nothing in common with his ideas about the perfect society still revere him, if for no other reason than that they share a common hatred of the United States. Most important, he can tap into nearly unlimited financial resources from those who believe they will benefit from chaos." *Holding up my side.*

"And don't forget about the scientific elite that Jeremiah has attracted to his movement," Laura said. "The Science Center always was the heart of New America, and now it's all that remains of it." *Crucial point won.*

Reyes shook his head and smiled. "What could they possibly do?"

"I don't know," Laura said, "but if you continue to sit on your hands, when you do find out, it may be too late." *Point, game, match.*

The limo took them back toward the airport. They planned to stay the night at the nearby Hyatt so Laura could visit with some old friends from the United Broadcasting Corporation.

"Do you ever think about the farm?" she asked.

"Sometimes," Steve replied as an image rose in his mind of the stately three-story farmhouse, the big barn, the rolling pasture, the smell of the horses, and the night sounds of the animals and insects. Forty-five minutes west, in the foothills of the Blue Ridge Mountains, they had lived in the Garden of Eden for nearly four years before the snake had reappeared and ruined everything.

"It's for sale," Laura said.

"The farm? How do you know?"

"I flagged an Internet real estate site to notify me when any farm in that area meeting certain specifications came on the market. I got an e-mail message about three weeks ago."

"What do they want for it?"

"A little over four million."

"Wow."

"Yeah."

"You thinking about buying it?"

Laura just shook her head, which he took to be a sign that she didn't want to talk about it now.

"So what did you think of our little meeting with the government weenies?" she asked.

"I thought I did a good job of putting them in their place," Steve said, trying to maintain a straight face.

"They just don't get it, do they?"

"It's Washington, Laura. Everyone here has so many balls in the air, they wouldn't even notice someone digging their grave."

"He'll be coming back, you know," Laura said.

Steve nodded. "Trent Dillman of Sioux Falls, South Dakota, a.k.a. Jeremiah the terrorist Prophet, returning to the scene of his greatest triumph. But what's he going to do then? He can't raise the banner of New America again. Even our foot-dragging government wouldn't stand for that. It'd squash him right away."

"I agree. So we can expect his next move to be something unique and demented. Whatever it is, both of our sons will be right in the middle of it. David doesn't have a choice. I can't even comprehend Thomas's thinking."

Thomas has left a trail a mile wide, Steve thought. Ariana had gone to the South Dakota Science Center to work undercover and keep an eye on him. For the moment, he was safe; Reyes and his group hadn't even asked about him.

"I should go out there alone," Steve said.

"No way. I didn't hesitate to run from Jeremiah when we were trying to protect David and ourselves. But I won't hide from the bastard now. I admit I'm afraid, but I'll do anything to free Thomas and David, even if I have to die doing it."

Steve looked out the window into the past. "When Peter was attorney general, he called me to Capitol Hill one day to persuade me to join a covert action team he'd assembled to kill Jeremiah. It wasn't legal, but Peter understood better than anyone else that time was of the essence. I had a lot of doubts then, even though I eventually went along, as you know. But I remember something else Peter said that day."

"What?"

"He said the only way to truly stop Jeremiah was to 'drive a stake through the fucker's heart and bury him in an unmarked grave.' "

"I remember. It was a brilliant idea, Steve, then and now."

11

Thomas entered the cavernous university library and sought out the reference desk. The sound of his shoes on the wood floor echoed loudly and he worried that all the students sitting at the study tables would somehow know of him and his purpose.

A middle-aged clerk lowered her head slightly, peered over her bifocals, and asked, "Yes?"

"I'm interested in learning about New America," Thomas told her. "In my studies so far, I've found a reference to a speech made by Theresa Dorfler in Pierre about eighteen years ago. I think a local television station filmed the event. I don't suppose there'd be a copy of the tape on file?"

"Are you a student here?" the librarian asked.

"I will be this fall. I'm working at the Center this summer as a janitor."

"What's your name?"

He hesitated, thinking once again that his choice hadn't exactly been smart. "Thomas Dorfler."

The librarian seemed truly surprised. She leaned forward and asked in a confidential tone, "Are you related to Theresa Dorfler?"

"I think she was my grandmother."

The woman's mouth hung open momentarily. Then her fingers flew over her keyboard. She looked at the monitor and made a notation on a small piece of paper. "Follow me," she said, leading the way toward the library stacks.

He followed the matronly librarian down an aisle between shelves stacked high with videotapes. Consulting her note again, she stopped, reached up, and pulled out a rectangular black plastic box. She handed it to him and said, "You'll find the speech on this tape, which also includes footage of other historic events of that time. There should be a Table of Contents keyed to the VCR clock."

"Can I take this out of the library and view it in my room?" Thomas asked.

"Do you have a library card?"

"No."

"Then come with me and we'll get you one."

After entering various information into the computer, she printed out a card and handed it to him. "Good luck in your research. You should know that Theresa Dorfler's speech generated much controversy back then."

"Why?"

"Jeremiah's rabid supporters thought the speech was staged to embarrass him. But I believe that a majority of New Americans already had become disillusioned with him. New Americans never were a monolithic group. In fact, there was a significant diversity among them. Not all of them supported everything that Jeremiah did."

"But he claimed to be a prophet of God. How could they think he'd make mistakes?"

She smiled indulgently. "I came here with my parents in the great migration of nineteen ninety-six. I wasn't much older then than you are now. My parents were committed socialists, attracted by Jeremiah's idea of the Wealth Exchange, which never really got off the ground." She gave him a warm motherly smile. "The New America movement had many facets, Thomas, and generated much controversy. Then and now. Everyone has to make up his or her own mind about whether it had any lasting value."

After he ate lunch in the cafeteria, Thomas went to his room to view the videotape. He planned to watch all of it and then go to work.

He fast-forwarded directly to his grandmother's speech. *My grandmother! A person that three months ago I didn't even know existed.* So much had happened in such a short time that he knew his life would never be the same again.

Theresa Dorfler carried herself with dignity, although she walked with the aid of a cane. That day nearly two decades ago, she had been dressed head-to-toe in black. A camera close-up allowed Thomas to see her piercing blue eyes, proud face, and beautiful silver hair.

A small crowd had assembled around her as she stood on a platform located on a sliver of land extending out into a lake just east of the capitol in Pierre. In impeccable English, she told the camera, "I came here to find my daughter, Katrina, and my grandson, Walter the Second. He was born in Munich on March ninth of this year and about two weeks later Katrina returned to Rapid City. My friend here, Steve Wallace, saw her there on the twenty-third. After that, I heard from Katrina until the end of May. And I've not heard from her since."

Thomas's mouth hung open in astonishment. His grandmother was talking about him and his real mother! The camera focused on Steve, who looked young and fit, then went back to Theresa.

"Katrina may be alive," his grandmother continued, "and if she is watching, I ask her to contact me and return home with me to Germany. And if Jeremiah is listening, I ask him to come forward and explain to me what happened to my daughter.

"I have to tell you that I fear the worst about Katrina, and even my grandson. Jeremiah knows what has happened to them. He's the father of Katrina's child, and he is my nephew."

His grandmother shook her head and smiled thinly. "Oh, I know what Jeremiah said on American television! That he doesn't know my Walter or me. That's not true! His mother, Frieda, was Walter's sister. Jeremiah's name once was Trent Dillman, and he came to live with us in Germany when he was a teenager. We took care of him. So he owes me an explanation! And if I don't get it soon, I'm going to believe the worst about Jeremiah."

She made a parallel between Jeremiah's movement and National Socialism, telling the audience that a good idea often can go bad when put into practice. "Everyone has to make up their own mind about what's right and what's wrong," she said, causing Thomas to think of the librarian's comment.

"I'm going to Rapid City today, and I'll stay there for a while," Theresa concluded. "The American Army has found many bodies in caves, and I have Katrina's dental records with me. General Franklin has promised me his help. And I know the American Army, which has protected our freedom in Germany for half a century now. They are good men, and I trust them."

Thomas pressed the "Pause" button, trying to absorb everything he'd seen and heard. Most startling were his grandmother's open hints that Jeremiah had had something to do with her daughter's death. *Her daughter, my mother.*

When the tape resumed rolling, a photograph of his mother flashed on the screen as an announcer identified Katrina Dorfler and provided a brief biography. Thomas pressed "Pause" again and stared at the image—that of a handsome, proud woman with an inviting smile, a youthful image frozen for all time. Now he knew whom he resembled physically. But what did he believe?

Her Chinese handlers agreed with Melanie that Jeremiah probably would return to the United States, specifically to the area formerly known as New America. They thought it most likely that he would hide out in the extensive cave system underlying the Black Hills in the southwest corner of the state, as he had done before.

The Chinese smuggled her into the U.S. aboard a diplomatic flight, provided her with a valid Canadian passport so she could move about freely, and assigned a bodyguard to protect her and report back to them.

She had told them honestly that Jeremiah would likely kill her if he ever saw her again, and she assumed they knew why. They had also believed her when she said that only she could get close to David and learn whatever Jeremiah's son and successor knew.

Melanie and her bodyguard, a giant named Xu, flew from San Francisco to Minneapolis, and then drove a rental car to Pierre, South Dakota. They checked into the Marriott Hotel at the Science Center, one of the few places in South Dakota large enough to get lost in while they refined their search plans.

Xu said that many Chinese students secretly loyal to Beijing either worked or studied at the Center. They would help protect them and help look for Jeremiah. If it didn't appear that the Prophet was in the central part of the state, they would move on to either Sioux Falls or Rapid City.

To avoid vigilant eyes, Melanie entered the complex inside a large trunk that Xu carried easily, as if it were empty. To fight off the feeling of claustrophobia and images of being buried alive in a coffin, Melanie listened intently to conversations and sounds. Xu checked into the hotel and spurned help from a bellboy. The hum of the elevator comforted her. When Xu opened the suitcase in their suite, Melanie gratefully crawled out and looked around at the spacious accommodations.

"Nice," she said, regaining her confidence. She would be very comfortable here while the Chinese tracked down Jeremiah and David. Then she'd turn the tables on everyone.

The old man rolled the wheelchair close to the door, leaned forward, and knocked loudly. He sat back and smiled, knowing that the boy inside probably had his eye to the peephole, wondering what a crippled old man could want.

Thomas opened the door and asked, "Can I help you?"

He frowned and cupped his hand around the ear containing a hearing aid.

In a much louder voice, Thomas asked again, "Can I help you?"

With two quick thrusts of his hands, he propelled the wheelchair into the room. Then he wheeled about expertly and scrutinized the boy.

"I think you're looking for the hospital," Thomas said, "but you've taken the elevator to the basement. I'll call someone to come get you."

"I see you got my package, Thomas. Otherwise, you wouldn't be here trying to learn about your heritage." He jerked his head toward the TV. "Your mother and grandmother were beautiful, strong women. It's sad how they were used in the end."

"Who are you?" Thomas asked hesitantly.

He stood, noting with satisfaction that his sudden movement clearly startled Thomas, who stepped back a pace.

Jeremiah pulled off a skullcap to reveal curly hair dyed a youthful light brown. He peeled latex off his face and removed rubber appliances from around his eyes, nose, and mouth. He walked closer to Thomas so that their faces were only inches apart.

"I'm Jeremiah, your father."

Thomas staggered backward until his legs hit the edge of the bed, causing him to drop helplessly onto the mattress.

"Don't be afraid," Jeremiah said. "The disguise is one of the many precautions I take to avoid being captured." He looked around the room and shook his head. "This is a real shit hole, Thomas."

"How did you get here? How did you know I was here? How do I know you are who you say you are?"

Jeremiah shoved the only chair close to the bed so he could sit and face his son. "You've got a lot to learn about going underground, Thomas. I imagine everyone knows you're here, including Steve Wallace and Laura Delaney. You can expect a family reunion very soon."

"What do you want?" Thomas asked.

Jeremiah frowned at the timidity and fearfulness Thomas exhibited. Designating a successor was proving to be a harder job than he'd imagined.

"I want the truth to be known, Thomas. For example, in the film you were watching, important background details were left out."

"How did you know I had this videotape of my grandmother? That I was watching it?"

"I know many things," Jeremiah said enigmatically, further confounding Thomas. "As I was saying, Steve Wallace and my other enemies cruelly manipulated your grandmother. They told her that your mother was dead and that I had killed her. She made their speech for them, and it was very effective, as were all their efforts to tarnish my reputation and alienate my followers."

"Did you kill my mother?"

"Of course not. Katrina was my first cousin, the daughter of the man I worshipped. We were lovers and she carried my child—you, my son. Why would I kill her? In fact, Wallace killed her and she was dead at the time Theresa made that speech. When we were attempting to flee New America after it was overrun by the United States military, Wallace and other FBI agents intercepted us and there was a fierce gun battle between them and my men. Katrina was killed and you were captured. I escaped with only my life and David, who Laura had abandoned to my care."

He paused, having now told the same story to both of his sons. He scrutinized Thomas carefully, although he had viewed his photograph many times over the years. The boy was tall and thin, not yet filled out. *With proper training, he could be a powerful man,* Jeremiah thought. Thomas had dark hair like Katrina's, and that same quizzical look of hers that could be both endearing and disconcerting.

"My mother tells a different story," Thomas said finally.

"You mean Laura? Of course she does, and you have to make up your own mind about the truth. I met Katrina when we were both eighteen, and she was my lifelong love. Your mother, grandfather, and grandmother were founders of the world's greatest revolutionary movement.

"At the same time, Thomas, I'll confess to you that I am but a mortal man. God speaks to me, but I am not a god. I met Laura when I was in my late twenties. In fact, at the beginning of that very videotape you were watching, you'll see us together at the Kremlin in nineteen ninety-one, years before I began my first campaign in the United States. Laura was one of the most beautiful women in the world, of course, and I had an affair with her off and on for years. I'm not proud of my sexual promiscuity outside the bonds of matrimony. It's only a coincidence that Katrina and Laura became pregnant at about the same time."

"But you and my real mother were never married, is that right?"

"Katrina and I were married in a secret ceremony soon after she gave birth to you in Munich and returned here to New America. My heart always belonged to your real mother, Thomas."

Thomas shook his head. "Did they know about each other? My mother and Laura."

"Of course. They were even friends. Here, see for yourself." Jeremiah reached over and took a manila envelope from the wire basket attached to the side of the wheelchair. He handed it to Thomas, who opened it and took out several photographs.

"Those are prints from a surveillance camera that filmed your mother and Laura during one of their frequent conversations in a cabin where we lived together."

"All three of you?"

"It was an unconventional arrangement, Thomas, although Biblical patriarchs had many wives. It's not a reason for jealousy or hatred among consenting adults."

"But Laura said you raped her in Texas and kidnapped her to New America."

Jeremiah shrugged. "She looks happy in those photographs, doesn't she? I know you've watched the university's orientation video of my tour of the Science Center many years ago. Did it look like Laura was there against her will?"

"I don't know who to believe," Thomas said, his voice cracking. "It's all very confusing."

"By design, I assure you, Thomas. In Laura and Steve's book about their efforts to defeat me, they also go to great lengths to rewrite the history of my movement, portraying me as the villain and themselves as saviors of America, as well as victims."

"They did live in fear and always were afraid that someone would try to kidnap me."

"Did anyone ever try?"

"Not that I know of."

Jeremiah nodded emphatically. "But Steve Wallace's organization, the Gemini Group, twice tried to kidnap David, and almost killed him once. In fact, David and I left China a week ago after assassins broke into our compound and killed several of my followers. Who really had cause to live in fear, Thomas?"

"Steve and Laura were always very good to me," Thomas said.

"Laura is a good person who simply tried to preserve her marriage and her reputation. You can't fault her for this little lie. It's too bad your Grandmother Dorfler is dead. She could tell you how they tricked her into telling those lies you just viewed."

"How could they make her say things against her will?"

"With threats of prosecution, both here and in Germany, for not revealing Walter's plans and activities over the years. Also, they promised her she could rebury Walter in Munich. Your grandmother was a devout Catholic and wanted that very much. But the Americans reneged on that promise later and Walter is still interred in Quebec City, where Wallace killed him."

Jeremiah could see he had overwhelmed the boy with this different version of events, and he pressed the advantage. "I'm sorry it took so long for us to be reunited, Thomas. But you understand I would have been jailed or killed had I come back to the United States earlier."

"So why did you choose to come now?"

"Circumstances often dictate our choices. I was in ill health for many years. I'm now recovered, thank God. For political reasons, the Chinese are no longer interested in protecting me. There was the assassination attempt. And, of course, I must complete the mission God has given me." He gave Thomas several seconds to digest this large and controversial topic. "Over the years, many people—certainly Laura Delaney and Steve Wallace among them—have challenged my status as a prophet of God. If you listened carefully to my video tour of the Science Center, you'll know that I addressed that topic."

Thomas nodded. "Yes, I remember. Vaguely."

"My view is that if one believes in God, there is no choice but to believe that the Almighty Lord can speak through a man if he wants to. Those who see me as a charlatan apparently don't believe that."

"Maybe they believe the concept, but not you."

Jeremiah laughed warmly. *This kid has more spunk than David does.* "Good point. You'll have to decide for yourself, Thomas, as does everyone. Although volumes have been written about New America and me, I can condense the whole philosophy into only a few sentences.

"God spoke to me and I relayed his words to those who would listen. Evil is man's choice, and modern man has willingly chosen evil. God instructed me to lead the faithful to a new nation, where God's laws would be strictly observed as a condition of citizenship, where all men and women were to be treated equally in all ways, where government would be limited and direct, and where the acquisition of knowledge, not money, was to be the highest good. No matter what you've been told or read, Thomas, that is what my mission is all about. It's very simple, and I'm very proud of my life and my efforts."

Thomas struggled for a response. "But why all the violence?"

"You mean the violence I committed, or that which was committed against me?" He could see the question startled Thomas. "I'm an advocate of revolutionary ideas, as was Christ, whose teachings were not all that different from mine. The power elite in America wasn't about to give my followers and me free rein to worship as we pleased, to exercise our rights of free speech and free movement. My followers didn't invade South Dakota, Thomas. They moved here freely, bought or built their own homes, and participated actively in the electoral process.

"There has never been a peaceful revolution in the history of the world, including the American Revolution. The United States of America was born in violence and today is held together only by the threat of violence against those who insist on their freedoms."

"As I understand it, you were committing terrorist acts long before New America was founded," Thomas said.

"One man's terrorist is another person's patriot, Thomas. Just as the American colonists attacked symbols of British rule, as they did at the Boston Tea Party, so did I attack American symbols of decadence, including rampant crime, economic inequality, and a corrupt political system. Millions flocked to my banner.

"As the Lord said to the first Jeremiah, 'I have set you this day over nations and over kingdoms, to pluck up and to break down, to destroy and to overthrow, to build and to plant.' "

"And you have the same mission?"

"God's goals don't change, Thomas."

"Why then did New America fail?"

This kid's a hard sell. "The evildoers ignore God, obviously. New America was simply overwhelmed by the military might of the United States." Jeremiah leaned forward to impart a confidence. "A friend of mine recently criticized me, pointing out that at one time a bomber loaded with nuclear weapons and piloted by New Americans penetrated defenses over Boston, New York, and Washington, D.C., and could have completely destroyed those cities."

"What happened?"

"A man named Joe Lambert aborted that mission, as I instructed him to do. It's part of the public record, Thomas. You can read about it. I'll give you references if you like. I will also tell you that I've now forsaken such violence as being counterproductive. I plan to take up the cause again and influence the development of mankind, but only by gathering the faithful unto me, while the non-believers suffer their own fate."

"What are you going to do?"

Jeremiah stood, thinking that he'd accomplished enough for one day. "I will need to know more about you and where your sympathies lie, Thomas, before revealing such matters to you. For all I know, you would just run home and tell Steve and Laura."

He had hoped for a denial, but Thomas switched to another topic. "I read your *Lamentations,* which seemed to predict the switching of me for David and substantiate the version of events as my mother described them."

Very, very good, Jeremiah thought. Thomas had saved that surprise for last, demonstrating cunning and tactical skills. What else could he expect from a child with Walter Dorfler's genes, raised by the likes of Laura Delaney?

"I'm afraid you've misinterpreted the word, Thomas. Let me recite one of my laments, which I recall well: 'Why O Lord choose me to be thy Messenger, knowing I would be abused by so many; that the Two closest to me would betray me, as Thomas did Christ, stealing my trust and stealing the Child who would carry on Thy Work in the future? What benefits your plan, O Lord, to deny Thy own Words?' The two betrayers were Steve and Laura, and you are the child stolen."

Thomas shook his head in confusion. "I'll have to read it again."

"Indeed, Thomas. Study the Word, and heed God's promise: 'A Remnant will remain, sayeth the Lord, even though the Nation be scattered to the ends of the Earth. A Nation is an Idea, not a boundary. That which binds New Americans cannot be broken by time and distance. It is the Word and it will endure all; out of this Remnant, a rich tapestry will be woven, I promise you.' That also is from my *Lamentations,* verse nine."

Jeremiah took a roll of gauze from the wheelchair storage basket. He stood in front of a mirror and began to expertly wrap it around his head. Then he sat down in the wheelchair and rolled it toward the door.

"Will I see you again?"

With his hand on the doorknob, Jeremiah smiled broadly to himself. "If you like, Thomas. I'll get back to you."

12

THE REVELATION TO JEREMIAH

CHAPTER THREE

1 The Angel of the Lord restored me to human form following my flight of discovery. Exhausted, I fell into a deep sleep and experienced a vivid dream.

2 I walked in a beautiful Garden where God's chosen people were in the form of productive plants, bearing the fruits of sustenance, both material and spiritual.

3 I, Jeremiah, Prophet of the Lord, Servant of the Chosen People, Champion of New America, recount this divine vision for the benefit of true believers preparing for an evolutionary transition.

4 In this renewed Garden of Eden, a gentle wind created an ethereal music that tuned all my senses to the Universal Purpose.

5 I walked on pristine Garden pathways that protected the plants from encroachment and conveyed a sense of design and order,

for living things flourish best in a safe and beautiful environment. These unobstructed pathways also were vistas into the future.

6 They facilitated cultivation and served as a conduit for water and nutrients converted by the plants into fruit and the very breath of Life.

7 I walked in the Garden for an immeasurable time, during which the pathways became increasingly clogged with nonproductive Life. Such Weeds have no pedigree and are the bastard children of the Earth. They propagate, without limit or purpose, and aggressively and greedily consume limited resources necessary to sustain the Garden's productive plants. They limit man's vision.

8 Furthermore, such congestion and overcrowding lead to destructive competition and violence. This situation promotes pollution, restricts freedom of movement, and creates a babble of competing interests that prevent consensus and promote chaos, which are the most deadly diseases that can afflict a Garden.

9 The wise Gardener eliminates the Weeds, for not all forms of Life have a Right to Life.

10 Remember the earlier lesson: even God is an Evolved Life Form, a natural byproduct of the laws of the Infinite Universe. Wherever Life arises spontaneously and develops no worthwhile purpose other than to consume, propagate, and die, it is not sanctified, nor does it have value.

11 The Earth is God's Garden, and Jeremiah is God's appointed Gardener. God has directed Jeremiah to weed His Garden.

12 Does the Gardener mourn for the Weeds or show them mercy? No, he methodically and relentlessly cuts them down or poisons them. His concern is only for the Greater Good of all. His

mission is to minister to those beautiful and vibrant plants that absorb and convert the Light of Heaven into purpose and meaning.

13 The Gardener's chief concern is to select the most effective Herbicide, seeking an agent that kills all the Weeds but spares the productive plants and all the essential seeds that have been produced over countless generations.

14 The Gardener must first Immunize the productive plants, so that the killing agent passes them by, as Moses did mark those houses of the Faithful in Egypt, that they be spared the plague.

15 In the Garden that has been weeded, cultivated, and nourished, the Gardener and his many helpers can then work without distraction, and take advantage of all the resources that were not harmed by the Herbicide.

16 The Gardener shall appoint Soldiers of the Lord who remain constantly on alert and rush to stamp out any resurgent Weeds that sprout in God's Garden.

17 If the Gardener does his job thoroughly, the Garden is restored to the pristine, dewy condition that existed at the Time of Creation.

18 Here the Tree of Life will grow again, and the Chosen Few will eat its fruit.

13

They entered the Buster Franklin Memorial Hospital at the Science Center with Laura lying on a medical gurney pushed by two husky male "nurses." A white sheet covered her body, a surgical cap concealed her hair, and an oxygen mask obscured most of her face.

Disguised as a bent-over old man with wispy white hair and matching mustache, Steve shuffled alongside the gurney, holding his wife's hand. He effected an absent-minded look at the same time he kept his eyes open for any sign of trouble.

While the young "private secretary" with them handled the registration process, the two nurses wheeled the gurney down a hallway to their assigned quarters.

Once inside the two-bedroom hospital suite, Steve and Laura temporarily held their positions as one of their bodyguards inserted an electronic sensing device into a wall socket while the other swept the area with a laser scanner.

A few minutes later, the first bodyguard said, "The place is clean, boss. No computer tabs or cameras."

Laura sat up and swung her legs over the side of the gurney. She pulled off the surgical cap and fluffed out her hair. Steve straightened up and quickly shrugged off the worn tweed jacket.

"These rooms for cancer patients undergoing treatment are about the only places in the whole complex where the walls don't have eyes and ears," he said, sitting on a sofa. He thought he smelled chemicals, but then decided he'd only imagined it.

"I guess they assume the sick and dying have no agenda other than survival," Laura said, taking off the hospital gown to reveal shorts and a T-shirt.

"That, and the fact that many of the patients here are rich and influential foreigners," Steve said. "The people who run the Science Center can't afford to offend them."

Their "secretary" entered the room without knocking, and Laura smiled at Ariana. "You look great as a redhead."

"How was your trip?" Ariana asked, taking off fake glasses.

"The flight was as smooth as silk," Steve told her.

"But the landing was a bit bumpy," Laura said wryly. "Talk about the airport that was supposed to bring people from all over the world to see New America—grass is growing in cracks all over the runway."

"We had men posted along the road to the Center," Ariana said. "According to our lookouts, no one paid any special attention to an ambulance coming from the airport. That's a routine occurrence here."

"We'll be in the greatest danger when we leave this room," Steve said. "Even though we'll use a variety of disguises, someone might spot us." He'd tried to keep Ariana under wraps at the Gemini Group, but many organizations could have her photograph.

"I don't think Jeremiah's people will try anything," Ariana said. "They know the FBI's here undercover, too."

"Who's running that operation?" Steve asked.

"Byron Mitchell, the Bureau's deputy director."

"I'll check in with him as soon as possible. Meanwhile, everybody has to keep their guard up."

In a voice laced with anxiety, Laura asked, "Where is he? Where's Thomas?"

"He's got a job as a janitor and a temporary room in the basement," Ariana answered. "Apparently he plans to enroll in the university this fall. To the best of our knowledge, he's never been out of the Center in the ten days he's been here."

"How are you avoiding him?" Laura asked. "If the two of you bump into each other, he'll blow your cover."

Ariana held out a cell phone. "Our people following Thomas make certain our paths don't cross."

Steve took a deep breath. "Ariana says he's going by the name of Thomas Dorfler, Laura."

"Oh, my God," Laura said, as if she'd suffered a body blow. "Why? What does he hope to accomplish? I don't understand!"

"He's suffered a double whammy, Laura. His father is a hunted terrorist who killed his mother. Maybe it's his way of connecting to her. It could also be his way of signaling to certain elements here."

That statement obviously stunned Laura, who said in disbelief, "Steve, you can't possibly believe he'd try to meet with Jeremiah if he comes here." She turned to Ariana. "Has anyone contacted Thomas while you've been at the Center?"

"No one who aroused our suspicions." Ariana paused and reconsidered. "Well, one of our guys spotted an old man in a wheelchair in the hallway leading to Thomas's room."

"Did he meet with Thomas?" Steve asked.

"I don't think so," Ariana replied. "I mean, he had bandages all around his head and apparently was lost. Two hospital orderlies showed up and took him away."

"How did he get to Thomas's room?"

Ariana shrugged. "Obviously, he got by our guys. We have one posted near the elevators and another one around the corner from Thomas's room. But they have to move around now and then so as not to attract attention from building security. That's when the old man went down the elevator into the basement, I suppose. Punched the wrong button, probably."

"Why are you concerned about this old man?" Laura asked Steve.

"History. Paranoia. Take your pick."

Laura said, "Either one is enough to convince me we need to find Thomas and get him out of here . . . fast."

Ariana returned to their hospital suite at four o'clock that afternoon, the time at which Thomas began work as a second-shift janitor.

"One of our undercover people in the janitorial department will arrange for Thomas to clean a small dining room on the twelfth floor used by the hospital staff for working lunches," Ariana said.

In preparation, Steve and Laura went into the bedroom to put on one of several disguises Ariana had placed in their closets, along with other clothes they would need. For security reasons, neither of them had brought along a suitcase, not wanting to be saddled with baggage or to leave behind evidence of their presence.

"You're kidding!" Laura said as Steve handed her a hanger holding a nun's black habit.

"It hides everything except your face, and no one looks a nun or priest in the face," Steve said, putting on a priest's collar.

Neither would anyone consider it odd to encounter the ecclesiastical couple in the hospital hallways. One bodyguard went ahead to the twelfth floor, while the other followed closely behind them. As they arrived in front of the passenger elevators, two couples waiting there glanced briefly at them. Steve smiled and one of the women dipped her head deferentially.

On the twelfth floor, Father Steve and Sister Laura got off first. People they encountered in the hallway gave them a wide berth, ducked their heads, and hurried on.

The bodyguard who had gone ahead waited for them near the dining room. He opened the door and followed them inside. Steve knew that the trailing bodyguard would remain in the hallway, in case they had unexpected visitors.

Steve sat down at a table littered with glasses, plates, utensils, uneaten food, meeting agendas, and notepads. While they waited, he tugged on the tight collar and watched Laura nervously pace about the room.

Twenty minutes later, they heard someone put a key into the door lock, causing the inside guard to flip off the light switch. As soon as Thomas stepped into the room and turned on the lights, the guard slipped behind him, shut the door, and locked it.

Thomas's initial fright soon gave way to understanding, and recognizable pique. "I should have known. You probably had people on my tail all the way, didn't you, Dad? Or should I call you Father?"

Steve chuckled, although he would be pleased with either acknowledgment. "It took us a day or so to catch up with you."

Laura took Thomas in her arms and held him until he gently struggled free and said, "You make a great-looking nun, Mom."

"And look at you! A janitor."

"I've found my calling," Thomas said, attempting to strike a light note.

"Let's sit down," Steve said as he arranged three chairs into a circle, "and you can tell us what's going on." He was thinking that Thomas seemed different, and not just because of the gray work uniform and the employee ID badge clipped to his shirt pocket. Their son looked uneasy and uptight.

"I just needed to get away by myself," Thomas said, sitting rigidly in his chair.

"Why come here, of all places?" Laura asked.

He shrugged. "I'd never been out this way. I wanted to see what New America was all about."

"This is South Dakota," Laura said emphatically. "New America was nothing more than a fascist colony."

"I'm not so sure of that," Thomas said.

"Not sure?" Laura echoed. "What do you mean?"

"I'm not certain all New Americans were fascists."

Steve intervened in a calm voice, "Why the name change, Thomas?"

Laura punctuated his question. "Yes, why?"

Thomas shrugged. "I needed an alias. It was the first name that popped into my mind, probably because I'd been thinking so much about my . . . birth mother."

"Oh," Laura said, and it seemed to Steve that she suddenly shrank in size, looking like a nun who'd been cloistered all her life.

He asked the next question casually, "Has anybody contacted you since you've been here, Thomas?"

Thomas looked away. "Just the people I work for."

"You could be in great danger here," Laura said. "Jeremiah has left Beijing. He could be on his way to the Center."

"What's he going to do to me?" Thomas asked flippantly. "Kill me, kidnap me?"

"Yes," Laura said, as if it were an obvious conclusion.

"I don't know why. I've never done anything *to* him, and there's nothing I can do *for* him."

"He could try to recruit you, to indoctrinate you," Steve said, disturbed by Thomas's uncharacteristic defiance. "Jeremiah has always thought of his crusade as a family enterprise. That's why he sent you that package of information that started all this. Read his so-called writings, including *Second Revelation,* which he and his people are now publishing on the Internet. He obviously wants a trustworthy successor."

Thomas smirked. "I'd be the last person he'd trust. He doesn't even know me. And I don't know him."

"You're not missing a thing," Laura said, her voice dripping with sarcasm.

"What are you here for, Dad?" Thomas asked. "Are you and your people going to try to capture Jeremiah, or kill him?"

Steve instinctively decided to soft-pedal the efforts of the Gemini Group. "We'd have to get in line for either of those jobs, Thomas. In fact, the FBI has specifically told us they're in charge here. We're only interested in protecting you."

"Come home, Thomas," Laura pleaded. Steve watched his wife revert to character as she flashed that warm smile that always captivated everyone. "You're still accepted at Dartmouth. You've got a bright future ahead of you. Don't you still want to study the law?"

"No, I've changed my mind. I may go into a scientific field instead, and this is one of the best places in the world to study."

"Why did you change your mind?" Laura asked.

Thomas leaned forward, rested his forearms on his knees, and sighed with typical teenager boredom. "I don't know, Mom. I just did."

"Well, you're coming back home," Laura said, standing abruptly, "whether you like it or not!"

The look on Thomas's face startled Steve. He'd seen such an expression the first time he'd met Katrina Dorfler, when she had defiantly refused to give them any information about Jeremiah's whereabouts.

"I'm eighteen, remember," Thomas said. "I'm a man. You can't force me to do anything." He directed another appeal to Steve. "Even the law's on my side."

"Thomas, do you realize how foolish you're being?" Laura cried.

Steve immediately intervened, wanting to head off a confrontation that could spawn lasting bad feelings. "He's right, Laura." He looked intently at her, trying to communicate without speaking. *This is not the right technique, nor the right time.* The white portion of the nun's wimple framed Laura's face in an oval, almost like a portrait. He watched her features soften as she began to nod her agreement.

"You're right, Thomas," she said. "You're an adult and you get to make your own mistakes in life. Believe me, staying here will be the biggest one you'll ever make."

Out in the hallway, Steve resisted an impulse to put his arm around the lovely nun walking beside him. They returned to the elevators, where their bodyguard had taped an "Out of Order" sign on the doors. As Steve and Laura approached, he removed the sign and pushed the "Up" button. The trailing bodyguard got on just in time and blocked two other men from edging their way through the closing doors.

"What are we going to do now?" Laura asked in a quavering voice.

"I don't know, Laura."

The next morning, Laura stood in their bedroom looking at her image in the mirror above the chest of drawers. *Today we'll be tourists*, she thought. *On vacation in July, hoping to visit the local sites*. Accordingly, she wore cuffed navy shorts and a short-sleeved cotton blouse with light blue vertical stripes. She fiddled with a straw hat, finally deciding it looked best cocked to the right. The front of the brim turned slightly down and would shade and hide her face, along with the large-framed sunglasses she'd wear.

She stared at herself, wondering now why they had even bothered with the plastic surgery years ago. She could still recognize Laura Delaney-Wallace from Austin, Texas, and so could certain knowledgeable people if they looked close enough. They'd had it done in the aftermath of David's kidnapping, hoping to maintain their anonymity at least on the streets so they wouldn't be recognized and hassled by the media and ordinary citizens.

She saw Steve approach from behind her and smiled as he grabbed her buttocks and put his chin in the crook of her shoulder, looking at her in the mirror.

"You've got a gorgeous ass," he said.

"It sags," she responded playfully as she turned and put her arms around his neck so their noses touched. "Are you repulsed at making love to a fifty-seven-year-old woman?"

"I'm just happy that I'm still able to do it."

"Like fine wine, you've improved with age," she said, even though they hadn't made love since Thomas disappeared. Over the years, they'd had an active and satisfying sex life, but no more children. After David was kidnapped, they gave up their plans to have a large family. *Jeremiah has influenced our lives in so many ways,* she thought sadly.

"You're still as beautiful as you were in the Miss America contest," Steve said.

She pushed him away, laughing. "Give me a break. That was nineteen seventy-eight, remember?"

"I'm serious."

"Seriously, what are we going to do now?"

"I think I'll stick around for a while," he said. "You can go back to New York if you want to."

"You're not getting rid of me that easily," she said emphatically. "Tell me what we're going to do."

"We'll watch and wait."

"Have any of your people or the FBI seen Jeremiah?"

"No, but I think he's already here."

Her mouth dropped open. "Why?"

"Intuition you develop after a lifetime of interrogations, or negotiations with people who have a hidden agenda. Thomas lied to us."

The questions tumbled out. "What do you mean? Do you think he's seen Jeremiah? How could you believe that? That would mean Thomas has decided to . . . " She clamped a hand to her mouth to stifle any more words.

"Maybe there's another explanation, Laura. We'll find out soon enough."

14

The beeper hooked to his belt began to vibrate and Thomas turned off the vacuum cleaner. The LCD read: "Go to Suite 3030 for extensive cleanup."

"This whole job is an extensive cleanup," he muttered, hoping it wasn't another toilet that had overflowed.

He put the vacuum in a storage closet, took a service elevator to the thirtieth floor, walked to the suite, and knocked on the door. A young man about his height and age opened the door.

"You requested a janitor, sir?" Thomas asked, acutely aware of his new role as deferential servant. Before, he had always been a member of the exclusive class, like this guy with the curly blond hair and money to stay in this luxurious hotel suite.

"Yeah, c'mon in."

Thomas walked into the room and immediately looked for the mess. Instead, he saw two burly men, whose type he recognized instantly. Bodyguards. The training he'd received from Steve immediately took over, and he backed toward the door, calculating which of the three he would have to deal with first.

"Give us some privacy, guys," the young man said. The two men gave him a sullen look, glanced curiously at Thomas, and left. One walked out the door into the hallway and the other went into one of the bedrooms, where he left the door cracked open slightly.

"How can I help you?" Thomas asked, fingering his beeper, which had a button for distress calls.

"We're supposed to talk, Thomas."

"How do you know my name?" Thomas asked, as the young man walked behind the bar, opened the door to a small refrigerator, and took out two cans of beer.

"My name's David. We're half brothers, or so I'm told."

Of course! Jeremiah is here, and David naturally would be with him. Then another thought occurred to Thomas: *With Steve and Laura also here, it's a potentially explosive situation!*

"How do I know you're telling the truth?" Thomas asked.

"Sit, have a beer, and let's get this over with. Why should I lie? Jeremiah—our father—visited you two nights ago. I understand you've recently become a student of the movement. I've been tested on that subject all my life. If you don't believe me, ask me anything."

Thomas took a stool in front of the bar, carefully assessing this guy who claimed to be his brother. David resembled Jeremiah physically, including the powerful upper body, slender nose, and deep blue eyes. Although David projected a level of maturity beyond his years, he had none of Jeremiah's self-assurance. Instead, his brother's eyes and facial expression reflected caution, calculation, and cynicism.

"Don't worry about your job or anyone looking for you," David said. "I'm sure that's been taken care of."

Thomas wasn't surprised. He'd already been impressed with Jeremiah's demonstrated skill and knowledge. The so-called Prophet had somehow escaped from China, entered the United States, and boldly come to the Science Center—all while being sought by the best police and intelligence agencies in the world. And he also knew every move his sons made.

"Where is Jeremiah now?" Thomas asked, popping the tab on the can.

David shrugged. "I'd be the last to know, although he's obviously somewhere nearby."

"David, aren't you afraid the FBI will find out you're here and arrest you?"

His brother drained his beer and turned toward the refrigerator. "You ready for another one?"

"No."

"How about some peanuts?"

"I'm okay."

David sat again on the barstool and rested his forearms on the counter. "I'm not wanted for anything, Thomas. I've got an American passport, since I was born in the United States. On the other hand, I imagine the FBI would like to have me in custody so they could inject me with chemicals and try to find out Jeremiah's location. That would be a waste of their time, however, since he didn't tell me where he was going."

"Is that why you have the bodyguards? To protect you from the FBI?"

"That, plus they report everything I do back to Jeremiah. I've always had bodyguards."

Thomas nodded glumly. "Me too."

"Even now?"

Thomas wondered how open he should be with David. "I'm probably being watched, maybe even followed—by the FBI, or the Gemini Group. Do you know about them?"

"Yes."

"They'll soon know you're here, if they don't already."

David drained away about half of his second beer. "I've always been a puppet on someone's string. For all I know, Jeremiah could be using me as bait in some grand scheme I haven't even thought of."

"I understand that feeling," Thomas said.

"I come and go as I'm told," David continued. "My friends were chosen for me, even my school. My studies were monitored so I didn't encounter any counterrevolutionary ideas. I'm watched all the time. Putting me in jail would be redundant."

He's smart, handsome, and dangerous-looking, all at the same time, Thomas concluded, although his instincts also told him that David might be unpredictable, and undependable. Still, they had so much in common. He wanted them to be friends . . . like brothers should be.

"Steve and Laura invented a cover story about being in a witness-protection program," Thomas said. "They told me that's why I needed bodyguards."

"You didn't know their true identities?" David asked skeptically.

It does sound dumb and naïve, Thomas admitted privately. "Not until a few months ago, when Jeremiah blew the whistle on all of us. I'd studied about him in school, but frankly, I didn't pay much attention. It seemed ancient history to me. And if I read about Steve and Laura, or saw photographs of them, I didn't make the connection. They've aged, of course, and they've had plastic surgery. We lived in a cocoon, anyway," he said bitterly.

David laughed and held up one hand for a high five. "We truly are brothers, Thomas. You ready now for that beer?"

"Yeah," Thomas replied as he returned the high five.

David put two more beers on the bar and took a bottle of bourbon from the shelf in front of the mirror. He put two shot glasses on the bar and filled each with the brown liquid.

"We're being put to the test," he said, mounting the barstool again.

"Test?"

"Yeah. Jeremiah shatters your little universe and you run out here, which I find amazing, quite frankly. It's probably just what he wanted you to do."

Thomas looked in the mirror behind the bar, considering the stupid person he saw reflected there—a janitor.

"Don't feel bad, Thomas. Basically, the same thing happened to me. Someone gave me Laura and Steve's book and forged a note from her."

"Who?"

"Either a woman I know, or perhaps Jeremiah." David shook his head in a manner indicating it wasn't important. "All of a sudden, a half-dozen assassins attack our house and we're on the run." He waved one arm to encompass the room. "Here we are, and I don't know why, except that I can make several educated guesses."

"I'd appreciate hearing them," Thomas said.

David sipped the bourbon, followed by a long swig of beer. "Jeremiah's healthy again and back to the old terrorism-and-prophecy game, and he wants to involve his two sons in the family business. One of us gets to be the inheritor, but which one? And what happens to the other one? To discover the answer to these questions, Jeremiah puts us to the test."

Thomas looked toward the bedroom with concern. Through the slightly open door, the bodyguard might be able to overhear their conversation.

As if reading his brother's mind, David said, "Jeremiah won't punish me for telling the truth, Thomas, although he'd lecture me about the cynicism." He smiled darkly. "And then I'd get rid of these bodyguards for ratting me out, and they know it."

"You said Jeremiah is healthy again. What exactly was the matter with him?"

"Heart disease. He had a transplant several months ago. Don't ask me why, but it convinced him that microbes are somehow involved in the battle between good and evil."

"What?"

"You heard right. He even made me get a flu shot. He's also studying the habits of birds." David laughed, winked conspiratorially, and whirled his finger in a circular motion beside his head. "That's our dad."

"Explain what you mean when you say he's going to put us to the test," Thomas urged.

David shrugged. "Maybe he'll pit us together in some gladiator contest. Survival of the fittest. It's a big part of his belief system."

"You're not serious?"

"Oh, yeah. Well, not about the gladiator thing. It'll be more subtle than that, but maybe just as deadly." David laughed at his own black humor.

"I take it you're not really interested in being part of your father's movement?"

"I take it that you are," David responded. "Otherwise, you wouldn't have come here. If you weren't intrigued with Jeremiah and his plans, you'd leave."

Thomas threw back a shot of Jack Daniel's. He coughed and said in a high, squeaky voice, "You know what? We should get out of here."

"Where do you want to go?" David asked.

"There's a student hangout in downtown Pierre called the Hitching Post. I hear it's a jumping place."

"I'll put on my cowboy shirt," David said mockingly.

"I'll take any kind of shirt," Thomas said, reaching for the telephone on the bar. "I'll call in sick."

In the bedroom, David searched his closet, although he knew there were no cowboy shirts. He grabbed a pair of jeans for Thomas and two clean button-down shirts.

"You're not supposed to leave the suite," his bodyguard said.

"Fuck you."

"We can't protect you in a downtown bar."

"Then I should get some competent bodyguards."

"I won't let you go," the bodyguard said.

David dropped the clothes on the bed as he took off his shirt. "Then let's you and I get it on, motherfucker. I've taken down better guys than you in Saturday-night brawls with Chinese gang members."

The bodyguard held up both hands. "C'mon, David."

"Listen, Clyde, just go get your asshole partner in the hallway and we'll all go down to the parking garage, get the car, and head to town for some fun."

"My name isn't Clyde."

"Look, I've just met my only brother. We want to hang out and party. You guys can have a good time, too. Later, we'll find some chicks. So what do you want to do, Clyde? Fight or fuck?"

David's eyes lit up as he and Thomas walked into the Hitching Post, a bar-and-pool joint on a side street in downtown Pierre. The stimulating smell of stale beer and cigarette smoke hung in the air. A long, horseshoe-shaped bar took up the center of the main room. Booths lined the outside wall. In the back were a dance floor, the kitchen entrance, and a hallway leading to the rest rooms. A doorway in the middle of the interior wall led to the poolroom.

Customers had to shout to be heard over the loud music. David put his mouth close to Clyde's ear. "You guys stay here."

He and Thomas went into the poolroom and slid into a booth against the back wall, where the music wasn't so deafening. A buxom waitress wearing short shorts that revealed lots of butt cheek took their order for Coors and Jack Daniel's.

"Any places like this is New York?" David asked Thomas.

"Maybe, but no slot machines."

David whistled. "Look at those two cowgirls playing pool. Wow-wee! We'll have to introduce ourselves later."

"Let's hope the cowgirls don't come with a pair of cowboys," Thomas said.

David laughed. "So what? It ain't a good evening out without a good fight or a good fuck."

"Did you date a lot of Chinese girls?" Thomas asked.

"Oh, yeah, but I'll tell you about that some other time. You been here before, Thomas?"

"No."

David looked around. "So no one would expect you to come here." Even if they'd been followed, long-range listening devices wouldn't work well in this place. "Let's get back to our earlier conversation."

"Sure."

Before they could begin talking, the waitress returned with their drinks.

"Just keep 'em coming, honey," David said. "We're here to celebrate."

"What are you celebrating?" she asked, content to loiter near their table.

David held up the bottle of Coors. "Belated birthdays." He and Thomas clinked bottles. The waitress smiled and reluctantly moved toward a beckoning customer.

David leaned toward his brother. "You came out here of your own free will, Thomas. You've met Jeremiah. I'm certain he gave you the indoctrination speech about his personal relationship with God, as well as the righteous nature of the former New America. You're still here. What does that mean, Thomas?"

"I never had a plan. I'm playing it by ear."

"I figure Steve Wallace and Laura Delaney are here too, right?" David couldn't bring himself to call Laura his mother.

"Yeah, they showed up yesterday, in fact."

"I read their book. What kind of people are they really?"

"The best," Thomas said with conviction.

"I assume they're also rich," David said. "Wouldn't they have set you up someplace else?"

"I could be living in my own condo in New Hampshire, getting ready for the fall term at Dartmouth. I might even get my folks to buy a ski chalet in the White Mountains. Maybe a summer cabin on Lake Winnepesaukee."

"Are you shitting me?" David asked, sitting back.

"No."

"So you'd rather be out here in the former New America. Have you looked around this area? It sucks. Who in hell would want to live out here?"

"It's complicated, David, and then it's not. I wanted to meet my biological father and learn more about my birth mother. Aren't you curious about Laura?"

David belted back the bourbon and signaled the waitress for a refill. "Yeah, I am. I just don't have your options. Jeremiah isn't going to put me up at Dartmouth, or anywhere else. He ain't gonna write me a check and say, 'Have a good life, David.' I only got one choice." He wondered again what had happened to Melanie. "And that might bring us into conflict, Thomas."

"No, I won't let that happen."

David laughed at his brother's continuing display of naïveté. "I'd gladly change places with you, pal. What I won't do is let you take my place at the cost of my life." He held up a hand to stop Thomas from responding immediately. "I'm not saying you want that to happen. I'm saying it could happen. You don't know our father at all. I do."

"Look, David, I can only tell you this. I came out here to get away, to try to understand who I am. I'll admit that some of Jeremiah's ideas are intriguing to me. For the first time in my life, I'm thinking about everything. Questioning everything."

David took possession of another shot glass of Jack from the waitress. "Okay, Thomas. Just remember we're brothers. Don't do anything without telling me first."

"I promise."

That's good enough, David thought. With Melanie gone, Thomas could be his ticket out. He just didn't know how right now.

"Enough about all that," he said. "Let's get ripped. Let's mosey over and introduce ourselves to those cute cowgirls playing pool. I don't see any cowboys hanging around."

Thomas grinned. "I'll follow in your wake and take whichever one you don't want."

"That's right brotherly of you, Thomas."

As they stood up, David focused on a banner attached to the front wall—"END OF THE WORLD CELEBRATION, LAKE OAHE, JULY 4, 2018."

"What the hell is that?" he asked.

"You got me," Thomas said.

The waitress overheard them and explained. "It's something the radical students from Thompson University cooked up," she said. "You know, New America groupies."

"We know all about them," David said. "Hey, we're switching headquarters to that pool table where the two young ladies are playing. Can you bring over our drinks over there?"

"Sure thing, sweetheart. Also, I'm off on the Fourth. If you want, we could go out to the lake and celebrate, and see if the world moves."

David grinned, thinking that he was beginning to like life in America.

15

Steve asked Ariana to repeat herself.

"Thomas and David went to a local bar last night and got drunk."

"Unbelievable!" Laura said, shocked. "Did you even know that David was here?"

"Not until we saw them together in the Science Center lobby," Ariana said, "as they were on their way out."

"Steve, how is that possible?" Laura asked. "It means Jeremiah is here. David is here. How could they get into this complex without someone seeing them? Where are they staying? My God, they weren't so brazen as to rent a hotel room, I hope!"

"This place is bigger than the Pentagon, Laura. People sympathetic to Jeremiah have always controlled parts of it, including the security forces and the state-of-the-art computer system that runs nearly everything."

"Why hasn't someone gotten rid of them?"

"You can't fire people or put them in jail because of what they believe or don't believe, Laura. That would make us just like Jeremiah." She was too distressed to think clearly, he knew.

"You were right yesterday, Steve," Laura said, sitting on the edge of an easy chair in their room. "Thomas lied to us, and he's seen Jeremiah. Now David. He's obviously decided to join them."

"Not necessarily, Laura," Steve said, trying to project a more optimistic scenario. "Thomas lied to us for understandable reasons. Yes, he's curious about his biological father and his half brother. Does that mean he's thrown in with them? No. And we don't know everything about David's situation, let alone what he's thinking."

Laura stood suddenly, smiled, and walked over to Steve. "Our boys are finally together! Don't you see—we can get them aside and persuade them to come back to New York with us." Her voice rose with excitement. "We'll send them to deprogrammers. We'll move to a totally secure location. It'll all work out, Steve, won't it?"

Steve looked at Ariana, who had purposely stayed out of the conversation. She got his nonverbal message and delivered the bad news: "It won't be so easy to snatch them, especially David. He has two large and undoubtedly efficient bodyguards. Reinforcements are probably nearby. Like Steve said, Jeremiah's supporters control the security operation here."

"There has to be some way we can pull it off," Laura said, her exuberance dashed. "Steve, get an assault team in here. Helicopters. Whatever it takes."

"I don't think the FBI would allow us to take Thomas and David, anyway," Steve said gently.

"Why not?"

Ariana rescued him again. "Because they're using them as bait, Laura."

"Oh, goddammit," Laura said, roughly running her fingers through her hair. "Politics, politics, politics! Fuck the FBI! Steve, this is about our family and nothing else. If we sneak around here, afraid to step on someone's toes, we'll lose our sons—and you'll be responsible!"

She had never threatened him before, and he took her at her word. He didn't disagree with her, anyway. "We'll keep them in sight, Laura. Ariana, we need to develop a plan to abduct them, if necessary."

"Where did they go last night after they left the bar?" Laura asked hesitantly, almost as if she didn't want to hear the answer.

"They came back here," Ariana said.

"Were they alone . . . except for the bodyguards?"

Ariana cut Steve a quick look and said in a low voice, "They picked up two girls at the Hitching Post. Our guys following them were blocked at the security checkpoint. They called for backup, but David's bodyguards hustled the boys into the Center through a delivery dock and storage room. We only know they're someplace inside the Center."

Laura appeared too stunned to speak, Steve saw, assuming that she was thinking of her sons as men with sexual needs. He quickly steered the conversation to another subject. "We need to get the boys wired, Ariana. Not just so we know what they're up to and where they are, but also to try to learn Jeremiah's plans. We can't let our personal circumstances cause us to forget that he's probably planning a new terrorist campaign."

Ariana headed for the door. "I'll get right on it, Steve."

A surreal scene prevailed near sundown in a state recreation area bordering on Lake Oahe, formed when the Missouri River was dammed northwest of Pierre. As the three of them stepped out of their rented motor home, Laura estimated the crowd to already be in the thousands. It filled the park and spilled over into the adjoining prairie of gently undulating hills and wild grasses.

Each wore a costume appropriate for the July Fourth "End-of-the-World Celebration" organized by those who'd read the first three chapters of *The Revelation to Jeremiah*, with its prediction of the end times.

Laura had on a full-length, black-and-white skeleton costume made of cool cotton. Ghastly white face paint contrasted with her black lipstick and a black skullcap. Steve's entire face had been painted with a likeness of the so-called ROSE flag once carried by Jeremiah's mercenary army—a curved swastika inside a circle. A loose-fitting, waist-length red cape symbolized the flag and hid the Sig-Sauer and shoulder holster he wore.

Ariana's yellow mesh bodysuit left little to the imagination. Three purple fabric flowers covered strategic spots and matched the color of her recently dyed hair. Although the costume qualified her as a spring nymph, Laura thought of Ariana as luscious bait.

In casual conversations with several employees at the Hitching Post, one of their spies had learned that a barmaid planned to attend the celebration with David. Unfortunately for Laura's grand scheme to spirit away both boys, Thomas had elected to work his second-shift janitorial job. Nevertheless, Steve had come up with an alternative plan.

They followed the flow of a crowd composed mainly of people wearing equally bizarre dress. Laura calculated that for most of those who'd shown up, the "End-of-the-World Celebration" called for a bacchanalian party, not a religious observance.

She saw that in clear violation of the prohibitions of *Second Jeremiah*, many in the predominantly young crowd openly carried beer and wine refreshments, and coolers presumably filled with reserves. The pungent smell of marijuana hung in the festive air. Ominous music from Wagner's *Ride of the Valkyries* blasted out of a boom box and caused the hairs on the back of her neck to stand on end.

"David and his date are about a hundred yards ahead of us," Steve said, holding a palm-size cell phone to his ear. "She's dressed in a cowgirl outfit, they say, but David's just wearing white shorts and a blue tank top."

Laura's fear and frustration of recent days translated into superstition as she tried to attach meaning to everything. Did David not want to be identified with this group, with its ties to his father's *writings*? Or did he want to stand out as different so he would be recognized?

Laura squinted at a sign warning people not to approach the buffalo herd that roamed a privately owned pasture north of the state park. A footnote pointedly noted that buffalo could run as fast as thirty miles an hour.

Yet the center of the so-called celebration had been established dangerously close to several dozen buffalo that milled about restlessly, bothered by all the noise. Several broken posts supporting a fence lay on the ground, allowing the revelers to step over strands of barbed wire.

"Let's stay behind the fence," Steve said, taking her arm and steering her to the side.

"We'll move closer to David," Ariana said and walked away behind two costumed men who had suddenly materialized near them.

"Keep in touch," Steve said, holding up his phone.

Laura scanned the faces in the crowd, looking not only for David, but for anyone who looked to be dangerous, or seemed especially interested in them. She knew how quickly they could come under attack. For added security, she put her hand inside the black bag hanging from a shoulder strap and fingered the .32 Colt she'd practiced with a thousand times. *For a day like this?*

Steve stepped in front of her as a park employee moved in their direction. The man carried a trash bag and a pole that had a sharp metal end.

"I see him," Steve said softly.

The man stooped over to pick up a discarded beer can. He put it in his bag and walked closer to Steve. "Director Mitchell wants you to know we're here in force," he said. "What are your plans?"

"To talk with our son David and see if we can turn him around."

"We'd like to be in on that."

"David wouldn't cooperate for certain then. At least give us the first go at him."

"I'll pass your request on to Mitchell."

"Tell him I'll brief him later, in the motor home. You know where it's parked."

Steve and Laura elbowed their way through the crowd until they had a position directly behind a portion of upright fence. Farther out in the pasture, a dozen men in costumes began to dance around a blazing bonfire. Even as the July sun set, Laura detected a chill in the air; either that, or the cold feeling came from within.

The barefoot dancers wore buckskin trousers and had bizarre, multicolored designs painted on their torsos. Attached to their arms were long feathers, complemented by head coverings representing various kinds of birds. As they flapped their arms, stomped, and skipped, the dance vaguely resembled an Indian ceremony, Laura thought.

She heard a chant sweep the crowd: "The birds know all, see all. Know all, see all, know all, see all." It went on and on until the chanters began to intone a softer mantra: "Damn the Dominant Creature, damn the Dominant Creature, damn the Dominant Creature."

One of the bird dancers abruptly ran directly at the buffalo, causing several of the beasts lying on the ground to rise and mill about restlessly. Suddenly one of the shaggy behemoths wheeled about and held its ground, pawing at the earth and wagging its great horned head. The birdman slowed, spread his wings wide, and walked deliberately toward the buffalo, which initially backed up but then charged ferociously, impaling its tormentor and flipping him into the air as if he were a rag doll.

A gasp of horror escaped Laura, but others cheered and howled their approval as the buffalo continued to maul the birdman, who soon lay motionless on the ground.

A man standing beside them spoke to no one in particular: "Fear not death, for the end time is near, and all who believe in Christ and Jeremiah will be resurrected to eternal life."

David sipped his beer and watched paramedics attend frantically to the man who had been gored by the buffalo. State policemen had moved the raucous crowd back behind the fence, which park employees had hastily repaired.

Father's movement sure attracts a lot of strange people, David thought. It wasn't a group he aspired to lead. With enough money, he could isolate himself and the world could go to hell on its own. He just wanted to party until the end.

"Is this totally bizarre or what?" someone said. David looked to his left, expecting to see the barmaid Malibu. But she'd disappeared. Instead, he saw a tall, gorgeous woman who might as well have been naked, considering the meager coverage provided by her yellow bodysuit.

"Who are you?" he asked.

"Nice outfit," she replied, smirking as she gave him the once-over. "You captured the college-boy look just right."

"Thanks. What are you supposed to be?"

"Hot."

She's beautiful and funny, David thought, forgetting all about Malibu.

"I'm Ariana. What's your name?"

"David. You from around here, Ariana?"

"You're not a religious groupie, are you, David?"

He laughed cynically. "I'm only here for the entertainment."

"I think that's peaked. I know where there's a real party."

"Any more like you there?"

"Believe me, I'm more than you can handle, David," she said, walking away and crooking her finger at him.

He couldn't believe his luck. Ariana was nearly as beautiful as Melanie and she couldn't be much older than he was.

"I'm coming," he said, following after her. Then reality set in and he stopped and turned, expecting to see his two bodyguards right behind them. But the guards were gone, too. At first he was puzzled, then overjoyed with his good fortune, thinking the crowd had separated them. He pulled off the highly visible blue tank top and dropped it on the ground, then hurried after the goddess in the yellow suit.

"Nice pecs," she said as he caught up. "But it's a bit early to get undressed."

"You got a car, Ariana? I came with someone else."

"Better than that, I came in a motor home. There's a case of Coors in the refrigerator."

"Ariana, you're the woman of my dreams. Tell me you have some heroin or coke and I'll propose to you."

Ariana shook her head in disgust and picked up the pace as she moved expertly through the crowd. David hurried to keep up, periodically glancing over his shoulder, fearful that his bodyguards would spot him.

Ariana jogged into the parking lot, approached a motor home, opened the door, and bounded inside.

David ignored the steps and leaped after her. A man standing to the side of the door shut it immediately. David saw two others like him. Security types.

Two people were sitting on a sofa. A tall, gray-haired man with a swastika on his face stood immediately. The pretty, older woman in the skeleton suit sat deathly still, staring at him.

"What the fuck!"

Those were the first words Laura heard from the son she hadn't seen in seventeen years. She'd dreamed many times about this meeting, rehearsing in her mind what she would say and do. She had planned to take David in her arms and explain everything, to begin planning their lives together from this point forward. Now she felt rooted to the sofa, incapable of moving. She could only stare at her long-lost son, who stood before her wearing nothing but shorts and holding a can of beer in one hand. Sweat glistened on his chest, and he hadn't shaved in days.

Steve held out his hand to David. "I'm Steve Wallace. You won't remember me, but I helped change your diapers for a year and thought of you as my son."

David's mouth fell open as he said, "I've heard about you and your organization, the Gemini Group." Then he smiled cockily. "You may be the only person in the world that Jeremiah's afraid of."

Steve turned toward Laura. "And this is your mother, Laura Delaney-Wallace. I believe she'd appreciate a hug from you."

David hesitated, so Laura stood, walked forward, and put her arms around her son, but she still couldn't say anything. She could only sob quietly.

David pushed her back gently, and she saw the bewilderment on his face. "Don't be afraid, David. You're safe now. This can be the first day of a wonderful new life."

David turned away and walked toward the kitchen area. He looked accusingly at Ariana. "I suppose you work for him?"

Ariana, who'd put on a long, baggy T-shirt, replied, "Yep."

David opened the refrigerator and looked inside. He took out a bottle of Heineken and said to her, "You also lied about the Coors. Now that's really unforgivable."

He sat in a recliner, drank greedily from the green bottle, and said, "I'd expected the FBI first."

"We're a private sector group," Steve told him. "We have to work harder. But if you don't deal with us, you'll be talking to the FBI soon enough."

"Then let me answer all your questions so I can be on my way," David said. "No, I don't know where Jeremiah is, and I don't know what he has in mind specifically. I read your book, Mom and Dad," he said, snickering, "and if you really know Jeremiah as well as you say you do, you know he wouldn't tell me any of his plans."

Laura still couldn't find her voice. She stared in amazement at her son as if she'd had no previous experience with a teenager. She had expected—hoped, at least—that he would be reserved and well-mannered.

"Do you consider yourself the inheritor?" she asked finally.

She couldn't help smiling at David's explosion of laughter. Then he sat forward, put his elbows on his knees, stared at the floor, and shook his head. He looked up, directly at her, and said, "You don't know anything about me at all, do you, Mom?"

Laura had had many images of him, and now she had to struggle to suppress some of them that popped into her mind uninvited.

"We're still learning about you," Steve said affably. "If the idea of being Jeremiah's successor strikes you as hilarious, then you obviously have good judgment."

"You think so?" David asked snottily.

"Yes, I do. Jeremiah's schemes didn't work before and they won't work again. He'll always be a criminal on the run. The forces opposed to him are out early this time, and in force. They mean business. If you follow him now that you're of legal age, you'll either be killed, put in jail, or even executed. I can make you a much better offer. Come with us and we'll protect you."

Laura watched David's eyes narrow. He tried to laugh but couldn't bring it off. "No one can protect me from him," he said. "You know that."

Laura responded firmly, "Yes we can, or at least we can do a better job than anyone else in the world. I'm not saying it will be easy, or without danger. But there's a good chance that with us, you can have your own life—be free to live as you choose."

"All that takes money. Lots of it."

"We have lots of it," she persisted. "Name your price."

David seemed to tear up, and Laura knelt in front of him. "Tell me what you want."

"I just want to be free," he said.

"Where do you want to live?"

"I don't know. Would you buy me a condo?"

"Anywhere."

"Pay for my college education?"

"Anywhere."

"What would I have to do in return?"

"Only one thing. Help us get Thomas out of here, if you can."

David stood, walked to the refrigerator, and got another bottle of beer. He ogled Ariana on his way back to the recliner.

"Haven't you talked to Thomas?" he asked as he screwed off the bottle cap and began guzzling.

Still on her knees, Laura replied, "He won't listen to us."

"I haven't seen Jeremiah since we got here," David offered, "but Thomas has."

Laura narrowed her eyes and stood. She returned to the sofa and sat down, crossing her arms. She looked up at Steve, whose intuition had been right—Thomas had lied to them.

"What's Thomas's interest in all this?" Steve asked.

David leaned against the wall. "Some people like to see how long they can hold their hand over the fire before they get burned."

"Thomas has had no real experience with Jeremiah," Steve said. "Right now he just sees his newfound father, who undoubtedly has presented himself as a misunderstood and persecuted martyr."

"Oh, he's good at that," David said.

"What about Melanie Thurston?" Steve asked.

Laura saw David straighten up immediately. "What do you mean?"

"Where is she?"

"She disappeared the day before our home in Beijing was attacked."

"Do you know anything about another son of Jeremiah's, other than you and Thomas?" Laura asked.

"You're kiddin'!" David said. The somber look on her face soon caused his smile to fade. "No, I've never heard of anyone else," he answered.

Laura took a checkbook out of her purse and began to write. She tore out the check, stood, walked over, and handed it to David. "Take this. It's a check for a million dollars."

"No way!"

"Help us get Thomas out of here and it's yours."

"And if he won't come?"

"Make your best effort and the check is still yours," Steve replied.

"What do you want me to do?"

"Talk to Thomas. Feel him out. We need to know what he's thinking so we can better appeal to him." Steve paused. "I want you to wear a device that records and transmits at the same time."

"If Jeremiah or his people find out about this, they'll kill me."

"We'll protect you to the best of our ability," Steve said. "If you agree to do this, I can promise you that the FBI will be on your side, watching out for you. As for tonight, you find your bodyguards and tell them you got separated in the crowd."

David took another drink of beer. He looked at each of them in turn and then turned to Ariana. "I don't suppose the offer of a sleep-over still stands."

"In your dreams, sonny."

David shrugged, then said, "I . . . okay, I guess you folks got a deal."

16

Just before two the next afternoon, David knocked on Thomas's basement-room door and his brother soon opened it.

"David. I wondered what happened to you! Did you go to that Fourth of July thing on Lake Oahe?"

"Yeah," David said, walking into the room.

"How was it? I saw a TV news report about them hauling some guy away in an ambulance. They said he'd been killed by a buffalo."

"It was totally bizarre, believe me. What did you do yesterday?"

"Just worked. It was time and a half because of the holiday, and I also get today off. You wanna do something?"

"Sure," David said, looking around at the dingy basement room, trying unsuccessfully to spot the bugs and cameras someone had certainly installed.

"Did Malibu go with you yesterday?" Thomas asked.

"Yeah."

"She's hot."

"To trot. Which reminds me, Thomas, did you poke that other girl we took up to my suite night before last?" He wanted to give Laura a jolt about her favorite son. She was listening to their conversation as it was picked up by the sophisticated computer chip hidden inside one of the buttons on a shirt they'd given him. He wondered how they'd known his size.

Thomas shook his head. "We just made out. I didn't have any condoms with me."

"You should've knocked on my bedroom door," David said, perversely enjoying the game in progress. "I've got dozens in five different colors."

"I'd be up to going back to the Hitching Post this afternoon," Thomas said.

"Second time's lucky, Thomas. Sounds good to me." First, he needed to earn his money. And he wanted to do it in Thomas's room, in the likely event Jeremiah also was listening. Maybe he could cover his ass that way, too.

"There were a lot of Jeremiah's followers at that Fourth of July thing. Of course he wasn't there. Thomas, the last time you saw Jeremiah, he said he might get back to you, right?"

"Yeah, but he hasn't."

"What would you do if he did? If he asked you to be on his team." *Be on his team. I'm a master at turning a phrase.*

"I don't know," Thomas said as he turned away, walked to a nightstand beside the bed, and picked up a book.

He's acting weird, David thought.

"David, have you seen a photograph of my mother, Katrina Dorfler? I found one in this book. Take a look. She's beautiful."

David took the book and opened it to the marked page. He glanced from the photograph to the slip of paper on which Thomas had written: *Be careful, this place could be bugged.*

"You're absolutely right," David replied, hoping to imply a double meaning with his eyes. "Your mother was a beautiful woman." *And her son is smart, too. He'd thought this through earlier.* David considered that he might help save Thomas from Jeremiah just because he'd begun to like his brother a lot. Maybe they could go away together.

Thomas took back the book and closed it. "Let's go."

"Ready, but let's get lunch here in one of the cafeterias first.

Okay? I need to get something in my stomach before I begin pouring Coors in it." Actually, David wanted to hold open the option of trying to ditch his bodyguards again. It would be easier to get rid of them in the Science Center than in a downtown bar.

In the ground-floor cafeteria, they made their way through the serving line, filling their trays. David walked toward a table in the back, far removed from any other diners. One bodyguard stayed by the door and the other sat several tables away with his own tray of food.

Before David could begin eating, Thomas handed him a note: "I didn't want to talk about this in the room."

People are listening, anyway. "What is it?"

"A note some huge Chinese guy slipped me in the hallway. It's for you. I have no idea how he knew you were my brother, or that you were even here."

David shook his head. "Thomas, we're both way in over our heads. Remember that."

He opened the note and began to read. Then his heart went into overdrive. "Did you look at this?" he asked Thomas.

"Yeah. It wasn't in an envelope. I thought at first it was for me, anyway. Who's the woman who signed the note, David? Another romantic conquest?"

David reflexively put his hand over the button transmitter and stood immediately. "I gotta go to the bathroom."

As he prepared to enter the men's room, David told the trailing bodyguard, "Wait out here, please."

Inside, he read the note again, carefully. Then he tore it up, pushed open the stall door, dropped the pieces in the basin, and pushed the flush lever. He ripped the button off his shirt in time to add it to the vortex of disappearing water. Next, he washed his hands in the sink, all the time staring at himself in the mirror.

Back at the table, David sat down, looked around cautiously, then leaned toward Thomas. "In the bathroom, I just flushed a listening device given to me by Steve and Laura. I told them you'd met with Jeremiah." He shrugged for Thomas's benefit. "They'd already arrived at that conclusion and they had me on the hot seat. It was either do what they wanted or go directly to jail without passing go."

"Although I can guess, what do they want?" Thomas asked, seeming to be more peeved at his parents than at his brother.

"They want you out of here. Me, too. It's a good idea, Thomas, believe me." He wouldn't say anything about the million-dollar incentive right now.

"I'm starting to like it here, David. I don't even mind my lousy job. For the first time in my life, I'm free. I thought you'd understand."

"I do, Thomas, I do. It's just that this isn't the right place, with Jeremiah lurking in the shadows. You and I can go somewhere else together and be totally free. I've got money. Lots of it." Maybe he'd never tell him where it came from.

"I don't know."

"Think about it. Listen, we gotta go, *now*. They'll figure I already ditched the transmitter. Steve and his guys'll be here any minute." *If they aren't watching already.* "You got any ideas about how we can get away, Thomas?"

"Yeah," his brother said, standing.

In the hallway outside the cafeteria, David's bodyguards hung back about twenty feet. He half expected FBI agents to materialize. *Or that Ariana bitch.* Thomas suddenly thrust a key in the lock of a door marked "Employees Only." They hustled inside ahead of the bodyguards, and Thomas turned the deadbolt to the locked position. As the bodyguards began banging on the door and yelling threats, David looked about the small room containing cleaning supplies and equipment.

"There're some advantages to being a janitor in a place like this," Thomas said, unlocking a three-foot-high, rectangular metal door in the middle of one wall. "You learn about the working guts of the place. Look in here."

David stuck his head into a lighted, vertical shaft about six by three feet. He couldn't see either the top or bottom. A steel ladder was anchored to the concrete wall alongside the opening.

"It's to give repairmen access to sewer and water pipes, and electrical equipment," Thomas explained, putting one leg through the opening. "I'll go down a few steps on the ladder. You go up."

When his turn came, David swallowed hard and followed. When he had both hands and feet on the ladder, he cautiously moved up several steps, allowing Thomas to swing the door shut and latch it. The bodyguards continued to pound on the outside door.

Lightbulbs inside wire cages lit up the shaft, but David still couldn't make out the top or bottom. *Christ, I'm dead if I fall.*

"Start climbing up," Thomas said.

"Where are we going?"

"The note I gave you said you should call room twenty-seven-thirteen when you were ready to meet, right?"

"Yeah."

"Then you were to go to that floor and not worry about the security cameras."

"Jesus, you mean I gotta climb up this ladder twenty-seven stories!"

"It's the only way I know to get up there without being seen. I'll get out on the seventh floor, which is a hospital waiting room. I'll make the call for you on a pay phone and leave a message that you'll be in the employees-only room on that floor, and that you'll come out when someone knocks and asks for you by name."

David couldn't think of a better alternative. Besides, he'd already committed himself, so he focused his attention solely on climbing the ladder . . . very carefully.

Melanie Thurston stood behind the door to the hotel suite on the twenty-seventh floor, holding a 9mm automatic that already had a round in the chamber. At the first rap on the door, she looked through the peephole and saw her burly Chinese bodyguard Xu standing beside David. She quickly opened the door and they stepped inside.

"My God, what are you doing here, Melanie?" David asked. "Why did you disappear on my birthday? I thought maybe he'd killed you."

She laid the gun on the hall table and glanced briefly in the mirror above it. After receiving the telephone message from Thomas, she'd quickly changed into a white sports bra and tight, light blue shorts.

Melanie put her arms around David's neck and kissed him passionately. He disappointed her by not responding with equal fervor.

Instead, he pushed her away and said, "Jeremiah's here! So is the FBI. And Steve Wallace and Laura Delaney and God knows who else. They could have followed me."

"I don't think so. If they knew I was here, they'd have come for me by now. Besides, Xu's many talents include electronic expertise. He's already checked this room for surveillance equipment. Friends who work in the Center temporarily disrupted the security camera transmissions on this floor while he went to get you."

Xu listened to her explanation with a smirk on his face and then went into his bedroom, as she'd earlier ordered him to do. Last night they'd slept together and Melanie was still sore from the brutal sexual assault that was Xu's version of love-making.

"What have you done to your hair, Melanie?"

"Do you like me as a brunette, David?" She slipped her arm through his and steered him into the center of the spacious suite and then toward the bar.

"Where did you get the bodyguard?" David asked.

"He's courtesy of the Chinese government, which would like to capture Jeremiah first, or at least to know what he's up to."

"I'd say the Chinese are grossly outnumbered here."

She walked behind the bar and took two beers from the refrigerator. "Let's have a few drinks and talk. Do you know where Jeremiah is?"

He sat on a barstool. "I haven't seen him since we arrived about a week ago and he put me in a hotel room three floors above you. How did you get in here without being seen?"

She walked behind him and rubbed the muscles in his back and shoulders. She felt his tension. "Jeremiah's not the only one who has a network of supporters, David. Besides, no one expects me to be here, including Jeremiah, so no one's looking for me. I'm sorry I left so abruptly on your birthday, but I'd been warned that Jeremiah might leave Beijing. I was afraid he'd kill me."

"You were probably right. He found videotapes of us . . . you know . . . doing it."

"I apologize, David," she said, walking behind the bar. "I should have told you about those tapes. I was naughty." She tried to look contrite, but burst out laughing. "I used to look at them late at night and fantasize. Would you like anything else? From the bar, or in the bedroom?"

"Bourbon, I guess. I could really use some opium or heroin. I understand the Colombian here is eighty-percent pure."

She smiled seductively. "Many wishes will be granted to you today, David. So tell me everything that's happened to you here." She poured his bourbon, perched on a stool beside him, and began to rub his inner thigh. "Don't hold anything back. You know you can trust me. I'm not in Steve and Laura's camp, or Jeremiah's. I only care about you."

He hesitated, but then did as she asked, and related the details of his meeting with Steve and Laura.

"You poor boy," she said as she began to rub his crotch. "You thought this Ariana woman was going to fuck you, but she left you all frustrated. Let's go into my bedroom. I've got a surprise for you."

A bong lay on the nightstand beside the king-size bed. Melanie lit it, took a deep drag, and handed it to David. "It's that Colombian you talked about," she said. "Now, how about you and I try out this bed?"

An hour and a half later, David lay on his back, sweaty, sexually satiated, and slightly stoned. Melanie had used the alcohol and narcotic sparingly, reasoning that she needed to keep her wits about her.

"So, have you decided to throw in your lot with Steve and Laura?"

"She's my mother. I'm certain she'd never do anything to harm me. They promised to protect me. And they're rich. She wrote me a check for a million dollars. All I have to do is persuade Thomas to go with me into hiding."

Intrigued, Melanie asked, "Where's the check?"

David nodded toward the floor. "In my billfold in my pants."

Melanie laughed at his audacity and his stupidity. She moved to the edge of the bed, bent over, and snatched his jeans off the floor. She took out his billfold, opened it, and examined the check. *Unbelievable,* she thought.

"I guess I could cash it," he said.

"I have a better idea. Endorse it, and I'll deposit it in a Cuban bank account I've opened for both of us. Once it clears, no one can get it back, including Laura. The Cubans are very protective of their banking system."

"That's a great idea, Melanie."

She sat cross-legged on the bed, facing him. "A million sounds like a lot of money, David, but it isn't. You know what a villa in the south of France costs?"

"No."

"Tens of millions. I'm not saying you shouldn't keep this money, but you might also consider that it has strings attached."

"What do you mean?'

She handed him the check and a pen from the nightstand. "Sign your name on the back while I explain it to you. Laura's going to want to keep in close touch with you and Thomas, her two sons. It's only natural. The problem is, it would restrict your freedom. I don't think your mother and Steve will allow you to do as you please. Party, drink, do dope. Do you?"

"Maybe not, although she doesn't seem the type that would be overly protective. Besides, I wouldn't mind getting to know her."

Melanie took back the check he'd endorsed and put it on the nightstand. "You should know your mother. It's just that I want us to be together, to have a private life of our own. And I especially want us to have enough money that we never again have to be dependent on anyone. Isn't that what you want too?"

"Yeah, sure. You knew Laura before, didn't you, Melanie? Say, did you leave her book for me to read, that day we both got a massage?"

She planned to let him wonder about that. "Laura and I were friends once, but she accused me of kidnapping you, as you know from reading the book. It's true I was with Jeremiah when he kidnapped you, but I didn't have anything to do with it."

Slurring his words, David said, "I believe you, Melanie. We got to get out of here. All hell's about to break loose."

"I understand, sweetie, but we've got to be careful. You know what Jeremiah's capable of. I can't tell you how many people I've known that he's killed because they crossed him. Including Thomas's real mother, Katrina Dorfler." *Maybe David would pass on the news and give Jeremiah another headache.*

David sat up. "I knew it, I knew it! He said Wallace killed Katrina Dorfler, but I didn't believe him then. Everything he says is a lie."

"You're right, but it's not wise for you to break with your father right now, David. Jeremiah's not afraid of the FBI, the Gemini Group, or the Chinese. He'll give them the slip and do whatever it is he's going to do."

"What should I do?"

"What should *we* do. I've got a plan, David. We need to carefully play both ends against the middle until we see who comes out on top. Which reminds me, that's my favorite position."

She pushed him down on the bed and climbed on top of him, so that their faces nearly touched. "You and I are alike, David. Jeremiah used both of us. He started using me sexually when I was twenty-three, not much older than you. The only reason he kept me alive in Beijing was so I could take care of you."

"He's always thought of me as a mindless robot," David said bitterly.

"Exactly. And we need to take our revenge together. We need to be together. Look, I know it bothered you at times that we had sex."

He moaned. "It didn't seem right when I was younger, Melanie."

She smiled sweetly, looking into his bloodshot eyes. "It was never wrong, baby, because I've always loved you. Sexual desire is nothing to be ashamed of; it's something to be satisfied. No one's too young to learn how to love completely. I don't know where you got that idea. Be honest, David—can you imagine any woman satisfying you more than I do?"

"No," he said, and began to cry.

She lay off to the side and pressed his face into her bosom. She rubbed the back of his head and repeatedly kissed his forehead. "We've been through too much together not to stay together, David."

"I know."

"I love you. I want us to get married."

He drew back. "Are you serious?"

"Absolutely. And if you're still worried about the age difference in a few years, we'll make an arrangement."

"Arrangement?"

"You'll have my permission to take younger women into our bed. Perhaps I'll even watch, or join in, if you like. Now wouldn't that be exciting? Two women at once."

He drew back, astounded. "You wouldn't be jealous?"

"It's the other women who will be jealous of me," she purred. "The point is, it will work, David, and you'll be gloriously happy. I won't be a nagging wife. Anything you want, I'll make possible. But first we need money, and lots of it."

"Where can we get it?"

"From Jeremiah."

"No way!"

"Remember the day you turned eighteen and he talked about giving you access to billions?"

"Yeah?"

"Take him up on it."

"I don't understand."

He really isn't his father's son, she thought. *He can't even see the obvious.* "Embrace him, and then you'll have the means to be free of him."

"I still don't understand."

The heroin had clouded his mind. Melanie rolled out of bed onto her feet. She bent over and grabbed his hand and pulled him after her. "C'mon, get up, David! We're going to take a shower and then I'll tell you what you're going to do tomorrow."

17

Laura awoke to the sound of Steve's voice. She rolled over in bed and saw him sitting in a chair, talking softly into a cellular phone. He wore his shoulder holster and gun.

"Did you sleep at all?" she asked.

"Not much," he answered, putting down the phone.

"Who were you talking to?"

"Mitchell. The FBI's frustrated that they haven't turned up any leads on Jeremiah's whereabouts. And they're really unhappy with Thomas and David for yesterday's prank."

She sat up in bed and scooted back against the headboard. "Did they find them?"

"Thomas finally showed up in his room last night but we never did find David. Mitchell's patience has run out. He plans to take Thomas into custody today and initiate a room-to-room search for David, if necessary. Mitchell's asked a federal judge for a warrant to search the entire Center."

"Will he get it?"

"Yeah, if he can convince the judge that Jeremiah might be here. David's presence alone is prima facie evidence of that."

"Maybe it's just as well," Laura said. "Someone needs to bring this all to a head."

In the middle of the night, Thomas bolted awake, sensing that someone was in his room. He saw, or imagined, a shadow moving across the wall toward the door. His heart racing, he turned on a lamp but saw no one. He resisted an impulse to check inside the three armoires and switched off the light. He lay back and closed his eyes as he tried to dispel the nightmare. *Maybe a cloud moved across the moon,* he thought. Then he sat up, wide awake now—his basement room *had* no windows.

About noon the next day, Thomas put on his janitor's uniform and clipped to his shirt pocket the ID badge featuring his photograph and employee number superimposed over a hologram. He left his room and went to the administrative office of the university's biology department. He asked for Karla Maypole, the graduate teaching assistant and student mentor he'd met at the freshman orientation session. A secretary referred him to a room in another hallway.

In addition to the room number, the door had a nameplate reading "Cellular Biology." Through a narrow, vertical window to the left of the door, Thomas saw Karla and a man sitting at adjoining desks. He knocked and entered.

"Karla, you may not remember me. I'm Thomas. We talked after the freshman orientation last month."

She stood and held out her hand. "Sure I remember you. How could anyone out here in the former New America forget the Dorfler name?"

He wished she hadn't said that in front of her colleague, a young man with an elongated head who studied him intently through quarter-inch-thick glasses. "I wonder if we could go somewhere and talk." When she hesitated, Thomas said, "About biology, of course. I'm possibly interested in studying in the field."

Karla smiled. "Sure. There's a lunchroom just down the hall."

He followed her out the door and couldn't help but admire her figure through the tight jeans she wore. He figured Karla to be in her early twenties. There undoubtedly had to be a boyfriend.

"You have a job in the janitorial department?" she asked, looking at his uniform.

He felt ashamed. "It's just a summer job. I needed some extra money."

They each got a soft drink out of a coin-operated machine and sat down at a table in the back of the room.

"What can I tell you about the biology department?" Karla asked.

She has the most incredibly clear complexion, he thought, and then mentally chided himself for forgetting his purpose. "I might be interested in studying about wildlife, especially birds, or even microorganisms." Two subjects that interested Jeremiah, according to David.

"Well, let's see. There's zoology, which is the general study of animals, including aviary species. Any particular kind of birds you're interested in?"

He shook his head, unable to be specific.

"As for microorganisms, that's a wide-open field, not unrelated to my area of study."

"What's that?"

"The study of cells. How they develop, their composition, function, and life span. You could specialize in any number of areas. Genetics is the big field, of course. Every cell contains DNA, which works in different ways in different types of cells. You could easily relate microorganisms to cellular biology. Bad bugs get inside cells and appropriate their reproduction mechanism. That's how they multiply and spread."

"Give me an example." Thomas said.

"Bacteria that cause colds, viruses that cause flu."

"You mean like HIV?"

"Exactly. Once researchers understood the cellular structure of HIV, they were able to develop a vaccine for it. In fact, it may be possible eventually to use good viruses to deliver beneficial genetic material to cells. "

"Exactly what do you study, Karla?"

She tucked an errant strand of hair behind one ear. "Enzymes. The Science Center is the best place in the world to study in my field."

"What about the relationship between birds and microorganisms?"

She frowned, briefly creating lines in her otherwise wonderfully smooth forehead. "That's not my field, but birds are infected with bacteria and viruses just like humans are. It probably varies from species to species. I could do a computer search for articles and books. Would that help?"

"I'd appreciate that, Karla." It would be a chance for them to meet again. Maybe eventually he could ask her for a date.

She flashed him a friendly smile. "It sounds like you might have found your calling, Thomas."

"Maybe."

Karla looked at her watch. "I gotta go. Give me a call later this week and I'll tell you what I've found."

"Great," he said, unable to take his eyes off her full, soft lips that he imagined would be wonderful to kiss.

David woke up with a pounding headache. He opened one eye and saw Melanie leaning over the bed, tugging at his arm. "Wake up, lazy bones."

"What time is it?" he asked, opening the other eye.

"Time to go."

"Go where?"

"I'm leaving, don't you remember? And you've got business to attend to."

She pulled him from bed and he rushed to the bathroom, dropped to his knees in front of the toilet, and vomited. Then he palmed cool water onto his face and put on a white terry cloth bathrobe that had been hanging behind the door and went back into the bedroom.

"You do remember our little talk last night after we showered?" Melanie asked, as he walked back into the bedroom.

"Yeah. Maybe."

"Try to think. How can you contact me in New York?"

He struggled to remember. "At the Great China Wall restaurant on Canal Street."

She kissed him on the cheek. "Good luck, David."

He watched, stupefied, as her Chinese bodyguard came into the bedroom and took a large trunk from the closet. Melanie knelt in the open trunk, lay on her side, and pulled her knees up to her chest. Xu closed and locked the lid. "This is how we come, and this is how we go," he said, chuckling triumphantly.

David vomited again and then put on yesterday's clothes. He went to the bar in the living room and made himself a Bloody Mary. He sat on a barstool and considered various plans. As soon as he left the room, everyone would know his whereabouts. If he wasn't killed today, it would be a miracle.

The vodka-and-tomato-juice pick-me-up helped clear his head. He called his room on the thirtieth floor, knowing that the bodyguards had a scrambler attached to the phone in case someone had bugged it.

"Where have you been?" one of them asked. "Why'd you ditch us yesterday?"

"Because I didn't want you watching me get a blow job, Clyde." That was partly true.

"Jeremiah wants to see you."

The message came over the phone like a death sentence. *Oh, Christ, he is going to kill me!*

He gave Clyde the room number on the twenty-seventh floor and fixed another Bloody Mary. A half hour later, someone banged on the door. David opened it and saw Clyde dressed as a waiter, standing behind a serving cart piled high with dirty dishes. The bodyguard wheeled the cart into the room and pulled up one side of the white tablecloth.

"Get in," he said, pointing at the open storage area.

As Clyde wheeled the cart out of the room and down the hallway, David thought about the irony of the similar way in which he and Melanie had departed.

Lying on his side, he could see the carpeted floor. The cart stopped and David heard Clyde push the elevator button. Judging by the sensation and the time lapse, David decided they were going down to the basement level. Clyde pushed the cart out of the elevator and David caught glimpses of a tiled floor. A muscle cramp began in his back from being nearly doubled over inside the cart.

Finally they stopped. He heard a door squeak open. Clyde pushed the cart inside and pulled up the tablecloth covering. David crawled out and looked around at a room crammed with air ducts, pipes, and machines that produced a whirring noise.

Clyde smirked. "Stay here, asshole."

David walked around the room, which had no windows and only the one door. He squatted in a corner, his forearms on his knees, and silently repeated Melanie's instructions to himself.

He stiffened with tension as someone put a key to the door. He stood up, expecting to see his father enter, but it was . . . Thomas!

"What the hell are you doing here?" he asked.

"My supervisor sent me down here to mop up a water spill," Thomas replied. "What's going on?"

Jeremiah's going to choose between us, David thought, considering that a bad sign. *What happens to the loser?*

From behind a concrete block wall, Jeremiah stared at his two sons through a peephole disguised as a water faucet on the other side of the wall. He had resided comfortably in a bunker beneath the Science Center ever since he and David had arrived.

He knew that many factions had undercover agents in the Center, including the FBI, the Gemini Group, the Chinese, the Russians, and others. But no one from these organizations had supervised the construction of the Science Center, as he had twenty-two years ago. A special work crew, commanded by an architect and engineer, had constructed a large underground facility, adding several secret entrances and escape tunnels.

When the work had been completed, Jeremiah assembled the designers and their crew for a celebration, during which all of them were served poisoned drinks. Today, only he and a few of his most trusted confidants knew about the bunker.

Jeremiah smirked, thinking that while he was right here under their noses, the FBI drilled holes in the Black Hills and installed cameras and listening devices in underground caverns. *The Bureau is just as stupid and predictable as ever.*

He pressed a button and a section of the concrete block wall swung out, pivoting around a center support pole. Because the blocks were staggered, the open section of wall appeared to have large teeth on each side.

"Hello, boys," he said, amused at the way each of them stiffened. A look of sheer terror spread over David's face, as it should. "Follow me, if you will."

Turning, he walked past several bodyguards and one disciple who, dressed as a janitor, resembled Thomas. This lookalike would reseal the door inside the room to make certain there were no telltale marks and then leave the area for the benefit of anyone watching.

Jeremiah walked down a flight of stairs and opened a foot-thick metal door leading into a narrow corridor that extended eighty feet to another formidable door. Security cameras placed strategically in the corridor conveyed images to monitors in a room where his people could activate gas jets and stationary machine guns should any intruders attempt to breach the underground bunker. The latest X-ray equipment scanned everyone passing through the corridor for weapons or electronic devices.

After entering an elaborate code on the far door keypad, Jeremiah and his sons entered another hallway that led to a V-shaped intersection, where other hallways split off to the right and left. In all three hallways, doors led into rooms that led into other rooms and other hallways. He'd had this mazelike quality built into the bunker to confuse and sidetrack invaders.

In the event of an invasion, an alarm-activated mechanism would cause doors to slide out of the walls and block off strategic corridors, thereby trapping his enemies, who then could be either gassed or gunned down.

Jeremiah walked to the right toward an armed guard who opened a door.

"These are my living quarters," Jeremiah said, ushering David and Thomas in ahead of him. Except for a lack of windows, it resembled a modestly appointed condo. "All the rooms down here tap into the Center's facilities for heat, air conditioning, water, and sewage disposal. It's very comfortable."

Jeremiah sat in a high-back chair and watched with amusement as his sons sat at opposite ends of a sofa, as if they feared touching each other.

"Do you think Abraham, Moses, Isaiah, Jeremiah the first, John the Baptist, and Jesus Christ were paranoid schizophrenics?" he asked suddenly, intentionally intending to befuddle them.

"Of course not," Thomas answered immediately, although David only shook his head wearily.

"I was wondering, because that's what my enemies say about me when I claim that God speaks to me, as he did to those Old Testament patriarchs and prophets, and to his only begotten son. The point is, anyone who denies that God speaks through me imposes limitations on the Creator and calls into question the validity of much of the Christian Bible. Is my logic refutable?"

Each shook his head, although Jeremiah really hadn't expected either of them to challenge him.

"God made a covenant with Abraham and all of his descendants for all time. These descendants shall be as numerous as the stars, God said, clearly indicating that the spiritual descendants of Abraham would inhabit the earth and eventually colonize the universe. God said to Abraham, 'Behold, my covenant is with you, and you shall be the father of a multitude of nations.' Genesis seventeen, verse four. As Paul wrote to the Galatians, Abraham is the father of all who profess belief in Jesus Christ and his teachings.

"I am in that line of descent, and you are my progeny. I want to be faithful to the Biblical tradition, at the same time being mindful of the difficulties each generation of Abraham's descendants experienced in finding someone to carry on the tradition. Jacob and Esau fought bitterly over the issue, as did Joseph and his brothers, who sold him into slavery in Egypt. So it may be with the two of you and I might yet be forced to look elsewhere for he who believes as I do."

He could tell by the look on their faces that they understood his meaning. *But they don't really,* he thought, wondering if his men had yet found the boy called James. Against all odds, James's caretaker continued to elude them. *That boy is the ideal me,* he thought. *That boy is me.*

"So what is this covenant, you might ask? It's in the Bible for anyone to read and study. Obey the Lord's commandments. Avoid the temptations of the devil. Treat your fellow man as yourself. Do not lay up treasures on earth. Render unto Caesar that which matters not. Prepare for the Day of Judgment. Besides ancient Israel, what other nation on earth has paid allegiance to these goals?"

"New America," David said immediately.

Jeremiah offered his son a congratulatory smile, but he recognized the nature of David's knee-jerk response.

"Then why did so many people oppose New America?" Thomas asked.

"Good question, obvious answer. The majority of men and women pay only lip service to God's commandments, Thomas. They have no intention of observing them. It's always been the case. When God created Adam and Eve and placed them in the Garden of Eden, he told them they could eat from any plant or tree in the garden, including the tree of life. They and their progeny were created to be immortal. God had one rule: Do not eat the fruit of the tree of knowledge of good and evil. If they did so, he warned them, they would die.

"One rule, which Adam and Eve immediately violated. They tried to avoid personal responsibility by claiming to have been tempted by the serpent representing evil.

"When we allowed no rule-breakers in New America, when we deported them or punished them, or executed them in the case of capital offenses, yes, we were called fascists, Thomas. Yet I can only refer to the word of God for justification. God destroyed Sodom and Gomorrah, symbols of evil. He told Joshua, 'Neither will I be with you anymore, except ye destroy the accursed from among you.' Do you believe these words, or do you reject them?"

Thomas squirmed on the sofa, crossing and recrossing his legs. "I'm not sure."

Jeremiah frowned and shook his head in an expression of disappointment. "You're not sure? You've clearly illustrated the problem, Thomas. People just don't want to obey the word of God. They'd rather indulge their selfishness and self-interest and die, as opposed to obeying God and living forever. I never denied anyone the right to choose evil. I just said they couldn't be one of us. What's wrong with that?"

"Nothing," Thomas said.

"When the United States government and its military tried to abolish New America, we fought them with all the weapons at our disposal, as the Lord instructed ancient Israel to do on numerous occasions. As God said to Abraham, 'I will bless those who bless you, and him who curses you I will curse.' "

Jeremiah watched Thomas nod thoughtfully, while David massaged his eyes and exhaled audibly. *David undoubtedly has a hangover,* he thought. *It might be time for me to cut the boy loose.*

"New America was ridiculed when we rejected capitalism and consumerism for the Wealth Exchange," Jeremiah said. "We were scorned as Communists for believing in real economic equality and state planning. Yet it always seemed to me that the system we tried to implement most reflected Jesus' teachings. As the apostle Paul wrote to his own son, 'The love of money is the root of all evil.'

"So in New America we replaced the love of money with the love of knowledge." Jeremiah looked upward. "The Science Center is a monument to our belief that the pursuit of knowledge will allow man to again eat the fruit of the tree of life. As Job said, 'But if they obey not, they shall perish by the sword, and they shall die without knowledge.' "

"At freshman orientation, I watched a videotape of a tour you conducted of the Science Center a long time ago," Thomas said. "The way you blended science and religion was fascinating and unusual."

"Thank you," Jeremiah said, pleased with his eldest son's interest. "Religion and science usually are considered antithetical. I believe they are inexorably linked. As God revealed to me recently, he too evolved, as shall we the people until we are reunited in him. My enemies also consider this heresy. But I believe it is my mission to lead mankind to the next evolutionary level. As Paul wrote to the Corinthians, 'I tell you this, brethren, flesh and blood cannot inherit the kingdom of God, nor does the perishable inherit the imperishable. Lo, I tell you a mystery. We shall not all sleep, but we shall all be changed.'

"The only remaining question is whether the two of you will have a role in helping to shape this evolutionary change. That's why I called you here today."

To his surprise, David responded immediately, "I know you've been disappointed in me, Father, and I've been disappointed in you."

Jeremiah initially bristled, but his anger rapidly dissolved into curiosity. David seemed suddenly energized.

"It wasn't easy growing up in China," David continued, "with you gone, preoccupied, or sick much of the time. In addition to lecturing about the movement, you might have taken a personal interest in me."

Jeremiah conceded the obvious. "That's fair, David. My own father ignored me also, but Walter Dorfler, Thomas's grandfather and your great uncle, treated me with kindness. And he indulged my bad habits as a youth. I'd forgotten about that."

"Well," David said, "perhaps you also forgot that Jacob, the grandson of Abraham, assembled his twelve sons and gave each a suitable blessing. Some, such as Judah and Joseph, he favored more than others. Nevertheless, all had a purpose and an assignment. From them are descended the twelve tribes of Israel. Perhaps there is a lesson to be learned here."

Jeremiah didn't like being lectured to, but David's response both startled and pleased him. David indeed had been listening throughout the years and had just demonstrated a remarkable skill for using the Bible and God's word to justify his own needs. *That talent has to be inherited,* he thought proudly.

"What do you want?" Jeremiah asked.

"An assignment with responsibility, command, and power," David replied, "so I can prove myself and become a man. If I fail, you can do with me as you like."

Jeremiah pursed his lips in contemplation. "A test. I agree." He pondered the alternatives and said, "There is an important mission to be accomplished in Europe, David. I'll give you that assignment, and the authority and resources to accomplish it."

"Thank you, Father."

Surprised and pleased with David's proposal, Jeremiah looked expectantly at Thomas.

"I have no idea of what my role is, or if I have a role," Thomas said cautiously. "It's all new to me, and a little overwhelming."

"That's a fair response," Jeremiah said, thinking it also was a diplomatic one. He sensed an analytical intelligence in Thomas far superior to David's. "You've only recently come to know me, Thomas. And you were raised in the home of my enemies. Soon you'll have to choose between us. Making choices is what life is all about. If you follow me, you walk on the Lord's path in the greatest of all adventures. Anything else you might do with your life pales into insignificance."

"You may be right."

"You can accompany me to the north country, if you like, Thomas. There we can appreciate the many splendors of the changing seasons and the ebb and flow of life. It'll help you make up your mind. We'll leave as soon as it's dark."

Jeremiah stared at his sons for several minutes, considering it likely that one or both of them would eventually betray him. Unlike Christ at the Last Supper, however, he didn't know which one. Not yet, anyway.

18

THE REVELATION TO JEREMIAH

CHAPTER FOUR

1 Verily, as I previously reported to my disciples, the Angel of the LORD revealed to me the secrets of Life and the Universe, and the nature of the Apocalypse to come.

2 Having become one in a flight of geese flying high above Earth in the form of a cross, I received an epiphany from a Passenger who, previously unknown and undetected, resided within my avian body.

3 Earth's Dominant Creature, the Passenger said, is but a vessel, and each vessel is a battlefield.

4 Once again in the company of my winged comrades, we soared high above the Garden of Eden, searching for the agent that kills Weeds and spares the productive plant. With the red glow of the sunset before us, we ceased our rhythmic flapping and glided

toward a landing in a watery marsh, where we would seek sustenance and rest.

5 But Earth's Dominant Creature arose suddenly out of hiding and threw tiny round balls of steel at us, which missed many but tore through my body, causing much pain and damage, so that I plummeted to the ground.

6 I, Jeremiah, though in the form of a Bar Goose, knew Death. Yet, in complete validation of the greatest promise of Christ, my soul and whole being passed unchanged into another form, that of my usually silent Passenger.

7 Round as a ball, covered with many flexible hairlike projections, invisible to the eye, and lighter than air, I floated on the wind along with billions of my brethren. We constituted an army with a solitary mission: to invade, colonize, and kill the Enemy of All. A shimmering letter A floated in the clear protoplasm of the most virulent microscopic warriors.

8 The Angel said to me: "You are a soldier without animosity or mercy, whose duty the LORD directs, as He does all who help fulfill His design."

9 In this Army of the LORD, only I, Jeremiah, Agent of Change, possessed consciousness, so that I might record the events of the battle for those who believe, and will survive the coming plague.

10 We soldiers of the Mighty God Our Father floated on the wind, seeking to do battle with the Enemy. Suddenly, a vortex of air sucked many of us into the Dominant Creature. We encountered a forest of fibers coated with a sticky, toxic substance that bound and destroyed thousands in our invading force.

11 The surviving Viral Warriors were swept into an oval-

shaped chamber that roared with the currents of gases inhaled and expelled. Here the enzymatic protuberances of my Being latched onto a compatible docking mechanism projecting from the wall of the breathing chamber of our host.

12 As if a magical key had been turned, I gained entrance into a cell where tranquility and efficiency reigned. To my great surprise, I again changed shape and merged the essence of my being with that of my host, and together we produced more Viral Warriors.

13 My sons and daughters burst through the cell's protective bubble, seeking other docking stations where they also could reproduce. It became a battle to control the life forces of our host.

14 Antibody soldiers appeared, wielding weapons of tremendous destruction. They attacked ferociously, enveloping us, and covering us with a bonding agent that sucked out our essence. We counterattacked with chemicals.

15 The battle raged throughout the vessel for days. Soldiers of both armies were swept along a torrential river, dark and thick, that ran through major and minor channels, even backwaters, carrying sustenance to the specialized organs that comprised the Dominant Creature.

16 In the ebb and flow of battle, each side gained an advantage here and lost it there. The Enemy showered the battlefield with chemical weapons introduced through the same air and liquid channels that facilitated our access. In response, we changed shape to neutralize the weapons.

17 Similar battles occurred in each of the Earth's Dominant Creatures, except those immunized by agents of the LORD.

18 The Soldiers of the LORD won most battles. Their victories caused tremendous heat and hemorrhage within the host, and the

breaching of cellular walls, which ruptured as if hit by an artillery shell. Such Pyrrhic victories brought only death for all combatants, however, because the battlefield itself was the life-sustaining mechanism for all.

19 On those few occasions when we lost a battle, millions of dead Viral Warriors were washed from the vessel in a foul-smelling yellow river. Not all who survived were the Chosen Few, for Evil has its resources, too.

20 It is not for soldiers to reason why, but only to carry out the judgment of the LORD, who has twice found cause to cleanse the Earth. Before, he chose flood as the Agent of Death, and saved only Noah and a Chosen Few.

21 I awoke on the morning after the battle in the form of those I had fought, and I knew the fate of those who had neither Faith nor Purpose. Now it is my mission to lead the True Believers into the modern-day Ark of Salvation.

19

Steve and Ariana approached a group of FBI agents standing in a hallway outside the Science Center security office and computer control room.

"Hi, Byron," Steve said to FBI Deputy Director Mitchell, who nodded curtly in recognition and continued talking in a low voice to three subordinates. With his lean, rugged looks and muscular forearms, the FBI's second in command could have been a lumberjack in another life, Steve thought.

Mitchell handed a clipboard to one of his agents and walked over to where Steve and Ariana stood.

"I understand you got a search warrant," Steve said.

"A limited search warrant," Mitchell replied. "The judge declared most of the hospital off-limits. He also gave the Center's administrator veto power in the case of scientific laboratories if he can show cause that search techniques could destroy valuable experiments, or perhaps cause the release of dangerous pathogens."

Mitchell couldn't totally hide his distaste at having to brief the head of a private intelligence-gathering organization. His rationale, Steve knew, was the expectation of a quid pro quo.

"What about Thomas and David?" Steve asked.

"I hoped you could tell me," Mitchell said. "We haven't seen David since he and Thomas gave us the slip day before yesterday."

"Thomas was in his room last night and most of this morning," Ariana said.

"We know that," Mitchell said testily. "And he went to work this afternoon after talking to a university teaching assistant in the biology department."

"Do you know what they talked about?" Steve asked, adding, "It might give me a clue as to his whereabouts."

"According to her, he was interested in microbes, birds, and viruses," Mitchell said, his laser-blue eyes homing in on Steve. "Put all that together for me and I'd undoubtedly be horrified."

Steve understood Mitchell's meaning.

"I gather Thomas has disappeared also," Ariana said.

"I think you already know that, Ms. Cicero," Mitchell replied.

Steve gave Ariana a look, wishing she would refrain from goading the man.

"As he went about his janitorial duties, our agents followed him, but they lost him in the basement area. You know how they lost him? He went through a door that locked automatically before my men could follow."

Someone had deliberately blocked the FBI men, Steve assumed. "What do the security cameras show?"

Mitchell, whose face looked to have been carved from rock, snorted derisively. "Nothing, of course. I've got the Bureau's best experts trying to understand this computerized security system. Apparently the walls, floors, and ceilings throughout this place contain the latest in computer chip sensors and transmitters. Not just super-thin silicon wafers, but even DNA chips. Some feed into phone lines and cameras, others transmit by radio waves. The people who run this system know everything, and they also know how to make it look like they know nothing."

We've only been fooling ourselves, Steve thought. Despite their best efforts to bypass the Center's pervasive surveillance system, Jeremiah's people knew they were here. They'd avoided an attack only because he and Laura weren't the targets. Not at this time, anyway. Jeremiah's priority was to find a successor. He couldn't kill them at the same time he tried to convince Thomas and David that he was a reasonable guy.

"I've got to get going," Mitchell said impatiently. "We have a security tape of Thomas taking an elevator up from the basement. We're concentrating on the hotel. We think that's where David has been staying."

"They're not in the hotel," Steve said.

Mitchell turned back. "How do you know that?"

"I don't, for certain. But the clues point in a different direction."

"Clues?"

"Nothing happens here by accident," Steve said, "including Thomas having been given a room in the basement." He turned to Ariana, who looked as confused as Mitchell. "You told me that our people tailing Thomas once saw an old man in a wheelchair in the hallway near Thomas's room."

"Yeah. He was lost. Some hospital orderlies came to get him."

"But our guys never saw him come into the basement," Steve said. "They just assumed he'd slipped by them somehow."

"Why are you suspicious about this?" Mitchell asked.

"Do you remember Davey Schropa, Jeremiah's boyhood friend?"

"Vaguely."

"Schropa was elected governor of South Dakota after Jeremiah's followers became a majority in the state. That was just before Jeremiah declared New America's independence. I was there when agents conducted a chemical interrogation of Schropa."

Mitchell grabbed Steve's arm and steered him away from Ariana. "Are you telling me those rumors we've heard for decades are true, Steve? That when Peter Thompson was attorney general, he authorized an assassination team to kill Jeremiah? That you were a member of that team? That you guys abducted Schropa?"

Steve wasn't about to sully Thompson's reputation. "Let me repeat, I was there."

"Christ, Steve. You guys signed Schropa's death warrant!"

Steve felt the hurt of Mitchell having gouged open that old wound. He motioned over Ariana so she could hear the rest of it. "Schropa hadn't seen Jeremiah since they graduated from high school. They met again, here, in nineteen ninety-six, at the groundbreaking ceremony for the Science Center. According to Schropa, Jeremiah came disguised as an old man in a wheelchair."

"He used the same disguise again!" Ariana exclaimed.

"I think that's a good possibility," Steve said.

"It's a wild theory," Mitchell protested, although not with conviction.

"In the tape you have of Thomas getting on the elevator in the basement today, was there a clear view of his face?" Steve asked.

Mitchell frowned and said, "No, and that bothered me."

"I think you should concentrate your search in the basement. Jeremiah had this place built. He always called it the crown jewel of New America. I'd guess there's a secret room down there, or even an underground bunker."

Shortly before midnight, FBI agents discovered the hidden door in a concrete block wall inside one of the basement utility rooms. The stairs leading down clearly indicated the existence of some type of bunker deep underground.

The agents took their time working their way into the labyrinth, fully expecting to encounter sophisticated booby traps. Even so, several of them were killed and injured when they interrupted invisible electronic beams, activating explosive devices, gas emissions, and stationary machine guns.

In response, the FBI used robotic probes, electronic jamming equipment, and explosives. By daybreak, they had disabled or destroyed all the booby traps and searched the entire bunker, but found no one.

"They knew we were coming," Steve told Mitchell. The bunker

had served its purpose. As usual, Jeremiah had planned ahead—decades ahead, in this case."

"What I don't understand is how they got by my people outside," Mitchell said. "They've been stopping every individual and vehicle since mid-afternoon yesterday."

By dawn, they'd found out how. Just when they thought they'd searched every inch of the bunker, an agent found a cleverly disguised tunnel. The three-foot-diameter concrete tube outfitted with rails extended five miles out from the Science Center. At the far end, they discovered an abandoned electromagnetic "train" consisting of several "cars" on which passengers lay as they were transported to the end of the line. A disguised door opened into a gully where those escaping couldn't be seen from the Center, not even by observers using night-vision binoculars.

"Shit, we didn't have our perimeter far enough out," Mitchell said in disgust. "They probably walked and crawled along this gully until they got to a vehicle that was waiting for them. Even so, we had cars at every intersection for ten miles around. Someone had to have seen them. We'll catch up."

Not if they got into one of the new helicopters that hardly make noise, Steve thought.

He went back to the bunker, looking for Ariana. They had no reason to stay here now. He'd have to decide where they would hunt for Jeremiah next.

Ariana had stayed in the bunker along with FBI evidence specialists combing Jeremiah's hideout for any clues to his whereabouts.

It took Steve twenty minutes to find her. "They come up with anything yet?"

"Nothing important." She motioned for him to follow her to a table where FBI agents had bagged and tagged evidence. She pointed at a plastic bag. "It's the shirt portion of Thomas's janitorial uniform."

Steve could only think that his son now wore another uniform, at least figuratively.

"Let's get out of here," he said. "I've got to deliver the bad news to Laura. She's been calling me on my cell phone all night."

"I'll go with you," Ariana said.

Laura knew that Steve had bad news for her by the look on his face.

"Thomas and David are gone," she guessed.

"Yes. Like I told you on the phone, Jeremiah has a bunker in the basement, with an escape tunnel extending five miles out into the prairie."

"But we don't know for certain that Jeremiah forced Thomas and David to go with him," she said, trying to convince herself as much as her husband. "The boys may have left together. That was the plan. We need to see if there's a trail and if we can pick it up."

"We found part of Thomas's uniform in the bunker," Steve said. "He was there, Laura. I can't imagine Jeremiah letting him go his own way. Can you?"

Ariana, who had been checking the electronic jamming equipment in the room, said, "We'll know soon enough."

"What do you mean?" Laura asked, watching her take a thin, rectangular object from her pocket.

"That's Thomas's ID badge!" Steve said. "Where did you get it?"

"I was the one who first found his shirt in the bunker, Steve," Ariana told him. "I palmed the badge and stole it."

"Why, for God's sake?" Laura asked.

"Because it's a special badge I had made," Ariana said. "Steve, you told me we had to get Thomas wired, so we'd know what he was doing."

"I remember."

"I called on some of our experts"—she held up the badge—"and this is the result."

Laura and Steve crowded close to Ariana as she peeled a tiny square of clear plastic off the badge.

"What is it?" Laura asked.

"The latest DNA microchip," Ariana explained. "All-natural protein that's undetectable by any scanner. It generates its own small electrical field, then records but doesn't transmit."

"How did you get it on his badge?" Steve asked.

"Actually, I broke into his room in the middle of the night and switched badges."

Ariana carefully placed the microchip on a small glass slide embedded with fine, intricate circuitry. She took a palm-size computer from an inner jacket pocket and gently inserted the slide into a port.

The DNA chip had recorded Thomas's entire day, beginning with his session with Karla Maypole, the biology teaching assistant. Mitchell had accurately reported their conversation about birds and microbes.

"I wonder what it means?" Laura asked.

"I'm not certain," Steve replied, "but microbes could indicate some kind of biological agent. Maybe that's what Jeremiah has in mind."

Sitting at a dining table in their hospital room with Steve and Ariana, Laura listened to the surprise in the voices of Thomas and David as they were thrown together unexpectedly. Her blood ran cold at the sound of Jeremiah's voice. As Jeremiah took his sons on a tour of his underground lair, she tried to imagine what they must have been thinking. Surely they felt trapped and compelled to do anything their father demanded.

Laura listened in disbelief as Thomas complimented Jeremiah on his blending of science and religion: ". . . fascinating and unusual," her son had said.

Her horror was compounded when David asked for "an assignment with responsibility, command, and power, so I can prove myself and become a man." *A man?*

Thomas appeared less certain about his "role," but he didn't object when Jeremiah invited him to the "north country."

As Ariana switched off the computer, Laura buried her face in her hands.

She felt Steve's comforting touch on her back as he said, "It doesn't mean anything, Laura. They had to go along to survive."

She wiped away the tears as she raised her head and looked at him. "Not David. He sounded as if he'd given great thought to his preferred assignment. He betrayed us, Steve. He took our money and betrayed us. I'll stop payment on that check."

"No," Steve replied. "The money will create a trail. Wherever it winds up, David will show up eventually."

Laura nodded, acknowledging that Steve at least was thinking clearly. "What can we do now?"

"There's no reason for us to stay here any longer," Steve said. "Ariana and I will try to figure out where the north country is. I want you to go back to New York, Laura, in case either David or Thomas tries to contact us there."

Laura didn't argue. She wanted to go home and retreat into the cocoon of their condo high above the streets. They had come here to rescue their sons and do away with Jeremiah, but he had defeated them on both counts.

20

Jeremiah stared at the laptop screen, trying to digest the contents of a memo from one of his aides while at the same time fighting to stay awake. His eyes opened wide, however, as he felt the airplane dip sharply left and begin to descend. The computer clock read 6:10 A.M.

Just over four hours ago, they'd boarded the executive jet in Aberdeen, New America. The pilot had filed a flight plan for Winnipeg, Canada, but they'd drifted off course on purpose.

The whine of the landing gear dropping woke Thomas, who lay in a fetal position across two seats. He sat up, looked across the aisle at Jeremiah, and asked, "Where are we?"

"The northwestern part of Quebec Province, not far from James Bay."

"What's here?"

"You'll see."

Colonel Emilio Picard greeted them as they stepped off the plane. "Jeremiah, it's been years."

"Yes, far too long, Emilio. I was sorry to hear of your father's death. He was a great man."

"He had a good life, even though he didn't get to realize his dream."

"There can still be an independent French Quebec," Jeremiah said. "Time is on our side, Emilio. Now, I want you to meet my son Thomas. Thomas, this is Colonel Picard."

"Colonel," Thomas said deferentially, extending his hand.

"Colonel Picard commands a battalion of Canadian soldiers conducting maneuvers in this area."

"My father was a general," Colonel Picard told Thomas. "He helped mastermind the armed rebellion of two thousand five when the French-speaking citizens of Quebec tried to form a separatist government. The freedom fighters were defeated, as you know. There is now a black mark beside my family name and I am forever destined to remain a colonel."

"Only in the Canadian Army," Jeremiah said.

"What is your pleasure, Jeremiah?" Colonel Picard asked, motioning toward a black Mercedes. "We can drive to the site you wanted to see, or the driver can take us back to my quarters, where you and Thomas can rest for several hours."

Jeremiah sucked in the cold morning air. This far north, the overnight temperatures dipped into the forties, even in July. "Sleep is for those lacking purpose in life, Emilio. We have important business to attend to."

Thomas thought it odd that Jeremiah sat in front beside the uniformed driver, a sergeant with a freckled face and a reddish-colored handlebar mustache.

"Thomas, I knew Walter Dorfler, your grandfather," Colonel Picard said. "He was an impressive man, wasn't he, Jeremiah?"

"Indeed he was, Emilio."

"You've seen photographs of him, Thomas?"

"Yes."

"Then you know he was a big man with a flowing mane of white hair. He had a presence about him. In another time, he would have been a king."

"When did you meet him?" Thomas asked.

"In the mid-nineties. I wasn't much older than you then, although already I was a lieutenant in the army. Walter and my father were great *amis*, and they had many friends in common all over the world. They got together through the Omega Project, isn't that right, Jeremiah?"

"Yes. In case you don't know, Thomas, the Omega Project was a worldwide effort to establish communication between people who held the same beliefs. Later, it focused upon identifying promising young scientists. Your Grandfather Dorfler was a pioneer in using the Internet, even going back to the times when only the military and intellectuals were aware of its potential."

"And this network of people still exists?" Thomas asked.

The balding, thin colonel with the beaklike nose nodded with conviction. "Your grandfather planted a lot of seeds, Thomas. Some of them are still bearing fruit in the second generation."

"What do these people do now?"

Jeremiah turned to look into the backseat. "They prepare for a new and better world, Thomas."

Colonel Picard took out a saxophone-shaped pipe and began stuffing the bowl with tobacco from a pouch. He cracked open a side window before lighting the pipe, but the sweet aroma filled the car anyway. "Thomas, in the battles to come, there will be many different roles for many different people," the colonel said. "Most of my soldiers are about your age, in fact."

Thomas looked at Jeremiah. "You told me the movement had given up violence."

"It has," Jeremiah said, staring straight ahead.

"Armies can do more than just fight, Thomas," Colonel Picard said, as he blew smoke toward the window opening. "They can maintain order, ensure the peace, dispense justice. Even provide administrative services."

Jeremiah turned to look directly at Thomas. "In certain circumstances, even a small army can be a powerful force," he said.

Thomas remained silent for the rest of the trip, looking out the window at the endless pine forests on each side of the narrow, two-lane road. *What have I gotten myself into?*

Thomas thought their destination might be a military training area, but eventually the driver simply stopped the car on the shoulder of the road near an oval-shaped meadow surrounded by the ubiquitous evergreens.

Jeremiah got out of the car. Thomas followed, and the driver handed him a jacket and a pair of rubber boots.

"Where are we?" Thomas asked.

"Out in the middle of nowhere," Jeremiah replied. "There's nothing for hundreds of miles except trees, tundra, and wildlife. Canada has four million square miles of land, but only forty million people. It's a prototype of the world to come."

"Follow me," Colonel Picard said, striding out across the meadow.

Thomas followed grudgingly, thinking that a body might never be found in this desolate place. He turned to look back at the car and saw the driver standing watch on the road with a submachine gun. The waterproof boots made walking on the wet, spongy ground easy. Jeremiah wore similar boots, black ski pants, and a thigh-length black coat.

"Why is it safe for us to be here?" Thomas asked him. "We're near a Canadian army post, aren't we? Canada and the United States are close allies. Aren't you worried that someone will recognize you? I mean, everyone's after you, aren't they?"

"Everyone's after *us,* Thomas. Before you make that final, big choice, think about it. You're committing various crimes just by being with me."

"I know."

"To answer your question, we're safe here because we're among friends. You still don't understand how many followers I have worldwide, do you?"

Thomas played the devil's advocate. "But they have to be a small minority, don't they? What can they do? Do you plan to set up a separatist nation in Canada?"

"No."

They arrived at the other side of the meadow. Thomas could see through a narrow stand of trees into another clearing of marshland leading to a lake in the distance. A thin blanket of fog lay over the land. He and Jeremiah followed Colonel Picard into the trees, but they stopped short of emerging on the other side.

The colonel looked at his watch. "We've got about ten minutes to wait."

It seemed an eternity and Thomas tried to ask more questions, but Jeremiah told him to be quiet.

He looked around carefully and initially saw nothing unusual—except for the hundreds of ducks and geese wading in the marsh, pecking at the ground, preening, flapping their wings and communicating in shrill voices. With a powerful beating of wings that seemed to move the air even from a distance, dozens of them would occasionally take flight.

An explosive sound off to their right startled Thomas so badly he thought his heart would race out of control. At first he feared he'd been shot. Then a half-dozen men on each side of them rushed out of the woods, startling him even more. He'd been unaware of their existence.

The men ran toward the birds, who took to the air in numbers so large they temporarily blocked the sunlight, or what little there was of it on this gray day.

Not all the birds could fly, however. Many were caught in nets that had appeared as if magically.

"The ground was salted with corn," Jeremiah explained, "which is what attracted so many birds. Radio-controlled explosives hurled the nets out of those gray metal boxes."

Thomas looked in the direction of Jeremiah's pointing finger and then out into the meadow, where Colonel Picard directed the actions of men dressed in camouflage. They went from one group of trapped birds to another. At each location, they knelt near the birds briefly before cutting open the netting to free them. The emancipated ducks and geese took to the air in a panicked rush of wings and loud, squawking protests.

"What are they doing?" Thomas asked.

Jeremiah didn't answer his question directly. Instead, he said, "The ducks that spend the summer here and farther north include blue-winged teal, old squaw, scoters. They're as varied in migratory habits as their plumage. The teal winter primarily in the southern United States. Some of the old squaw may fly as far south as Mexico, even South America. About two thirds of the scoters are west-east migrants. Some go to the Chesapeake Bay area and the rest to the Pacific Coast. Do you know how many North American ducks migrate each year, Thomas?"

"No."

"Over a hundred million. And we're just talking about ducks on this continent, not worldwide. Other waterfowl, including the different colored snow geese you see here, also number in the millions. Barnacle geese that spend the summer on the Queen Elizabeth Islands in the Arctic Circle fly to England in the winter. Other geese, called brants, fly from Siberia to the Aleutian Islands and as far south as western Mexico. From Alaska, they may cover three thousand miles in one nonstop flight over the Pacific Ocean. In short, Thomas, birds are world travelers, constantly on the move, and not just during seasonal migrations."

"How do you know all this?" Thomas asked.

"How? By studying. Why? Because sometimes a most important tool of social change can be right underfoot." He smiled and looked up at the sky. "Or overhead."

"A graduate student at the Science Center told me that certain birds carry bacteria and viruses. Is that true?" Thomas asked.

Jeremiah turned toward him, his smile broadening. "Yes, I believe it is, Thomas."

• • •

She had waited seventeen years for this telephone call. *David is coming home today!* Laura had no idea of how he'd obtained her phone number, or even knew she was at home. And she didn't care.

She scurried about the penthouse, picking up anything that wasn't in its regular place—this morning's *New York Times*, a coffee cup, a napkin, and a book lying open on a nightstand. She ran her finger over the tops of several pieces of furniture and wished she had time to dust, maybe even to vacuum. She critically assessed the bathrooms and worried about soap scum in the sink and dental-floss splatters on the mirror.

She sighed, threw up her hands, and implored the heavens to take away this curse of obsessive thinking. She walked slowly to *his* room and stood in the doorway, remembering it as it was on the day David had been kidnapped. It had contained a crib and playpen. Toys had been scattered about on the floor. The wallpaper had featured the innocent, friendly animals of the jungle. Near the window there had been a rocking chair where she sang songs to David on nights he couldn't sleep, or when he cried. *Hush, little baby, don't you cry. . . .*

In reality, the room was as Thomas had left it months ago, except that she had made the bed, picked up his clothes, put away his books, and shut the lid on the antique rolltop desk he'd loved so much. The framed photographs hanging on the wall were of Thomas with Steve and herself and with some of his friends. In her fantasy, Laura saw both boys coming home soon and sharing the room.

She turned away slowly, went into the living room, and examined her appearance in a wall mirror. Earlier, she had planned to go to the Gemini Group offices, so she was already dressed in a white linen suit and yellow floral blouse. She freshened her makeup and then sat on the love seat so she could see the front hallway. One of her bodyguards sat behind a desk to the right of the door. She heard the other one in the kitchen, scrounging around in the refrigerator.

She hadn't even thought to tell David to take precautions so he wouldn't be followed, but then he would already know to do that, having been raised by Jeremiah. It occurred to her that David could be merely running interference for Jeremiah, but she stopped the thought from fully forming.

It seemed to her that the minute hand on the clock took an eternity to move from one mark to the next. Finally, the doorbell rang and the guard looked through the peephole. He buzzed open a glass-enclosed anteroom just outside the front door so David could step inside and be scanned for weapons.

When David came into the hallway, he saw her immediately and walked into the living room. She tried to move forward deliberately and not to rush. She put her arms around him and held him close. He patted her on the back but without any rhythm, as if uncertain of whether to continue. With her face pressed against his neck, she became aware that he had a different smell. Different from Steve and Thomas. The smell of a stranger.

She stood back and looked at him. He wore an expensive taupe-colored summer suit, a patterned tan shirt, and mahogany loafers. He was going to be a very handsome man—a heartbreaker, as her mother would have said. Laura quickly put out of her mind thoughts about her son's love life.

"How did you get this telephone number?" she asked, leading him to the large sofa. "It's unlisted and automatically changes every month."

"Thomas gave it to me, along with your address."

"Do you know where Thomas is?" she asked, trying to keep the anxiety out of her voice as they sat down.

"Only that he's with Jeremiah."

"Is he with him willingly?" That wasn't clear to her even after listening to the conversation that had taken place among Jeremiah and his sons in the bunker.

"He really didn't have a choice."

"And why aren't you with them?" He didn't know about the secret recording and Laura wanted to see how much information he would volunteer; how much he trusted her.

"I've got other business to attend to."

"Jeremiah's business?"

"Actually, it's my business."

"Where? Here in New York?"

It seemed to her that David wanted to tell her, and didn't want to tell her.

"It's in Europe, in fact. That's all I can tell you right now, Laura."

"I'm not trying to pry," she said apologetically. "Steve is right. We can't force either you or Thomas to do anything you don't want to do. I learned that the hard way out at the Science Center."

"I'm sorry. If there'd been more time, I might have persuaded Thomas to come with me. It's still possible."

Despite what she had indignantly told Steve, Laura didn't plan to ask David to give back the million-dollar check. Not after his news about Thomas. "I want you to know that Steve and I will always be here for you, David. All we want is what's best for you. You have to make your own choices."

He laughed and leaned back against a corner of the sofa, crossing his long legs and smiling easily. *He's much more relaxed than he was that night in the motor home,* Laura thought. *Best of all, he came here of his own free will.*

"Everyone lectures me about my choices," he said. "I wonder if it's occurred to anyone that I might want to do something totally different than what's been outlined for me. I don't mind making my own mistakes."

She moved closer to the edge of the sofa so she could turn sideways and look directly at him. "I have no agenda, David. God doesn't have a mission for me, and I have no idea of how to make it a better world, other than to play my very small part in life to the best of my ability."

He nodded resolutely. "We can agree on that."

Encouraged by his response, she pressed her advantage. "I know that Jeremiah indoctrinated you with his ideas all the time you were growing up, and you probably have feelings for him. He's your father. But not everything he says is the gospel truth."

Her inadvertent slip of the tongue caused her to cover her mouth and then break out in laughter. David leaned back his head and did the same. They guffawed until the bodyguard in the kitchen came to the doorway. Laura waved him away.

There were so many things she wanted to say that she had to restrain herself. Nevertheless, she rose and walked to a credenza on which lay a photo album.

She sat down beside him, opened the album, and pointed to a photograph of a baby. "This is you when you were about six months old, crawling on the floor in your room. Would you like to see the room? It's not the same, of course. It became Thomas's—after he came to live with us."

"Not right now," he replied, turning the page.

"That's you and Steve at our favorite deli on Lexington Avenue. And the three of us in Central Park. See, you're between us, just learning how to walk. Oh, here's your first birthday. I made the cake." She paused to catch her breath and choke back tears. "You lived here once, David. Jeremiah's people kidnapped you from us. We didn't kidnap Thomas and kill his mother. Katrina Dorfler and I respected each other. We were friends."

"I never believed him. I always figured the truth was something else. The world's not even the way he describes it."

"Jeremiah's a consummate liar," Laura said, rushing her words. "He'd never have been able to kidnap you without help from that bitch, Melanie Thurston."

Laura gasped, realizing too late her mistake. Then she calmed down. *David doesn't know that I know about Melanie and him.*

"What did you think of her?" David asked, earnestly.

The relaxed smile had left his face, Laura noticed, but he didn't seem angry, only intensely curious. She chose her words carefully: "Like so many others, Melanie was attracted to Jeremiah's movement. He used her for his own selfish ends. God knows what he did to her in China." *But you know, David.*

David looked troubled and Laura put her hand on his arm. "You can trust me, David. I won't lie to you. I never loved Jeremiah. He stalked me, and raped me. He kidnapped me. He tried several times to kill my husband Steve, who I love dearly. Jeremiah kept me imprisoned in New America. Do you know how all that makes me feel about him and those who helped him?"

He didn't respond, but he slowly nodded his understanding. Laura hoped she had accomplished her purpose delicately enough. She would never tell him about the videotapes she had of him with Melanie. He could never look her in the eyes again if he knew that she knew.

"David, I wish none of this had ever happened. I wish both you and Thomas had had a normal life, that Steve and I were just any ordinary married couple. This penthouse is worth millions, but it's really a prison with guards where we have lived in fear for nearly twenty-five years."

"I understand completely, Laura."

"Now it's different," she said, trying earnestly to project unbounded optimism. "Jeremiah won't succeed this time, no matter what he has in mind. He may still have a fanatical group of followers, but most people around the world know exactly what he is—a murderer and a terrorist. They'll catch him this time, David. You don't want to be near him, or part of his inner circle. You're free now! You're here. Steve and I have many resources. We're wealthy. We can protect you until this nightmare is over."

David stood and walked to the sliding door leading to the balcony. Laura rose and eagerly followed him, her hands clasped as she awaited his decision.

"I don't want to just move to another cage," he said finally. "I understand what you're saying, Laura, but I never underestimate Jeremiah. I'm not certain the wisest thing to do right now is to break with him openly. That might put me in even more danger, and you, too. It could backfire."

Secretly, she couldn't disagree with him. "What do you want to do? How can I help you? Do you need more money? A safe house? Protection?"

"How about a cell phone, I can use anywhere? I could call you."

Thrilled beyond belief, Laura walked quickly to the living room credenza, picked up her cell phone, and handed it to him. "It's the latest model designed to prevent anyone from listening in."

He took the phone, and put his arms around her. This time she felt him hug her without hesitation. "Don't worry, I'll be fine. I came here because I want to get to know you, to be part of your life. I'll be back soon. Everything will work out. Then we can make some plans together, Mom."

21

"Why Quebec City?" Ariana asked Steve as they sat side by side in the Gemini Group executive jet.

"Canada qualifies as the north country," Steve answered.

"So does Alaska. Besides, there's a lot of Canada."

"It's just a hunch, Ariana. Yes, Jeremiah could have been talking about another place on earth. Maybe Siberia, or Scandinavia. You could also make a case for Vancouver, with its significant Chinese population. But Jeremiah has a lot of history in Quebec City. Besides, it's a short hop from there to New York, and it's on a direct line to Europe, where David is supposed to be heading. We can go either way if things don't pan out."

He and Laura had once been on a similar flight from Washington to Quebec City when he'd been an FBI agent and his superiors had sent him there to check out Claude Dumont, a rich French-Canadian separatist suspected of pouring millions into Jeremiah's terrorist campaign.

Steve smiled, remembering how the stewardess had looked askance at them as he and Laura went together into the same closet-size bathroom. Even in the midst of a national crisis, they couldn't contain their passion for each other.

They'd hit a bonanza on that trip. They didn't turn up Jeremiah, who, they later discovered, was actually at Laura's northern Virginia farm. They found Walter Dorfler instead. The aging German fascist lay sick in his bed at the Hotel Frontenac. Both he and Laura questioned Dorfler while a camera crew from the United Broadcasting Corporation filmed the interrogation.

Dorfler told them nothing that helped them find his nephew Jeremiah, but he revealed a secret about the self-styled Prophet that turned out to be prophetic. According to Dorfler, Jeremiah had a tendency to become obsessed with the women in his life, especially those who spurned his advances or wouldn't do as they were told.

Jeremiah had become so infatuated with his first cousin Emma Dietze, a famous international tennis star, that Walter had ordered his own niece killed to keep Jeremiah focused on the terrorism projects. Dorfler's daughter Katrina fell hopelessly in love with Jeremiah and, against his wishes, became pregnant. When she inadvertently let slip the secret about Emma's death, and the fact that she had helped Laura escape from New America, Jeremiah killed Katrina in a rage.

Worst of all, the terrorist bastard had risked his life several times so that he could possess Laura against her will.

Ariana reflexively grabbed Steve's arm as the jet hit an air pocket. "God, I hate bumpy flights," she said.

"Talking about airplanes, Mitchell told me earlier today that a private jet flew out of Aberdeen last night shortly after Jeremiah escaped. The pilot filed a flight plan for Winnipeg."

"Did it arrive there?" Ariana asked.

"The tower log says yes, but FBI agents and Canadian police can't find the plane."

"He continues to make everyone look like a fool. What else is the FBI up to?"

"I told Mitchell we received information through informants that Jeremiah planned to go to the 'north country.' I also said we'd been tipped off about some operation he's got going in Europe."

Ariana grinned. "So the FBI knows everything we know, but just not how we found out."

Steve gave her a tolerant look. "Stealing evidence from a crime scene is a felony. On the other hand, failing to protect one's sons would be a major ethical lapse."

She surprised him by squeezing his arm and saying, "Life's complicated, isn't it, Steve? Sometimes you can't tell the truth for fear of hurting someone you love."

They landed at the airport northwest of the old walled city. Ariana rented a car while Steve made several phone calls.

"What does your crystal ball say now, master?" she asked as she drove toward the airport exit.

"Drive northeast on the Interstate," he said, smiling. "Your aunt was a lot more respectful when she and I worked together, you know."

"That was the last century, Steve. It's a new generation now."

"You're telling me. That reminds me, do you have a boyfriend?"

"I have several male friends," she said pointedly.

"Are you serious about anyone?"

"You know the old story, Steve. All the good guys are taken. Do you know of anyone interested in a tough-talking, gun-toting babe who chases bad guys all over the world?"

Steve didn't answer immediately as he looked over at the St. Lawrence River to their right. "If you want to, we can stop at a church I know of where miracles are granted to the faithful. You can pray for a good man."

"Where is this church?"

"It's another eighteen miles. Sainte Anne de Beaupré."

"Never heard of it."

"It's a famous pilgrimage shrine, named after the grandmother of Christ. People who are ill come from all over the world seeking to be cured. Or to have their faith restored."

"Do you still have faith?"

He knew his faith in his sons had been shaken. "When we cornered Walter Dorfler here back in nineteen ninety-five, he took a cyanide tablet and committed suicide. The Germans, who are always sensitive about fascism, wouldn't allow his body to be returned home. They were afraid it would become a shrine for neo-Nazis. He's buried in a cemetery near Saint Anne's."

Built in a hilly area north of the St. Lawrence, the church's twin three-hundred-foot granite steeples, topped by crosses, could be seen from miles away. Ariana drove past the church grounds, packed with tour buses that unloaded the curious, the devout, and the infirm. Steve directed her to turn into a graveyard and park in front of the caretaker's office.

Inside, Steve asked for Monsieur Pampalon, and presently a slight, elderly man appeared. He wore a black suit shiny with wear, and his white hair and beard were cut to the same length.

He respectfully took off his beret. "Mr. Wallace. I haven't seen you for many years. We've both grown older, I see."

"Yes, sir. Monsieur Pampalon, this is my assistant, Ariana Cicero."

The old man bobbed his head respectfully in her direction.

"Monsieur Pampalon, you told me on the phone that there had been visitors recently to a certain grave."

"Late last evening," the caretaker said, leading the way into his office. He pulled down a shade to cover the glass portion of the door. Steve and Ariana sat down and watched Pampalon unlock an ancient file cabinet. He took out a videotape and inserted it into a VCR/TV set.

For nearly twenty years, Steve had sent the caretaker a modest monthly stipend that he earned by maintaining a hidden video camera near Walter Dorfler's grave. Any movement near the grave interrupted an infrared light beam that activated the camera. The investment had never paid off until today.

On the videotape, an old man and a young man got out of a black limo and walked to the grave. No effort had been made to disguise Thomas, who wore jeans and a green coat. Not so Jeremiah, who played his favorite role—that of a stooped old man with long white hair. He hobbled about with the aid of a cane.

The small talk between them at the gravesite consisted largely of Jeremiah telling Thomas about the highlights of Walter's life and what a stand-up guy his grandfather had been. Thomas asked if any family remained in Germany, and Jeremiah said he'd give him some names and addresses later.

When father and son turned back toward the limo, Steve heard Jeremiah say, "We'll relax this weekend, Thomas, and then travel to the city where I struck a blow at the devil's army."

Ariana pressed the slow-motion button on the remote as the limo drove away. "I'll get the license number and maybe we can trace the car and figure out where they went from here."

Steve and Ariana scoured the area around Dorfler's tombstone and grave for nearly twenty minutes, searching for other clues.

"I don't see anything," Ariana said.

"Me neither." Steve had hoped that Thomas might have dropped a note, protesting his kidnapping.

As they got into their rental car, Ariana asked, "Why did Jeremiah come here? He had to know you'd put this high on your list of surveillance sites."

"I guess he balanced the risks against the rewards."

"What could he hope to gain?"

Steve looked at her as he put the car in reverse gear. "Thomas. It's part of the web Jeremiah is weaving. He's linking Thomas to the Dorfler family and its tradition of intrigue and terrorism."

Ariana nodded her understanding. "What now?"

"Back to the crystal ball, although Jeremiah may have left us an important clue." *It's almost as if he did it on purpose,* Steve thought, *as if this were some game.*

• • •

Maybe it wasn't wise to have visited my mother, David thought as he got in the car waiting for him on a side street near the condo. On the other hand, Jeremiah obviously had known where Steve and Laura had been living all these years—*the same place I lived before he had me kidnapped.*

Why hadn't Jeremiah sent someone to kidnap Thomas? David wondered. Was it an experiment to see how his son would turn out if raised by Steve and Laura?

He gave up trying to think like his father. Besides, Laura's comments about Melanie had confused him even more. He'd had a love-hate relationship with Melanie since he was ten years old. He had often wished she'd stop using him sexually, then feared that she might.

That had changed now that he was a man. She hadn't shrunk from betraying someone as dangerous as Jeremiah . . . which meant she could be capable of betraying him, too. Yet she had come to him at the Science Center with a plan for them to be free and together. She also had his million-dollar check, which he'd stupidly endorsed.

"Where are we going now?" the bodyguard riding shotgun asked insolently. The three of them, including the driver and the guy sitting next to David in the backseat, had grumbled all the way from Washington to New York. They kept telling him that Jeremiah had the route planned precisely according to a timetable that couldn't be altered. They were supposed to drive directly to Dover Air Force Base and board a C-5A cargo plane bound for Germany. The National Guard flight crew were "sympathizers."

That wasn't as surprising as how they'd gotten to Washington, David recalled. The private jet that took off from Sioux Falls belonged to an international oil company and there were a congressman and several oil industry lobbyists on board! When he and his three bodyguards boarded, no one even looked at them, nor did anyone speak to them during the entire trip.

"You need any more clothes?" the same bodyguard asked in the same critical way he'd objected when David had them pull over at a men's shop on the way to Laura's penthouse. He had wanted to look nice for his mother.

"If I do, I'll tell you where to stop and you'll do it," he replied, thinking the time had come to take control of this situation. "I report directly to Jeremiah, and I'm taking over in Europe." *That's a stretch.* "You three take orders from me."

He glared at the one sitting beside him. The bodyguard grimaced and looked away, to David's great satisfaction. "If you don't like working for me, or you go around my back, I'll get rid of you." He'd let them worry about what he meant, although he knew the threat was meaningless.

They drove to the Chinese restaurant on Canal Street and parked out front in a loading zone. He told the bodyguards to wait in the car and none of them objected, although one got out and stood off to the side of the building.

Inside, David told the hostess he had an early dinner date with Ms. Melanie Thurston. She took him through a doorway covered with hanging beads, gave him a business card, and pointed to a pay phone.

Perplexed and not too happy with the run-around, David called the number written on the card. A woman answered and he asked for Melanie. Several seconds later, she picked up the phone.

"Where are you?" he asked. "How come you're not at the restaurant? You said we'd meet here."

"I didn't know exactly when you were coming, did I?" she replied, as if talking to a child. "We have to be careful, you know. How'd it go at the Science Center?"

He couldn't resist bragging. "He gave me a major assignment in Europe and access to a bank account containing five million bucks."

"You did well, David. Didn't I tell you? Where's the bank?"

"Zurich."

"Which one?"

"The Swiss Union Bank."

"How are you supposed to get to Zurich?"

He told her and she convinced him they should travel separately for security reasons. That was why she hadn't met him at the restaurant, she said, and he privately conceded her point.

Melanie asked where he would be staying and he gave her the address Jeremiah had given him. Melanie spoke to someone in the background, but he couldn't hear the words.

"I'll meet you at the bank day after tomorrow. Ten A.M."

Outside, the bodyguards were happy to learn they could still make their connection in Dover. David was equally happy that Melanie hadn't deserted him. Laura had been wrong. Not only was Melanie trustworthy, she loved him. Melanie had been right when she said that Laura wouldn't understand their relationship. *No matter,* he thought. *Laura will come around someday and accept both of us—me and my wife.*

22

The giant cargo transport took off from Dover Air Force Base at dusk, laboring mightily to catapult itself into the air. In the windowless cabin high above the cargo hold, David shoved rubber plugs into his ears in an attempt to shut out the angry roar of the four engines. He visualized the ocean waters below, with narrow, dark rivers of riptides running outward against the shore-bound waves. If this behemoth dove nose down, would it submerge, bounce, skip, or simply shatter into a million pieces? He shrugged fatalistically and lay down across the seats to sleep.

They landed the next morning at Rhein Mein, a former American air base that had been returned years ago to the German government, although U.S. military planes still had landing privileges there.

A taxi took him and his bodyguards the short distance to Frankfurt International Airport, where they blended into a throng of travelers descending to the underground railroad station. They purchased tickets providing them with a private compartment in the Class A coach. Before boarding, David bought a sandwich and soft drink from a platform vendor. He bit into a piece of juicy wurst just as the train lurched forward on its trip to Switzerland.

That afternoon a car picked them up at the Zurich train station and drove them to a château built into the side of a hill overlooking the city. Jeremiah had given David the address, although he had told him nothing about the property, such as who owned it.

The French-style château came with a full complement of servants, one of whom showed David to his bedroom, which appeared to be the master suite. French doors on two walls opened to sitting balconies. He walked out onto the one closest to the road they'd traveled. Two hundred yards to his right, he saw an intersection he'd noted as they had driven by.

He bent over the balcony railing and inspected the support legs; they were made of iron and had a lattice design that served as a trellis for climbing vines. They could also serve as steps.

He took out the cell phone Laura had given him and punched in a number he had seen on the side of a taxi at the railroad station. Then, exhausted from jet lag, he collapsed into bed and immediately fell asleep, dreaming of the many promises of tomorrow.

At 7:00 A.M. the next morning, David neatly folded his New York suit and put it into an oversized backpack, along with underwear, socks, his mahogany loafers, and a pair of cool, wraparound shades he'd picked up in an airport shop.

Wearing only running shoes and shorts emblazoned with a Nike swoosh, he went out onto the balcony. He dropped the backpack to the ground before climbing down. He walked directly toward an iron gate leading out to the road, knowing full well that it would be locked and that he'd encounter a guard before reaching it.

A young, fair-haired guard came jogging from a corner of the building.

"Where are you going so early, sir?" he asked, his English overlaid with an accent.

"Running," David said, noting the submachine gun suspended by a shoulder strap so that its snub-nosed barrel pointed at the ground.

"I'll get someone to go with you," the guard said, turning away.

"No, that won't be necessary."

Although he appeared not much older than himself, the guard said, "But it could be dangerous."

"Do you know who I am?"

"Yes, sir."

"Then you should know to obey my orders without question. I'm here to take charge in Europe, you understand? Now, unlock the gate."

Looking properly chastised, the guard hurried to the task. But he made one more effort. "Can I follow behind at a discreet distance, sir?"

David walked through the open gate and looked down the road, seeing that the taxi had already arrived. He gave the guard his best stern, imperial look. "Yes, you can. But cover up that gun with your shirt."

David slipped his arms through the backpack and began jogging toward the taxi, looking back once to see that the guard still stood near the gate, trying to button his shirt over the gun. David reached the taxi, opened the back door, and jumped inside. On the way into the city, he changed his clothes.

David entered a coffee shop in Zurich's financial district and sought out a small table in the back of the room. He ordered breakfast in English, which prompted his waitress to bring a copy of *USA Today* along with his coffee. He pretended to be interested in reading the newspaper, only because he could hold it in front of his face, if necessary.

A front-page story nearly pulled his eyes out of their sockets, however. The exclusive article quoted unnamed sources within the FBI, the White House, and the Congress, to the effect that Jeremiah, the terrorist prophet, had returned to the United States after leaving China. After nearly being captured in South Dakota, he might have fled to Canada, the writer said, *accompanied by his two sons!*

The reporter outlined Jeremiah's past terrorist campaigns in the United States and quoted the opinions of several terrorism "experts" about plans the Prophet might have in mind for the near future.

Toward the end of the article, the writer sketched David and Thomas's lives, pointing out that government officials had cooperated for many years with Steve and Laura in keeping secret Thomas's identity and location. The author ended his piece by reviewing several old controversies, including Laura and Jeremiah's relationship, the details of David's kidnapping, and the fate of Katrina Dorfler.

Then the journalist nourished a new seed of sensationalism by writing that "FBI officials fear that Jeremiah may be in the process of training his sons as successors to the revolutionary ideology concocted by Jeremiah's uncle, the infamous German neo-Nazi, Walter Dorfler."

The eternity of two and a half hours finally passed and the Swiss Union Bank opened its doors to customers.

David told the receptionist he had an appointment with Herr Ernest Schoeck, the bank official whose name Jeremiah had supplied. As he waited, David looked anxiously around the lobby, but didn't see Melanie. Should he have mentioned her name to the receptionist?

An attractive, older woman appeared and asked him to follow her to Herr Schoeck's office. As they waited for an elevator to the second floor, David fretted again about how he'd find Melanie. Maybe she would be waiting for him on the street after he withdrew the money. Maybe an intermediary would contact him.

On the second floor, they entered Herr Schoeck's office and David's escort introduced him to another receptionist and then left. The receptionist told him to have a seat and that Herr Schoeck would be with him momentarily.

No sooner had he sat down than the door opened and in walked Melanie.

"Here you are, David," she said, sitting beside him. For the benefit of the receptionist, she said, "Sorry I'm late."

His mouth hung open as Melanie put her lips to his ear and whispered, "My name is Madeline and I'm your companion. Don't make any more of it than that. Bankers are wise to the ways of the world. You're a rich, important young man. Act the role."

He tried to be both mature and nonchalant as he glanced sideways at her, noting how the tight, navy blue suit clung to her luscious figure. A broad-brimmed hat and large sunglasses hid much of her face. The aroma of her perfume generated goose bumps on the back of his neck. When she crossed her long legs, the rustle of her nylons caused him to swallow a lump in his throat. She wet her lips with her tongue, causing him to imagine the taste of her lipstick. Her fingers touched the back of his hand and David could scarcely contain himself. Whatever doubts he'd had about Melanie disappeared completely.

She turned her head toward him again and spoke softly. "Ask Schoeck for three million in Eurodollars in a briefcase. Large-denomination bills. Then ask for a back way out and a private limo. He'll do it all for you."

And Herr Schoeck did, quickly and efficiently, as soon as David rattled off the nine-digit account number and the passwords Jeremiah had made him memorize—*Israel plus.* The banker called for a private car service while they had coffee and chatted. Herr Schoeck naturally paid most of his attention to *Madeline.* Ten minutes later, he showed them into a stairwell leading from his office to the ground floor. A security guard held open a door and they exited onto a cobblestone street and found the car waiting. Beyond the old buildings across the street, David saw boats plying the Limmat River.

In the backseat of the limo, he hugged the black leather briefcase, which even smelled expensive. He couldn't believe the withdrawal had been made without a hitch. "Where to now? Why didn't we just empty out the account?"

"We don't want to be too greedy," Melanie said, glancing sharply at the driver, "or do anything that would arouse your father's suspicion. We'll get the rest of the money later."

David understood that Melanie didn't want to say Jeremiah's name. More and more, he appreciated her maturity and wisdom, as well as her many other talents.

Melanie gave the driver an address and they were taken a short distance south of the city to a charming two-story *gasthaus* overlooking Lake Zurich. While she handled the check-in, David looked around the hotel, admiring its Old World ambience. Later, he and Melanie would visit the bar and have dinner in the adjoining restaurant, he decided.

In their room, on the second floor, David let out a *whoop!* They had three million Eurodollars in a briefcase and no one knew of their whereabouts. *Finally, I'm free!*

Melanie climbed all over him, smothering him with kisses, caressing him with one hand and taking off her clothes with the other. He responded in like manner. Things were different now. He lusted for her as she maneuvered him toward the bed, which creaked loudly as they flopped down on it, both still struggling out of their clothes. He pushed her onto her back, jerked off her panties, and entered her with gusto. He exploded within seconds.

"Don't worry about it," Melanie said as he rolled off to the side. "We've got all the time in the world, David. No one knows we're here. Don't you feel great?"

Their faces nearly touched as they lay on their sides and talked. "I really do, Melanie. I'm out of China, traveling all over the world. First America, now here. I got away from him. I have money. You. We can do anything we want." He sat up, excited by the multitude of thoughts competing for space in his head. "You were right, as usual, about not taking all the money today. I'm supposed to go to Geneva tomorrow and give some guys a million bucks for a job they're doing for Jeremiah."

"What kind of job?"

"I didn't ask. Jeremiah wouldn't have told me, anyway. It doesn't matter."

"Are you supposed to contact Jeremiah?"

David laughed. "I was."

"You should. You need to string him along. Remember the plan."

"What if he asks to see me? Or asks about the other two million?"

"Tell him you need the money for operating expenses. Tell him you don't trust the people you met here, or your bodyguards."

"That's no lie."

"Tell him you're setting up your own operation, with your own people. Jeremiah can't object to your taking control of the situation and acting like a leader. The good inheritor."

David had a sudden inspiration and the words tumbled out. "We'll rent a château! Get our own bodyguards. Hire people who are loyal to us. We'll keep drawing out the money in small amounts. I'll stay in contact with Jeremiah, asking him for more responsibility. Make him think I can run the show over here. He's got even more millions, I'm certain. Probably stashed in other Swiss banks. Maybe I can get to it before they get to him."

"Before who gets to him?"

"The FBI, the Gemini Group, the Chinese, whoever. He's not going to get away this time. That's what Laura thinks, and so do I. Even the newspapers are writing about him."

Melanie sat up and propped a pillow between her back and the headboard. She put her feet on the mattress and rested her forearms on her knees. "You went to see Laura in New York?"

"Yeah. Here's the thing, Melanie. She's rich, too. She offered me more money."

"Did you mention me?"

"No," he said, lying easily.

"Let's not tell Laura about us just now, David. We need to pick the right time."

He desperately wanted Melanie's approval. "So what do you think about my plan?"

She smiled broadly, leaned over, and kissed him. He admired the way her breasts swayed with the motion. "It's a great plan, David. I'd actually thought about something similar, but you beat me to it," Melanie said. "You're not only handsome and a stud, you're smart, too."

He held his fists high in the air. "I'm the man, I'm the man!"

"Of course we'll have to be extremely careful," she said, "and I'll have to stay in the background. I'll take care of finding us a permanent place to stay and hiring new bodyguards and servants. I've already set up a separate bank account for us and deposited Laura's check. I'll handle all the money. Okay?"

"Sure. You're right that we need to be careful, Melanie. Jeremiah has people all over Europe, too."

"What's Jeremiah up to? Did he ever let you know?"

"Not really. You know him, he talks in parables like he thinks he's Christ. After we left Beijing, we went to this army base out west. On the way, he talked about Genghis Khan, the Black Death, and how good always comes out of human disasters. We stopped by some big lake and he pointed out huge flocks of ducks and geese and told me how they fly all over the world and no one pays any attention to them."

"Have you been reading his revelation from God?"

"Are you kiddin'? It's just more bullshit. You remember that on my birthday I had an audience with him and he talked about microscopic bugs. The guy's Looney Tunes."

Melanie frowned. "Yeah, I remember."

"He even made me get a flu shot in China. Said the flu would be bad all over the world for several years."

After he and Ariana left the Sainte Anne de Beaupré graveyard to return to the airport, Steve called Laura from the car and her news frustrated him. Although David had visited her in New

York, she hadn't gathered any additional information about his destination in Europe, nor did she have him followed when he left.

Steve didn't criticize her openly, however, because he understood her emotional state. Her long-lost son had unexpectedly come home, and she couldn't very well establish a lasting relationship with him by acting like a policewoman. Even he had broken the law to protect his sons, Steve reminded himself.

Still, he wanted desperately to know David's destination in Europe so he could prevent him from doing anything irreversible. Maybe the CIA would spot him there.

"Are you going to tell me about this clue as to Jeremiah's whereabouts?" Ariana asked.

"Jeremiah told Thomas they would visit another shrine where, quote, I struck a blow at the devil's army, unquote."

"Where's that?"

"Maybe Atlanta."

"If I remember my terrorist history correctly, that's where he abducted two teenagers in a suburb and hung them. As I recall, the boys had been accused of assault and rape."

"Jeremiah videotaped his kangaroo court and the execution and sent the film to Laura, who at the time was host of UBC's newsmagazine show *American Chronicle.* As justification for his actions, he claimed that the two kids were apprentices in the devil's army of criminals who were waging war on America. That statement also led to our first clue about his real identity."

Steve recalled the FBI task force established in 1995 to hunt down Jeremiah. It included Dr. Michael Ellsworth from the Bureau's Behavioral Science Unit. Ellsworth had come across the same description—comparing criminals to an invading army—in literature distributed at a survivalists' exposition in Seattle. That put them on Jeremiah's trail. Except for himself, Ellsworth and every member of that task force had died or been killed years go. *Why couldn't Jeremiah have died of heart disease?*

Steve called FBI Deputy Director Mitchell from the plane and told him about his latest hunch. Steve thought that Mitchell, although polite and courteous, seemed clearly underwhelmed. Nevertheless, the deputy director said he would alert the Atlanta office.

"Do you think Jeremiah's taking Thomas on a sentimental tour of sites where he committed terrorist acts?" Ariana asked, incredulous. "I know he's an egomaniac, but that doesn't make sense."

"It might if he has other business in Atlanta."

"Such as?"

Steve took a turn at sarcasm. "I'll check my crystal ball when we get to New York."

23

Melanie swung her legs over the side of the bed and sat up.

"You going somewhere?" David asked.

"No," she said, reaching for the telephone on the nightstand. "I know the people who run this place. They can be trusted—that's why we came here. I thought I'd call down for some good local beer, and schnapps. You gotta try the schnapps here, David."

"All right! Now you're talking."

As she picked up the receiver, Melanie thought, *I could really use a drink, too, after what he just said about microscopic bugs and the flu shot.* "Also, David, this is Switzerland. Drug use is legal and drug sales are kinda legal. How about some top-quality heroin?"

"Let's party hard," he replied enthusiastically. "Later on we'll have dinner and go dancing. Do they have nightclubs in Switzerland?"

She kept her back to him as she placed their order with an assistant manager who was on the Chinese payroll. So that she'd have time to think, Melanie kept the phone to her ear even after the manager hung up. As she had put together David's account of his various conversations and travels with Jeremiah, the Prophet's latest writings, the "job" in Geneva, and the news of a flu shot, a sudden realization had struck her with the intensity of a bolt of lightning. *Jeremiah has a biological weapon! And there's a vaccine, too!*

Within ten minutes, a room-service waiter delivered the beer and schnapps. Shortly after draining a beer and taking two stiff shots of one-hundred-proof schnapps, David achieved an erection and they "made love" again while Melanie schemed.

She had never planned to stay with David. She had used him sexually in the beginning as a knee-jerk, reckless way of getting even with both Jeremiah and Laura. Only later, when her rage abated, did she consider the possibility that David might become a vehicle by which she could get rich, and get away. With prodding from her, David had actually demonstrated ingenuity and backbone lately. He truly thought he had independently arrived at the plan to string Jeremiah along while siphoning more money out of the terrorist's bank accounts. She'd control David with sex and drugs, and he'd give her control of the money. It could amount to five, ten million; maybe even more.

At the same time, she would have to juggle the Chinese, who had added her to their payroll. They had helped her get out of China, made it possible for her to travel safely within the U.S., allowed her to stay in their New York consulate offices, and flown her to Switzerland on a Chinese government jet covered by diplomatic immunity. They actually owned the *gasthaus*. They had invested in her in the hopes that she would discover Jeremiah's plans . . . and now she had done just that.

What would they pay for this startling new information? she wondered. *Maybe billions.* But then they'd undoubtedly want to get rid of her. If she could give them the slip, then she could hold an information auction. Who could help her? The Swiss banker Schoeck had devoured her with his eyes. What would he do for a taste of the real thing?

David finished at about the time someone knocked. Melanie put on a robe, opened the door only a few inches, and smiled. The same room-service waiter who had delivered the beer and schnapps now held out a brown paper bag. She took several bills from her robe pocket and they exchanged items.

She put the bag on the table in front of the fireplace and David immediately leaped out of bed. He sat down at the table, took out the heroin and a pipe, and expertly lit up.

He inhaled deeply and asked in a high-pitched voice, "Where did you get this shit?"

"Like I said, it's a wide-open city. If you've got enough money, you can buy anything."

"I'm gonna like it here," he said.

They sat on each side of the small table and shared the pipe as they continued to drink beer and schnapps. The light coming through a small window off the sitting room gradually dimmed as the sun set.

"You said you were supposed to meet some guys in Geneva, David, and pay them to do a job. It sounds dangerous. Tell me the details so we can figure out if it's safe for you to go there."

He shrugged. "It's simple. About noon tomorrow I'm supposed to go to room two-two-three at a certain hotel near the train station. I knock and say, 'A.C. is here.' They ask, 'Who's on first?' I say, 'I don't know.' They say, 'No, he's on third.' I say, 'What?' They say, 'Second base.' If the conversation goes exactly like that, I give them the money."

"And you don't know who they are or what they're going to do?"

"Nope. I'm supposed to return to the château after the delivery."

"We may alter the plan slightly," Melanie said.

They never made it to dinner, nor did they go dancing. Early in the evening, David passed out on the bed and began to snore loudly.

Melanie took a hot shower to clear her mind. She dressed and sat at the table smoking a cigarette and staring at David lying in bed. When a plan had fully taken shape in her mind, she picked up the phone and asked for her favorite room-service waiter. A half hour later, he passed a thin, rectangular box through the door in exchange for money.

Melanie opened the box and took out a syringe. She sat on the edge of the bed and took David's hand in hers. She looked at both sides of his lower arm. Nurses had always taken blood from the underside of her arm, but she didn't like that idea. What if David reared up in bed when she jabbed him? He could break the needle off in his flesh.

She rubbed a big vein on the back of his hand until it seemed to increase in size. Then, shifting her body so as to put her left side against his chest, she held his right hand with her left, and used her right hand to position the needle above the vein. She took a deep breath and shoved it in.

David moaned and squirmed a bit, but then settled down. She lowered his hand and arm to the bed so she could grasp the needle cartridge with her left hand and slowly pull out the plunger with her right. She smiled with relief as blood flowed into the cylinder.

Melanie placed the syringe back in its box and put the box in her purse, reminding herself that she needed to refrigerate it immediately.

She put the briefcase on the table and opened it. She took out several banded batches of bills amounting to about fifty thousand Eurodollars and casually tossed them onto the bed. *He deserves some payment for his efforts.*

She would have preferred to move David to a secret location, but she knew it would be impossible to evade the Chinese lookouts. Since they would keep David under surveillance, that dictated her actions. She'd deal first with the Americans. They had more money, anyway.

Melanie bent over and kissed David on the cheek. "Bye-bye, boy. It's been fun."

She wondered if the extremely helpful room-service waiter could get her out of the *gasthaus* without being seen. If he wouldn't do it for money, he'd undoubtedly be interested in her other assets.

• • •

In a bucolic suburban setting northeast of downtown Atlanta, Jeremiah and Thomas strolled casually through the visitors' center at the national headquarters of the Centers for Disease Control.

"There are actually eleven CDC centers located around the country," Jeremiah said, "although the Center for Infectious Diseases is located here. If you look at these displays, you'll see information about all the exotic viruses that so excite novelists and moviemakers looking for an agent of disaster."

He stopped in front of a glass case containing an artist's drawings of various viruses and read from the explanatory information displayed in large print: "In the last century, these viruses included Bolivian hemorrhagic fever, the Marburg virus and, of course, Ebola, and HIV. Although deadly, most of these viruses could be contained and controlled because they were spread primarily by contact, the exchange of body fluids, or through readily identifiable vectors."

"What's a vector?" Thomas asked.

"Rats and ticks that carried the bubonic plague, mosquitoes that transmit malaria; control them and you can control the disease. However, there also are virus reservoirs that can't be totally controlled for a variety of reasons. Viruses can lie dormant in such reservoirs for thousands, perhaps even millions, of years. Take chimpanzees, for example. They harbor an ancestral simian immunodeficiency virus that is harmless to them. Ordinarily, this virus wouldn't leap the barrier between species. But environmental degradation in the last century drove monkeys into closer contact with humans, especially in the rain forests of Africa, South America, and Southeastern Asia. Monkeys and man shared common food and water supplies. Monkeys bit people. Until about ten years ago, monkeys were hunted for food in parts of Africa. The SIV virus was transferred to humans by one or another of these means and mutated into a form of HIV so it could survive inside its new host. When scientists understood the transmission chain and mapped these related viruses, they were able to develop vaccines."

Jeremiah walked to another display. "But this is what I really brought you here to see, Thomas. The real killer, the artillery of viruses—influenza, the common flu bug. It has a complicated genetic structure, meaning that it's much older than most other viruses. Aquatic birds are a reservoir for influenza A subtypes, which have caused all the great influenza epidemics in history."

He watched various emotions cross Thomas's face, ending with an epiphany. "They weren't banding those birds in Canada, were they?"

"No, Thomas. Not there, or at any of the dozens of other locations around the world where we've trapped migratory birds."

Thomas struggled for answers. "You're drawing blood from them to determine if any new viruses have formed?"

"No," Jeremiah said, enjoying the conversation, which probably would be similar to that he could have with ninety-nine-point-nine percent of the blissfully ignorant people on earth. "In fact, however, that's what scientists right here at the CDC do. They periodically analyze the blood of aquatic birds. Do you know that new strains of influenza usually arise in China or Southeast Asia and then spread to the rest of the world?"

"No, I didn't know that."

"It's true. Do you know why? Even today there are many places in poverty-stricken rural Asia where farmers raise pigs alongside ducks and chickens. There's also likely to be a pond nearby where wild ducks land and feed. As the scientists here know, certain flu viruses can be spread from the wild birds to domestic fowl, and then to pigs, which serve as a mixing vessel. A hybrid type-A flu virus is produced and transmitted to humans. The same process occurs in Third World marketplaces that sell live animals caged in close proximity to each other. Once humans are infected, the virus can become airborne. Then it becomes extremely difficult to contain."

"Most people don't die from the flu," Thomas said.

Jeremiah walked a few paces to his left and pointed at another display. "Most people are ignorant of history, which is why history repeats itself so often. As you can read here, the so-called Spanish influenza of nineteen eighteen killed twenty million people and infected another two hundred million. That was one in every seven people alive at that time. Read the last line on that chart, Thomas."

Thomas leaned closer and read aloud: "A new and virulent form of influenza that appeared suddenly today could cause a death rate equal to a third of the world's population."

Jeremiah quickly did the math for him. "That would mean a hundred and sixty million deaths, Thomas, and maybe ten times that many sick people susceptible to a wide variety of secondary bacterial infections that could kill them."

"Wouldn't scientists just develop a new flu vaccine?"

"It takes about six months to detect a new virus, map its genetic structure, prepare a vaccine, test it for effectiveness, and distribute it worldwide."

Thomas, his lips trembling, said, "You've discovered a new flu virus and are injecting it into migratory birds."

"And they'll spread it around the globe in their travels. It's already too late to stop it, Thomas. It isn't possible to kill all the world's birds, is it?" The stark look of terror on his son's face gave Jeremiah great satisfaction.

Two small boys ran between them, yelling in delight while their parents followed, trying to shush them. Jeremiah smiled and took Thomas's arm, steering him off to the side so their conversation couldn't be heard.

"There's been incredible progress in the last two decades in genetics and cellular biology, Thomas. Certain scientists at the New America Science Center have led the way, as they have in so many fields, including organ transplants, for which I'm eternally grateful. No, Thomas, we didn't discover a new virus, we made one."

"Oh, my God!"

Jeremiah resumed strolling around the exhibits, although his eyes catalogued all his people placed strategically around the CDC. "Viruses are actually very fascinating, especially when you consider that they may possess a form of intelligence."

"What do you mean?" Thomas asked, in a gloomy voice.

"Influenza viruses are generally content to maintain a symbiotic relationship with their host reservoir, Thomas. They reproduce within limits so as not to kill the host, which would be tantamount to burning down your own house. It implies discipline and self-awareness, wouldn't you say?"

"I've never thought about it."

"When a new virus enters the human body, it's just looking for a warm place to eat and reproduce. In layman's language, a flu virus has a couple of proteins on its exterior, called hemagglutinin and neuraminidase." He pointed at a display case featuring an artist's rendition of the flu virus. "They're usually portrayed as spikes, although they can take many forms. The first protein is a docking agent that allows the virus to get inside a human cell and reproduce. The other protein cuts sialic acid off the baby viruses, so they don't clump together. What flu vaccines and drugs do, basically, is try to neutralize these two proteins so the virus can't produce and move around the human body.

"That's when it gets interesting, because the virus reacts by mutating. It's called 'antigenic shift,' which changes the configuration of these proteins, making the vaccines and drugs ineffective, or only partially effective. Isn't that amazing? I'd call this viral intelligence, wouldn't you? Or at least an incredible instinct for self-preservation. What if human beings had this same capability? Does the lack of this advantage doom the human race to extinction in this war with all the different forms of viruses and bacteria?"

Thomas could only shake his head in shock and disbelief, which disappointed Jeremiah. Like so many other pedestrian thinkers, his son apparently lacked vision. He couldn't see that the coming battle would be like a cleansing rain. The human race would emerge stronger and accomplish a great leap forward on the evolutionary road. If the boy didn't grow up shortly, he wouldn't live long.

"What happens now?" Thomas asked.

"We go about our business. We certainly didn't come here to look at the scientific displays."

24

In the Atlanta airport, the three of them set up shop in an airline club lounge, trying to figure out what to do next.

"Steve, do you really think we should visit the site where Jeremiah hung those two teenagers?" Laura asked. "That was nearly twenty years ago."

"Who'd have thought he would have visited Walter Dorfler's grave?" Ariana asked.

"I was just lucky about that," Steve said. "Instead of Atlanta, Jeremiah could have been talking about Los Angeles. That's where he officially launched his terrorist activities in nineteen ninety-five. Before we go off on a wild-goose chase, let's talk about what he might target in this area."

"How about military facilities?" Ariana asked.

"There's a naval air station and a small army post," Steve said. "I can't think of anything else."

"It's the state capital," Laura added. "Jeremiah has killed politicians in the past, although he usually went after high-profile national targets."

"What about some big convention?" Ariana asked. "Or visiting foreign dignitaries?"

"Let me check today's events on the CNN Web site," Steve said, manipulating the mouse on his laptop. While he waited for the site to come on-line, he glanced around at the other frequent flyers who packed the lounge. Some in the reserved, businesslike crowd were here to eat and drink or, like him, get on the Internet. Others chatted on the many phones scattered throughout the lounge, probably speaking to someone in their office, or family members at home. He doubted that most of them would even remember Jeremiah, let alone have any idea of his plans.

"Anything?" Laura asked.

"Nothing that leaps out at me," Steve said, when his laptop suddenly announced, "You've got mail."

Steve checked the mailbox and said, "It's from a CIA agent I know who's stationed in Brussels. I sent him an e-mail earlier, tipping him off to rumors of something ominous about to happen in Europe and asking him to keep us posted about any developments."

"Why would he do that?" Ariana asked.

"He's retiring next year," Steve answered. "He'd like to work for the Gemini Group as a consultant."

"Someone might call that bribery," Laura said, grinning. "What does he have to say?"

"An unidentified woman called the American consulate in Zurich just before midnight yesterday, their time," Steve replied, "and asked them if they wanted to bid on information about Jeremiah's plan to release a new biological weapon on the world."

"I knew it!" Laura said, scooting to the edge of her chair.

"Did the woman say where he was going to do this?" Ariana asked.

Steve continued to read the screen. "Apparently not, but she claims to have a blood sample from someone who's been vaccinated against the agent."

"Wow!"

"This has to be top-secret information," Ariana said, dumbfounded. "What did you offer to pay this guy?"

"A big signing bonus, which obviously just got bigger. He also says there's frenzied activity on both sides of the Atlantic among those watching the situation—politicians, diplomats, the military . . ."

"Maybe we should go to Zurich," Laura suggested.

"Maybe," Steve replied. "Ariana, why don't you check on flights?" As she walked away, he turned to Laura and said, "Tell me what you're thinking."

"I'm kicking myself for not questioning David at length about his so-called assignment in Europe," she said.

"I can't believe he knows about this, Laura."

"It doesn't make any difference. He's somehow in the middle of it, Steve, and he could be arrested, or killed."

A woman called the American consulate. Only one name and image popped into Steve's mind, but he wasn't about to mention it to Laura.

"What's the matter?" she asked, looking at him intently.

"I was just trying to imagine what Jeremiah will do. It's always been hard for me to think like a sociopath."

"He might threaten to use a biological weapon just to cause panic around the world," Laura said, "and give himself a negotiating base. He's done that before, remember. This time, he'll probably want his own continent."

"Here's an even worse scenario," Steve said. "What if this woman sells this information to the highest bidder and some rogue nation or outlaw group uses it for its own purposes?"

The computerized voice announced more e-mail. Steve felt Laura move closer to him so she could lean in and read the message too. The CIA agent wrote that the woman had called the consulate a second time and given them the address of a hotel in Geneva, and the room number where they might find several of Jeremiah's men. They could identify them by exchanging code phrases in the proper order.

Steve opened the attached file and they both read lines that appeared to be part of a comedy skit. "I think this is an old, old Abbott and Costello comedy routine," Laura said.

Steve chuckled. "Yeah, I remember it. It must date back to the nineteen fifties."

"That's just like Jeremiah," Laura said. "You remember when he called the *New York Times* just before an explosion destroyed the New York Stock Exchange. He told them stocks 'were going up' in a few minutes."

"He's about as funny as the plague."

"I don't understand why the caller would give up these people," Laura said.

"To enhance her credibility, maybe. Maybe for money. Or maybe she's just afraid of what might happen."

Ariana returned and read off departure times for Zurich that she'd jotted down in a small notebook. Several flights left within the hour. Steve showed her the email messages.

"I think we should go as soon as possible," Laura said. "David could be the contact, or one of those people in that hotel room. We've got to save him, Steve."

"The Swiss police, the CIA, the FBI, and God knows who else already have that hotel surrounded, Laura. They're not going to let us in on the action."

"We can't just sit here, especially since we don't even know that Jeremiah's here. Maybe he's in Europe."

Steve leaned back on the sofa. "I don't think so."

"Why?"

"A hunch."

"Here we go again," Ariana said, grinning.

"When I was in the FBI, we were taught never to ignore any clue, no matter how insignificant it seemed. Take kidnappings, for example. There is a whole field of study devoted just to ransom notes—the writing style, phraseology, references, the type of threat, the drop-off place and plan, even the paper stock. This minutiae often added up to a profile of the kidnapper—how he thought and what he might do."

"Do you find something significant about these guys using lines from this old comedy routine to identify each other?" Ariana asked.

"Maybe."

"Like I said, Jeremiah's done this before," Laura reminded them. "When he dynamited a convention of tobacco lobbyists in Florida, he called me on the phone and said they were 'going up in smoke.' "

"Exactly. His communiqués always have a double meaning. If David is the person who's supposed to contact these people in Geneva, why did Jeremiah select this obscure comedy routine?" Steve asked. "There has to be a reason that appeals to his twisted mind."

They studied the Abbott and Costello skit again.

Laura shook her head in confusion. "It's funny, but it's about baseball."

"Stadiums, crowds, first, second, third," Steve said, trying desperately to make a connection.

"Who's on first," Ariana repeated, puzzled.

"What's in Geneva?" Steve asked, following her line of thought.

Despite the circumstances, Laura couldn't resist saying, "What's on second."

All three laughed giddily, as if they were punch-drunk. Then Steve sobered up suddenly. "Who. Who. Who."

"I got it. You're an owl, but you're not wise."

He ignored his wife's feeble attempt at humor. Then it came to him. "Think of it as an acronym. W.H.O." He looked from Ariana to Laura and said, "World Health Organization."

"That could be the target in Europe!" Ariana exclaimed.

"Maybe Jeremiah plans to have his people steal a biological agent there," Laura said, suddenly serious.

"Not if he already has a new one. But maybe it has a double meaning." He stood, so excited that his hands had begun to tremble. "Give me the acronym of a similar organization located in Atlanta." He'd already thought of one, but he wanted to see if it would occur to them, too.

Laura stood. "You don't think . . ."

"I do."

Steve led the way out of the lounge, nearly breaking into a run as he placed a call on his cell phone.

"Several of the government's leading scientists in the field of virology work here," Jeremiah said, continuing his lecture to Thomas. "I think it's the best lab of its kind in the world, although much can be said for the expertise of the World Health Organization, the Pasteur Institute, the Deutsches Rheuma Forschungszentrum, and others. Additionally, there are many fine scientists working in government labs around the world, or at pharmaceutical firms, universities, and private laboratories." He smiled wickedly at Thomas. "Naturally, we have all their names and locations in a database. We're paying many of them a visit today."

"What are you going to do?"

"Eliminate them, of course, just in case one among them might come up with a universal antiviral agent."

Thomas had only a moment to be stunned as Jeremiah walked toward a door marked "Employees Only."

"Where're we going?" Thomas asked, running to catch up.

"To work. Follow me and do as you're told," Jeremiah said brusquely.

Thomas saw him nod at one of the center's security guards, who swiped an access card through a reader and held open the door for them. On the left side of the hallway, white-coated technicians worked in laboratories. At the end of the hallway, the guard took a tangle of keys off his belt, disarmed a fire alarm, and opened an exit door.

Thomas stepped outside into the oppressive summer heat, although he felt chilled. He followed Jeremiah along an elevated walkway into a warehouse where laborers unloaded boxes from the back of trucks and stacked them on pallets.

Sweat began to form on Thomas's face, although Jeremiah seemed calm and collected despite his black shirt and trousers.

"Do you know where to find the vulnerable point in a well-guarded facility such as this?" he asked Thomas, but then immediately provided the answer: "Low-paid employees, such as security guards, clerks, janitors, food-service people, and laborers. Many in the economic and social underclasses harbor a lot of resentment against the economic system and the upper class. Give these oppressed people enough money and you can focus that resentment to help achieve your own goals. That's how I blew up the New York Stock Exchange years ago."

Jeremiah proceeded farther into the warehouse to a central point where workers were off-loading the boxes from the pallets onto four conveyor belts extending through the walls into the main building. Thomas stared briefly at three bound and gagged men lying on the floor. One wore a security guard's uniform.

"Given the fact that highly contagious medical specimens and samples are sent here regularly, they are taken by these conveyor belts to airtight rooms and opened by specialists," Jeremiah said. "Fortunately for us, these conveyor belts serve secure rooms strategically located throughout the facility. Today we're making a special delivery."

He reached down, picked up one of the metal boxes by its handle, and set it on a table, then dialed a combination lock and opened the lid, revealing a brick-shaped object wrapped in plastic. "Take a look, Thomas."

"What is it?"

"The latest plastic explosive. We want to do maximum damage to the buildings, people, and records here. Go ahead, turn the dial on the timer to fifteen minutes."

"I can't do that!"

"*Can* and *will*. You sought me out, Thomas. Exercise your free will and make a choice. It's time for you to either fully commit yourself to the movement or become one of its obstacles."

Although his eyes never moved from Thomas's face, Jeremiah held out his arm and a bodyguard slapped a gun into the Prophet's hand. Jeremiah pulled back the top slide and released it, injecting a bullet into the barrel.

"Time is wasting, Thomas."

Everyone stared expectantly at him, including several armed guards wearing CDC uniforms. Thomas couldn't really think. He just knew he had to do as ordered, or die. He didn't have the guts to be a hero. He gulped down his Adam's apple and turned the dial to fifteen.

They walked out of the warehouse, down the steps, and around the trailers parked at the loading docks. Their driver stood beside the already open back door of the gray Ford sedan they'd arrived in. Idling in front and back of the car were two large sports utility vehicles. As Jeremiah shoved him toward the car, Thomas felt the hot heat of shame on his face.

The FBI didn't share Steve's enthusiasm about the relationship between esoteric acronyms, so they sent only a car and driver to pick them up at the airport and take them to the Centers for Disease Control.

As they exited Interstate 85 onto Lindberg Drive and headed east, Laura felt the sound waves of a massive explosion shake the car seconds before she heard the rumbling noise.

"Oh, my God, we're too late!" Steve yelled.

Laura looked ahead through the windshield and saw black smoke billowing above the tree line. As they neared an intersection, she looked off to her left and saw a gray Ford and two black Explorers parked on the right-hand shoulder of the northbound street. Rubberneckers, she assumed, and then did a double take upon seeing a man standing next to the open back door of the Ford, facing directly toward her, although looking off into the distance. She'd never forget that face.

She screamed, "It's him, Steve! It's Jeremiah!"

Steve followed her pointing finger and then directed the driver's attention. The FBI agent activated the car's siren and swung out around several cars stopped in front of them for a red light. He bullied his way left through the intersection, causing several on-coming cars to brake and swerve suddenly to avoid a collision.

"The bastard had to stop and admire his handiwork," Steve said in disgust. "That'll cost him his life."

With tires squealing and spewing gravel behind them, Jeremiah's three-car caravan accelerated back onto the road as Steve grabbed the microphone and broadcast their discovery: "Suspect Jeremiah spotted northbound on Briarcliff Road between Interstate Eighty-five exits thirty and thirty-one." He asked the driver, "Where could he be going?"

"Don't know. Possibly to DeKalb Peachtree Airport," the driver replied, pinning the accelerator to the floor.

Steve broadcast the airport as the possible destination while their driver closed on the trailing SUV. A pervasive wail of sirens filled the air as several emergency vehicles and fire trucks raced by, going in the opposite direction. Most drivers already had pulled off the road.

Suddenly the SUV in the lead turned left and then sharply right onto the Interstate. Laura feared they'd overturn as their car slid up the on-ramp, but the driver made a skillful correction. By the time they merged into traffic, he'd closed the gap and rammed the trailing SUV, causing it to shoot across two interstate lanes and run a car off the highway onto the grassy median.

The FBI agent whipped their car into the passing lane alongside the Ford and then sideswiped the vehicle carrying Jeremiah—*and probably Thomas*, Laura thought desperately. She looked past Ariana sitting beside her but couldn't see through the Ford's blackened windows.

Their driver jerked the steering wheel to the right again and hit the Ford, knocking it onto the shoulder.

"Steve, can you see Thomas?" she yelled.

Before he could reply, his head jerked back violently against the headrest. The SUV they had passed had recovered and rammed them from behind, causing their car to fishtail and then go into a sideways slide. As the driver turned the steering wheel to regain control of the car, Laura saw the SUV out of the corner of her eye as it came alongside and plowed into the driver's door.

She screamed as the car slid off the road and down an embankment. Then they began to turn over, and over, and over.

Laura didn't know how much time had passed before she regained her senses. It could have been seconds, minutes, or hours. Even so, her disorientation lasted until she realized that the car had come to rest on its roof and that she was suspended upside down by her seatbelt.

The mayhem of the road battle had been replaced by a deadly quiet, broken only by Ariana's moans. Laura pushed aside the deflated airbag and fumbled for her seatbelt release button. Only a few inches separated her head from the roof. When the belt gave way, she fell to her side and then managed to get her knees on the roof.

She could see the back of the driver's head, but not Steve. The passenger's door had been torn off. Steve's seatbelt was still coupled to the anchor, which had broken loose and now dangled ominously in the air.

She felt the driver's carotid artery but found no pulse, and she panicked as she smelled the pungent odor of gasoline.

"Ariana, can you hear me?" she cried, pressing a thumb to Ariana's neck and feeling a wild, erratic heartbeat. "We've got to get out of here." She undid Ariana's seatbelt and helped her twist around to her knees. "Are you all right?"

Ariana looked at her with shocked eyes. "I think my arm is broken."

As Laura tried to crawl over the front seatback and out the passenger's-side door, she realized that the roof had caved in partially, making the opening too small for them to get through.

Now the smell of gasoline seemed overpowering.

She looked around desperately, noting that the car lay at an angle, with one side slightly higher than the other. She reached past

Ariana and pushed the electric button that opened the window on that side. Amazingly, the window whined up into the door. She shoved Ariana out the opening and crawled after her.

She knelt beside Ariana, who sat on the ground cradling her left arm. The car had come to rest on its top at the base of a berm. Laura looked up at the Interstate and saw a whirling blue light on top of a vehicle parked on the shoulder. She waved excitedly and shouted for help until it dawned on her that the light sat atop one of the SUVs parked behind the gray Ford they'd chased. A man stared down at her, while another man waved on passing cars.

Now truly panicked, Laura stood and walked unsteadily to the other side of the overturned car.

She couldn't initially comprehend any of what she saw there. Steve lay motionless on the ground. Thomas knelt beside him, stroking his father's face and crying softly. Jeremiah squatted nearby, casually holding a handgun.

He stood and said, "It's kind of anticlimactic, isn't it, Laura? Steve's neck is broken. I think the car rolled over him. I didn't even get to kill him . . . after thinking about it all these years."

Speechless, Laura rushed over and dropped to the ground beside Steve. She looked into his face and knew immediately he was gone forever.

"He's dead, Mom!" Thomas wailed.

The man who had stared down at her from the side of the highway suddenly appeared beside Jeremiah. "We got to get out of here, now!" he yelled.

A gunshot rang out and the man fell to the ground. Laura looked over her right shoulder and saw Ariana pointing a gun.

She looked back at Jeremiah, who had pulled Thomas upright as a shield. The terrorist had wrapped one arm around her son's neck. His other hand held the gun to Thomas's head.

"Let him go!" Ariana shouted, her left arm hanging limply at her side.

"Don't shoot!" Laura screamed. "You'll hit Thomas!"

Jeremiah began backing up the hill. "I don't suppose you'll come along with us right now, Laura, since you have to make funeral arrangements and all. But since you're a widow now, you can expect me to come courting."

Keeping Thomas between him and Ariana, Jeremiah reached the car where another one of his soldiers shielded both of them while they got into the backseat of the Ford. The soldier jumped into the front passenger's seat and the car gunned onto the highway.

Laura heard the gasoline ignite and turned to see flames engulf the car. Like Ariana, she began to run, but within only a few steps the explosion knocked her down. Even though she lay flat and covered the back of her head with her hands, the heat waves washed over her with all the force of the devil's breath.

25

THE REVELATION TO JEREMIAH

CHAPTER FIVE

1 The LORD graciously bestowed upon me a vision of the Garden as it will be after the Weeds are destroyed. Beauty, order, and purpose will prevail, where before there had been only selfishness, ignorance, chaos, and Evil. The underlying principles of the earthly Garden of Eden will coincide fully with those of the Infinite Universe, where all is orchestrated according to immutable laws and God's purpose.

2 The ingredients of this restored Heaven on Earth included vast open spaces, unpolluted air and water, and a serenity compromised only by the sounds of nature. The diverse forms of Life were greatly restricted in number and lived in absolute harmony, as they did in the original Garden of Eden. Gone were the screeching voices of hubris, ignorance, and greed, along with the grating sounds of commerce. It amounted to blissful happiness and ultimate freedom

for the True Believers dedicated to achieving God's Purpose for Mankind.

3 The natural Herbicide approved by the LORD killed many Weeds, and the Gardener and his helpers guarded diligently against their resurgence, for the seeds of Evil always lie dormant in the soil, awaiting nourishment.

4 The LORD's agent of destruction had attacked the Weeds with precision and without mercy, sparing only the strong and the Chosen, as well as the many granaries storing the produce of the ages, and the greenhouses where experimentation to improve the Garden is forever ongoing.

5 In the renewed Garden, all living things are allowed to once again partake of the fruit of the Tree of Life, which grants Immortality.

6 Those who use nourishment from this fruit to extend their roots farther into the soil of the Ultimate Purpose of Mankind will know only sunlight and cleansing rain all their lives, and their seeds will be renewed generation after generation, until they merge with the Godhead.

7 Those who consume the fruit for Evil and selfish purposes once again become Weeds in the Garden of the LORD.

8 The LORD's Gardener also has a mission to distribute needed nutrients equally to all areas of the Garden. Different areas of the Garden are assigned different purposes, but if any area is inadequately tended, Weeds take root there and spread aggressively throughout the Garden.

9 The Garden is diverse in productive plants, but their purpose is as one.

10 In the renewed Garden, experiments with Hybrid Plants seek

to increase productivity, survivability, and longevity. In such greenhouses, the Gardener and his assistants probe the very nature of Life and the many influences on the Garden.

11 Sprouts from the Garden will be planted in other hospitable ground in God's Universe, according to His instructions to be revealed to my Successors.

12 Yet the Gardener knows full well that the Serpent of Temptation will continue to slither throughout the Garden, tempting those eating of the fruit of the Tree of Life.

13 The Serpent's hissing whisper urges seedlings and mature plants alike to use this fruit to further selfish goals. The Serpent leads those it seduces not on the LORD's Way, but rather down the Garden Path where the signposts read: Money, Power, Sexual Excess, Mindless Consumption, Encroachment on Thy Neighbor's Plot, and Narcissism That Knows No Limits.

14 The Serpent and its den of writhing offspring are located in that portion of the Garden previously designated as the united states. Here began the rot and blight that eventually infected all plants in the LORD's Garden.

15 The productive plants of the Garden call out to the Gardener, "Slay the Snake!" Woe, but even though the Serpent be chopped into many parts, each part regenerates itself whole, so that Evil is increased tenfold.

16 The LORD has told His Prophet that the Serpent is as much a part of the Universe as is the Eternal Good, and that the Evil the Serpent represents can be defeated only by those who consume the designated fruit and chose the LORD's Way; against this, the Snake has no lasting power, for its strength lies solely in Temptation. Man alone is responsible for his own actions.

17 Furthermore, the Serpent changes forms and is not always easily recognized.

18 In a dream of inevitable and irreversible future events, I, Jeremiah, the LORD's Gardener and your Faithful Servant, encountered Nine Strangers in the Garden, and a pleasant and productive conversation took place.

19 As I walked away, I turned to wave good-bye, but my new friends were gone, and in their place I saw a multiheaded Serpent and recognized all its faces, not only my Enemies from the present, but from the past also, including the Dead.

20 I rushed to smite the Serpent but it turned into a shrub among the rows of productive plants. I jerked it out by its roots, but another popped up several rows over; and then another, and another. Everywhere the Serpent's offspring flourished, they grew at the expense of their neighbors.

21 Flowers of various bright colors bloomed on the shrub, but the petals had sharp, jagged edges and a bristly pistil, which, upon close examination, again revealed the faces of my Enemies who would nourish the Weeds of the Garden.

22 Therein, sadly, I again saw my Fate. Remember that this is a Revelation from the LORD. It will be. But there will be many Gardeners, and each will have many Helpers. The nature and necessity of the battle between Good and Evil will not always be understood by everyone, but it will be ongoing, and its end is predictable.

23 Those who believe in me shall know God, understand all, and have Eternal Life.

26

David woke up feeling as if he'd been stricken with a bad case of the flu. He tried unsuccessfully to focus his eyes on the ceiling. In struggling to get out of bed, he rolled over something shaped like a brick and nearly as hard. His urgent need to get to the bathroom didn't allow him time to investigate further.

On unsteady legs, he wobbled into the bathroom and performed the usual morning-after routine—vomiting, urinating, and trying unsuccessfully to have a bowel movement. The heroin always plugged him up, but he knew the cure—a breakfast beer.

Taking a bottle of Hefe-Weitzen from the refrigerator, he gulped greedily at the dark unfiltered beer as if it were mother's milk. In fact, he suffered from dehydration. The effects of his lifestyle had become as familiar to him as the lyrics from a favorite song.

When he lowered the bottle, he became aware of a string of dried blood on the top of his right hand. The skin around it had taken on the yellowish tint of a developing bruise. *I probably cut myself somehow last night,* he thought.

He struggled back to the bed and flopped down, landing squarely on several of the same hard objects he couldn't concentrate on earlier. He picked one up and looked at a brick of Eurodollars wrapped in plastic. He stared stupidly at several similar bricks lying on the bed, until reality set in.

He sprang from bed and frantically dashed around the room, looking for the briefcase Herr Schoeck had given him at the bank so he could carry away three million Eurodollars belonging to Jeremiah. The adrenaline rush cleared most of the cobwebs from his mind. He sat at the table, took another slug of beer, and lit a Marlboro.

He chuckled. Of course. Melanie had left the money for him—for *them,* rather—while she deposited the rest of it in the joint bank account she'd opened, the account they would fill with Jeremiah's money until they milked him dry.

Wait! He had to deliver a million Eurodollars today to the hotel in Geneva, otherwise Jeremiah's people would come looking for him. He grabbed his watch off the nightstand and stared in disbelief at the time. He had only two hours to get to Geneva for his noon appointment.

Melanie probably was on her way to take him to the train station. He went into the bathroom and showered so he'd be ready to go immediately when she arrived. After he dressed, he picked up the phone and called the front desk to check for messages. Maybe she'd been delayed.

The front desk had no messages for him.

Where can she be? He became alarmed. What if Chinese agents had picked her up? Or the CIA, maybe the Gemini Group? They all had her photograph.

Who could he call for help? He thought about his bodyguards waiting at the château. They had probably already told Jeremiah he'd disappeared. Several excuses came to mind. He could say he'd gotten drunk and been robbed . . . but then Jeremiah wouldn't give him any more assignments, or access to the bank accounts.

Wait a minute. Why panic? So Melanie was late. So what? He'd get to Geneva when he got there. No big deal. The boss didn't have to keep to a schedule, but his subordinates had to wait. *Melanie will show up in a few minutes. I'm her sex machine, her man, and her protector. We're going to get married.*

He sat down at the table, fired up the bong, and took a few hits to smooth off the rough edges. He felt better immediately. When Melanie arrived, he'd be calm, cool, collected. Ready for their morning tumble. Better yet, they could do it on the train in rhythm with the swaying of the passenger car.

By mid-afternoon, his optimism had vanished entirely. He paced the room and thought about calling Laura for help, but what could he say? That he needed more money, that he'd temporarily misplaced her million bucks? If he told Laura that Melanie had the money, his mother could say, *I told you so.* No, he couldn't run to Momma at the first sign of trouble. Or to Daddy.

As darkness descended over the *gasthaus* window, David got sick again and vomited. He thought about leaving, getting something to eat, going to a nightclub. Then he remembered who he was. He really shouldn't be out and about in case Melanie had been picked up, interrogated, and broken.

If that were the case, they'd be here by now. He sighed deeply, unable to avoid the truth anymore: Melanie had taken the money and ditched him. He picked up a batch of the Eurodollars. *This is nothing more than a tip.*

His hands shook as he called room service and asked for the waiter who had served them last night. When the man arrived at the door a few minutes later, David asked him, "Are you the guy who delivered some stuff here last night?"

"Yes, sir."

"Have you seen the woman you gave it to?"

"No, sir."

"Can you get me some of the same stuff?"

"Yes, sir."

"How much does it cost?"

"How much do you want?"

• • •

Before they had driven a half mile from the crash scene where Wallace had died, two police cars appeared behind them. Despite the whirling blue light on the roof of the Ford and the misleading information the driver had put out over the emergency radio band, the police cars appeared to be chasing them. Jeremiah knew he and Thomas would never make it to the airport now.

He took a cell phone from his pocket and pressed a program button that immediately initiated a conference call to several of his supporters in the area. While the connections were being made, he glanced at Thomas, who sat doubled over, sobbing into his hands. Jeremiah shook his head in disgust. First David and now Thomas. There'd been an obvious dilution of the gene pool in the second generation.

When everyone was on-line, Jeremiah calmly asked for assistance.

"Where to, boss?" the driver pleaded. "There's a cop car right on our bumper!"

"Take the next exit ramp," Jeremiah ordered as he listened to instructions on the phone. "Then right."

As he'd been trained to do, the driver angled onto the exit ramp at the last minute without braking. But the driver of the blue-and-white didn't shoot by as planned. Jeremiah grabbed the roof-level handgrip as they slid around the corner at the bottom of the ramp. Out of the corner of his eye he saw a Suburban coming directly at them. The timing had to be just right.

Through the back window, he saw the Suburban crash into the side of the cops' car, causing it to spin around several times and hit an oncoming car.

Jeremiah knew they'd bought only a few minutes of grace. Law enforcement knew their general location and the area would soon be sealed off as tight as a drum.

Jeremiah listened to the voice on the other end of the cell phone, then relayed instructions to his driver: "There's a small L-shaped shopping center coming up on our left and a florist's shop near the end of the shortest wing. Drive around to the back entrance."

He grabbed Thomas's shirt collar and jerked him upright. "Act like a man!"

Thomas fixed him with steely eyes and said, "I'm acting like a human being."

That remark enraged Jeremiah, who used the edge of his fist to hit Thomas on the side of his head. The blow opened a gash in the boy's eyebrow. Jeremiah looked at the bodyguard sitting opposite the driver. "You take care of him when we make the transfer," he said, jerking his head toward Thomas.

The car stopped only long enough for the three of them to get out of the car and into the back of the florist's cargo van. The Ford went one way and they went the other.

Chaos reigned on the street running in front of the shopping center as marked and unmarked police cars and other emergency vehicles raced by, the high-torque whine of their engines only a decibel or two below that of the sirens. Cars driven by ordinary citizens lined both shoulders of the street.

Their driver turned the other way and drove through an upscale residential area. They wound their way through a maze of streets that might have existed anywhere in Ireland—Blarney Court, Shamrock Lane, Cork County, Dublin Avenue.

On the other side of the subdivision, they caught a left-turn arrow onto a four-lane thoroughfare taking them even farther away from the Interstate. They traveled several miles before turning onto another side street. Several blocks later, they pulled up to a security gate and guard post.

Jeremiah sat quietly on the floor of the van and looked daggers at Thomas, although he didn't fear that the boy would cry out—not with the bodyguard's ham-sized hand clamped over his mouth.

The gate opened and they drove into the world of the super wealthy, where million-dollar mansions sat at the end of long driveways that ran through canopies of towering oaks and lodgepole pines.

At one of these driveways, the florist's van pulled up to a mammoth iron gate, which, as if by magic opened, as Jeremiah continued to talk on the cell phone.

The van dropped them at the rear of the house, where they couldn't be seen from the street.

Thomas followed Jeremiah into a huge, well-stocked pantry and then through a commerical-grade kitchen with many stoves and ovens on each side of a rectangular food-preparation table. Suspended above the table were skillets, pots, pans, and other cooking utensils.

At the end of the counter, Jeremiah turned on the faucet above a sink. He soaked a dishcloth under the stream of water and handed it to Thomas. "Put this on your eye."

At the far end of the kitchen, Jeremiah pushed through a swinging door and Thomas felt the bodyguard's meaty hand on his back, propelling him in the same direction.

On the other side of the door, Thomas glanced to his left and saw a dining room dominated by an immense, polished mahogany table. The deep-red velvet padding on the high-backed chairs matched the heavy gold-trimmed drapes covering a tripartite window overlooking a flower garden.

"This way," Jeremiah said brusquely, opening a massive door.

Thomas walked ahead of him into a library; books lined all of one wall and part of another—most of them law books, he saw. Framed photographs and awards adorned an end wall. A large desk faced a fireplace, while a smaller desk sat off to the side, like an obedient puppy.

Thomas heard voices and looked through the open French doors leading to the patio. A man stood there with his back to them, and Thomas saw the profile of a beautiful young woman wearing a cream-colored skirt and frilly white blouse.

The man turned and walked into the room. "Jeremiah," he said in an affectionate, booming voice as he wrapped his arms around the Prophet.

Still holding the dishcloth to his eyebrow, Thomas stared at the young busty woman who also came in from the patio. She gave him a patronizing look in return. He thought of Karla Maypole and wished he were sitting in her biology class at the Science Center.

"Thomas, this is Judge Zachary Hewitt," Jeremiah said, introducing the elderly man, who wore gray, pinstriped pants, a midnight-blue textured vest over a heavily starched white shirt, and a polka-dot, blue-and-white bow tie.

"This is Allison, my assistant," Judge Hewitt said, casting an admiring glance at the strawberry blonde. "She was just about to attend to other duties."

As Allison left the library, the barrel-chested judge openly admired her swishing gait. Then he walked over on spindly legs and held out his hand to Thomas, who reached for the bony, liver-spotted claw. "So you're one of Jeremiah's sons," he said. "What happened to your eye?"

"I'm Thomas Delaney-Wallace," Thomas said, defiantly looking into the intelligent, laserlike eyes. The judge's long white mane reached nearly to his collar

"Really." Judge Hewitt took a cigar from his vest pocket and put it in his mouth, where he rolled it from one side to the other. "I assume you're in mourning for your stepfather, then."

Taken aback, Thomas couldn't fathom how the judge knew about Steve's death. "How did you . . . " he began.

"It's all over the television news," the judge explained, walking to one section of bookshelves. He flicked what appeared to be a light switch, and two shelves of books rotated one hundred and eighty degrees, revealing a well-stocked bar. The florid-faced judge reached for a bottle of amber liquid and asked, "Anyone else want some bourbon?"

"You know I don't drink," Jeremiah said affably as he sat down in one of three leather chairs arranged around the coffee table. "And neither should you, Zach. It's bad for your soul, and your health."

"I'm seventy-six years old, Jeremiah. My longevity can be attributed in some degree to drinking expensive bourbon since I was fifteen." Having proudly made that announcement, Judge Hewitt walked over to Thomas and handed him a glass. Then he limped across the room and dropped heavily into one of the leather chairs.

Thomas looked defiantly at Jeremiah and took a drink. The high-octane bourbon burned all the way down to his stomach, generating a coughing spell. Then he sat down in the third chair, holding the glass as if it contained poison. With his other hand, he placed the blood-soaked dishcloth on the end table.

"Are you really a judge?" he asked. "What are we doing here?"

"I assume you're hiding from the FBI and the cops," Judge Hewitt said, a twinkle in his eye. "And this is a helluva good place to hide, son. No law enforcement officer would dare drive down these streets aiming a listening device at the houses. Hell, the mayor of Atlanta lives just three houses to the east. And you don't have to worry about anyone knocking on the door with a search warrant. If they did, I'd have Supreme Court Justice William Blakely all over their ass in ten minutes."

"Judge Hewitt was appointed to the Federal Appeals Court in nineteen ninety-eight by President Bill Clinton," Jeremiah said.

The judge leaned forward and said mischievously, "You might remember him, Thomas. He conducted foreign policy on the telephone while his girlfriend gave him oral sex. I admire that kind of concentration."

Thomas frowned and could only vaguely remember a history class reference to some sex scandal during the Clinton administration.

"Why am I here?" Thomas asked, looking first at Jeremiah and then at the judge.

"You're one of us, Thomas," Jeremiah answered. "Everyone knows you're with me. You came out to the Science Center to join my movement."

"That's a lie!"

"Is it? You came with me willingly when we left there."

"I really didn't have a choice, did I?"

"You were with me when my colleagues injected various migratory birds with the new influenza virus."

"I didn't know what they were doing."

"Let me contribute to your education, Thomas," Judge Hewitt said, lighting up the cigar he'd been chewing on. "Ignorance of the law is no defense in court."

"Your fingerprints are all over the bomb materials used to destroy the CDC," Jeremiah said, calmly continuing his recitation of Thomas's transgressions. "You even set the timer that ignited the explosives."

Thomas snorted. "With a gun to my head."

"That's not what the others present would testify," Jeremiah said. "You might even be implicated in the death of Steve Wallace."

Thomas stared hatefully at Jeremiah.

A bourbon glass in one hand and the cigar in the other, Judge Hewitt cocked his head, stared at Thomas, and said, "I think this young whippersnapper already has failed the test, Jeremiah. I'd get rid of him. You don't need a successor anyway."

"You may be right, Zach, "Jeremiah said, as if Thomas weren't present. "I just wanted someone to supervise the day-to-day details of the movement so I could think big thoughts. It's the same reason you have law clerks."

Judge Hewitt chuckled. "That's not all I use my law clerks for, Jeremiah." He leaned forward and bared long yellow fangs at Thomas. "You wouldn't believe the view when Allison is bent over that desk, Thomas. It's enough to give an old man a heart attack."

"I can't believe that a federal judge would be involved in terrorism," Thomas said, glaring at Hewitt.

"I'm Jeremiah's ally *because* I am a judge," Hewitt said philosophically. "You can't imagine the number of people who've stood in front of our appeals bench over the years, Thomas, nor all the stories of perfidy I've listened to for decades. After a while, any reasonable man comes to a couple of conclusions: Most people aren't worth a hill of beans; and the world will be changed only when someone changes it."

"Amen," Jeremiah said, smiling at Thomas.

"So the logical thing to do is to kill millions of innocent people," Thomas said, settling grimly into the argument. Steve's face appeared in his mind, and he knew the man he still thought of as his father would want him to fight this battle. "What if this deadly virus kills you?"

Judge Hewitt laughed loudly and looked at Jeremiah. "You haven't told him about the vaccine, have you?"

"No."

The judge held out an empty glass to Thomas and said, "Go fill this up, sonny, and I'll continue this enlightening lecture."

Thomas hesitated, but then did as he'd been told only because he wanted to hear more. He left his partially empty glass at the bar when he returned with the judge's second drink.

"Man is just another form of life," the judge said, accepting the bourbon. "He likes to think he's special and unique, which is why he invented God in his own image and concocted the idea of eternal life and heaven." He grinned at Jeremiah. "None of my opinions apply to Jeremiah's revelations, of course."

"No offense taken, Zach," Jeremiah said, chuckling.

"Man even tries to play God, Thomas. We manage, thin out, and exterminate other life forms all the time, especially the ones we keep under lock and key for our amusement. Whatever we do to them is always for their own good, you understand. At the same time, of course, we continue to think we're unique in all the universe. Fact is, Thomas, the vast, vast majority of humans are nothing more than animals. Most of them even lack the dignity and self-sufficiency of most species. Most humans do nothing more than take up space on this decaying planet. They eat, breathe, defecate, reproduce, and then rot in some fancy casket that prevents them from fertilizing the soil and finally being of some use."

Thomas couldn't believe his ears, although he was beginning to understand the purpose of this discussion. Jeremiah wanted him to know there were many others who thought like he did, including important, influential people. That, and the fact that he could escape from right under the noses of the cops.

"If you took all the great inventions of the world and assigned them to the individuals who conceived and implemented them, you wouldn't have enough people on hand to fill a quarter of the football stadium when Georgia plays Georgia Tech," Judge Hewitt declared, laughing so hard he slopped bourbon onto his pants.

Jeremiah hunched forward and stared somberly at Thomas. "For decades, we've drawn up lists of intellectually superior people. We're in the process of making them an offer most of them won't refuse. When the earth is cleansed of rubbish and flotsam and old ideas, we'll start over, Thomas. A hundred years from now, the results will be spectacular, I assure you."

Judge Hewitt stood unsteadily. "And I'll be known as a contributor to that society, Thomas. I'll consider that a great legacy." He drained the bourbon from the glass. "Now, I've got to go upstairs and get together with Allison, if you know what I mean." He winked at Thomas and slowly left the library.

"Are there many more drunks like him in the movement?" Thomas asked sarcastically.

"He's a brilliant man. Don't judge lest you be judged."

"Did God reveal that line to you?"

Jeremiah ignored the insult. "When I was ill all those years in China, Thomas, the world pretended I no longer existed. It gave me time to communicate on the Internet with thousands of my supporters around the world. You'd be absolutely astounded at the people in our ranks, Thomas. Increasingly, however, I sense that you just can't wrap your mind around the movement's many dimensions. I probably expected too much from you. Zach may be right that I'm wasting my time trying to groom you." He paused, and then offered a carrot. "I can understand you're upset that Wallace is dead. He raised you to this point in time. Now you're either mine or you'll be joining him shortly."

Thomas cringed as Jeremiah stood suddenly and said, "I'll have one of my men show you to an underground bunker located off the basement wine cellar. It has a special air-filtration system and many other amenities. I gave Zach the construction plans, in fact. You can stay in there for a couple of days and make up your mind before I leave."

"Where are you going?"

"To my command center. There's a helicopter pad out back of the house. Day after tomorrow, a helicopter will pick up Judge Hewitt and fly him to a private airport, where he'll take a jet to a judicial conference in Washington, D.C. I'm going with the judge. There's only one more open seat."

Thomas watched Jeremiah leave the room. The bodyguard held open the door for his leader and then crooked his finger at Thomas.

27

Laura and Ariana sat side by side in the Gemini Group's corporate jet, while Steve's body lay in a coffin that rested in the aisle at the rear of the plane. Laura couldn't help turning in her seat now and then to look back at it in disbelief. She expected Steve to appear at any moment, and sit across from her . . . though she knew that wouldn't happen since she had watched the men at the funeral home prepare his body. And that was all that was left—a body. He'd gone somewhere else.

Her cell phone rang and she took it from the pocket of her jacket. She put it to her ear and listened, punctuating the conversation with terse remarks such as "Thank you" and "I appreciate that" and "Yes, he was" and finally, "A memorial service would be nice."

"Who was that at this hour?" Ariana asked, looking at her watch. "It's past midnight."

"President Ellison. She extends her sympathy and wants to have a state funeral for Steve at the National Cathedral."

"You agreed?"

"To a memorial service next week."

"It's quite an honor."

Laura sighed. "I suppose so." In fact, it really didn't matter. Nothing mattered anymore. She recalled lines from a poem: *Lock the doors, turn out the light, and take to your bed, for the one you loved is dead, and the world will never again be right.*

"They probably think the memorial service will help them rally public support for the hard times ahead," Ariana said.

She's wise way beyond her years, Laura thought, looking sympathetically at Ariana's red, swollen face and the cast on her left forearm.

"In another lifetime, I interviewed President Bob Carpenter after he'd declared martial law," Laura said. "Jeremiah had set off a bomb at a convention in Florida, killing thirty-one members of Congress." She frowned, mentally looking back over the years. "I expect the government will have to do something radical like that again."

"And not just our government," Ariana said. "The FBI guys in Atlanta said that scientific laboratories all over the world were attacked."

"It's clear evidence that Jeremiah has a new biological agent," Laura said. "He's trying to eliminate all the laboratories and people who might find a way to neutralize it."

Ariana squeezed her hand. "We'll survive somehow, Laura, and so will David and Thomas."

My sons. They are the only reason not to take to my bed and pull the covers over my head.

In a small interrogation room at the American consulate in Zurich, Melanie Thurston sat and stared across a narrow table at Dexter Vinson, the local CIA station chief. *In retrospect, I didn't play this as smart as I should have,* she thought.

"Let's go over this again," Vinson said. "You claim to have a blood sample from an individual who *might* have been vaccinated against a biological agent Jeremiah *may have* developed. And you want the United States government to pay you for this sample?"

I shouldn't have abandoned David at the gasthaus, she thought. Her greed had overcome rational thought. She appreciated the irony of it all, since Jeremiah always had preached about the evils of pride and avarice. She had greedily fled with three million of Jeremiah's dollars, along with a million of Laura's, and mentally added to that figure more millions—perhaps even billions—she *might* get for selling the valuable information and blood sample. Maybe she should have gone back to the Chinese, but they still didn't think like capitalists.

"We know for certain that this blood sample you allege to have wasn't taken from Jeremiah himself," Vinson said, "because the terrorist whose bed you shared all these years in Beijing was positively identified only hours ago in Atlanta, Georgia."

Soon after she had arrived yesterday, they'd put her on ice, but she still knew that something terrible had happened, what with all the grim-faced consular employees scurrying in and out. The secretary who'd brought her a mug of coffee had obviously been crying. When Melanie asked what was the matter, the woman had referred to "awful events" in the United States and around the world.

Obviously, Herr Schoeck hadn't heard the news at the time she'd dropped by the Swiss Union Bank and asked him to redeposit the Eurodollars in her numbered account in Cuba. She had facilitated the process by giving him a phone number in Havana where she could be reached later.

"Whatever Jeremiah did in Atlanta, it didn't happen in Geneva," she said, "because of the information I gave you."

Living in China all those years, she had become an expert at reading facial expressions. And although Vinson wore a mask of indifference, he acknowledged the truth of her statement with a slight elevation of one eyebrow.

"I assume the blood sample came from Jeremiah's son David," he said.

"Assume," she said, mocking his earlier attempt to belittle the reliability of her information. In truth, it had been a calamitous mistake for her to abandon David. Now *everyone* undoubtedly was

searching for him, if the Chinese hadn't already taken him into custody. Knowing them, however, Melanie knew they would watch and wait for a while.

"Why don't you just tell me where David is," Vinson said, smiling kindly as if doing her a favor. "I'll make certain you're not charged with any crimes and that you get into our witness protection program. You can lead a very comfortable life, without fear."

If they found David, they'd get their blood sample and Herr Schoeck's name. David would give up that information for a beer and a dime bag of heroin. They might even find and confiscate her money, although the Cubans were very protective of their lucrative role in the post-Castro world as money launderer for the rich and the crooked.

She should have done as she'd promised David, which was to give the Chinese the slip and rent a château for the two of them somewhere in Europe. That way, she could have kept him hidden and happy. Greed and a thoughtless act had landed her in this sterile room.

"We'll find David in only a few hours."

They have to be scouring the city, she thought. The first thing they would do would be to distribute photographs of her and David to all hotels and *gasthauses* in the city and surrounding areas. The room-service waiter she had bribed wouldn't keep her secret very long if Vinson got hold of him.

"You can't keep me here against my will," she protested, playing the helpless damsel in distress. "I'm entitled to see a lawyer."

"Why? Have you committed a crime?"

"I have constitutional rights."

"Not when the national security of the United States is at risk. I can hold you for as long as I like."

She thought about offering him sexual favors, but she sensed that tactic wouldn't work with this man. She had only one trump card left to play. "Look, before I came here, I put the blood sample in a refrigerator. I left a letter with a courier service for it to be delivered after four o'clock this afternoon." She looked dramatically at her watch. "The letter goes to the Chinese consulate and tells them where to find the sample before it deteriorates." Everything she said was true, except for the details. She had left the tube of blood in a refrigerator in a hotel room, and she had left the letter and mailing instructions with the concierge in the lobby.

"If the Chinese get the sample, why would they pay the outrageous price you're asking?"

Ten billion had seemed like a nice figure at the time she'd announced it. Now she would dicker. "Look, let's make the price an even billion, deposited in the numbered bank account I gave you."

"That's a lot of money," he said. "I'd have to contact Washington for approval."

Naturally, he's trying to buy time. "Look, I know the Chinese. They won't share any information about the blood analysis with anyone. They love to sit on their secret information instead of giving it away, like America does. They'll see this secret as a way for them to survive the coming plague, while the United States becomes a gigantic hospital ward. As for David, don't pin all your hopes on finding him alive. Jeremiah's people *may* already have found him. Besides, he's got a bad drug habit and I think he might be in a mood to overdose. How much time do you think you have, Agent Vinson?"

An hour after they landed at Dulles International Airport, the company limo pulled up to the front gate of a country estate. Laura stepped out of the backseat to punch a code into the keypad. The gates creaked open noisily, interrupting the pervasive quiet before dawn, when even the insects and birds were silent. Perhaps in respect to Steve.

She had been living here in 1995 when she met Steve and fell in love with him. They had planned to live on the farm forever, but Jeremiah had kidnapped her here and they'd been afraid to come back. When it became obvious that Thomas and David were on their own in the world and that she couldn't protect her sons forever, she had begun to yearn for the farm. She wanted to bask in her memories of the happy times she and Steve had shared here.

So when the farm had come on the market recently, she bought it. She had planned to surprise Steve with the news after they returned from Atlanta. Now he would never know, *or would he?*

As a result of her telephone call from the plane, the grave site behind the house had already been prepared. The four bodyguards who lowered the coffin into the ground had known Steve for decades, and even these hard men shed tears of sorrow.

"Do you want us to cover the casket, Laura?" one of them asked.

"Not right now, Shawntel. I'd like to be left alone for a few minutes."

A red glow on the eastern horizon announced the impending sunrise. The air already had that heavy feel to it, as it always did in August, and Laura knew it would be a hot, debilitating day.

She'd thought briefly about reading an appropriate passage from the Bible but had rejected that impulse, largely because Jeremiah and a never-ending host of religious charlatans had so perverted God's word that it no longer had any meaning to her.

Instead, she began talking—babbling, really—as if Steve were alive, or at least listening.

"Maybe this isn't much of a funeral, Steve, but it seems right. There'll be the memorial service at the National Cathedral. Besides, you understand that I can't go into mourning for days. You know there's no time to waste. I wanted to talk with you alone, Steve, so you can help me decide what to do."

Maybe he would, in time, if she talked along enough. "Like you, Steve, I had many lives," Laura continued. "I was a girl and a daughter. My life was centered on my parents and the ranch in Texas. When I got to be a teenager, I drifted into another life, full of uncertainty." She paused, trying to remember just what it had been like. "Selfishness, impetuousness, lust, and lofty dreams consumed my thoughts. Then I became an independent young woman of the world." She laughed at the preposterousness of the idea, although she had believed it at the time. "In truth, I was scared to death. I don't know how I even survived. It was as if I had one foot on each of two escalators that started out parallel and then diverged. One carried ambition, the other, dreams of romantic love and family." *It's a good analogy,* she thought. She hadn't been walking purposefully then, just standing still while unseen forces moved her through life. "I hopped on the ambition escalator for a while, and that seemed like a good life for a long time. I even became rich and famous."

She paused, almost ashamed to bring up the next topic, but he already knew. "The first time I got married, it was for convenience's sake." She shook her head at the stupidity of it all. "Then I met you and learned about true love. I became a mature woman and a whole person. That was the life I'd always wanted . . . the life I'd searched for while leading other lives. I hoped our life together would never end. I prayed many times that if we had to die, we would die together.

"You proposed to me—not far from this spot—when we were working in a flower garden. It wasn't all roses, as you know." She startled herself by laughing at the unexpected pun. "I learned about fear and terror, and physical and emotional pain. I learned what it was like to lose hope, and then regain it.

"I became a mother and finally felt whole, despite the circumstances of my pregnancy. You were always there like a rock for me, for David, and then for Thomas. They were *our* sons, even though Jeremiah was their biological father. Even though we had David only for a year, his heart and soul belonged to us. I always believed that, Steve, and I still think it will be so again.

"I'm sorry we never had other children—enough to form a baseball team, like we wanted to do. You remember the day we talked about that? But our love grew anyway. We developed a deep friendship based on understanding and respect. We truly became partners in every way. I gained some wisdom and learned the true purpose of life—which is to love and be loved. Other things are important, but love is the core of it all.

"I hope our life together was your best life, too, Steve. I pray you've just entered another dimension and that we'll be together again." Tears gushed from her eyes. "I really hope that, Steve, I really do."

Laura sank to her knees and took a deep breath. "Now I'm starting the last phase of my life here on earth . . . without you. The future is cloudy and dark. Wisdom and hope seem to have deserted me once again. I feel guilty for having survived longer than you did, Steve. I don't know where David and Thomas are, and I don't know how to save them. If you couldn't do it, Steve, what chance do I have?"

She dug her hands into the fresh dirt beside the grave and looked down at the coffin, trying to visualize Steve lying on that satin cushion. Terror stabbed deep into her heart. "Help me, Steve! If you can hear me, talk to me sometimes. Maybe late at night when it's very quiet. If you can't tell me what to do, just nudge me in the right direction. Be there even if I don't know it. I love you and I know you love me. I have to believe that, Steve. If love doesn't survive life, then what's life for?"

Laura stood in the entryway of the house and looked around. Memories flooded back as Ariana came out of the kitchen carrying a cup of coffee, which she handed to Laura.

"Can I go out and pay my respects to Steve now?" she asked.

"Sure, but don't take too long. We're leaving as soon as I make a couple of telephone calls."

"Leaving? We haven't slept for twenty-four hours, Laura. I'm exhausted, and so are you."

"Sleep on the plane or stay here. It's your choice."

"Where are you going, Laura?"

"To Zurich. I just buried my husband. I don't intend to bury either one of my sons."

28

Before they left for Zurich, Laura called President Ellison's chief of staff and asked him for a favor, in honor of her husband's sacrifice on behalf of the nation. Steve had nearly caught Jeremiah in Atlanta, while all others had ignored his warnings. The White House couldn't very well deny Laura anything immediately preceding a memorial service designed in large part to serve political ends.

"Why do you want to meet with the Swiss ambassador?" Ariana asked as they buckled themselves into their seats aboard the aircraft preparing to leave Dulles International Airport at midday Wednesday.

"A hunch."

Ariana chuckled, causing Laura to smile and ask, "What's so funny?"

"Do you remember how Steve played hunches? He was right more times than he was wrong."

"I know. He taught me how to do it." She'd learned another lesson from him, too: *Be prepared in case your hunches pay off. The consequence is not always what you expect.* Steve had had a hunch many years ago that their bodyguard, Maria Inglesias, actually worked for Jeremiah. Although he'd been right, the trap he set nearly got him killed. He'd had a hunch that Jeremiah would visit a certain doctor in Rapid City, and that hunch had resulted in his capture by Jeremiah. Steve had languished in a New America jail for months. *And Steve had a hunch that Jeremiah would be in Atlanta.*

At 2 A.M. local time, she and Ariana entered the Zurich airport terminal. Sydney Wellington, U.S. ambassador to Switzerland, met them. She introduced herself and her companion, Dexter Vinson, local CIA station chief. The four of them went into a private conference room and sat around a table.

"First, please accept my condolences regarding the death of your husband," said Wellington, who projected a vigorous, patrician bearing despite being well into her seventies.

"Thank you, Ambassador Wellington. I know what an inconvenience it is for you to come here this early in the morning, so I'll come right to the point. My husband had been told that a woman contacted the consulate here in Zurich late Monday night and claimed to have valuable information concerning Jeremiah and a new biological weapon."

Wellington looked to Vinson, a steely-eyed African-American who looked to be in his thirties. "We've been interrogating her for two days," he admitted.

"Is it Melanie Thurston?" Laura asked.

Clearly startled, Vinson asked, "How did you know that? How do you know any of this?"

Laura knew only one woman close enough to Jeremiah to have gleaned some secrets about him. Couple that with the fact that Thurston was close to David, and it couldn't be anyone else. "I want to talk to her."

Vinson shook his head emphatically. "That's not possible."

"What does she want?"

"We're down to a billion dollars and safe passage to Cuba," he replied with distaste.

"Originally, she wanted ten times that amount," Wellington said pleasantly.

"Are you going to pay her?" Ariana asked.

"Maybe," the ambassador said. "Apparently she kept a diary during her years in Beijing. She's given us enough tidbits to believe that it would be very valuable."

"What does she know about Jeremiah's new biological agent?" Ariana asked.

Wellington looked first at Vinson and then spoke directly to Laura. "Ms. Thurston originally claimed to have a refrigerated blood sample from someone who has been immunized against the new agent that Jeremiah apparently plans to set loose. A letter went to the Chinese consulate yesterday afternoon telling them the location of the sample."

"Ms. Thurston thought this was her ace in the hole," Vinson said. "She apparently hoped to start a bidding war between us and the Chinese. We called her bluff and followed the Chinese to the location of the blood sample, and beat them to it."

"And?" Laura asked.

"The blood was improperly drawn," Ambassador Wellington said. "It coagulated, and apparently that destroys some of its properties. The lab people are still analyzing it, but obviously we need to find the donor."

"You know that person is my son David," Laura said.

"And Melanie knows David's location," Ariana said, addressing Vinson. "Why haven't you gotten it out of her?"

"Who says we haven't?" Vinson answered.

Laura sat back and momentarily considered the various Machiavellian possibilities. "You didn't care if Melanie had a letter sent to the Chinese. You wanted to get together with them and deal. That way, everything would be on the table—the blood sample, the biological agent, the vaccine, what Melanie knows about Jeremiah and his supporters within the Chinese government and around the world. Even what David knows."

"It is indeed a delicate political situation, dear," Ambassador Wellington said in her best little-old-lady voice.

Laura was beginning to dislike the old bat. "And it's about to get worse if you don't take me to my son."

"What do you mean?" Vinson asked, a frown creasing his forehead.

"I'll call a press conference here at the airport. Widow of an American hero reveals to the world that the United States and China know that Jeremiah has a biological weapon. The two governments may even have enough information to manufacture a vaccine. I'll pose innocent questions such as: 'Why haven't the people of the world been warned? Will the United States and China share their information with scientists in other nations?' That sort of thing."

Ambassador Wellington smiled as if she was presiding over a tea party. "That would cause panic and rioting all over the world, dear, as well as create more diplomatic crises."

"I imagine it would."

"Why would you do that to your own country?" Vinson asked, incredulous.

Laura locked eyes with Ambassador Wellington. "Because I'm a mother whose son has gone through hell and I want to rescue him at any cost. Play along with me and you'll get what you want, and more."

Ambassador Wellington put her hand on Laura's, smiled warmly, and said, "Let's go see your son, dear."

Near dawn, they arrived at the *gasthaus* to find both Chinese and American officials still engaged in a standoff after nearly twelve hours. Politicians, diplomats, spies—even military officers in civilian clothing, Laura assumed. All of them here to protect their own turf, while an apocalyptic storm gathered.

But there was one present who represented no one but herself. Melanie Thurston stood out among the American contingent not only because she was the only female, but because she wore a skin-tight red suit trimmed in black, with the skirt slit halfway up her thigh.

Laura walked over and stood in front of her, causing Melanie to blanch and back away.

"Don't worry, I'm not going to hurt you," Laura said, roughly grabbing Melanie's arm and steering her aside. "Not that you don't deserve it."

"It's been a long time, Laura," Melanie said, regaining her composure. "Did you get my packages and letters over the years?"

Laura struggled to control herself. "I saved everything, Melanie. In fact, you may see yourself on the Internet any day now."

Clearly startled, Melanie asked, "What do you mean? You're not talking about the videotapes surely. That would be rather embarrassing for you and David."

"Oh, his face will be fuzzed, but not yours. It's clear evidence that you're a child molester. I plan to file criminal charges against you in the United States for rape of a minor. If the government buys information from you, I'll go to court to put a lien on the payment. I'll mount a public relations campaign against the use of taxpayer dollars to pay blackmail to an American traitor and criminal. I'm certain you remember all my media contacts, Melanie."

Melanie tried to control her trembling lower lip. "I don't believe you."

Laura leaned closer so that her lips were near Melanie's ear. "It gets worse. I'll use the considerable resources of the Gemini Group to find you wherever you're hiding in the world, and out you. I already know about Cuba and your secret bank account. I'll have you followed every time you move. The U.S. government might even tacitly support me, so it can get back most of its money after Jeremiah's followers find you and kill you."

Melanie, looking terror-stricken, clamped a hand over her mouth to stifle a cry of anguish.

"There's only one way you can save yourself."

"Anything, Laura. Anything!"

Laura hissed, "Never, ever, contact David again. And tell me right now the name of the highest-ranking Chinese government mole who protected Jeremiah during his exile in China and fed him inside information."

Melanie frowned. "That would be Wang Ho, minister of the interior."

"Good. No matter which side you're traded to tonight, Melanie, don't ever mention his name. Do we have a deal?"

"If I do as you ask, you'll leave me alone?"

Laura smiled and turned away. She knew that the Americans or the Chinese would wring every drop of information out of Melanie eventually. Then they might even drop her in a hole. With some luck, Laura would have just enough time to outflank all of them.

"What did you say to her?" Ariana asked.

"I told her she was getting too old to wear red. Ariana, I want you to find a secure phone and call one of our contacts in Beijing. Have him contact Minister of the Interior Wang Ho and tell him that Melanie Thurston is about to give him up. Tell him that we can get him out of the country and set him up in the United States in return for information no one else has."

"What are you doing, Laura?"

"Buying bargaining chips for the future."

On the second floor of the *gasthaus*, one of Vinson's agents inserted a key in a lock and slowly opened the door. He and another agent silently entered the room, while Laura stood anxiously in the hallway with Vinson and two Chinese officials.

When one of the agents waved them in, Laura went first. She rejoiced in her good luck. *I've found him and he's alive and . . . not well.*

David sat in a chair near the window, wrapped in a blanket even though the room seemed stifling hot to her. He hadn't shaved, his eyes were bloodshot, his skin blotchy. Beer and liquor bottles littered the table and floor, along with scattered drugs and drug paraphernalia.

She bent over to put her arms around her son and tried not to recoil at the body odor. He obviously hadn't bathed recently, either. "What are you doing here, David?"

"Having a party." He tried for a light note, but the smile dissolved into a pathetic look of distress.

"Well, the party's over and it's time to pay the piper. Melanie used you. She stole your money, including, I assume, the million dollars I gave you. She tried to sell her information to the U.S. government. The good news is, she's out of your life forever. Swiss cops busted Jeremiah's terrorist group that planned to blow up the World Health Organization in Geneva, so he knows you've betrayed him. You have only one place left to go, David"—she stood—"home, with me."

He looked around the room. "I figured the guys outside would eventually come get me."

"So you thought you'd kill yourself with drugs first?" she asked.

He looked up at her. "Something like that."

Outside the *gasthaus*, Laura huddled with Vinson and Cao Zengke, China's ambassador to Switzerland.

"Here's the deal," Laura said, trying to project a no-nonsense demeanor. "I'm taking David home with me to northern Viriginia. Before we leave, both of you can have a qualified person draw a sample of his blood."

"I object to David being returned to the United States," Cao said, "where we wouldn't have access to him and all the information he undoubtedly possesses about Jeremiah and his plans."

"Whatever information David has will not be anyone's proprietary information, Ambassador Cao," Laura said. "I intend to see to that. This is a worldwide crisis, and no country, including mine, should solely benefit from it."

"I'm a great admirer of you and your husband, Mrs. Delaney-Wallace," Cao said smoothly. "Certainly you have my deepest condolences and those of my government concerning the death of Mr.

Wallace. Nevertheless, although I believe you intend to be fair, I'm not as trustful of your government and the CIA."

"You're certainly not taking David with you," Vinson said to Cao.

Damn politics, diplomats, spies, and testosterone, Laura thought. "David is sick, as anyone can plainly see. He needs medical attention, and he needs to go home so he can rest and recuperate." She paused, mindful also of the needs of the world. "I'll accept this compromise. We'll take David to a Swiss hospital, where my people will guard him. You get your blood sample, and later you each get a couple of hours with David. He will tell you everything he knows."

Vinson shook his head. "There are established interrogation protocols. This violates all of them. We can't depend on him to tell the truth under those circumstances."

Laura was beginning to really dislike this guy. "Gentlemen, you don't seem to understand. We're going to do it my way, even if I have to call President Ellison and hold a press conference."

"I don't appreciate the fact that you continue to threaten your own government," Vinson said testily.

"And I don't appreciate your shortsightedness, Mr. Vinson. First off, no one knows more about Jeremiah than I do. Did either one of you live with him in a cave for nearly a year? Did he kill your husband? He killed Steve in Atlanta, just as sure as if he'd fired a bullet into his head. Steve and I were there fighting your battle because you and your governments were too stupid to figure out where Jeremiah would go."

She had their attention. "Now, I will guarantee you that David will tell you the truth, because only I will know the moment he lies. Right now he has no reason to lie. Finally, don't forget the most important thing: David knows next to nothing about what's going on now as compared to my other son, Thomas, who was with Jeremiah in Atlanta. With him against his will, by the way. Jeremiah held a gun to Thomas's head and used him as a shield; otherwise, Ariana would have killed Jeremiah right there."

Both men hung on her every word.

"Either Jeremiah or Thomas will come to me," she concluded in a low voice. "To no one else. If you want my cooperation, gentlemen, we'll do things my way."

As the car took them to a local hospital, Laura silently spoke to her husband: *Thanks, Steve. I couldn't have done it without you.*

29

The helicopter flew silently in the dark over the Shenandoah Valley and touched down briefly in an isolated meadow near New Market, where frightened but determined young cadets from a nearby military school had skirmished with Union troops during the Civil War.

Jeremiah led a blindfolded Thomas to a waiting van and helped him inside.

"Where are we?" Thomas asked as they sat beside each other on a bench seat.

"You don't need to know that right now," Jeremiah told him.

Mulling over recent developments, he remained silent as they drove east across a mountain range and then north on a narrow blacktop road running along the base of the western slope. The driver eventually turned left onto a gravel road and zigzagged up the side of a mountain past several lookout posts until they came to a gate, which two armed sentries opened immediately. At the end of the lane lined by scrawny pine trees, a sprawling log cabin blended nicely into the surrounding forest.

Inside the cabin he pulled down Thomas's blindfold and told

one of his men to show his son to an upstairs bedroom. "Put him in the one next to mine."

Jeremiah went into a den and sat down before a computer. He read and answered several e-mail messages. His jaw muscles clenched spasmodically over the news received from General Zhang in China and verified by other sources in Europe. The CIA had David and Melanie in custody in Zurich, and Laura had flown into the city from the United States, presumably to negotiate David's release.

He had received news at Judge Hewitt's in Atlanta that the attack on the World Health Organization had been foiled, and now he understood why. David had failed his mission, undoubtedly because Melanie had turned his head. He wondered if she had been at the Science Center, although none of his people had seen her there.

No matter, he thought. He'd had years to think about this mission and to plan painstakingly for all eventualities. David's capture had negative and positive sides, in fact. It ended forever his dream that his and Laura's son would take over the movement. On the other hand, it would lull the opposing forces into a false sense of security. The vaccine David had received in China would effectively treat most of the viruses, but not all of them. David was only one of many Trojan horses.

He couldn't help but smile at the thought of Laura, however. Beautiful, intelligent Laura. She hadn't wasted any time grieving over Steve. What a worthy adversary; more so than the various government agencies he dueled with regularly. He admired her beyond calculation. He meant what he had told her at the scene of the crash in Atlanta: He would come courting again.

After dinner, Jeremiah and Thomas sat in the living room gazing at a fire crackling in the large stone fireplace.

"I'm truly happy you decided to come along, Thomas," Jeremiah said, not under any illusion that his son had willingly accompanied him. Thomas simply wasn't ready to die. The strong human instinct to survive had perpetuated the species for thousands of years. But he could still turn Thomas around; biological ties were strong and complex.

"Tell me what you're thinking, Thomas. And try not to lie."

"That wouldn't do me any good, since the Lord would tip you off."

Jeremiah couldn't help but smile. "That's right."

"In March, when I turned eighteen, there was no way I could have imagined everything that has happened to me since."

"You've been catapulted into manhood, that's for sure."

"It seems to me that what you're going to do is inevitable. Migratory birds will start to move south any day now, won't they?"

"Indeed. In the far north, they're flying to staging areas right now, allowing the viruses to spread among them."

"And it will be a different world after the . . . catastrophe, won't it?"

Jeremiah stood and walked to the fireplace. He took a poker and strategically moved several logs so the fire could renew itself. Sparks and flames shot up, spreading a delightful smell of aged cherry throughout the room. He cherished the ambiance of the fire, even though the air conditioner hummed in the background.

Then he sat down again, staring at the hungry flames. "I won't attempt to fool you, Thomas, and tell you I know exactly what's going to happen, or even that we'll prevail. There will be a fair amount of chaos when people start dying by the hundreds of thousands. Medical facilities will be overwhelmed. There will be mass migrations, hysteria, looting, and crime. There will be natural survivors I don't control, and they'll immediately seek to impose their will on others. Mankind has an unlimited capacity for cruelty and self-interest.

"There will be wars, and many people who didn't die of the plague will be killed. Whole continents may be depopulated for centuries.

"The strongest forces that oppose me, especially those in the United States and Western Europe, may successfully combat the new viruses, at least in part. The rich and the strong always survive in disproportionate numbers. Even we won't totally escape the danger."

"What do you mean?" Thomas asked, clearly alarmed.

"My people developed multiple influenza viruses to complicate the task of those who will seek to prepare vaccines and new drugs," Jeremiah said. "That's why we attacked those scientific labs around the world. But we only crippled them, we didn't eliminate them. Additionally, one or more of our manufactured viruses could mutate into a form for which even we don't have a vaccine. My scientific advisers warned me about that in the beginning."

"So we could die, too?"

"It's possible, Thomas. Big gambles carry big risks. As far as I'm concerned, the potential rewards are worth the risks. Besides, I have faith that this is what the Lord wants me to do."

"That's a big comfort to me, too," Thomas replied.

"Tomorrow I'll show you around the facility, and you'll discover that we've taken every step conceivable to protect ourselves against all possibilities. Some very intelligent, innovative, and dedicated people who work for me have been planning this event for decades. Nevertheless, we may have to stay here for quite some time."

Jeremiah leaned forward, put his elbows on his knees, and stared intently at Thomas. "I keep saying *we,* Thomas, assuming that you will want to remain here in this safe haven. Beyond your instinct for survival, I'm going to need a far greater commitment from you very shortly."

"I understand."

He didn't have any more time to waste on the boy. "If you like, I'll let you go in the morning. Someone will fly you home."

"To New York?"

"If you wish, but your mother—I should say Laura—has purchased a farm in Virginia, where she lived many years ago." *You can be buried beside Steve.*

"How do you know that?"

"I have a first-class intelligence network, Thomas. First class.

Remember Judge Hewitt? Remember Colonel Picard in Canada? Mine is not a movement of ignorant mercenaries and opportunists—not that such people won't be useful at first. You need to understand that the heart of the movement consists of tens of thousands of people who think and believe as I do. That's what the authorities who opposed me never could get into their heads. There are people who want to change the world and the course of human history and will do anything to achieve those goals."

"Change it for the better?"

Jeremiah shook his head emphatically. "Yes, yes, Thomas. I fear you're one of the many young students who went to school and graduated but didn't learn anything. The last thousand years of world history has been a sad, disgusting chronicle of man's ignorance and inhumanity. Tens of millions of people were butchered in the name of greed, nationalism, imperialism, racial superiority—and especially, religion. The last century was one of Godless mayhem, although of course, the madmen, murderers, looters, and rapists all claim God is on *their* side.

"I hope you listened closely to Judge Hewitt. Eliminating seven-eighths of the world's population will not destroy anything essential to mankind's survival and evolution. In fact, if the resulting situation is managed properly, we can achieve a renaissance overnight."

The vision of the Garden of Eden that lay in the future so energized Jeremiah that he stood and began pacing from one end to the other of the large rug covering the richly polished pine floor.

"The beauty of the viruses we'll use to cleanse the human race is that they won't destroy our warehouse of knowledge developed over the ages. The archives, libraries, universities, hospitals, and laboratories will be untouched."

He suddenly sat on his haunches directly in front of Thomas. "And my people, *our* people, can easily organize and rule those who survive the plague. In time, they'll thank us. They'll worship us as the founders of a new civilization."

He stood again. "Think of the new world, Thomas. I won't allow nation states, competing political philosophies and competing religions, because they are the seeds that produce hatred and war. We will have a world government that strictly enforces the law. God's law. The Commandments God dictated to me and that I published in *The Book of Second Jeremiah.* Obey or die.

"As I'd planned to do in New America, I'll eliminate money and materialism as the sole incentives of man and replace them with the quest for knowledge. We'll learn more about the secrets of the universe in our lifetime than *they* would have learned in a thousand years."

"*If* we survive."

Like so many others, Jeremiah thought, *Thomas has no vision. He can only nurture his fears*. "Mankind needs this test of its mettle, son. In the beginning, there were only a few hundred men, and they survived. Other life forms on earth survived under even harsher conditions. Think about our friends, the birds. They have no political organization, no health-care or educational system, no army, no judiciary, and no religious philosophy. Yet like many other life forms, they were here before us and they may survive us. On the other hand, man has the gift of intelligence. If he can't survive the coming battle, he doesn't deserve to exist."

"What will happen to David?" Thomas asked. "And to my mother?"

"I'm not sure, Thomas. In a way, that may depend on you."

Jeremiah smiled as Thomas looked stunned. He could literally see the hatred, the defiance, and the hope drain out of his son's body. He might yet mold Thomas into a figurehead successor. *A lightning rod, if you will.*

"I'll see you in the morning," Jeremiah said and walked toward the stairs leading up to his second-floor bedroom. The bodyguards, inside and outside, would make certain Thomas didn't wander off.

As he thought back to his youth, he understood how Thomas felt. Jeremiah remembered what his Uncle Walter Dorfler had done to keep him in line when he wasn't much older than Thomas. Walter had killed Emma Dietze, the woman Jeremiah had loved even more than he did Laura Delaney.

If Walter hadn't done that, I would have abandoned the movement for a life of wealth and idleness. But Walter had been right, and Jeremiah didn't hate him anymore—any more than Thomas would hate him once he became intimately involved in this greatest of all social experiments.

Laura watched out the kitchen window as Ariana and David stood talking near the larger of the two barns. Then Ariana walked up the hill to the house and entered through the kitchen mudroom.

"Do you want some fresh coffee?" Laura asked.

"Yeah."

Laura poured two cups and set them on the hexagonal table that stood in the space created by the turret. Wraparound windows gave them a panoramic view of the front yard. "What were you two talking about?"

"He's interested in moving into the apartment on the second floor of the barn," Ariana said.

"That's where the farm manager and his family usually live. We'll need someone like that now that we're living here full time, especially since I plan to buy a couple of horses."

"What you mean is that you don't want him up there alone?"

"Exactly," Laura replied, chuckling over the fact that her motives were so transparent.

"I understand where he's coming from. Even though I'm nearly ten years older than he is, we speak the same language."

"As opposed to the language spoken by an old lady."

"Give me a break, Laura. A lot of people would mistake us for sisters."

"Now you're buttering me up."

"What I'm saying is that you're his mother and you want to protect him. But don't smother him. He needs privacy. He's a young man. What he's been through in life makes him older than his chronological age."

Laura sipped the hot coffee. "Good advice, excellent analysis. I admit to wanting to keep him under my thumb so he doesn't run away—or, worse yet, kill himself with booze and drugs."

"He's been clean for nearly a month," Ariana said. "Let's let him commit another offense before we jail him permanently. If he slips up, we may have to get him into some kind of treatment program. I'll keep a close eye on him, and so will the bodyguards."

"Speaking of which, we'll need to make this place into a fortress. Assume that Jeremiah knows we're all here."

A hard, determined look came over Ariana's face. "We've deployed the latest security equipment around the farm, including laser beams that not only detect intruders, but also can be used as weapons against them. I've had the pond in the pasture drained and the drainage pipes permanently sealed. We'd done a sound-wave analysis of the property to reveal any tunneling. The bodyguards make nighttime sweeps of the surrounding area, especially the foothills to the west, to identify any observation posts or movement. He won't get in here again, Laura."

Laura held her tongue, thinking of how many times someone had promised her that over the years. *Even Steve, God rest his soul.*

"What's going on around the world?" she asked.

"I've kept in touch with Mitchell at the FBI and he's very cooperative—probably because he ignored several of Steve's tips and hunches that turned out to be right. I imagine the director and the attorney general had a talk with him."

If they'd listened to Steve and sent an army of agents and federal marshals into Atlanta, Jeremiah could be in jail now, Laura thought. *Or, better yet, dead.*

"September is the beginning of the flu season in parts of Asia," Ariana said, "and scientists will be monitoring every outbreak there. They're already trapping birds all over the world and analyzing their blood."

As they'd analyzed David's blood, Laura thought. Already, government scientists suspected that her son wasn't fully protected. *It's just another sword that bastard is holding over his own son's head.*

"The scientific community apparently thinks it can quickly come up with a vaccine, or several vaccines," Ariana said. "By using these vaccines in combination with certain drugs, they think they can save a large percentage of people who are infected."

"What kind of drugs?" Laura asked, hopefully. She wanted to live, too, especially since she had important work to do.

"They're called plug drugs. As I understand it, they bind to a protein on the surface of a virus and prevent it from spreading. Scientists have known about these drugs for several decades, but they've never been able to perfect them. They don't work all the time in all people, and sometimes they merely minimize the effects of the flu."

"It sounds like only a partial solution," Laura said, disappointed.

"Even so, I've arranged to have several different brands mailed to us," Ariana said. "I suggest we take them anyway."

What about Thomas? Laura wondered. *Is he already fully protected?*

"I'd like you to look into converting the third-floor ballroom into a sterile room," Laura said.

"What do you mean?"

"I'm thinking we could remodel it, building a shell inside it that's airtight but equipped with the latest air-filtration system. There must be something that can filter out the tiniest airborne particles, including viruses and bacteria. Find out who the experts are in the field and get them in here as soon as possible. Don't spare any expense. I want that floor fixed up so we could all live there for a year or more, if necessary."

Most people in the world weren't aware of the looming catastrophe, Laura knew. Governments everywhere were keeping a lid on the information that Jeremiah might set loose a modern-day plague. They were afraid of inducing panic and riot, and they wanted to get their defenses in place first.

Even so, she'd read and seen news reports speculating that the recent attacks on scientists and scientific facilities might be the work of Jeremiah or other terrorists preparing to use biological weapons. It wouldn't be long before the whole world knew. In anticipation of a widespread social collapse, Laura had begun to convert a large percentage of her assets into gold, cash, and precious stones, which she planned to store on the farm. Just in case.

"Let's transfer the Gemini Group headquarters from New York to the farm," she said. "There's room, I think. If not, we'll put up another building when we have to."

"Are you asking me to move in here?"

"That's a silly question, Ariana. Of course. You're family as far as I'm concerned. Is there someplace else you want to go?"

"Nope. Here's fine with me."

"How's the arm and everything else?" Laura asked.

"No problems. The cast comes off tomorrow. Oh, by the way, do you remember the woman who contacted Steve and said she had information about Jeremiah's health and his plans . . . and a third son?"

"Yes, Steve told me he had arranged to get her to New York,"

"She apparently made it. The New York office received an e-mail from her. Untraceable, of course."

"What does she want?"

"A permanent hiding place."

Laura shook her head in amazement. "Bring her here."

Laura relented and allowed David to move into the barn apartment.

"It's my first bachelor pad," David said jokingly, as he showed her around. Laura hadn't been in the apartment since Seth and Gladys Schuyler had managed the farm decades ago. Its only distinguishing feature was the large picture window overlooking the north pasture. Once it had been the second-floor opening through which farmhands threw alfalfa bales into the loft.

"Thanks for all the new furniture," David said. "Especially the stereo set. If you see the barn shaking in the middle of the night, you'll know I'm playing some tunes."

Downstairs in the walkway between the horses' stalls, Laura slipped her arm around his waist. "I want you to be happy here, David. I'm sorry you didn't have a normal life . . . and that things may get even harder in the days to come. Right now, all of us need to stay here on the farm and take care of each other."

"I understand. Maybe Ariana can find something for me to do."

"You like her a lot, don't you?"

"Yeah. I wish I were a few years older."

She would always have trouble dealing with his sexuality, Laura knew. *Every time I think of him with a woman, the videotapes will play in my mind. I should have that Thurston bitch killed.* Unfortunately, the U.S. government had Melanie under wraps and wouldn't reveal her location to anyone. Laura couldn't even find out if they'd agreed to her blackmail demands.

The Gemini Group had Minister Ho in a New York apartment, thanks to Melanie's information. They'd mined a wealth of information from him already. Laura planned to trade it for guarantees of their safety, if necessary, and she planned to eventually use a tidbit or two to take care of Melanie Thurston, once and for all.

After she left David and walked toward the house, she looked over at Steve's grave, marked by a simple white cross until the tombstone could be delivered. She frowned. There were flowers propped against the cross. *Maybe Ariana put them there.*

She angled off toward the grave. As she drew closer, she recognized a bundle of red roses. Squatting, she pulled out a white card wedged into the middle of the flowers. A thorn pricked her finger, which she put in her mouth to suck the blood. As she read the note, she straightened up ramrod stiff: *Laura, remember the time I predicted that our son would one day lead New America and that you shouldn't mistake the first battle for the last. Those two prophecies may yet be fulfilled. As I said in Atlanta, I'll come courting soon.*

Laura turned slowly in a circle, studying the land for as far as she could see. A bodyguard stood near the corner of the smaller barn, looking away from her, toward the front fence line. Far off toward the northeast corner of the pasture, she saw a four-wheel-drive pickup. She couldn't make out the features of the two bodyguards sitting in the cab. They had a commanding view of the north two-thirds of the hundred-sixty-acre farm.

Laura put the note in her pocket and walked quickly toward the house, going around to the front porch entrance so she could see the guards down by the gate.

"Good afternoon, ma'am," said the bodyguard stationed permanently on the porch. He cradled an assault rifle in the crook of one arm. She smiled perfunctorily at him and went inside, where she walked to the fireplace in the living room and took out the note. She scanned it again quickly and then used a match from the mantel to set it on fire. She dropped the flaming piece of paper into the fireplace.

In response to a telephone call from Laura, FBI Deputy Director Byron Mitchell and three other FBI agents arrived at the farm the next morning in a black limo.

He paid his respects at Steve's grave, and Laura asked him to walk with her into the north pasture. A light breeze spread the distinctive aroma of autumn, which included a hint of decay.

She slipped her arm through Mitchell's, even though she didn't know him that well. She thought the gesture would serve her purpose. "Can I talk to you in complete confidence?"

He looked over his shoulder at the agents trailing a respectful distance behind and said, "Go ahead. I'll stop you if I don't think I can keep it to myself."

"I'd like to have a special bomb made."

Mitchell stopped and turned toward her, a stupefied look on his face. "Why?"

She smiled to put him at ease, then again linked her arm

through his and continued walking. "A hunch, not unlike the one Steve had about Jeremiah being first in Quebec City and then in Atlanta."

Mitchell sighed audibly and looked at the ground. "Believe me, I got raked over the coals for ignoring those hunches."

She smiled. "I don't blame you." She did in part, but she wanted to be ingratiating today. "Do you know the history of this farm?"

The lean, balding agent looked around. "Everyone at the Bureau knows what happened here."

"Do you know how Jeremiah got out of Atlanta?" she asked, and saw Mitchell's facial muscles begin to twitch.

"Not a clue. He still could be there, for all I know. Obviously, the guy has an extensive network of supporters and safe houses. We did everything except go door to door."

"Constitutional rights are a necessary pain in the ass, Steve used to say."

"He was right, as usual."

"I think Jeremiah has left Atlanta. I think he might come here to this farm."

Mitchell looked at her. "Why would you think that?"

"Because he has always had an obsession with me. He's come here several times before, as you know. David is here. As Ariana and I told you during our interview, Thomas wasn't willingly with Jeremiah in Atlanta."

"If that's true and Thomas escapes, he might come looking for you. Does he know you've moved here?"

"I'm not certain, but Jeremiah knows. He's not beyond using Thomas as bait, believe me."

"I won't make the same mistake twice," Mitchell said. "I'll blanket this area with men and equipment. If Jeremiah comes within a fifty-mile radius, we'll know it."

"He knows that, too," Laura said, standing toe to toe with the Bureau's second in command. "That's why I'd like to have the bomb, Byron. Just in case he slips through your lines and gets close to me or my son David."

Confusion and disbelief competed for space on the FBI chief's weathered face. "You don't mean you'd kill yourself to kill him?"

"I hope it doesn't come to that."

"We'd rather have him alive, for obvious reasons. We need all the information we can get about this biological agent."

"I understand, and I'm only talking about a last resort. Besides, if he's dead, his organization will start to crumble. Those in his ranks with the slightest bit of doubt will want to bargain with the authorities."

"Why not let me wire you instead, Laura? If he gets close to you, we'd know his precise location. We'd capture him right away and you wouldn't have a scratch on you."

She turned and resumed walking, not bothering to take his arm this time. She had known it wouldn't be an easy sell. Maybe she should have contacted one of the Gemini Group's experts on explosives. But then Ariana would find out, maybe even tell David, and she would never persuade them to go along with her plan. Besides, the FBI should be involved.

As Mitchell caught up with her, she said, "It's strictly a precaution in case he does one of his Houdini tricks, like he did here at this farm when an army of FBI agents surrounded it. Like he did in New America when it was surrounded by the U.S. Army." She turned to face him. "Like he did in Atlanta. Are you going to look me right in the eye, Byron, and tell me for a fact that he couldn't do it again?"

He blinked. "What kind of bomb are you talking about?"

"Something small, nonmetallic, about the size of my middle finger, although a little bit bigger around. Something pliable like the old plastique. Powerful enough that when it exploded, it would kill everyone within a three-foot radius, even if it had to blow through something semisolid."

"Give me an example."

Laura carefully phrased her response so both of them could ignore reality. "Let's say I slipped it into a guy's back pocket and it exploded when he was walking beside Jeremiah. I'd want it to kill both of them."

Mitchell absorbed all this, nodding his head.

"The bomb would have to be undetectable by any metal-scanning device or X-ray equipment," she added.

Mitchell crinkled his forehead in contemplation. "Given all the latest technology, it's possible to make a bomb like that." He looked over her shoulder, not wanting to meet her eyes. "Still, if they did a full-body search, including body cavities, you couldn't hide it."

"I've thought of that. Leave it to me."

"How soon would you need this bomb?"

"As soon as humanly possible. I don't think there's much time left."

30

After Jeremiah had gone to bed the night before, Thomas had checked out all the unlocked rooms in the two-story cabin, so he didn't know what to expect the next morning when Jeremiah said they would tour the "facility."

Jeremiah led the way along the first-floor hallway and opened a closet door at the end of it. With the push of a button, a trapdoor in the floor opened automatically, revealing a flight of stairs. Thomas gingerly stepped down into a tunnel. Although lights lined the walls, the tunnel curved and he couldn't see all the way to the other end.

"It runs into the side of a mountain," Jeremiah explained.

"Which mountain? Exactly where are we?"

Jeremiah didn't answer. Instead, he sat behind the steering wheel of one of several golf carts parked in a large circular area surrounding the stairs. He patted the seat beside him and Thomas climbed in.

The battery-powered cart hummed along an asphalt surface for several hundred yards until they came to an imposing steel door beside another group of carts.

Jeremiah got out, walked to a device beside the door, and submitted to a retinal scan. The foot-thick door clicked open immediately. An armed guard on the other side put considerable muscle into pushing the door open wider so they could step into a glistening steel chamber.

"It's basically like the holding area at the entrance to the bunker under the Science Center," Jeremiah explained. "We're being scanned for weapons, bomb material, and other contraband. If you have any cavities, Thomas, we have an excellent dentist on staff."

Thomas smiled feebly at Jeremiah's joke as the opposite door opened automatically after they had apparently passed the various tests. They stepped over an elevated threshold onto a steel-plated walkway with a handrail on one side. Jeremiah walked to the right and Thomas followed, noting that the walkway appeared to circle a large metal building. On their left were a series of entrances leading into glass-enclosed offices and laboratories. The latter included exotic-looking machinery and several recognizable computer mainframes.

He looked up at a geodesic dome and had the impression of being inside a stainless steel egg. *Only God knows what ideas are being hatched in here*, he thought.

Jeremiah nodded and spoke to several individuals they passed, including two women in lab coats. For some reason, Thomas considered women to be out of place here.

Jeremiah turned onto an exit ramp, then stopped and faced Thomas. "Let me tell you how this place came to be. We're inside a natural cavern beneath the Appalachian Mountains, which, as you should know, extend from Alabama to Canada. Because of the way these mountains were formed eons ago, such caverns are the rule rather than the exception. In my business, with its never-ending need for invisible, impregnable hideaways, it pays to become a student of geology.

"Years ago, my followers bought several hundred acres in this area, which borders on a national forest, so naturally there aren't many people or communities nearby. We built the cabin on one side of the mountain. Directly across the mountain in another valley, we constructed a large warehouse and put out the word that our new company assembled steel plates and girders for use in construction projects. That way, no one was suspicious of all the flatbed trucks that drove in and out of the area. We made it look like they unloaded raw materials and transported finished products, but in truth, they primarily hauled away excavated dirt and rock."

Jeremiah looked around admiringly. "It was a significant engineering challenge to build this facility and escape detection at the same time. It took nearly four years, after which the manufacturing company officially went out of business. We converted the space into a storage warehouse, although we actually keep various weapons there."

"What goes on here?" Thomas asked.

"Research, the gathering and storing of information, planning, and communication with our colleagues around the world. This enclosed facility constitutes a self-sufficient city, with its own air-filtration system, water system, and food supplies. We could live here comfortably for three to five years."

"You mean in case the viruses mutate, as you said they might?"

"Exactly. Please follow me, Thomas."

They entered a room filled with computer workstations not unlike those Thomas had seen in the university section of the Science Center.

Jeremiah introduced him to Dr. Hakim Wakilpoor, whom Thomas thought to be Indian or Pakistani. The thin, dark-skinned doctor wore a white lab coat.

"Dr. Wakilpoor heads up our computer operation," Jeremiah said. "He and I go way back. You won't ever meet anyone in the computer field who's more talented."

"Thank you, Jeremiah. And it's a pleasure to meet you, Thomas," Dr. Wakilpoor said in British-accented English. "Any time you have questions about the computer system, call me on extension fifteen or come to my office down the hall. Right now, step over here and we'll do a retina scan on you."

Thomas followed Wakilpoor to a workstation, where he was directed to sit down and look into a device. "It's not unlike an eye exam," Wakilpoor told him, "but it will take far less time."

In fact, it took only a few seconds, after which the doctor sat in front of an adjacent computer, his fingers flying expertly over the keyboard. Then he announced, "That's done. Whenever you come here to use a computer, Thomas, just look into the retinal scanner attached to the side of the CPU and you'll have the access Jeremiah has authorized."

Then Jeremiah showed Thomas to a computer terminal in a cubicle that provided privacy from the other users.

"Go ahead, do the retinal scan," Jeremiah said. "I assume you have some familiarity with computers."

Thomas couldn't help bragging, "Actually, I know a lot about computers."

"Good. Then I suggest you go to the site map and browse those areas that intrigue you. I think you'll be surprised at the scope and complexity of our operation, although none of the information you can view is sensitive in nature. You will have to earn the right to move beyond the introductory level."

With that, Jeremiah left abruptly. Thomas clicked on the site map and read through a table of contents. He skipped over the introduction, Jeremiah's biography, speeches, and the Bible books he'd written, and opened a directory titled *Birds*.

As he entered various other folders and files, his mouth fell open. The voluminous information provided elaborate descriptions of aviary species, including photographs and short videos regarding their physical characteristics and appearance, food preferences, indigenous diseases, mating rituals and breeding habits, life span, staging areas, migratory routes, and feeding grounds. When he touched a speaker symbol on the monitor, it broadcast each bird's voice.

Within the "Migratory Routes" file, Thomas selected North American ducks, such as those he'd seen in Canada, and immediately viewed a three-dimensional representation of flight lanes as well as a video of flight formation and landing techniques.

After looking through various files for nearly an hour, he could guess at the contents of the restricted levels of information. They would likely contain details about the types of viruses injected into different species of migratory birds—information so valuable at this point in time that a price tag couldn't be placed on it.

He excitedly opened the "Viruses" directory, most of which contained the type of information he had viewed in the visitors' center at the Centers for Disease Control. Again there were three-dimensional drawings of viruses and detailed information about their pathology. Restricted areas undoubtedly contained details of the genetic makeup of the viruses—perhaps even the structure of the vaccines that counteracted them.

Mainly out of curiosity, he clicked into a directory called "Supporters" and found personal testimonials provided by individuals who shared Jeremiah's vision. Each disciple had an e-mail address, although a parenthetical notation indicated that the mail would be routed through an Internet service provider to protect the identity of the "army of believers."

Thomas rested his head against the high-backed chair, as exhausted as if he had performed manual labor all day. He had no doubt that the information in the central mainframe computer, or computers, could either destroy or save the world. And he, an eighteen-year-old kid, had partial access to it. Once, when Dartmouth had been part of his future, he had dreamed of one day being a lawyer with influence and power. Now that dream seemed like kids' stuff.

The decision isn't all that hard, he thought. Sure, Jeremiah had said he could leave, but Thomas figured the minute he accepted that alternative, he could expect to be executed. If he stayed and pretended to be gradually warming up to his role, he'd be safe, for the moment at least. And he'd acquire more and more knowledge about Jeremiah's plans, which would give him immense power. On the other hand, when he revealed his true face, Jeremiah would spare no effort to kill him.

He sighed. Either way, odds were that he could look forward to a short life. Staying here would allow him to survive longer than he would in the outside world. Besides, he remembered Jeremiah's remark at the side of the highway in Atlanta—that he would eventually go after Laura. Maybe even David would show up. Perhaps the three of them could accomplish what he couldn't do alone. Maybe they could find some way to get rid of Jeremiah and control his movement.

Control his movement? Why did he think that, instead of automatically assuming that the best course would be to destroy it? In his heart, Thomas knew the answer. Even if Jeremiah died or disappeared, the movement would not simply collapse and disband. The fanatics who believed in Jeremiah's twisted philosophy would always be there, including the wealthy and influential ones like Judge Zachary Hewitt. Someone would have to hunt them down one at a time. *Maybe it will have to be me,* he thought.

The day after she met with Bryon Mitchell and persuaded him to make her a unique bomb, Laura walked down the hill to the large barn and went up the stairs to the apartment at one end of the hayloft.

She knocked and David let her in.

"The place is a mess," he apologized. "I'm still arranging things."

"Are you comfortable here?" she asked as she sat down at a garish kitchen table he'd picked out of a catalog. The fifties-style, red Formica tabletop matched the color of the plastic covering the chairs. *What goes around comes around,* she thought.

"Yeah, I like it a lot here," David said, taking two cans of Pepsi from the refrigerator and sitting down opposite her. "It's mine."

"That and more," Laura said, picking up one of the cans. "I've changed my will so that you and Thomas inherit this farm and nearly everything else I own." She reached into her pants pocket and took out a plastic case containing a computer disk. "The will and all you'd need to know about me and my possessions are on this disk, a copy of which is in my lawyer's safe. It's the New York firm of Hardy, Durkee, Warren, and Brown."

David popped the tab on his Pepsi. "You'll probably outlive me, Laura. I don't want to talk about this."

"You know what's coming this fall, David. Death will be the primary topic of conversation around the world. I hope we all survive, especially you. You've just begun to live."

He nodded and said philosophically, "If you hadn't rescued me in Zurich . . ."

"You're welcome. Just don't kill yourself with booze and dope."

He laughed uneasily. "No way. Ariana watches me like a hawk. She says I can't even have a beer until Christmas, and then only one."

Laura chuckled. "Ariana's tough. She's fair, too. When I'm not around, I expect you to listen to her. She has my complete confidence and trust."

"How old is Ariana?"

"Twenty-eight, I think. Why? Are you interested in her?" To her surprise, the possibility of a romance between David and Ariana pleased rather than disturbed her. She wanted her son to know love.

"She thinks I'm just a punk, boozer, and dope-head."

"Try acting like a man and maybe she'll change her mind."

"Maybe."

Laura stood. She had planned to say a lot of things to David, but it didn't seem necessary now.

"I have some things to do," she said.

"Thanks for stopping by, Mom."

That was all she really needed to hear. *Mom.* Nothing else need be said about their relationship.

Laura started for the door to the stairs, stopped, and turned back toward David. "There are some horse magazines in a rack up at the house, in the living room. Why don't you read up on the subject and then look at the ads in the back? I might be willing to buy a couple of horses this month. We had horses when I lived here before. I thought maybe you could help take care of them."

David glowed with enthusiasm. "That would be great! Can we race them?"

Laura laughed. "That depends on many factors. But we certainly could breed them. There's money in good horseflesh, you know. Lots of work, too."

"Hey, I need a profession, right? It sounds better than going to college."

"I didn't mean it as a substitute for that," she said, pretending to be concerned.

They laughed and hugged, and Laura held on for as long as she dared.

Shortly after noon, Byron Mitchell arrived, as he'd promised to do in their morning telephone conversation. To get Ariana out of the way, Laura asked her to accompany an expert whom Mitchell had brought along to assess the security of the barn and the apartment where David was living.

After they were seated on a sofa in the living room, Mitchell handed her a black velvet pouch.

"Don't squeeze it," he said.

With shaking hands, Laura loosened the drawstring on the pouch, peered inside, and carefully extracted the plastic explosive device, which was about the size of a four-inch cigar. She calculated that it weighed only five or six ounces.

She held it delicately, almost afraid to breathe. "How does it work?"

Mitchell took the bomb back. Wedging the fingernails of one thumb and index finger under notches on each side, he pulled off a bullet-shaped cap. He tilted the remainder of the plastic capsule, and the inside slid out into his hand. "Feel it gently," he said.

Laura carefully touched it with her finger and felt a light coating of oil or grease, although it gave off no odor.

"It works according to the same principle as an atomic bomb," Mitchell explained, "which explodes when atoms of natural fissionable material are compressed. In this case, the man-made molecules release a small amount of energy and ignite the bomb material, which is the latest plastic explosive."

"My God, what if I accidentally sit on it, or squeeze it, or somebody accidentally bumps into me?"

"That's why it's inside this protective case. Also, there has to be a significant depression of the doughlike material, such as would occur if you put it in your fist and squeezed hard."

"What if someone rammed it on the end when it was out of the plastic case?"

Mitchell nodded. "That would do it. The best thing, though, would be to squeeze it hard, then either put it in someone's clothing, throw it in their car, or drop it at their feet. And then move away quickly. You'd have about fifteen seconds before it went off."

"How deadly is it?"

"It will do as you requested, which is to kill everyone within, say, a six-foot radius, and seriously wound those standing as far away as twenty feet."

"Guaranteed?"

"It was put together by the best people in the business. The coating is a special material that prevents dogs or machines from detecting the explosive."

The bomb business, Laura thought as she watched Mitchell slip the bomb back inside its casing and reattach the cap.

"What about X-rays?"

He shrugged. "Nothing's perfect. In or outside the plastic container, it would appear on X-rays."

Which wouldn't generate alarm if it appeared to be something other than what it was, Laura thought.

Mitchell handed over the velvet pouch and asked pointedly, "Is there anything you want to share with me, Laura?"

"I don't have anything to share, Byron. I just think that Jeremiah might pop up suddenly, as he's done so many times in the past. I want to be ready. I can't predict when and where it could happen—or even if it will."

He frowned and sighed. "I understand. In any event, try not to kill yourself. We'll always be nearby."

Laura showed him to the door and watched as two agents who'd obviously been on each side of the house escorted their boss to a black limo, which drove toward the barn to pick up the security expert.

Upstairs in her bedroom, Laura took a long, hot shower. When she finished and put on a robe, she picked up a phone and punched one of the stored numbers.

She sat in front of her vanity and combed her hair, but mainly she just stared at herself at the mirror until someone knocked on the door. She opened it and ushered Ariana inside.

"What's up?" Ariana asked, hooking her thumbs into the belt loops of her jeans.

"I just wanted to talk to you for a few minutes."

"Shoot," Ariana said, flopping into a chair. Laura sat on the edge of the bed, opened a nightstand drawer, and took out a computer disk. "I gave one of these to David today. It contains my will and reproductions of other important documents. I've left you a decent inheritance." She knew that Ariana's parents were dead and that the young woman was alone in the world.

"Gee, should I shoot you now or try to make it seem like an accident later?" Ariana asked, then grimaced at her own bad joke.

"Given the times, it seemed like a prudent idea," Laura said. "I've been lucky enough in life to amass a fortune. I want it to go to the right people."

"I appreciate that, Laura," Ariana said softly.

"I want something in return, naturally."

"What?"

"Your promise to stay here on the farm if anything happens to me. Take care of David—and Thomas if he returns. I don't want the Gemini Group to fade away. Its activities will be as important in the future as they have been over the past twenty years."

"I consider it my life's work, Laura. Don't worry about me suddenly switching careers"—she smiled—"even if I were to get rich somehow."

"I know you're young, Ariana, and that you'll get married someday and have a family. There's plenty of room on this property for you to build another house. That provision is in my will, too."

"Laura . . . "

Laura held up her hand to stop the protest. "Just one more thing, Ariana, and then you can go. In a week or two, some people I trust will arrive with several boxes of cash, gold, and precious stones. I want you to supervise construction of a safe in the basement floor. Something state-of-the-art that couldn't be opened even if someone found it. You and David come up with a combination known only to the two of you. And Thomas, of course, when he's free."

"You're really expecting bad times, aren't you, Laura?"

"Always plan for the worst and you'll never be sorry." Laura stood. "That's all. I'm going to lie down and nap for a couple of hours."

Ariana hugged her and said, "I love you, Laura. I've always loved you and Steve."

Laura held her at arms' length. "Especially Steve."

Shocked, Ariana backed away. "I never, ever came on to Steve! Besides, he thought you were the only woman in the world."

Laura smiled. "It was hard sometimes, though, wasn't it?"

She watched Ariana frown, look around, and jab the toe of her boot into the carpet. Finally she looked Laura in the face, smiled, and softly admitted, "Sometimes."

Laura chuckled to herself as Ariana did a slow turn and left the room. How could she blame anyone for loving Steve?

Laura punched another phone number, and soon thereafter came another knock on the door. She opened it to let in Shawntel, who had been on her and Steve's payroll for over twenty years, first as a bodyguard and then as an advance man and negotiator in business deals. He had helped dig Steve's grave, and he was an expert at disguises.

"You got everything?" she asked.

He handed her an overnight bag. She emptied it onto the bed and surveyed the contents.

"You'd best start with this," Shawntel said, handing her a vest-like article of clothing.

"I'll be right back," Laura said, taking the garment with her into the bathroom. She removed her blouse and bra and stared into the mirror as she slipped her arms through the short sleeves and pulled up the front zipper of the vext. The top half of it flattened her breasts, while padding in the lower half filled out her midriff and made it flush with her hips. That, plus the padded shoulders, gave her the appearance of a man.

She walked back into the bedroom.

Shawntel looked her over critically. "Not bad. This is next."

Laura did a double take. "Is it what I think it is?

"You gonna look like a man, you gotta have the right bulges in the right places."

Laura doubled over in laughter as she accepted the appliance and went back into the bathroom. She took off her slacks and put on the jockstrap with the plastic insert shaped like a man's genitals.

She dressed again and walked back into the bedroom.

"Well, well, if it ain't Mr. Loren."

Shawntel had always been a jokester, with a permanent twinkle in his eyes.

Laura stood in front of the full-length mirror. "The pants aren't tight enough to really show off my stuff."

"If you're walking down the sidewalk and seen a shapely lady coming at you, just hitch up your trousers. You've seen men do that, haven't you, Laura?"

"You're shameless, Shawntel," she said, although thoroughly enjoying this light moment. She knew it might be one of her last.

"Okay, now put on these size-eleven shoes, which I've fixed up inside so they'll fit you."

Even so, as Laura walked around the room, she felt awkward, as if she were wearing a clown's shoes. She stopped in front of Shawntel, who appraised her disguise. "Put on the dark blue windbreaker and you'll pass as a man . . . from the neck down," he said. "The problem, of course, is your face. Come over here and sit down in front of the vanity."

She looked at him in the mirror as he stood behind her.

"Your head ain't big enough," he said.

"Unlike most big-headed men," she shot back.

"Neither are your hands, but at least you got rid of the fingernail polish and clipped your nails."

"Actually, I bit them to the quick."

"I'll put a prop in your hands when we leave. That'll do the trick. Right now, we got to concentrate on your face. First, put on a layer of lotion."

While she did that, he held up a mask by grasping the hair attached to it. Laura turned halfway in the seat and felt the hair, the mustache, and their texture. "My God, it feels real!"

"It took me nearly an hour to skin him," Shawntel said with a straight face.

Rather than pulling it over Laura's head, Shawntel put the mask around her face. "There are Velcro tabs hidden in the hairline, which I can adjust," he said.

For nearly a half hour, Shawntel fitted the mask and used a variety of makeup materials to blend it to Laura's skin color around the eyes, nose, and throat. Finally, he combed the hair neatly into place and said, "Voilà."

Laura got up and walked to the large mirror, taking in her new image. *Not half bad*, she thought. It would be needed only long enough to get them out of the house and off the property without being tailed either by Ariana's people, the FBI, or anyone else who might be watching.

Laura packed several items of clothing in a sports-equipment bag that she handed to Shawntel. Then she went into the bathroom, took the velvet pouch off the shelf, and placed it in a zippered pocket of the windbreaker.

Walking to the west bedroom window, she stood and looked down at Steve's grave for several minutes. Then she and Shawntel left the bedroom. Downstairs, she stared at a man sitting on the sofa—a man she now resembled. Now she understood how the mask had been formed. Her lookalike stood and handed her a submachine gun. The prop.

Shawntel pulled aside the front door curtain so he could look out at the yard and main entrance. He said, "Let's go."

Laura followed him down the steps and quickly got into the car. Shawntel drove down the driveway and waved at the gate guards, who immediately let them through. As they approached the intersection with the north-south state highway, Shawntel playfully pointed his left index finger and thumb out the window at the two FBI agents sitting in a car parked on the shoulder. One of them "shot" back.

As they drove north, Laura looked through the window at the farm and doubted she would ever see it again.

31

They drove into Middleburg from the south, and Laura told Shawntel to turn east on the main street, which also was Highway 50.

"Drop me anywhere along here and head on home," she said.

"You can't be serious?"

"Yes, please do as I ask. When you agreed to help me get away from the farm, I told you I had private business to conduct without being spied on by the FBI."

He shrugged in acknowledgment. "You sure? I wouldn't advise it."

"I'm sure."

"You're the boss lady. You want me to stay in the shadows in case you need any help?"

She patted his arm. "Go on home to your family, Shawntel. I'll be fine. I'll call you when I need a ride home."

But that won't happen, she thought, getting out of the car in front of an antiques store. She left the submachine gun lying on the front seat floor, but remembered to bring the sports bag. She pretended to look into the store window until Shawntel's car disappeared from sight. Then she walked around the corner, down a block, and crossed the street to a Comfort Inn.

The desk clerk didn't look askance at her, so Laura assumed that the disguise continued to pass muster. She kept her speech to a minimum, saying, "Room, please," in a low voice. She paid in cash, took the key, and walked briskly down the hallway, then up the stairs. Inside her room, she laboriously shed her disguise and immediately got into the shower. She stood under cool water for several minutes to counteract the heat of the mask, which had left her hair sweaty and matted. Adhesive applied to several places had brought out a red rash on her face.

She pulled back the bedcover and lay down on the cool sheets for fifteen minutes before rising, doing her hair and makeup, and getting dressed. From the sports bag she took out a light blue shantung blouse with a wide collar and a black single-breasted jacket and matching skirt. The "dark-side" look suited her purpose and mood.

At a pay phone downstairs, just off the lobby, she called a cab and told the operator to have the driver pick her up at the back entrance.

"Take me to the Red Lion restaurant," she told the driver when he arrived.

Middleburg had a carefully cultivated, small-town look, although the proliferation of bed-and-breakfast inns, antiques stores, high-priced boutiques, and fancy restaurants were a tip-off to the wealth of those who lived in the surrounding countryside. Estates ranging from five to fifty acres dotted the rolling pastures in the mountain foothills. Among the country squires were congressmen, high-tech industry executives, Hollywood actors, and the multigenerational rich. Their leisure-time activities included riding to hounds.

Many of these people dined in the Red Lion, *the* place to be seen in the area. Since Jeremiah already knew she had moved here—he had even infiltrated her property—it seemed a good place to start, although she couldn't imagine the terrorist showing up in an establishment where a house photographer took snapshots of seated patrons.

Laura asked the hostess for a back booth in the nonsmoking area. She knew that someone might recognize her, although it seemed unlikely; she and Steve had been extremely camera-shy over the last two decades. Nevertheless, she walked through the room with her head high, boldly staring back at those who looked up. After all, she had come here to be seen.

In a booth with high-backed wooden panels, she studied the menu with interest. Everyone raved about the food here, and she felt starved. She began with the calamari appetizer and a glass of Cakebread Cellars Chardonnay. Sipping the wine, she made plans to take a cab later to Dulles International Airport and sit at a bar there. Surely Jeremiah's men had that place staked out. From there, she would go to one of the five-star hotels in downtown Washington, D.C. She thought it likely that somewhere along the route, someone would recognize her and report to him.

Her heart leaped to her throat when Jeremiah slid into the booth across from her. His once-blond, curly hair had turned gray, and lines crisscrossed his angular features. But the eyes—the mirrors into the soul—were the same: light blue and vacuous.

He seemed smaller somehow, not as lithe and coiled with energy as he had once been. Nevertheless, Laura could literally sense the danger that surrounded him like an invisible force field. As she had expected, he was dressed in black.

"Hello, Laura. It's been a long time."

With a trembling hand, she put the wineglass to her lips, seeking time and courage. "How did you know I was here?"

"A friend of mine called from a local motel and told me the oddest story. It seems he saw a man go into one of the rooms and emerge later as a beautiful woman."

Laura still struggled. "How did you know I'd left the farm?"

He gave her the look a schoolteacher gives to a not-so-bright pupil. "Laura, do you think I walked onto your farm and put the flowers and a note on Steve's grave? Even I'm not that brave."

She gasped as reality struck her like a slap across the face. "Shawntel!"

"He's a black man, Laura. In the new world, they want their own country," he explained indifferently. "Even though they have an entire continent now."

"But he'd been with us for years. One of your men even shot and wounded him!"

"I can't tell all my men about every undercover agent I've purchased over the decades. Shawntel understood. It actually increased your confidence in him, didn't it, Laura?"

The waiter brought her appetizer. "What would the gentleman like?" he asked.

"A glass of iced tea, please. And perhaps some of that great bread you bake here."

"Yes, sir."

"What did you have in mind for an entrée, Laura?"

"I've suddenly lost my appetite. How do you know I don't have a gun in my purse." *Or a bomb.* "I could kill you right where you sit. Then what would your whole movement have been about?"

"You didn't go through this elaborate charade to kill me, Laura. Then you wouldn't know what happened to Thomas, would you? And my followers would certainly kill David and Ariana in revenge. You left the farm so they wouldn't get hurt when I came for you. Isn't that right?"

"What do you want with us? I've never understood it."

"I'm an obsessive-compulsive personality, Laura."

"No shit."

"It's what makes me so good at planning, and it's what makes me want you. Part of it is the standard dream of all men. I wanted sons to follow in my footsteps. It seems I chose the wrong son, but that doesn't invalidate the prophecy. Thomas is also our son, isn't he, Laura?"

"It's unthinkable that he'd do your bidding," she said.

"He will, eventually. He doesn't have many other choices, does he? He's smart, independent, and tough-minded—some of the time. You did an excellent job of raising him."

"And if I go with you, I can save both of my sons?"

He sat back and beamed as his tea and bread arrived. "I've been telling Thomas what a wonderful world it will be in a couple of years. I believe we can all live for a long, long time, Laura. I've been talking to my medical advisers. As you know, I have a new heart. They have plans to transplant other organs, to manipulate my genetic structure to grow new bones and muscle—perhaps even new brain cells.

"They've predicted even more amazing advances in the future, including entire limb replacements featuring titanium bones, plastic replacement arteries and veins, platinum-fiber muscles, and artificial skin impervious to cancer. Eventually my whole body will be artificial, leaving only the natural brain. I'm convinced that if I can live another hundred years, ways will be discovered to preserve my brain forever, or to transfer its intelligence, memory, and experiences to an indestructible form. I plan to be the first immortal man.

"You can be part of this great adventure, Laura. You, David, and Thomas. It may even be possible for us to have more children. Remember that Abraham's wife Sarah was well beyond childbearing years when she gave birth to Isaac. Would you like that, Laura?"

Seeing the fanatical glow of belief on his face, Laura felt her spirits plummet into a black, bottomless void. Looking back on the year he had kept her a prisoner, she knew it was fruitless to delve into his mind for reason.

"All right, I'll go with you," she said, taking her purse from the seat beside her and putting it on the table. "First I need to go to the bathroom."

"Planning on leaving a note, Laura? The waiter will just destroy it."

"No, actually I need to attend to a female problem. I just started taking estrogen-replacement drugs. They cause me to spot now and then."

"Laura, Laura. We wasted so many years, but the future can be as bright as the sun."

The nearness of the cabin stunned Laura. *He's almost living in my backyard! It's another indication of his enormous resources.*

As they stood beside the car, Jeremiah said, "It's only about a hundred miles from here to the White House, Laura. I know we'll all be excited to move in there later on, when it's deserted."

Just inside the entryway of the cabin, Laura stepped into a glass cage as instructed, assuming that machines were scanning her body. She could almost feel her blood pressure rise. A guard whispered in Jeremiah's ear, causing the Prophet to frown and shake his head. Laura heard him say, "It's not necessary, I know about that."

Jeremiah took her arm and led her down a hallway past a large living room with gleaming pine floors, a centerpiece stone fireplace, and an open ceiling soaring to the rafters. Under the second-floor balcony overlooking the living room, another hallway led to other rooms in the back of the cabin.

Upstairs, Jeremiah opened the door to his bedroom suite and ushered Laura inside. She barely had time to remove her coat before he began kissing and groping her. She pushed him back, but forced herself to smile. "Slow down, big boy. I'd like to freshen up first, if you know what I mean, and then talk to Thomas. After that, I'm yours for as long as you like."

"I like your new attitude, Laura, although it makes me very suspicious."

"It's not complicated, Jeremiah. I want my sons to survive. I'll do anything to accomplish that. If you don't rush things, maybe it will eventually work out for us."

A collage of emotions formed on his face—suspicion, calculation, hope, and lust. "You can forget about Steve that quickly?" he asked.

"I'll never forget him, but I can't bring him back, and he can't save our sons." *Our sons.* Laura planned to use every subtlety, no matter how distasteful.

Jeremiah turned toward the door. "I'll send Thomas up. Don't take too long."

After he left, Laura went into the bathroom and looked at herself in the mirror. She didn't fully recognize the person who stared back. Jeremiah, a cunning and cautious person, probably didn't buy the whole charade, but she had gauged correctly that he would throw caution to the wind to once again pursue his insane, longtime lust for her.

She looked around the spacious bedroom, which included a king-size bed and a sitting area furnished with an easy chair, love seat, coffee table, and large-screen television. She stood in the middle of the room until someone knocked on the door.

Laura and Thomas stared awkwardly at each other for several seconds until he stepped forward and wrapped her in a tight hug.

"I've missed you so much," she said as she took his arm and pulled him toward the love seat, where they sat side by side, holding hands.

"Me, too, Mom."

"Tell me everything," she said.

He looked around the room warily and Laura understood that someone surely watched and listened. She could deal with that.

"I'm so sorry about Dad," Thomas said, tears spilling down his cheeks. "There was nothing I could do," he sobbed.

"Me either."

"I feel so stupid for running away from home like I did," he continued. "I thought it was about understanding my roots." He shook his head sadly. "Now, unfortunately, I do."

"We have no choice but to make the best of things, Thomas."

"Is that why you're here?"

"Yes," she said frankly, although she planned also to speak to the eavesdroppers, which perhaps included Jeremiah. "Steve is dead. I know for a fact that he would want all of us to survive as best we can."

"No matter what?"

"No matter what."

She took heart from a calculating look that flickered across Thomas's face. He dried his tears and looked intently at her. He had always been intelligent and she suspected that he was getting smarter by the day.

"I've been studying computer files since I've been here," he said. "There's voluminous information about the movement and the engineered viruses they've set loose."

"Good. Knowledge is power." She felt strongly that they were communicating on a level beyond their words.

Thomas asked, "Have you seen David?"

"He's at the farm I repurchased. Not far from here, in fact. It's north of The Plains about five miles. Ariana's there, too." She thought angrily about Shawntel and wondered if there were others like him.

"I'd like to see David again."

"You will." Laura stood. There were a thousand other things she wanted to say, but she couldn't, and she needed to get on with her task before she lost her nerve.

She took Thomas in her arms and whispered in his ear, "You're a man now, Thomas. Be a man. And if you get out of here and back to the farm, get rid of Shawntel and others like him."

He drew back and stared down at her. "Are you going to be okay, Mom?"

She flashed her most optimistic look and patted both sides of his face. "More than okay. Don't worry about me. Let's have breakfast together in the morning and talk some more. I'm tired now."

"I remember your philosophy, Mom."

"Yes?"

"Practice the Golden Rule, do as much good as you can, and never, ever forget the power of love."

"I love you, Thomas, forever and ever. Be strong. Always be prepared to seize the moment."

"I love you too, Mom."

"Did you have a nice talk?" Jeremiah asked as he stepped into the bedroom.

"Yes. You can depend upon Thomas to be a good student."

"With you here, I'm certain that will be true. I have something I want to show you." He went to the closet, opened the door, and walked in, sorting among the clothes hanging there. He pulled out a blue dress and held it up for her to see. "Remember this?"

Initially, Laura drew a blank and looked quizzically at him.

"It's a copy of the blue Scassi you once wore."

"At the ball in the Kremlin, in nineteen ninety-one!" Laura recalled, stunned.

"I'm sure it will fit you, Laura. Try it on." He carefully placed the dress on the bed. "I never got to dance with you then. I'll put on some Tchaikovsky."

How stupid, she thought, but complied. In fact, she disrobed right there, dropping her clothes to the floor. Naked, she picked up the dress and stepped into it. "Mind zipping me up?" she asked.

Jeremiah stood behind her and did as instructed. He also kissed each of her shoulders.

Then the swelling music started and they danced on the bare pine floor. As they whirled about, a smile touched Laura's face as she pretended to be dancing one more time with Steve.

Jeremiah stopped suddenly and unzipped the dress so that it dropped to the floor. He traced the outline of her nipples with his fingers. "My God, you're beautiful, Laura."

She began to unbutton his shirt and trousers, and he eagerly helped. Soon he faced her with an erection. She shoved him onto the bed and flopped down beside him, kissing his face and eyes as she reached between her legs and inserted a finger into her vagina, pushing aside the diaphragm she had inserted to keep the bomb in place.

Jeremiah tried to climb on top of her and she summoned all her strength to resist going over on her back. *No way is this bastard going to get inside me again!*

Her finger found the tip of the bomb and she jammed it at least an inch into the soft material. She began to count.

With both hands, she pushed him onto his back. “I want to be on top first.” *Five.*

“Fine by me.”

She squatted right over his heart and seductively cupped her breasts. *Ten.*

“Jeremiah, I’m going to fuck you . . . up.” *Fifteen.*

32

Thomas sat alone at the kitchen table, drinking a Coke and worrying about his mother, when an explosion caused him to jump to his feet. At first he thought it might be a grenade and that government troops had attacked the cabin.

He ran into the living room, where several men had sat reading or watching television. All of them were on their feet now, shouting and pointing upstairs. In one horrible moment, Thomas realized that the explosion had occurred within the cabin—inside Jeremiah's bedroom suite!

He took the stairs two at a time behind three bodyguards, who tried the doorknob and then kicked the door open.

Thomas stood in the doorway and immediately gagged at the sight and the sickening odor. The walls and floor, even the ceiling, were covered with blood and pieces of human flesh. The smoke lingering in the air gave off a strange acrid smell.

One bodyguard had lifted Jeremiah's naked body off the bed and carried it to the love seat. The other guard angrily shoved Laura's body off the other side of the bed, while using a pillow to beat out the flames that threatened to engulf the mattress.

Thomas looked at his mother's naked body lying faceup in the narrow space between the bed and the wall. He could contemplate the ghastly sight for only a few seconds before covering his eyes. A foreign, frightening moan gathered in the pit of his stomach and erupted upward, bursting from his mouth in the form of a prolonged scream. Amid the general shouting, cursing, and crying, it went unnoticed.

He looked again. Whatever the source of the explosion, it had ripped out the midsection of Laura's body, leaving her legs attached to her trunk by only a few strips of muscle and shreds of skin.

Thomas peered through the group of onlookers crowded around Jeremiah, whose midsection was a mangled mess of unrecognizable intestines and body parts. One badly broken rib pointed toward the ceiling. Thomas crowded closer and thought he saw Jeremiah's eyelids quiver. *My God, he can't still be alive?*

Suddenly someone shoved Thomas aside, causing him to stumble against the wall. A doctor with a stethoscope and bag knelt beside Jeremiah. A man Thomas knew only as Grumman, head of security, shouted at those in the room: "Get back! Get out! Let the doctor work."

The others obeyed him, although they stood outside on the balcony and continued to voice their comments and expressions of shock.

Thomas saw Grumman bend over Laura's body and heard him say, "The bitch had *a bomb* in her cunt. Jeremiah must have thought it was a tampon." The security chief righted himself and looked disgusted. "It's the only mistake I ever knew him to make in all the years I worked for him. Goddammit!"

Then he saw Thomas. "Get the fuck out of here!"

Someone outside on the balcony shouted, "She was his mother! He probably helped her kill Jeremiah!"

Many pairs of eyes looked at him in hatred, and Thomas felt helpless and afraid. His mother's words suddenly gave him courage: *Be prepared to seize the moment.* She had known what would happen, of course, and had tried to warn him.

"Shut up, all of you!" Thomas shouted. "You're not allowing

these people to help my father." Two men dressed in white pushed a machine on wheels through the door. They and the doctor began feverishly attaching tubes and wires to Jeremiah's body.

"Who are you to be giving orders?" Grumman said, distracting Thomas from his observation of the efforts being made to help Jeremiah while Laura lay unattended.

"Yeah!" someone shouted.

It's now or never, Thomas thought. "I'm Thomas Dorfler, that's who I am! Jeremiah's son. And for your information, Laura Delaney wasn't my mother! Katrina Dorfler was, and Walter Dorfler was my grandfather."

His outburst silenced everyone except the doctor, who issued terse but otherwise calm orders to his assistants.

Thomas shouldered his way past Grumman and walked out the door onto the balcony overlooking the living room, which had filled with people from the offices and labs inside the cavern.

He used his eyes to part the crowd on the balcony so he could put his hands on the railing. "I'm here because Jeremiah designated me as his successor. Months ago he asked me to come to the Science Center to join him." The lies came without thought. "Have you all forgotten the prophecy in *The Book of Second Jeremiah*? I am now in charge of the movement!"

A chorus of voices erupted, some angry and threatening. There were more than a few boos. Someone yelled, "Let him talk!"

Thomas again shouted for silence. "That's the prophecy! You who want to ignore the word of God, step forward and make yourself known to all." He trembled at this moment of truth, but gained confidence as no one moved or spoke. "God, speaking through Jeremiah, set the course. Any who abandon it now are heretics, cowards, and traitors. If this movement disintegrates into competing factions that give rise to chaos, then evil will triumph. Those are Jeremiah's words."

He waited with bated breath for someone to shout out that Jeremiah had distrusted him, but there were only a few low murmurs.

"I didn't even know Jeremiah was bringing Laura Delaney here."

He turned to stare at Grumman. "If our security had been up to par, this wouldn't have happened."

Grumman stepped forward. "Wait just a minute, kid."

Thomas faced him and snarled, "Call me a kid again and you're out of a job. You either make up your mind to fall in behind my leadership or you support some other faction. And if the movement breaks down now, it will fail. I know it, and you know it. If you believed in my father, you have to believe in me."

Thomas watched the beefy-looking security chief blink twice rapidly, then turned back to the crowd below. "Yes, we've suffered a terrible loss. It doesn't make sense, but we cannot understand the mind of God." He tried to think like Jeremiah. "Perhaps it's his way of testing us. Are we of so little faith that now we slink away into the darkness rather than march down the path of light and goodness?" He tried to *think and talk* like Jeremiah. "My father knew about this day. Read his *Revelation* from God. That's the reason he prepared me and my brother David to be his lieutenants." He had to save David too, if possible.

Thomas elevated his voice. "I promise you that we will march ahead without missing a step. Everything's changed, and nothing's changed. Jeremiah is dead, but he would want us to go forward. Christianity didn't fail because Christ died. It flourished because those who believed took up the crusade. Now, please go back to your work or to your rooms. We'll talk again tomorrow." *Like hell we will.*

The crowd began to break up, and Thomas turned back toward the bedroom just as the doctor and various attendants wheeled out a gurney. Plastic tubes stuck out of both sides of Jeremiah's neck and attached to a pump that emitted a humming sound.

"Where are you going?" Thomas asked.

Over his shoulder, the doctor said, "Jeremiah gave us detailed instructions about what to do in a situation like this."

Thomas couldn't think of any counterargument. He turned to Grumman, whose help he would need to get out of here. "Look, I'm sorry I shouted at you, Grumman, but we can't let panic take over the movement. We can't let it collapse." An exciting idea formed in his mind. "In fact, we can't let word of what happened here get out."

A look of confusion crossed Grumman's massive, scarred face. "What do you mean?"

"What do you think will happen around the world when members of the movement find out that Jeremiah is dead?" Actually, Thomas could sell this point because he believed it. "There'll be a dozen men who'll proclaim themselves as successors. They'll make alliances. They'll trade information, even with the enemy. Jeremiah's plan to cleanse the earth and begin a new civilization will be abandoned as they quarrel among themselves."

The stocky man with Popeye-size upper arms nodded slowly. "You're probably right."

"I'm not a kid," Thomas said, more gently this time, "but I don't know everything. I'll need a lot of help and advice if I'm going to hold this movement together."

"Okay, Thomas. I'll give you a chance. What do you want to do?"

Thomas walked back into the room, trying to buy a few minutes to think. He glanced briefly at Laura's body and choked back vomit rising in his throat. For the moment, he was beyond tears. "Put her in a body bag so no one can see her."

"What do you want to do with her?"

Thomas squared off in front of him. "She was never here."

"Huh?"

"She was never here, and she didn't kill Jeremiah with a bomb when they were in bed together." *God, how she must have hated him to have made this sacrifice.* "How would that look to his followers and the world? Let me tell you. Jeremiah's death would become a joke, and so would everything he stood for. We need to make certain her body is never found."

Grumman nodded, and relayed Thomas's request into a handheld radio transmitter.

He's tough, but not very smart, Thomas concluded. "We'll construct a heroic myth about how Jeremiah died. Better yet, we might even tell the world that he survived, that his medical team pulled off a miracle and saved him. He planned to be the prototype of the new man anyway. Right? You've read his writings."

Thomas recognized the look of a lie coming. Grumman said, "Yeah, sure."

Two men came into the room with a black body bag. Not wanting to watch them manhandle his mother, Thomas walked out onto the balcony, saying over his shoulder, "Bring the body to Dr. Wakilpoor's office. That's where we'll be." *The computer guru will be a harder sell,* he thought.

In Wakilpoor's office, Thomas continued and perfected his performance, feeling increasingly comfortable in the role of head man. "She didn't do this alone," he said conspiratorially to Grumman and Wakilpoor. "She had help, obviously. Someone made the bomb for her. Maybe she also smuggled a transmitter in here. I don't think we can rule out an assault on the cabin by government forces. Perhaps at any moment."

Grumman barked into his radio, demanding reports from the outside lookouts. "They don't see anything, Thomas, but that doesn't mean you're wrong."

"I assume Jeremiah had a contingency plan for dealing with an attack on this complex," Thomas guessed.

"Of course. There's a secret escape route for Jeremiah and the heads of the various divisions, including Dr. Wakilpoor."

Thomas turned to the doctor. "The computer files are invaluable, I'm sure you'll agree. If they fell into the wrong hands, everything would be lost."

"That's true," Wakilpoor said, but without any alarm in his voice. "But we've prepared for that. Any effort by inside or outside hackers to gain access to the computers will result in all files being deleted. I wrote the programs myself. Of course there are backup computers elsewhere."

How much should I push now? Thomas wondered. "The other

important thing, it seems to me, is the vaccine. Are there stockpiles here?"

"Yes, but not a lot," Grumman said. He held up the radio. "If I enter a code on this, they all go up in flames instantly."

Thomas took a deep breath. "Okay, this is what I propose. The three of us leave here now, just in case. I'd like to take a dozen vaccines with us." Hastily, he added, "We can easily destroy them, if necessary. Dr. Wakilpoor, you must come because you can't fall into the enemy's hands. I suggest you disable these computers, at least temporarily, and that we take along zipped files containing essential information."

"I'm not certain that would be wise," Wakilpoor said. "What if we were captured?"

"Then we'd destroy the disks," Thomas said. "What I'm thinking, though, is that if this is the beginning of a widespread government assault, we can't necessarily expect to get to the other computers, right? We don't want to be downloading essential information over telephone lines, do we? And we need to be in contact with our people around the world."

Dr. Wakilpoor hesitated, which Thomas considered a good sign. "We need to hurry."

"All right," Wakilpoor said. "I'll be with you in a minute." He sat in front of a computer terminal as Thomas steered Grumman out of the room and onto the exterior walkway. "Take me to my father. I'll spend a few moments with him and then we must leave immediately. Also, get me a gun."

"Why? Protection is my job."

"I don't intend to be taken alive in any firefight," Thomas said, hoping his bravado would allay Grumman's doubts.

"What types of weapons do you know how to use?"

"Any nine-millimeter." Actually, Steve had trained him extensively in the use of various types of weapons.

"I should notify the other division heads," Grumman said, "so they can come with us."

"No," Thomas said quickly. "We need to maintain tight security now, until we find out who was involved in this conspiracy."

"Oh, yeah," Grumman said as he escorted Thomas to another room off the walkway.

He left Thomas facing a bodyguard carrying a submachine gun.

"I want to see my father."

The gunman hesitated only briefly and then showed him down a corridor, where another guard opened a door leading into a surgical theater. Thomas saw a dozen gowned men and woman hovering over the gurney that had taken away Jeremiah's body. A strong smell of antiseptic filled the room. An unseen motor pumped rhythmically.

A man walked over to him and lowered his mask. Thomas recognized him as the doctor who had first arrived in the bedroom following the explosion. "Is my father alive?" he asked, faking a sorrowful look.

"Life and death are increasingly relative terms in these times," the doctor said. "In layman's language, his body is destroyed beyond repair, but he's not brain dead."

"So what are you doing?"

"Keeping his brain functioning as best as we can, according to his instructions."

"I don't understand."

"I don't mean to be rude, Thomas, but I can't take time now to explain it to you. How about tomorrow? Then I'll know more, anyway."

Thomas reluctantly backed out of the room. *Can they somehow save him? God, if that's possible, what about Laura!* He stood in the hallway, leaning against the wall. Tears streamed down his face, knowing that his mother was brain dead, given the amount of time that had passed. They'd ignored her in their frantic efforts to save that bastard. Even if he had ordered them to perform heroic measures to keep his mother alive, they would have ignored him—and they would have known his true allegiance.

The sobs that racked his body now were generated by guilt. One of the guards gently took his arm and led him to the exit.

Grumman and Dr. Wakilpoor were waiting. Grumman handed Thomas a Sig-Sauer. "Let's go," he said, striding off briskly down the walkway.

They boarded an electromagnetic train similar to the one they'd used to escape from the Science Center bunker. Two of Grumman's assistants placed the body bag containing Laura's remains across the last two seats. At the end of the line, Grumman opened a door into a shallow cave that faced into a densely forested area. He easily hoisted the body bag over his shoulder and led the way out of the cave.

A bright moon lit up the darkness, aiding them in carefully stepping over a minefield of rocks before they reached a hiking trail. As they began to walk single-file, their shoes scattered rocks and snapped twigs. The slight noises sounded like gunshots to Thomas. Two hundred yards down the path, they arrived at the edge of a gravel parking lot, empty except for a newspaper delivery truck that looked clearly out of place. When Grumman spoke softly into his radio, the truck lights flashed on and off.

Then he walked to the vehicle, slid open the side door, and unceremoniously dumped the body bag inside. It landed with a thud that profoundly distressed Thomas.

"Get in," Grumman said. "We'll take Interstate Eighty-one and drive toward Pennsylvania. There's a subheadquarters there. If we have any trouble along the way, I can order in a helicopter."

Thomas wasn't about to go to Pennsylvania. Did he have the guts to seize the moment again—especially when the moment called for deadly action, not rhetoric? The thought of Laura lying dead in the black bag steeled his nerves. He pulled the Sig-Sauer from his belt and injected a shell into the chamber. Grumman, who had already opened the passenger's door, heard the sound and wheeled around.

Thomas shot him in the chest and immediately stepped toward the open door and began firing at the driver. He shot three or four times before he remembered Wakilpoor behind him. He quickly swung the gun around, but the wide-eyed computer expert seemed rooted to the ground. Thomas looked at Grumman, who lay face-up on the ground. To be safe, Thomas fired another bullet into the man's body.

"My God, what are you doing?" Wakilpoor asked.

"Get in the back of the truck. Lie on your stomach. Do it or I'll shoot you, too!"

He ordered the doctor to take off his shoes and remove the laces, which Thomas then used to bind Wakilpoor's hands behind him. After gently repositioning Laura's body, he got out of the truck and knelt beside Grumman. He rolled the beefy bodyguard over and went through his pockets until he found the cell phone.

Thomas walked to the other side of the truck and pulled the driver out of the door and onto the ground. He climbed into the driver's seat, feeling the dead man's wet blood soak into his pants. He drove out of the parking lot, trying to recall Laura's directions to the farm.

33

THE REVELATION TO JEREMIAH

CHAPTER SIX

1 Remember the barely audible whisper you hear in the middle of the night as you lie in the crystal-clear darkness amid the thunderous quiet?

2 It is I, Jeremiah the Second, Servant of the LORD, Enemy of Injustice, the Scourge of Evil, Founder of New America, and Earth's Gardener.

3 Hear ye, for although I no longer have physical form, I am, and forever will be, by virtue of the grace of the Evolved God.

4 My death, well known in advance, is evidence of the existence of Evil, as well as the reality of Eternal Life. One is not possible without the other. Those who listen should choose wisely, for the consequences are beyond description.

5 Energy is the essence of Life and the Universe, yet in its highest form unseen, difficult to measure and quantify, and

impossible to destroy, although it can be transformed. So it is with the Human Soul.

6 Why, you ask, worry about the evolution of Mankind when the reward of death is Eternal Life? Because the soul of imperfect Man is imperfect, and will be until Mankind achieves immortality and perfection, and merges with the Godhead.

7 Therefore, my soul and all those that preceded me in death from the beginning of time immemorial will drift aimlessly in the Void, and remain incomplete. That is the real Hell, from which the Dead will be released only when Mankind achieves perfection by choosing the path the LORD outlined to me during my lifetime of service.

8 Perfection is knowing all, understanding all, and controlling all. Intelligence and the soul are interchangeable and reside in the brain in the form of electrical and chemical energy. Such energy can be preserved and replicated.

9 In its current state of evolution, the intelligent soul is limited because it cannot achieve perfection before the brain dies. Extend the life of the body and the brain, and perfection is possible.

10 Cells are composed of such common elements as proteins, enzymes, and amino acids arranged so; bone is but a framework, and muscle an elastic material to facilitate movement; blood is a liquid highway; internal organs are but small machines; sight is merely a series of mirrors reflecting images. All can be made, synthesized, altered, and improved.

11 But thought, comprehension, insight, reverence, obedience, love, and yearning never were material, and never will be. Why think ye that such abstractions cannot exist without a superstructure?

12 One more Vision granted to me by the LORD will I relate to you, the Faithful.

13 A ship sailed by anxious sailors approached the Horizon and dropped off into the Void. It fell, but not to the bottom, for there is no end of the Void. The ship simply falls forever and changes form many times, sailing through many dimensions for all of Eternity. It is a concept the imperfect soul cannot comprehend.

14 How can I explain to my beloved brethren that which cannot be measured by time and distance, nor viewed solely in three dimensions? How can I explain God and Infinity to you?

15 Maximum intelligence knows no limits or fear, and enjoys complete satisfaction, unlimited knowledge, rapturous joy, complete love, ultimate fulfillment, and Eternal Life.

16 To make progress toward this state, do your duty; duty and obedience yield great rewards. Follow my teachings, yet move forward without me. Face this challenge with resolve. Take a small step toward that which has been ordained for all time. In time, you will understand the inexplicable, and be rewarded for your diligence. Fear not Death.

17 I had a plan to become the Immortal Man, but alas, the dream exploded in love misplaced, for indeed Hate and Love are as intertwined as Good and Evil. Yet the ways of the LORD are mysterious, and what seems the end could be the beginning, because time bends and begins again. What was will be.

18 My earthly role is now vested in another, yet his identity has not yet been revealed by the LORD. Mistake ye not the pretender for the next Prophet.

19 My fate is not entirely clear to me now. I may drift aimlessly for eons, waiting with the other dead the blending and the Resurrection. I pray the LORD has another role for me in effecting the evolution of Mankind.

20 I, Jeremiah, bid farewell temporarily to all those who loved Me and followed Me.

34

Inside the farmhouse, David and Ariana pretended to watch a television movie that had started at midnight, although he assumed that she also was thinking about Laura and wondering what had happened to her.

They both jumped when a voice crackled over the intercom. One of the front-gate guards announced, "Thomas is here. He's driving a truck and has some guy tied up in back."

David raced out of the house, jumped off the porch, and sprinted toward the gate. As he drew close, he saw that two carloads of FBI agents had boxed in the truck. Thomas stood at the junction of the car headlights, surrounded by the farm's guards and the FBI agents.

David squeezed through the gate. "Thomas!" he shouted, elbowing his way through the armed men and wrapping his arms around his brother. "How did you find us? Is Laura with you?"

Thomas looked up the hill at the well-lit farmhouse. "So this is Mom's dream place. I heard about it many times when I was growing up. It looks just like the photographs."

One of the FBI suits grabbed David's arm. "We've called Director Mitchell. He'll be here in a few minutes. We took this from Thomas."

He held up the black nine-millimeter for David to see. "It's been fired."

Thomas said, "The guy tied up in the back of the truck is Dr. Wakilpoor, head of computer services for Jeremiah. Mitchell should be very interested in talking to him. I'll be up at the house with my brother. Don't touch anything else in the truck, please."

"I think you should wait here," one of the FBI agents said sternly.

"Give it a break, buddy," David replied. "He's not going anywhere. He came here, remember? Send Mitchell up to the house when he comes."

As they walked up the hill, David asked, "How did you get away from him? God, I know how hard that must have been. And you kidnapped this guy Wakilpoor, too? Jesus, I can't imagine you got away! Jeremiah'll be after you. Both of us, in fact. I'm glad the FBI is here and sending reinforcements." He grabbed Thomas's arm as they reached the front steps. "Laura's not here. She somehow slipped out about mid-afternoon without being seen. I even thought Jeremiah's people might have gotten onto the grounds somehow and kidnapped her. Have you seen her?"

"Let's go inside, David."

Ariana hugged and kissed Thomas. "The last time I saw you, that bastard Jeremiah had a gun to your head. Tell us how you got away. Where is he? Do you know where Laura is?"

"Sit down," Thomas said, blowing out his breath. "I've got bad news."

As Thomas tearfully related the astonishing events of the day, David dropped his head into his hands and sobbed mixed tears of joy and sadness. Both the father he'd hated and the mother he had begun to know and love were dead.

They turned toward the door as it opened and Deputy Director Mitchell walked in. He approached them in the living room as if treading on eggshells. David could tell that he knew about Laura.

"I'm sorry to intrude at a moment like this," Mitchell said, "but I have to talk to you, Thomas."

"Jeremiah is dead," Thomas said. "So is Laura. She killed herself and him with a bomb she smuggled into his headquarters."

David thought Mitchell looked to be in shock. "My God! She asked me to have that bomb made for her."

"And you didn't think about what she was going to do with it?" Ariana snapped indignantly.

The lanky FBI agent steadily returned her gaze. "I had my suspicions, although I didn't take it as a given that she would be killed, too. Laura was a strong-willed woman. If I hadn't helped her, she'd have found someone else to make the bomb. You know that." Mitchell shook his head. "I admit I never expected her to give us the slip."

David knew how difficult it would have been for anyone to kill Jeremiah, and he thought about the delicate way in which Thomas had described how Laura had accomplished her goal. He couldn't help but smile. Laura had considered Jeremiah's obsession with her, as well as his monumental ego, and played him like a fiddle. Despite his grief, David thought that Laura might have died happy. Although he hated to think it, it might have been better for her to go that way than to spend decades pining for Steve and running from Jeremiah.

"Do you know how Laura got away from here?" Thomas asked.

Mitchell looked briefly at the floor. "She wore a disguise and left with one of your bodyguards, Shawntel LeGrand. His partner apparently hid in the house for several hours before showing himself."

"Where is Shawntel now?" Ariana asked grimly.

"He's disappeared," Mitchell said.

Ariana collapsed against the back of the sofa and looked at the ceiling. "Christ, who can we trust? I'd get rid of everyone on the staff, but then we'd have the same problem when we hired replacements."

"Maybe not," Thomas said. "Jeremiah's disciples will be too busy to pay much attention to us."

"Which brings up the guy you brought with you," Mitchell said. "Wakilpoor."

Thomas handed Mitchell a small box. "I hope the files on these zip disks tell you everything you need to know about the movement. Otherwise, you can get it out of Wakilpoor. Also, you should have found some vaccine in the truck."

"Yes, we did."

"And if you'll bring me a detailed map of the mountains west of here, especially the area about forty-five miles south of Front Royal, I might be able to get you within a few square miles of Jeremiah's headquarters."

While Thomas studied the map that one of Mitchell's aides produced, David went into the kitchen to talk with Ariana as she made a fresh pot of coffee. Finally he said what was on his mind: "We have to get Laura's body back and give her a proper burial."

"Her body's in the truck out front," Thomas said, standing in the doorway.

Two FBI agents carried the body bag into the house and looked expectantly at the group of them.

"Put her on the dining room table," Thomas said, removing the candelabra and tablecloth. "We'd appreciate some privacy also."

After Mitchell and his agents stepped out onto the porch, Thomas unzipped the bag only far enough to reveal Laura's head.

David bent over the table and looked closely at his mother's face, which in death had taken on the appearance of a wax mask. She looked neither horrified nor triumphant. Just neutral. David felt comforted by Ariana's hand on his shoulder, although he could hear her crying softly.

The three of them stood that way for a long time and then sat around the table. Even though the smell of death was overwhelming, David tried to savor it out of respect rather than let it nauseate him.

"What are we going to do?" he asked, looking at Thomas, whom

David now considered the leader of their truncated family. Thomas obviously had more brains and guts than he did. David still couldn't fathom how his brother had talked his way out of Jeremiah's hide-out and then shot two men to death at close range. He only knew he couldn't have done it.

"We have to bury Laura," Thomas said. "I'd rather we did it ourselves."

Ariana looked horrified. "What do you mean?"

Thomas explained, "After the FBI examines her body, we should bury her beside Steve, without any church ceremony or public spectacle. Do for her what she did for him. I don't want their graves to become a shrine for some and an evil symbol for others."

At that moment, Mitchell stepped into the entryway and coughed delicately.

Thomas stood and faced him. "We were just talking about preparing Laura's body here and burying her alongside Steve. Your experts can look at her, but don't mangle her body any more than it already has been."

Mitchell nodded. "I can take care of everything."

"We should trumpet Jeremiah's death to the world," Ariana said angrily. "Everyone should know of the sacrifice Laura made, not just for this country, but for all the people of the world."

"Thomas did at least as much," David reminded her.

"It's not about glory and recognition," Thomas said. "And I disagree that we should announce the true details of how Jeremiah died."

Even Mitchell looks bewildered, David thought.

"What do you mean?" Mitchell asked.

"I think Jeremiah's top lieutenants bought my suggestion that the circumstances of his death would make Jeremiah the butt of jokes for decades to come," Thomas said. "They're going to construct some heroic myth about his death."

"I can easily envision that," David said. "They'll say the Lord called Jeremiah away for consultation. He'll be back later."

Thomas grinned. "Exactly."

"Which is all the more reason that we should tell the world what really happened," Ariana persisted.

"And then we'll truly be hunted for the rest of our lives," Thomas said, "which probably wouldn't last longer than a few more months. It's the kind of bragging rights I don't want."

"Thomas has a point," David said, looking apologetically at Ariana.

"What are you thinking, Thomas?" Mitchell asked.

"We don't confirm or deny their myth. But we do put out the word that Wakilpoor turned traitor. In the confusion surrounding Jeremiah's death, or his ascension into heaven, Wakilpoor and Grumman escaped with the movement's computer files and forced me to go with them. They planned to set up an alternative movement, but Wakilpoor killed Grumman. I escaped, and you captured Wakilpoor."

Mitchell's smile indicated that he liked this yarn. "We'll parade him before the media cameras but not allow him to say anything."

"He'll be so grateful for your protection, he'll tell you anything you want to know," Thomas said.

"The problem is, Jeremiah's supporters will know that all of you are here, anyway," Mitchell said. "They obviously have the place under surveillance."

"Why wouldn't we stay here?" David asked rhetorically. "Thomas and I inherited the farm."

"We don't have to hide," Thomas said, "We haven't committed any crimes, although it might help if you publicly threatened to prosecute us for something. David and I will respond by conducting a short news conference on the front porch."

"You are crazy!" Ariana said.

"I'm not too taken with that idea either, big brother," David said.

"We admit we were with our *father* on several occasions over recent months," Thomas said. "We deny knowledge of his plans, including the use of biological agents. We know nothing else and insist on our innocence. We'll admit that Laura has disappeared but deny knowing what happened to her."

David thought it over. "It would confuse the hell out of everyone and keep us in good graces within the movement."

"In which case, some of the new leaders may contact you," Mitchell said, smiling.

"Exactly," Thomas replied.

Even Ariana reluctantly acknowledged the brilliance of Thomas's plan. "Jesus, you are a convoluted thinker, Thomas."

"Please don't say 'just like Jeremiah,' " Thomas said.

"What did they do with his body?" Mitchell asked.

"I don't know," Thomas replied. "One of his physicians said it had been destroyed but that he wasn't brain dead."

David's imagination ran wild, and he saw the others frown as they also apparently mulled over the possibilities.

For Laura's burial, Ariana selected a long black dress with a delicate floral pattern. While she and several FBI forensics experts washed and dressed the body, David and Thomas stepped outside and watched two bodyguards begin to dig the grave.

Mitchell had a casket delivered just before first light broke in the east. When David and Thomas reentered the house, Laura's body lay in the coffin in the living room, with only the top half of the lid open. Someone had lit several aromatic candles.

While the bodyguards and FBI agents retreated respectfully to either the entryway or the kitchen, David and Thomas stood together, looking down at their mother. Ariana stood behind them.

"She looks okay," David said, fighting back tears.

"Yeah," Thomas agreed, placing a hand on David's shoulder.

Several minutes later, Thomas closed the coffin, and several bodyguards came forward to carry it through the kitchen and out the side door. They lowered it into the grave next to Steve's. Everyone present then folded their hands, bowed their heads, and stood as still as death.

Without moving his head, David glanced at the FBI agents and the bodyguards and knew that rumors of Laura's death and burial site would circulate, no matter if he and Thomas denied it. How would they lie their way out of that? How would they ever keep the curiosity-seekers and the loonies away?

He began to cry and tried manfully to keep from bursting into uncontrolled sobbing. If Laura hadn't come to Zurich to save him, he'd be dead now. She had given him his freedom, a home, and a purpose in life—he had grown increasingly enthusiastic about raising horses. He pledged to repay her by being a good man and staying sober.

"I want to repeat something my mother told me many times," Thomas said, breaking the oppressive silence. "It was her recipe for the good life: 'Practice the Golden Rule, do as much good as you can, and never, ever forget the redeeming power of love.' Also, I never got to say good-bye to my real father, Steve Wallace . . . who was the best man I ever knew."

"Amen," Mitchell said.

Ariana dropped a bouquet of flowers on Laura's casket. "Steve and Laura, I loved you both like you were my mom and dad," she said. "I wish you an eternity of happiness together."

David didn't know what to say, but suddenly the words poured out. "Jeremiah had no inheritors. Steve and Laura had two sons who loved them, and always will. That's the only legacy that matters."

Near dusk Thomas sat on the porch swing, giving it momentum now and then with the toe of one shoe. The crisp October night air reminded him of high school football games, when the urgent voices of players, coaches, cheerleaders, and fans rang in a din of excitement. He missed being a boy.

Ariana walked around the house, up the steps, and stood beside the swing. "Can I sit?" she asked.

"Sure."

"Whatcha thinking?"

"That it's so quiet off there on the horizon that you would never know a war is going on. I could understand it better if the sky was lit up by exploding bombs and antiaircraft fire."

"Yeah. At least the governments of the world finally told the people what's going on."

They had designated Ariana as their contact person with the outside world. Thomas had limited his involvement so far to a two-day debriefing by the FBI. Now the Bureau knew everything about Jeremiah that he knew, and probably more.

"I guess Wakilpoor's computer files and the vaccine were helpful?" he asked, glad that he'd hidden three syringes in his shirt pocket that night. At least he and David and Ariana had been immunized.

"There's a massive worldwide effort underway to manufacture and distribute the vaccine to every country," she said, "but apparently that's going to be difficult to do, even impossible in many Third World countries . . . at least in time to do any good. The flu has already hit and a lot of people are going to die."

"Jeremiah's legacy will be millions of dead in those countries—just the kind of people he always said he wanted to help most," Thomas added.

Ariana said, "The other problem is that rebel armies and guerrilla organizations already have taken the offensive in parts of Asia and Africa. Many of them undoubtedly had arrangements with Jeremiah, since their troops appear to be healthy. I just hope the superpower nations don't get dragged into some worldwide conflict."

"And I hope the viruses Jeremiah set loose on the world don't mutate. Then we're all in trouble."

"We're as safe here as we can be," Ariana said. "The latest air-filtration system has been installed in the house. As Laura wanted, the third floor has been turned into an airtight bunker, complete with enough water and food to last for a couple of years."

Thomas looked up at the sky, thinking that invisible death could be riding on the air currents right now and no one would know it. Even so, he didn't feel like getting up from the swing.

• • •

Thomas moved into Steve and Laura's old bedroom and converted the sitting room into a computer den. Late one evening, he worked on a word processing file in near darkness, save only the light coming from the monitor. A loud rapping on the door made him jump, as if the police had come for him. He picked up a handgun and walked to the door, which he kept locked. He looked through the newly installed peephole, relaxed, and let in his brother.

"I saw a light flickering up here," David said, sauntering into the bedroom.

Thomas grimaced as David flopped into a deep red, velvet-covered chair. His brother's jeans were filthy and smelled of horses.

"Do you sleep with those horses?" Thomas asked.

"If I was going to sleep with any animal around here, it'd be the one down the hall from you. You know, the tall, well-built filly. I'll bet she can turn it on in the stretch drive."

Thomas laughed softly. "You mess with Ariana and you may wind up a gelding."

"Ouch. I think she likes me, though."

"She feels sorry for you, is what." In reality, Thomas had noticed a certain spark between them.

David looked into the sitting room. "What are you hammering out on the computer at this hour? Or are you in one of those chat rooms, trolling for hot-to-trot thirteen-year-olds?"

"Do you ever think about anything besides sex?"

David stood and hitched up his jeans. "Nope. It's about all I'm interested in now that I'm on the wagon."

Thomas watched his brother walk into the computer den, bend at the waist, and read the words on the screen.

When David came back into the bedroom, he no longer seemed to be in a joking mood. "You're playing with fire, Thomas. This wasn't part of the plan."

"I never settled on a plan."

"The night we buried Laura, you said we'd go along with whatever myth they concocted about Jeremiah's death and blame Wakilpoor for snitching to the government. That's all."

"That's all we talked about then."

David walked across the room and grabbed the doorknob. He turned back and said, "I can't tell you what to do, Thomas. I hope you don't get yourself killed, but promise me you won't do anything to put Ariana and me in danger."

"I promise."

After David left, Thomas sat again in front of the keyboard. Ironically, his brother's visit had generated several new ideas. He finished the document and went onto the Internet. He accessed the www.Jeremiah2.com Web site and added the document he just wrote, titled: *An Epistle from Thomas, the True Inheritor, to the True Believers.*

Epilogue

The woman and the boy got out of the limousine and stared up at the three-story farmhouse. With the boy holding tightly to her hand, she walked up the steps onto the porch and rang the doorbell.

A beautiful young woman wearing a gun in a shoulder holster opened the door and said, "Come in. We've been expecting you. I'm Ariana."

A tall, dark-haired young man stepped forward and held out his hand to the visitor. "I'm Thomas," he said.

She looked at him keenly. "You favor your mother. I met her once in New America, many years ago."

Another, slightly taller young man standing off to the side said, "I'm David." He kept his hands in his back pockets.

"You have your mother's face," the woman said, studying him.

Thomas bent over and asked, "What's your name?"

The woman gently pushed the boy forward. "Don't be shy. Tell them your name."

"I'm James," the child said, looking up at all the tall people.

"Could we sit down and talk?" the woman asked. "Perhaps you have a Coke for James? I'm certain he'd like one."

Thomas led the way into the living room, while David disappeared into the kitchen and returned shortly with two Cokes, which he placed on coasters on the coffee table.

They all watched James pick up a bottle and drink eagerly. Then he set it down and licked his lips. "Are you really my brothers?" he asked.

"Yes, they are, dear," the woman said. "Now, I'd like to talk to them alone for a few minutes. Why don't you go sit on the porch swing? It's a beautiful day outside."

"I'll go with him," Ariana said.

"What's your name?" Thomas asked.

"My real name is Annabelle. I corresponded with Steve Wallace over the Internet and spoke to Ariana when I arrived in New York. She said that Laura wanted me to come here."

"James is Jeremiah's son?" Thomas asked.

"Yes and no. James was cloned from Jeremiah."

Thomas and David looked stunned.

"You can verify that through a DNA analysis," Annabelle said.

"After his heart surgery in Beijing, Jeremiah said something cryptic to me," David recalled, "about the donor not being chosen haphazardly."

"He planned to use James as an organ bank," Annabelle said, "perhaps taking his kidneys and liver next. At the same time, James would serve as an experimental model for various artificial organs."

"Did you know that Jeremiah is dead?" Thomas asked.

Her hand flew to her mouth. "I'd heard rumors. Praise the Lord, my prayers have been answered. Are you certain?"

Thomas frowned. "Almost."

"Jeremiah would have left no stone unturned in his search for James," she said.

"How did you get out of China?" David asked. "That couldn't have been easy."

"Steve Wallace arranged that. I thought it strange that I didn't hear from him when I arrived in New York. I didn't know he'd been killed until I read about it in the newspaper. I'm terribly sorry."

"Who else knows about James?" Thomas asked.

"I don't know exactly. A dozen or so members of the Science Center's medical team, certainly. Jeremiah was very adamant that it remain a closely guarded secret."

"That's good at least," Thomas said.

"Does James know any of this?" David asked.

"No, Jeremiah didn't want him to know, and I haven't found a good reason to tell him yet."

"Is he in good health? Does he know he's a clone?"

"No, he doesn't know he's a clone. Yes, he appears to be in good health, but of course he needs constant medical supervision to make certain that his artificial heart functions as it should. Mainly, he needs protection. You both can guess how valuable he would be to the movement."

"Have you and him been vaccinated against the flu?" David asked.

"Yes, Jeremiah made certain of that."

Thomas stood and walked to the fireplace, where he turned and looked at her. "Why are you doing this, Annabelle?"

"I love James and I want him to have a normal life, or as much of one as is possible, given the circumstances. I had hoped you two would have a certain sympathy for his plight."

"I have all the sympathy in the world for him," David said. "Jeremiah tried to make me his clone too, in a way."

"Look, I feel for the kid, also," Thomas said, "but we can't guarantee his safety here. Just by his presence, he may put all of us in even greater danger. Do you understand?"

"Yes. But I had to come to the two of you first. After all, you could think of James as your brother."

"No, he's a miniature version of our biological father," Thomas said. "Did you ever think of what he might grow up to be?"

"Perhaps someone like you two?"

Annabelle rose, walked to the front door, and opened it. "Come on back in, James. You can talk to your brothers now."

The serious, studious-looking boy sat on the sofa again alongside Annabelle. Ariana stood behind them.

"If you're my brothers, then who were our parents?" James asked.

David looked at Thomas, who said, "We all had different mothers."

"But the same father, obviously." James looked at his guardian. "Annabelle says she doesn't know, but I tend not to believe her."

Annabelle smiled. "James is precocious."

"Tell us something about yourself, James," David said. "What do you want to be when you grow up?"

"A veterinarian, maybe," James said. "I really like animals. That's why I was so happy we were coming to visit a farm. What animals do you have here?"

"Dogs. And I just bought two thoroughbred horses. I hope to breed the mare in the spring."

"I could help," James said eagerly. "I've read all about animal births. Who's your veterinarian?"

David frowned. "We don't have one yet."

James shook his head in concern. All the adults in the room began to laugh.

"You see, he's just a normal boy," Annabelle said.

"Are you both farmers?" James asked.

"Kind of," Thomas said.

"I haven't made up my mind what I'll be when I grow up," David said, grinning.

"That'll be a while yet," Ariana replied dryly.

"Okay, James, we'd like you and Annabelle to stay with us," Thomas announced suddenly. "At least until we can decide what's best for your future. If that's okay with you?"

James pursed his lips in contemplation. "That seems like a good decision. I'm anxious to learn more about my roots."

"That'll make you sick," David said.

"What?"

Thomas quickly answered, "He said families *stick* together no matter what, didn't you, David?"

"Absolutely."

"I've had a heart transplant, you know. My other heart didn't function properly, they said. I suppose the artificial heart could stop at any time."

"Don't worry about that, my dear," Annabelle said.

"It's only a machine," James reminded her.

"We'll all have to make the most of the time we have together," Ariana said.

"That's right," Thomas said. "There's important work to be done."

"You mean with the horses?" the boy asked.

"That, and doing as much good as we can, in any way we can. My mother told me that, and I've got some other ideas. Right, David?"

"Oh, yeah, you got ideas, Thomas. Lots of ideas. You know what the problem is with some ideas, James?"

"No, what?"

"They ain't worth horse dung. Our *father* taught me that."